Faye Kellerman was born in St Louis, Missouri, and graduated in Mathematics and Dentistry at UCLA. She began her career as a dentist but turned to writing after the birth of her first child in 1978. She has now published fourteen hugely successful novels featuring Peter Decker and Rina Lazarus, as well as a non-series thriller, MOON MUSIC, and a historical novel, THE QUALITY OF MERCY. She lives in Los Angeles with her husband, Jonathan Kellerman, also a bestselling thriller writer, as well as a psychologist, and their children.

headline

Stone Kiss

Faye Kellerman

headline

First published in Great Britain in 2002
by HEADLINE BOOK PUBLISHING

First published in Great Britain in paperback in 2003
by HEADLINE BOOK PUBLISHING

10 9 8 7 6 5 4 3 2 1

ISBN 0 7472 6538 0

Typeset in Plantin by
Letterpart Limited, Reigate, Surrey

Printed and bound in Great Britain by
MacKays of Chatham plc, Chatham, Kent

HEADLINE BOOK PUBLISHING
A division of Hodder Headline
338 Euston Road
LONDON NW1 3BH

www.headline.co.uk
www.hodderheadline.com

FOR JONATHAN—
thirty fabulous years with the guy, his cars, and lots of guitars.

For Jesse, Rachel, Ilana, and Aliza—
from kids to wise adults, thanks for all the excitement along the way.

And for Barney Karpfinger—
for eighteen years of service par excellence and invaluable friendship. What a great ride it has been!

1

It was the stunned, pale look of bad news. Decker immediately thought of his parents, both in their mid-eighties, and while their health wasn't failing, they had had some problems over the past year. Right away, Rina had the good sense to tell him that the family was fine.

Decker was holding his daughter's hand. Looking down at the little girl, he said, 'Hannah Rosie, let me fix you up with some videos and a snack. I think Eema needs to talk to me.'

'It's okay, Daddy. I can do it myself. Eema taught me how to use the microwave.'

'Nine years old and ready for college.'

'No, Daddy, but I can use a VCR and a microwave.' She turned to her mother. 'I got an A on a spelling test. I didn't even study.'

'That's wonderful. Not that you didn't study, but that you got an A.' Rina kissed her daughter's cheek. 'I'll be with you in a minute.'

'Whatever . . .' Hannah left, rolling her wheeled backpack into the kitchen.

'You should sit.' Decker regarded his wife. 'You're colorless.'

'I'm all right.' But she sank down into the couch,

hugging a blue-and-white-checked throw pillow like a life preserver. Her cerulean eyes skittered around the living room, first landing on the lamp, then bouncing off Decker's special leather chair, onto the white wicker rocker. Anywhere but on his face.

'My parents are fine?' he asked specifically.

'Perfect,' Rina reiterated. 'Jonathan called—'

'Oh God! *His* mother?'

'No, she's fine.'

Jonathan's mother was Frieda Levine. She was also Decker's biological mother, making Jon his half brother. Ten years ago, by accident rather than by design, Decker had met up with his maternal family, which included five half siblings. Ties had been forged: more than mere acknowledgments, but less than time-tested relationships. Decker still considered his only parents to be the two people who had adopted him in infancy. 'Then what's going on?'

They both heard the microwave beep. A moment later, Hannah came out, juggling a pizza bagel on a plate, a big glass of milk, and her backpack. Decker said, 'Let me help you with that, sweetie.'

Wordlessly, she handed her father the food and her schoolbag, skipping off to her bedroom, orange ringlets flying behind her. Like the faithful valet, Decker followed several steps behind. Rina got up, went into the kitchen, and started a pot of coffee. Nervously, she pulled off her head covering and unclipped the barrette holding a ponytail, shaking out a shoulder-length sheet of iridescent black hair. Then she tied it up again, but left the head covering off. She picked imaginary dirt off her jeans skirt, then moved on to the imaginary lint on her pink sweater. She gnawed the edge of her thumb, but that only made the hangnail worse.

Decker came back in, sat down at their cherry breakfast table – a bit scarred but still rock solid. When he carved it, he had used the best quality wood he could find, and it showed. He took off his blue suit jacket and draped it over the back of his chair. He loosened his tie, then ran a hand through rust-colored hair heavily streaked with white. 'What's with the Levines?'

'It's not the Levines, Peter; it's Jonathan's in-laws, the Liebers – Raisie's family. There's been a terrible incident. His brother-in-law Ephraim was found dead—'

'Oh no!'

'Murdered, Peter. They found him in some seedy hotel room in upper Manhattan. To add to the confusion, he was with his fifteen-year-old niece – his brother's daughter. Now, she's missing. The family's in shambles.'

'When did all this happen?'

'I just hung up with Jonathan about five minutes before you came home. I think they found the body around three hours ago.'

Decker looked at his watch. 'Around 4 p.m. New York time?'

'I guess.'

'What was this guy doing in a "seedy hotel room" with his fifteen-year-old niece in the middle of a school afternoon?'

A rhetorical question. Rina didn't answer. Instead, she gave Decker a slip of paper with Jonathan's phone number.

'It's horrible.' Decker fingered the paper. 'I feel terrible for them. But this call . . . Is it just a comfort call? I mean, Jon doesn't expect me to do anything, does he?'

'I don't know, Peter. I suppose he'd like you to work miracles. In lieu of that, maybe you should call him up and listen to what happened.'

'He can't expect me to come out there.'

'I don't know. Maybe. You have a pretty good track record.'

'A prisoner of my own success. I have a *job*, Rina. As much as my heart goes out to them – it truly is horrible – I can't leave at a moment's notice and run off to Boro Park.'

'Actually, Chaim Lieber and his family live in Quinton, which is upstate. His widowed father lives there as well. Jonathan's wife, Raisie, is Chaim's younger sister. It's Chaim's daughter who's missing.'

'In upstate?' Decker thought a moment. 'Is the family religious?'

'Yes. Quinton is a very religious enclave. The family's black hat, superreligious except for Raisie. She's Conservative like Jonathan.'

'The outcast,' Decker said.

'She and Jonathan were lucky to find each other.' Rina got up and poured two cups of coffee. 'They both came from the same background and have altered their lifestyles for similar reasons.'

'And her father lives in Quinton. By himself?'

'I believe so. Raisie's mother died around ten years ago. Don't you remember their talking about her memory at Jonathan's wedding?'

'No, but I wasn't paying close attention.' Decker stared at the number over in his fingers. 'Why don't you tend to Hannah while I do this?'

'Don't want me hanging over your shoulder?'

He stood up. 'I don't know what I want.' He gave Rina a kiss on the forehead. 'I know what I *don't* want. I don't want to make this phone call.'

Rina took his hand and squeezed it. 'Why don't you talk from the bedroom? That way I can get dinner started.'

'Fine. I'm starved. What are we having?'

'Lamb chops or salmon?'

'I get a choice?'

'Both are fresh. Whatever you don't want, I'll freeze.'

'Hannah hates fish.'

'She hates lamb chops, too. I have some leftover schnitzel for her.'

'Lamb chops, then.' Decker made a face, then went inside the bedroom and closed the door. He kicked off his shoes and stretched out on his California king bed, dialing the number. It wasn't Jonathan's home phone in Manhattan, so Decker figured that it must be either his cell or possibly his synagogue, located near Columbia University. His half brother was a Conservative-pulpit rabbi. On the sixth ring, he answered.

'Jon!' Decker said.

'Akiva!' A loud whoosh of air. 'Thank you so much for calling!'

'My God, Rina just told me. That's terrible! You must be going through hell!'

'Not as bad as my wife's family. At this point, we're all shell-shocked.'

'I'm sure you are. When did this happen?'

'About three hours ago. About four o'clock here.'

'Jeez. And what do the police say?'

'Not much of anything. That's the problem. What does that mean?'

5

'It means they probably don't know much.'

'Or aren't telling us anything.'

'That could be. I'm so sorry.'

There was silence over the line. Jonathan said, 'You didn't ask how it happened.'

'If you want to tell me the details, I'm here.'

'I don't want to burden you . . .'

But that's exactly what he was going to do. 'Tell me what's going on, Jon. Start at the beginning. Tell me about the family.'

'Oh my.' A sigh. 'Raisie comes from a family of five – two boys, three girls. Both of her brothers are older. Chaim is the eldest, then Ephraim, the one who was . . . murdered. Raisie's the oldest daughter. Chaim Joseph is a typical oldest son . . . reliable, responsible. He and his wife, Minda, have seven children. He's a good man who has always worked hard in the family business.'

'Which is?'

'Several retail electronic stores in Brooklyn . . . one on the Lower East Side. You know, TVs, stereo, cameras, computers, mobile phones, DVDs, etcetera. The second brother, Ephraim Boruch . . . the one who this happened to . . . he's had some problems in the past.'

'What kind of problems?'

'Relationship problems – married and divorced.'

'Kids?'

'None.'

Silence.

'And?' Decker prompted.

'Drug problems,' Jonathan admitted. 'Addiction and rehab.'

'That probably had a lot to do with his relationship problems.'

'No doubt. Ephraim has been divorced for ten years. His ex is out of the picture. She remarried and now lives in Israel. As for Ephraim, he's straightened himself out. He's been sober for the last two years. About that time, he also joined the family business with his older brother.'

'How's that working out?'

'Fine, as far as I know. He was always the favorite uncle of all the nieces and nephews. He especially got along well with his niece Shaynda, who is the oldest in Chaim's family.'

'The missing niece.'

'Yes, the missing niece. Shaynda, like Ephraim, has a rebellious streak. She has been typecast as the problem child in the family since grade school. She's a beautiful girl, Akiva, with incredible spirit, and maybe that's part of the problem. She has not walked the walk or talked the talk.'

'Specifically?'

'Skipping school, hanging out at the mall with public-school kids. A couple of times, she had sneaked out of the house at night. My brother and sister-in-law came down on her with an iron fist. Unfortunately, the tougher they got, the more Shayndie fought. She and the mother have a miserable relationship. But the shining light had been Uncle Ephraim. He and Shayndie seemed to have had this rapport. More and more, she began to confide in him. They began spending time together—'

'Hmm . . .'

'I know what you're thinking. I would have sworn up and down that it wasn't that at all.'

'Wasn't what?'

7

'That he wasn't molesting her. When they first started spending time, I thought it was odd – the amount of time they spent together. So did Raisie. We had a long talk with Shaynda because we figured no one else would. We asked her point-blank. When she said no – she seemed genuinely shocked – we gave a step by step of what to be aware of. After the conversation, both Raisie and I were satisfied that Ephraim really had the girl's interest at heart. We had no reason to suspect that Ephraim was anything more than just a loving uncle trying to reach out to his troubled niece.'

'But now you think differently.'

A long sigh. 'Maybe. The two of them were supposed to be going on an outing this morning . . . to the Met. To see the new Dutch/Vermeer exhibit.'

'This morning?' Decker paused. 'It's Thursday. She doesn't have school?'

'I don't know, Akiva. Maybe her mother gave her the day off. Maybe her allergies were acting up. I didn't think it appropriate to question my sister-in-law.'

'Of course. Go on.'

Jonathan stuttered a few times, trying to get the words out. 'Ephraim was found dead in a hotel room. Did Rina tell you that?'

'Yes.'

'He'd been shot, Akiva. He was also . . . naked.'

'Good Lord!'

'I know. It's awful!'

'Any sign of the girl? Clothes left behind? Personal effects . . . like a purse, maybe?'

'Nothing that I've heard.'

'Any sign of a struggle? Torn sheets? Things in

disarray?' Decker licked his lips. 'Blood other than from . . .' He wanted to say kill spot. 'Blood other than where Ephraim was shot?'

'I wouldn't know. The police aren't saying much. They claim that they're just gathering information at this point, but we all know what they're thinking.'

Defensiveness in his voice, but it was seasoned with anguish. Decker said, 'And what are the police thinking?'

'That somehow we're guilty. Of course, they have to ask the family lots of questions. But they've made all of us feel more like criminals than like victims. Believe me, Akiva, I didn't want to call you. I know it's unfair of me to call you. But no one here is able to handle this. Is there anything – anything at all – that you can say to advise us?'

Decker's head was awhirl.

Jonathan added in a gush of words, 'And if it's not too difficult, perhaps you could make a couple of calls? As one detective to another.'

The words hung in the air.

Jonathan said, 'I shouldn't be asking you this—'

'It's all right, Jon. I just have to think for a moment.'

'Take all the time . . .'

Decker closed his eyes and felt a headache coming on. 'Can I call you back in a few minutes?'

'Of course—'

Decker clicked off the line before his brother could add another obligation. He went to the bathroom, took two Advils, then treated himself to a needle-hot shower. Ten minutes later, he slipped on soft worn denims and a work shirt. With trepidation, he punched the phone's redial button.

'Hello?'

'Okay, Jon, listen up. First thing you need to do is to hire a lawyer.'

'Hire a lawyer?' Surprise in his voice. 'Why?'

'Because you don't like the way the police are questioning you. You need protection.'

'But won't that make us look bad?'

'It will raise a couple of eyebrows, sure. But weighing the pros and the cons, it's no debate. Go out and find the best criminal defense attorney in town, and see if you can get an appointment with him ASAP. See if he'll take you on if things get . . . complicated. You've got to entertain the real possibility that someone in your family knows more about this than he or she is letting on.'

'I can't accept that.'

'Fine. Don't accept that. Just listen to me, okay? And don't talk to the police without an attorney present. Just as a precaution.'

No response.

Decker tried to hide his irritation. 'Are you there?'

'Yes, I'm here. Sorry. I'm writing this down. Go on.'

Decker slowed it down. 'Jon, I don't mean to snap at you. I'm used to barking orders.'

'It's fine, Akiva. Believe me, it's wonderful to talk to you . . . to someone who knows what he's doing.'

'That remains to be seen. After you've talked to a lawyer, have him call me. I'll talk to him directly.'

'That's it?'

'For the time being.'

'What about the police, Akiva?'

'Let me talk to the lawyer first. New York law is different than L.A. law, and it would help all of you if I didn't act precipitously.'

There was a long silence. Decker knew what was coming.

Jonathan said, 'I know this is dreadfully wrong to ask, Akiva. But it would really help us out if you could maybe . . .'

'Come out for the weekend?' Decker completed the sentence.

'I'll understand if you say no.'

Decker said, 'Let me call you back in five, all right?'

'Akiva, thank you so much—'

'Wait until you get my answer before you thank me.' Decker hung up. Rina was standing at the doorway. 'You've been listening?'

'Just for a minute. I think you gave him good advice – about the lawyer.'

'I'm glad you approve. He wants me to come out there. What do you think?'

'I can't make that decision for you, Peter.'

'I know that. But I still want to know what you think.'

'How do you feel about flying?'

Decker shrugged. 'It's a big hassle now, but I'm not nervous if that's what you're asking.'

'If you don't go,' Rina said, 'you'll feel guilty.'

He cursed under his breath, soft enough that it wasn't offensive, but loud enough so Rina could hear. 'It isn't fair to get me involved.'

'No, it isn't.'

'It's a family member. If I uncover muck or deliver bad news, I'm going to get blamed.'

'Probably.'

'Definitely.' Decker smoothed his mustache, chewing on the ends. It was the one part of his body that was still predominantly red as opposed to gray. 'On the other hand, it's not just a murder. There's a missing girl.' Decker filled in some of the blanks to the story, watching his wife grow paler by the moment. 'The girl might have been a hidden witness to the murder. Or maybe she escaped before the whole thing happened. That would be the most favorable outcome.'

No one spoke. Decker rubbed his forehead.

'Dinner's ready,' Rina said softly. 'Can you eat?'

'Not a problem. What do I tell Jonathan?'

'It's up to you, sweetheart.' She sat down next to him. 'I love you.'

'Love you, too.' He looked at the ceiling. 'I suppose I could hunt around for a few days. By then maybe she'll turn up . . . one way or the other.' He faced his wife and kissed her cheek. 'How many miles do we have?'

'Actually, I have enough for you to fly free. Interestingly enough, I also have a companion ticket for Hannah and me if we do a Saturday-night stayover.' She patted his hand. 'And we do have two sons back East—'

'Just hold on!' Decker interrupted. 'My flying is one thing. You and Hannah are quite another thing.'

'I haven't seen the boys in a while,' Rina told him. 'I'd much rather fly with you than by myself.' She patted his cheek. 'You're a tough guy.'

'Real tough.' It *had* been a while since they had seen the boys. 'You'd like to come with me?'

'Yes, I would love to come with you.'

Decker thought a moment. 'I have a condition. Promise me you won't get involved.'

'Good heavens, why would I do that! I wouldn't

12

dare take any chances as long as Hannah's with me.' She smiled encouragement. 'Go call back Jonathan. I'll make the reservations on the other line.'

With great reluctance, Decker called back his half brother. After working out a few more details, he walked into the kitchen, where Rina had just hung up on the land phone.

'Jonathan wants to know when we think we'll be arriving.'

'I've booked us on the red-eye.'

'When?'

'Tonight—'

'*Tonight?*'

'It's Thursday, Peter. If we don't take the red-eye, we won't be able to leave until Saturday night, because I won't fly on Friday in case of delays. Too close to *Shabbos*. Besides, I figured you'd want maximum time out there.'

'Well, then, I'm going to have to start making phone calls.'

Over the line, Rina could hear Jonathan telling him to forget it if it was too hard. Decker interrupted him. 'We'll be there around six in the morning.'

'Give me the flight number,' Jonathan said. 'I'll be there. Even though it's been eight years, you won't have any trouble recognizing me. I'll be the one with the sheepish look on my face.'

Decker pushed up his seat tray in the locked position. 'Why do I have to use up my vacation time doing this?'

'Because you're a caring person?' Rina tried out.

'No, it's because I'm an idiot,' he snarled as he moved about in his seat, trying to get his long legs comfortable. Flying under the best of circumstances was now an ordeal. And this certainly wasn't the best of circumstances. 'I despise molestation cases—'

'Can you keep your voice down?'

Decker glanced around. People were staring at him.

Rina whispered, 'You don't *know* it's that.'

'Yes, I do know. The uncle was a sleazeball—'

'Peter, please!' Rina pointed to Hannah.

'She's sleeping.'

'She still hears things.'

'I'm resentful.'

'I know that. I am, too.'

Decker looked at her. 'You are?'

'Yes, I am. People take advantage of me because I'm such a softy. I'd like to say no, but then I'd feel bad about it. What can I do? It's the way I am. I was born with a "sucker" gene.'

'You and me both, darling.' Decker made a face. 'We'll give it a few days. In the meantime, we'll see the boys. That's not so bad.'

'No, that's the good part. Sammy's no problem because he's in the city. Yonkie has a bit more arranging to do, but he swears he'll be with us for the weekend.'

'You're excited.'

'Of course. So are their grandparents. They're beside themselves with joy.'

Rina's late husband's parents. Not his family. What the heck? They were nice people who had endured a horrible loss. 'At least I'm making someone happy.'

Rina patted his hand. 'Being with you, Peter. That's the good part, too.'

'You have this way of dissipating my anger.'

'Then why do you look so sour?'

'But sometimes I like being angry. You're robbing me of one of my few pleasures.'

'Don't worry.' Rina told him. 'After dealing with New York City traffic, Jonathan's family, my family, and Jews in general, I'm sure you'll have plenty to be angry about.'

2

They arrived at JFK on time, and ghastly tired, trudging out of a terminal now armed with men and women in camouflage, holding M-16 rifles – standard army issue. Not only was Decker bug-eyed from lack of sleep, but also he had gone back to the station house to finish up paperwork before he left for the airport. After rearranging schedules and appointments, he had managed to take off four days from work, coming back late Wednesday night. The most pressing business – a recent string of convenience-store robberies – was now under control with two perps in custody. Mike Masters and Elwin Boyd were handling that one. Dunn and Oliver could take care of the scheduled meeting with the D.A. in the Harrigan carjacking. As they were the lead detectives, they knew more about the case than Decker did. The Beltran arraignment for the GTAs wasn't scheduled until he got back. While Decker was gone, his pickup could be handled by Bert Martinez – now Detective *Sergeant* Bert Martinez – who had been promoted just three months ago.

Rina had planned the trip's itinerary. The trio would leave New York Monday night, then spend two days with Decker's aging parents in Florida. Visiting them was something he should have done awhile ago. Perhaps this unplanned trek was a wake-up call in disguise.

Jonathan was waiting for them at the baggage counter. He was thinner than Decker had remembered, his brother's beard now equal portions of brown and gray. Bleary red-rimmed eyes tried to focus under small wire-rimmed glasses. But his dress was sharp – a blue tone-on-tone, windowpane suit, white shirt, and a bright gold tie woven in a chevron pattern. After a round of genuine hugs and kisses – the appropriate cooing at Hannah, who was grumpy and groggy – Decker commented on his sartorial splendor.

'That's because we have an appointment in forty-five minutes,' Jonathan replied. 'You said get a great criminal defense lawyer, and that's what I did. He also happens to be a *frum* Yid. Early morning was the only time he could work us in. He's noted for discounting his time for Jews in trouble. But, as I talked to him, I could tell that he was intrigued by the case. I think he's curious to meet you.'

Decker grabbed a big black valise off the conveyor belt. Thank goodness for frames with wheels. 'One more bag. Why is he curious to meet me?'

'Because you're a cop . . . on the other side, so to speak.'

'That's our other bag, Peter,' Rina said.

Decker grabbed the second suitcase. They loaded up Jonathan's dented silver 1993 Chrysler minivan, Rina insisting that Peter sit in the front. Within a few minutes, they were on their way.

The air was cold and biting – typical March weather, Jonathan told him. Dark rain clouds hung above, heavy and gray like soiled laundry. Whatever foliage there was had yet to bloom and the naked branches swayed like cobwebs in a brisk wind. The highway was moving – one less thing to be concerned about – but because of the speed, the van took the potholes with spine-numbing jolts. To Decker's eyes, the surrounding area looked worn and depressed – a mixture of old factory buildings, some commercial retail shops, and unadorned, redbrick apartment houses. Graffiti littered the concrete walls of the roadway.

'Where are we?' he asked.

'Queens,' Rina said. 'Is this Astoria?'

'Not yet.'

'Doesn't matter,' Decker said. 'It all looks the same to me. Tell me more about the Orthodox lawyer.'

'He made time for us, Akiva. Time that he could ill afford considering he's representing Anna Broughder.'

Anna Broughder. The woman dubbed by the papers as Lizzie Borden II. She had been arrested for killing both of her parents by hacking them to death with a cleaver. She had claimed it had been done by a group of crazed druggies. Somehow she had escaped through the bathroom window, withstanding only a few minor scratches to the forearms and one rather large gash to her palm. A 200-million-dollar inheritance was at stake.

'Leon Hershfield,' Decker stated.

'That's the one. The case has had coverage in L.A.?'

'Front-page articles.' Decker tried to shake fatigue from his sleep-deprived brain. 'I didn't know Hershfield was religious.'

'He doesn't wear a *kippah* in court, but he's

18

self-identified as modern Orthodox.' Jonathan tapped the wheel. 'He's defended all the biggies. He's well connected.'

Decker glanced at Rina. 'Connected, as in Joseph Donatti.'

'Among others,' Jonathan countered.

'But Donatti was his biggest triumph.' The mobster had been indicted on three counts of murder along with lesser charges of fraud and racketeering. After the third hung jury, the state declined to try the case again. Evidence kept getting lost. The Donatti name always perked Decker's interest, although his curiosity wasn't at all limited to the old man. 'When was the trial? About six years ago?'

'About.' Jonathan gripped the wheel. 'Hershfield got him off.'

'That he did.'

'You said to hire the best, Akiva.'

'Yes, I did.' Decker raised his eyebrows.

No one spoke.

'Has Hershfield given you any advice?' Decker asked.

'He wants to talk to us before we talk to the cops. By us, I think he means my brother-in-law.'

'Is your brother-in-law going to meet us there?'

'Chaim's not in any state to talk to anyone. I told him I'd talk to Hershfield first.'

'Chaim must be beside himself.' Rina reached over and smoothed Hannah's curls. She had fallen back asleep, her eyes moving behind onionskin lids, her head upward, her mouth agape. She was snoring softly.

'The whole family's crazed,' Jonathan answered.

'How is the mother holding up?'

'Minda? She's . . . we had to tranquilize her. Normally, I would never suggest medication at a time like this, but she was out of her mind with hysteria.' Jonathan hedged. 'She and Shayndie had been at odds for a couple of years.'

'That doesn't mean anything,' Rina said. 'All parents and kids fight.'

'Their arguments were . . . vitriolic,' Jonathan said. 'I'm sure Minda feels as if this is all her fault. Of course, it isn't.'

Unless she had something to do with the disappearance, Decker thought. 'So Chaim and his father own some electronic stores.'

'Yes.'

'Equal partners?'

'I don't know. It's not my business.'

'Just asking questions. Do they do all right financially?'

'The stores have been around for over thirty years. I know that the last year has been tough – the strain of living in New York topped off by the economic slowdown. But I haven't heard about any major financial problems. Of course, they wouldn't tell me if there were problems.'

'Ever hear of any improprieties in the business?'

'No.' He bit his lip. 'I really feel for my father-in-law. He lost his son. Everyone is so focused on Shaynda – and rightly so – it's almost as if they've forgotten about Ephraim. Not only does my father-in-law have to deal with the pain of his son, but he's also worried about his granddaughter.'

'When's the funeral for Ephraim?' Rina asked.

'We're hoping that they'll release the body today so that we can do the *levaya* on Sunday. But I have a feeling it's going to take longer. *Shabbos* is going to be hell, everyone in a suspended state of animation. Unless they find Shayndie today . . .' Jonathan glanced at Decker. 'That's a possibility right?'

'Of course,' Decker answered. It was still too early to predict the outcome. 'They haven't any idea of where she might be?'

'We've tried everyone – all her friends, all the public-school kids, teachers, rabbi, homeless shelters near the area where the crime happened. The Quinton police have done a door-to-door search.' He blew out air. 'When I talk about it like this, it just seems so . . . so bad.'

'It hasn't' been that long, Jon. She may turn up on her own.'

'I certainly pray that's the case.'

'Anything that I can do?' Rina offered.

'No, Rina, thanks so much.' He tapped the steering wheel again. Decker realized it was his brother's nervous habit. They drove without speaking until the crenellated Manhattan skyline popped into distant view.

Rina was staring out the window.

Jonathan said, 'You haven't been here since September eleventh?'

'No.'

'I know,' Jonathan said. 'Even now I find it strange. Every once in a while, I'll look up, expecting to see the towers.'

Rina shook her head. 'It'll be so good to see my boys.'

'My mother told me you're staying with the Lazaruses for *Shabbat*,' Jonathan said. 'They're deliriously happy about seeing everyone. It's wonderful that you've remained in contact with them.'

'They're my sons' grandparents,' Decker said.

'You'd be surprised at the pettiness I see, Akiva. Pastoral counseling is sometimes a misnomer for refereeing.'

'I can believe that,' Decker said. 'The Lazaruses are nice people. I'm sure they get a lump in their throat every time they see me with Rina.'

'Actually, they adore you,' Jonathan said. 'I think they've co-opted you as one of their own. At least that's what my mother tells me.' He tapped the wheel and cleared his throat. 'I shouldn't be so possessive. My mother is your mother, too.'

They exited the highway somewhere in the middle part of town. The main avenues were still clear, so traveling was doable. But Decker knew that within an hour, the streets would be clogged with mean-looking vehicular metal that would make him wish he were battling rush-hour traffic in L.A. At least back home, the city was car friendly. New York streets had been built for buggies, not for delivery trucks and their drivers who felt it was their God-given right to double-park even if it meant jamming up the road-ways. And the street addresses never corresponded to anything. It was impossible to find a location unless you knew it was there to begin with. To Decker, an excursion through Manhattan was akin to one big scavenger hunt.

He sat back and looked out the window, thinking about Jon's words: 'My mother is your mother, too.'

'You know, it's funny, Jon. I think of you as my half brother. And the others – your brothers and sisters – feel related to them as well. But your mother . . . who is as much my mother as yours . . . I haven't made the connection yet. I probably never will.'

Jonathan nodded. 'I can understand that. There is this small issue called my father.'

'Maybe that's it. I'm sure I make her very uncomfortable—'

'Not really. She knows her secret is safe with all of us.'

'Psychologically then.' Decker laughed. 'I like your mother. I really do. But my own mother is still alive. It's unfair to expect a man to have more than one mother at any given time.'

'Not to mention a couple of mothers-in-law,' Rina added. 'My mother *and* Mrs Lazarus.'

Decker frowned. 'Yeah, that too. Two mothers, two mothers-in-law, two daughters, and a wife. I'm surrounded by all these estrogen-filled beings. Don't you feel sorry for me?'

'I would,' Rina answered. 'Except right now I'm cranky because of PMS.'

Her face was deadpan. Decker couldn't tell if she was serious or not. But he didn't question her. Never rouse a sleeping lion.

3

The sign said $16.83 an hour to park the car: Decker wasn't sure if he read it right, but then Rina said something about space in the city being at a premium. Space or no space, the rates were usurious. Since a typical leisurely paced business meeting could last two to three hours, Decker now knew why New Yorkers talked so fast.

Hershfield had the requisite Fifth Avenue address, and Jonathan miraculously found parking on a side street because it was still early. As soon as Rina unbelted Hannah, the girl woke up as cranky as a coot. Decker held her as they walked, the monolithic buildings blocking out what little light the sky had to offer. Rubbish cans and Dumpsters lined the sidewalk. With any luck, there wouldn't be a garbage truck blocking the van when they had to leave. Hannah whined as they walked into the granite lobby of the skyscraper and checked in with the security desk, manned by six gray-jacketed sentries. She complained she had to go to the bathroom.

'No public rest rooms,' the guard announced.

'What do you mean there's no public rest room?' Decker countered. 'This is a sixty-story building.'

'Security precaution. It's key only. Mr Hershfield's

office is on the forty-third floor. You can take the express elevator up.'

Rina grabbed Peter's arm and brought him over to a bank of elevators. 'Don't start.'

'Guy's an idiot. Do we look like terrorists—'

'Shhh. He'll hear you.'

'That's the idea.'

'I have to go to the bathroom—'

'In a minute, pumpkin,' Decker growled.

Moments later, as they were whisked up to the forty-third floor, Hannah moaned that her ears hurt. By the time they reached the first secretary, Hannah was saying that her bladder was about to burst.

'Can we use the bathroom?' Rina asked.

'Three floors down,' the secretary answered. 'Take the internal elevator and go to the right. Ask for Britta.'

'But there's one right over there,' Decker pointed out.

'Employees only. Fortieth floor, sir. That's where Mr Hershfield's offices are anyway.'

'I finally found a place more bureaucratic than the LAPD.'

'Come on, Peter,' Rina tugged at his jacket. 'Getting her angry won't help.'

'Listen to your wife.' Then she turned her back to them.

They waited at the elevators as Hannah whimpered in Decker's arms.

'Cry louder, pumpkin,' Decker told her.

'Peter—'

'Scream a little. Wailing's okay, too.'

Another elevator ride. By now, Hannah was complaining of nausea. She reached out to her mother.

Rina took her and marched over to the first person she saw. A fifty-plus woman with short clipped brunette hair and hoop earrings. She had round brown eyes and wore bright red lipstick. Over her black sweater was chunky jewelry. Half-size reading glasses sat on the bridge of her nose.

'I'm looking for Britta,' Rina announced.

'That's me.'

'They're looking for Mr Hershfield.' Rina cocked her finger in the mens' direction. '*I'm* looking for the bathroom. She's got to go, and apparently this floor has the only public bathroom in the entire building!'

'Lenore didn't let you use the forty-third-floor one?'

'No, she did not!'

'What a peach!' Britta stood and extracted a ring of keys. 'I'll take you, sweetheart. Poor thing.' She looked at the men. 'Is one of you Rabbi Levine?'

'I am,' Jonathan said.

'Third door on the right. Mr Hershfield's expecting you. Just knock. I'll get you coffee in a moment.' To Rina, Britta said, 'Come, dahling. I know what it's like to be captive to a small bladder. After I had my last child, I ruined outfits every time I sneezed.'

Decker watched the women disappear behind the sacred door known as the women's rest room. Then he and Jonathan found the office. A gold doorplate told them that Hershfield was a legal corporation. Jonathan knocked. A stentorian voice bade them enter.

His office was the size of a secretary's reception room. Then Decker realized it was the secretary's reception room. The desk held a nameplate that said MS MOORE. The person behind the desk definitely wasn't female. He was Ichabod Crane, alive and well and practicing law in the city of New York. His cheeks were so sharp that they almost poked out of the thin skin. His forehead was high and bare, with thinning dark hair combed straight back. His lips were two slash marks, his eyes were sunken in his brow. Still the orbs held a spark of mischief. He was superbly dressed – black crepe wool jacket, white shirt with French cuffs, and patterned tie of horses and gladiators – probably two-hundred-dollar Leonard tie.

Hershfield looked up at the standing figures. 'This is my receptionist's office. I get my best work done here at six in the morning when no one's bothering me . . . buzzing me every twenty seconds. Of course, that's her job . . . to buzz me, and to organize my professional life. I don't know why, but I find her desk much more conducive to work. Maybe because it isn't filled with my own garbage.'

Gathering up his papers, Hershfield stood, then took out a key ring. He opened an adjoining door. 'Come in.'

Good-size place, Decker thought. Not cavernous, but the plate-glass window view opened things up – an endless snapshot of steely, gelid air and rooftop machinery. The office itself was paneled in warm red mahogany. Sharing the wall space with the abstract oils were lots of diplomas and certificates. He had a small bookcase in the back of his desk, the shelves holding just as many Hebrew books as tomes on American jurisprudence. Of course, the firm had its own law library, so the references he had were the ones he probably used the most. His desk was rose-wood and brass, his desk chair tufted oxblood leather.

Two client chairs sat opposite the desk, upholstered in a subtle hunter green and maroon floral. In the middle of the room sat a sofa in the same pattern and two more client chairs, the arrangements separated by a sleek rosewood coffee table framed in brass. A corner leather wing chair rounded out the atmosphere. The parquet wood floor was almost entirely covered by a fringed, ornate Persian rug.

There was a knock at his door. Hershfield answered it, and Rina came in. She had applied some fresh makeup. She was wearing a navy sweater over a navy skirt, and black boots. Hannah was in her arms.

'And who is this *motek*?' Hershfield asked.

'This is Hannah.' Rina shifted the girl in her arms. 'You wouldn't have any orange juice on you, would you?'

'I'd have anything you want.' He buzzed Britta. The brunette came in holding a pencil. 'Could you run to Harry's?'

'No, I can't run. But I can walk.'

Hershfield ignored her. He turned to Hannah. 'What can I get you, *kleinkind*?'

'Are you hungry, sweetie?' Rina said to her daughter.

'No, just *grumpy*.'

'But maybe you'd be less grumpy if you ate.' Rina looked at Britta. 'Maybe I should come with you.'

'Sure,' Britta said. 'We've already done our bathroom bonding. Would any of you gentlemen like something?'

'Coffee,' Decker said.

'I'll go along with that,' Jonathan said.

'Mr Hershfield?'

'If it isn't too much work,' the lawyer answered.

'That's what you're paying me for, Mr H.'

The females left.

The man was all folksy and polite. In a courtroom, he was part Tasmanian devil, part wolverine. Anyone who came up against him got bit. Decker stuck out his hand. 'We haven't met formally, Mr Hershfield. I'm Peter Decker.'

'The Homicide detective I told you about,' Jonathan said.

'Actually, you're selling him short, Rabbi Levine. The lieutenant here is actually in charge of the detectives' division. Where do you work? Somewhere in the San Fernando Valley?'

'I see you've done your homework.'

'I'm nothing if not compulsive.'

'My division is in the West Valley – Devonshire. Do you know L.A?'

'I have a brother in Beverly Hills. Corporate law. He's got a beautiful house. It's got an entry hall that you could skate in. My brother's very successful.'

'It must run in the family,' Decker said.

'Me?' Hershfield made a face. 'I'm just a bulldog who believes in due process. Sit down, gentlemen.'

The gentlemen sat.

Hershfield smiled at Decker. 'So hiring counsel was your idea. I'm not surprised. You know what the police are capable of.'

Decker smiled back.

Hershfield said, 'Are you related to the victim?'

'No.'

'We're brothers.' Jonathan pointed to Decker, then to himself. 'Half brothers. The victim was my brother-in-law.'

'I'm just debating how much we should talk in

front of him,' Hershfield said.

'Technically, I can be subpoenaed and made to testify because I'm not a family member,' Decker said.

'It doesn't matter,' Jonathan said, 'because the family's not involved. I'm sure of it.'

'I appreciate your loyalty, Rabbi, but I think your brother has a point.' Hershfield shrugged. 'Look, Lieutenant Decker told you to call me because he thinks you might have a little problem. And you're here because you don't want a big problem. Very smart. So talk to me, gentlemen. What did you have in mind, Lieutenant, when you asked the rabbi to call me?'

'First, I was thinking about contacting the police to see if I can get anything specific out of the investigation. Sometimes agencies are open, sometimes they're protective. If I get some resistance, it would be nice to have a New Yorker to do some legal pushing.'

'If need be, I suppose that could be arranged.'

'I have a feeling you could arrange anything, Mr Hershfield.'

'Ah, Lieutenant. You make me blush.'

Britta returned holding a tray of coffee, creamer, and packets of sugar substitute. Rina was holding Hannah's hand and a tray with bagels and cream cheese. The two women set the food down on Hershfield's coffee table. Rina looked at the men. 'Hannaleh, maybe we'll eat this outside in the secretary's office.'

'Don't leave on our account,' Hershfield said.

'Of course not. It's just better all around. That way, we won't disturb anyone.'

'You know, there's a Disney store on Fifth Avenue around Fifty-fifth.'

'I'm sure there is, but I doubt if it's open at seven.'

'A very good point.'

'Come eat next to me,' Britta said. 'Alma's always late anyway.'

'She is?' Hershfield said.

Britta whispered, 'It's that time of life.' She nodded, then took some bagels and cream cheese. 'See you later.'

As soon as the door closed, Hershfield spoke to Jonathan. 'So why don't you tell me what happened from your family's perception? The lieutenant and I can fill in details from the police.'

Jonathan gave Hershfield a brief recap. Way too brief, Decker thought. Immediately, Hershfield went after him. 'So you have no theory as to what happened?'

'None.'

'Then something's missing.' He made a face. 'And your brother-in-law. Did he have any vices?'

Jonathan squirmed.

'Drugs,' Decker told him.

'Ah.'

Jonathan said, 'But he'd been sober for a while.'

'What kind of drugs?'

Jonathan sighed. 'Mainly cocaine.'

'Freebase?'

'Blow,' Decker said.

'Expensive,' Hershfield said. 'Where did he get the money?'

'The family has a business,' Decker said.

'Yes, I know. Electronic stores,' Hershfield said. 'And, Rabbi, you think the family gave him money to waste on blow?'

31

Jonathan sighed. 'I'm sure they helped him out of a couple of tight spots.'

'Or he helped himself,' Decker offered. 'He worked in the family business.'

'He only started working after he was sober,' Jonathan countered, defending him.

'Any criminal record?' Hershfield asked.

'One arrest.'

Decker looked at his half brother. 'That must have slipped your mind.'

'Possession?' Hershfield asked.

Jonathan squirmed. 'Soliciting an undercover police officer.'

'Jon, it would have been nice if you'd told me that over the phone.'

'I didn't think it was relevant. It happened ten years ago, right after his divorce.'

'But it does show what kind of man he was—'

'Ten years ago, Akiva.'

'Your brother is right,' Hershfield said. 'At the moment, everything is important.'

'What are you thinking about, Mr Hershfield?' Jonathan said. 'That Ephraim had a relapse of his drug use? That the setup was a drug buy gone haywire?'

'Is that what it seems to you?'

Jonathan didn't answer.

Decker said, 'You left out a couple parts, Jonathan. Ephraim was found naked.'

'They could have stripped him,' Jonathan said.

'That's always a possibility,' Hershfield answered. 'Then there is the other possibility.'

No one spoke.

'Yes, I would say that's important,' Hershfield said.

'Especially since he was supposed to be baby-sitting his fifteen-year-old niece.'

'My wife had previously asked Shayndie if any funny business was going on. She adamantly denied it.'

Neither Decker nor Hershfield answered.

Jonathan stammered, 'Yes, of course, it's a possibility that she was lying – or covering for him. But how would murder be part of that picture?'

Decker said, 'Maybe he had been threatening her, Jonathan. Maybe she had had enough.' He looked pointedly at Hershfield. 'In which case, she'll be needing a very good defense lawyer.'

'Then why go willingly with him to the art exhibit, Akiva?' Jonathan said. 'Believe me, Shayndie is an opinionated girl. If he was molesting her, she would have said something.'

'Not always, Jonathan. Especially if she was in love with him.'

Jonathan bristled. 'At this point, it's all speculation.'

Decker put a hand on his shoulder. 'I don't mean to upset you, Jon. But if I'm thinking of these kinds of questions, and Mr Hershfield is thinking about these types of questions, I'm sure the New York Police are thinking the same thing.'

'Now that is true,' Hershfield said.

Jonathan seemed to wilt. 'I'm sure you're right.'

Hershfield said, 'I'm intrigued about this relationship – uncle, niece. It is unusual, especially in that community where postpubescent girls are not allowed to be with single men except their fathers. Why do you think the girl's parents allowed such a relationship to flourish?'

Jonathan went on to explain Shayndie's problems.

'Ephraim seemed to have a special rapport with her. I never saw anything inappropriate.'

'How much time did you and your wife spend with your niece?'

'She'd come over for dinner on Sundays . . . spend an occasional *Shabbat*, although Chaim wasn't wild about that. He was often vocal in his objection. We're Conservative Jews, and my brother's Chasidic.'

'So to him, we're all goyim.'

'Probably,' Jonathan admitted.

'And your brother-in-law didn't like your entertaining his daughter because you're Conservative. But he didn't object to his unmarried, drug-addicted brother spending time with her?' He turned to Decker. 'What am I missing?'

Decker shrugged. 'You're more in the loop than I am.'

Hershfield said, 'You said that you and your wife had questioned Shayndie about her relationship with her uncle, your wife's brother. Why?'

'Just to . . . make sure.'

'So there was no . . . precipitating factor that led up to the questioning?'

'No, not at all. Raisie and I discussed the relationship, and we both decided that the girl should be talked to. You know as well as I do that in that community, sex is taboo.'

'So is an uncle–niece liaison. *Halachacally*, it's equivalent to incest.'

'As far as I know, he wasn't molesting her.'

'Let's switch gears for a moment,' Hershfield said. 'You told me that Chaim works with his father in the business. What about Ephraim? What did he do other than dabble in drugs?'

'Like I said, he'd been sober for over two years,' Jonathan insisted.

'All right. Have it your way. And he worked in the family business with his father and brother.'

'Yes.'

'Alongside Chaim?'

'Chaim's been in the business for twenty years, so he has seniority naturally. Ephraim knew that.'

'So there haven't been any problems?'

'Not that I know of. From my perspective, Papa was thrilled that his son finally showed some interest in family affairs.'

'All right. And what about the business? Is it solvent?'

'Akiva asked the same questions. Sure, it's been going through some rough times. Everyone's on edge and the economy isn't the greatest. But yes, as far as I know, the stores are solvent.'

'Any bad loans?' Decker asked.

'Not that I know of.'

'Any bad investments?'

'You'd be much better off asking Chaim.'

'I will do that,' answered Decker. 'And I guarantee you, so will the police.'

'Why would the murder have anything to do with the business? The stores have always run on a small profit margin. There's nothing there to get excited about.'

'I'm sure he's just trying to get a lay of the land,' Hershfield said. 'If I can talk frankly for a moment, Rabbi, you know that the Chasidim in your brother's area have been in trouble for embezzling public-school funds and transferring the money to the local yeshivas. Is either of your brothers-in-law active in local politics?'

'Not that I know. They're shleppers, Mr Hershfield. They make their money by dint of hard work.'

'Two years ago, Yosi Stern was indicted on drug-sales charges. I wasn't his lawyer. If I had been, he wouldn't be upstate right now. He used Chasidim to smuggle in ecstasy from Holland, then laundered the drug money through local yeshivas and businesses of the Chasidim. What would you know about that?'

'Nothing,' Jonathan said.

'And your wife's family?'

'My father-in-law would never permit it.' Jonathan was adamant. 'He's a camp survivor. He kept his wits about him the entire time by an unwavering trust in God. He's not only a religious man, but a good man.'

'The two don't always go hand in hand,' Decker said.

Hershfield got up and made himself some coffee. 'Let's take a break. Bagels, anyone?'

Jonathan dropped his head into his hands, but Decker stood up. 'I'm hungry.' He smeared some cream cheese over a poppy seed bagel. 'Anyplace to wash?'

Hershfield popped a panel door and a wet bar appeared. He held up a *becher* – a traditional washing cup. 'I am fully prepared.'

Decker washed and ate, cajoling Jonathan to do the same. Fifteen minutes later, after saying the grace over bread, Hershfield sat back in his desk chair. He was all-business.

'I have made a decision,' he announced. 'You'll like the outcome, I think. If you need representation, I'd be happy to fit you into my busy schedule. But there's a condition.'

'What's that?' Jonathan asked.

'If your family hires me, they're going to have to work *with me*. That means if I ask them questions, they will have to answer me truthfully.' He shook his finger at Jonathan. 'This isn't the *shuk*, Rabbi. This isn't haggling until we find a story we both like. I must know what's going on so I can perform the service to the best of my ability. Oftentimes, the subtleties of attorney/client privilege are lost on some of our black-hat brethren. They seem to consider it an insult to answer me truthfully. I will not deal with clients like that. At this point in my life, I don't need that *tsuris*. Am I clear?'

Jonathan nodded. 'I understand.'

Hershfield stood. 'I have a couple of very important depositions this morning. In the meantime, it is within everyone's best interest if your family refrains from talking to the police unless I am there during the questioning.' He turned to Decker. 'I'm sure this isn't the case with you, Lieutenant, but a few of your renegade comrades have played it pretty loose with Miranda.'

Decker was expressionless. 'If you say so.'

Hershfield laughed. 'And you're planning to contact your fellow brothers in blue?'

'I'd like to take a look at a report or two.'

'And you'll keep me abreast.'

'I'll do whatever I can, Mr Hershfield.'

'So what happens if your findings put you in conflict with your family obligations?'

'Yes, I've thought about that.'

'And?'

'And . . .' Decker looked at his watch. 'And I think it's time to go.'

4

It was still early, and the detectives weren't in yet. Decker left his name and number with a desk sergeant and on the squad room's phone machine. If no one called his cell back by nine, he'd just show up and deal with it in person. Hannah needed to settle down and so did Rina. Jonathan drove them into Brooklyn – traffic mercifully going the other way on the bridge. When the van got to Eastern Parkway – a main thoroughfare in the borough – things took on a familiar focus. It had been ten years since Decker had been here, but he had gotten to know the streets fairly well because he had been searching for someone in the area.

A missing kid, actually.

History repeating itself?

Maybe. That wasn't all that bad. That kid had turned up alive.

As they passed the avenues – Forty-second, Forty-third, Forty-fourth – Decker was surprised by how many people were up and about. Gaggles of bearded men – most of them bespectacled – dressed in black woolen suits, white shirts, and black hats, with their side locks, called *payot*, bouncing off their shoulders as they moved with quick strides down the sidewalks.

The boys and teens were miniversions of the men except for no facial hair. There were also dozens of kerchief-headed women bundled in coats pushing prams while trying to contain the multitude of children who surrounded them. Some had as many as ten children, the older daughters assigned the role of mother's assistant to their younger siblings. There were groups of school-age girls, toting enormous backpacks (some things were the same world over), garbed in parochial uniforms – long-sleeved white shirts, blue skirts with hemlines way below the knee. Their legs were encased in opaque tights, heavy coats on their backs.

The air was nippy now, so the thick suits and woolen coats and stockings were not only modest but also practical. But Decker knew that when summer arrived with temperatures soaring into the triple digits and 90 percent humidity, the Chasidish attire wouldn't alter much. The exterior coats would be gone, but still they'd sweat into their long-sleeved clothing, drenched and itchy with dark circles of perspiration under their arms and around their necks, faces moist with muggy air. Yet they'd accept their lot, endure the heat and the humidity, wearing the discomfort like ill-fitting shoes.

Regarding the girls, Decker couldn't help but think of Shaynda. All of these preteens and teens were so fresh-faced with their hair in pigtails, ponytails, or a long braid that trailed down their backs. None wore a drop of makeup or nail polish . . . even the adolescent girls.

Especially the adolescent girls.

What was Shaynda's big sin? Wearing nail polish or makeup? Hanging out at the mall? Breaking away and being with the public-school kids? It seemed so harmless, but not in this community. It would give the locals the wrong idea about the girl, making it hard for her parents to find her a proper *shiddach* – a match for marriage.

The streets were lined with stores catering to the Jewish trade – kosher cafés, pizza joints and restaurants, kosher meat markets and butchers, produce markets advertising day-old sales, a dress shop featuring discount *shaytles* – wigs. There were stores that specialized in *sepharim*, or religious books, and there were smiths that forged esoteric silver objects like torah *yads* – pointers that a prayer leader would use while reading from the holy scroll. Decker noticed a studio for a *sofer* – a scribe. Every other establishment seemed to be a *schtiebl*, or a small storefront synagogue. Maybe some of the places had changed hands, but the overall gestalt of the area was the same – except that the population seemed even *more* religious than it had been ten years ago. How was that possible?

Jonathan pulled the van curbside in front of a small two-story brick home on a block of small two-story brick homes. This was the house of Lazarus, the abode of Rina's former in-laws. As always, Decker wanted to wait in the car until it was over. The Lazaruses had gone through the ultimate tragedy, and he always felt as if he were a painful reminder of what shouldn't have been. Yet, as soon as the motor died, the short, squat couple flew out of the doorway with smiles so wide that they almost bisected their faces. They greeted Decker with a generosity of spirit that defined them as the lovely people they were. Heavy-breasted, apron-wearing, Mrs Lazarus hugged and kissed Rina; white-bearded Rav Lazarus pumped Decker's hand with vigor that defied a man of eighty-six. Both of them made over Hannah as if she were a blood granddaughter, greeting her with a plate of cookies and several wrapped presents. The little girl smiled, thanking them shyly, calling them Bubbe and Zeyde.

After everyone made nice, Decker took the suitcases into the house. The small living room was hot and stuffy and enveloped in the aromas of chicken soup, roasting meat, and the sweet smell of chocolate-chip cookies, reminding Decker's stomach that a bagel hadn't been much of a breakfast. But he'd satisfy the hunger pangs later. He looked at his watch, wondering when he could make a graceful exit. Rina caught it and came to his rescue.

'I know you have work to do. Go. I'll make excuses.'

'Are you sure?'

'Of course. The brother's still dead and the girl's still missing.'

'Try to have a good time,' Decker told his wife.

'You know, that just might happen. They've completely taken over Hannah's care. They even bought her a *TV*.'

'That's right,' Decker said. 'These people don't have TVs, do they?'

'*These people!*' Rina elbowed him. 'Well, now they do have a TV. So there!' Her smile was wide. 'I think I'm going to take a hot bath. Then I'm going to relax!'

Decker felt content. It was good to see Rina so happy. She always seemed calm and content in this ultrareligious environment. He had always thought of himself as the one and only giver, the person who had completely changed his ways to please her. Now he was aware that she, too, had adjusted her life to make a home with him. He kissed her modestly on the cheek. 'I want you to promise me something.'

'What?'

'That after you relax, you take off your shoes and relax some more.'

Her blue eyes were dazzling. 'That's a very good idea. I'll see you in about six, seven hours.'

'That's right. It's *Shabbos* tonight.'

'How much can you really find out in six hours?'

'Depends. I've solved cases in thirty minutes.'

'Really?'

'Really.'

'What's the longest it ever took you to solve a homicide?'

Decker laughed. 'Don't know. The files are still open.'

Quinton was a town divided. On one side of the main municipal park – Liberty Field – was an upscale upstate rural suburb. Two-story Federal-style brick houses were perched on large lots with SUVs and Mercedes parked in the driveways. Sinuous lanes and roadways were edged by tall trees and old-fashioned street lighting with fixtures that looked like a sprig of flowers. Some of the sidewalks weren't even paved. There were lots of big sycamores and oaks that would provide much-needed shade in the summer, although they were bare at the moment. The exceptions were the pines, and a few stately early bloomers with budding branches, greening the wood as if it were covered in moss.

Taft, Taylor, and Tyler streets held the local shopping. Lots of the usual names – The Gap, Banana Republic, Star$s, Ann Taylor, Victoria's Secret, Pottery Barn – chains, yes, but at least they were individual stores, not units housed under the one big roof with adjacent parking lots the size of Lake Tahoe. Here, the parking was the diagonal kind – on the streets and free. Decker commented to Jonathan about the absence of a mall and asked where Shayndie found one.

'There's one in the next town – Bainberry.'

'It's pretty here . . . old-fashioned.'

'This side is, yes.'

'This side as opposed to . . .'

Jonathan stared out the window.

'How far away are we from the religious side?' Decker asked.

'Don't worry. You'll know when you're there.'

Tree studded and filled with multicolored tulip beds, Liberty Field contained the requisite courthouses, the hall of records, the main police and fire stations, and a library. There was also a small lake, a botanical garden, an indoor skating rink, bowling alley, and a community center, where the Quinton High School production of *Pajama Game* was playing.

Traveling past the park, Jonathan steered the van onto a road sided by sylvan copses of denuded trees. Minutes passed; then new groupings of houses came into view. These were smaller, less adorned, and more functional. The driveways held cheaper cars and vans – sometimes even two vans. The lots were smaller and barer, and the shopping district was quite different from its upscale cousin. Except for the word 'Quinton' every now and then, it could have been interchangeable with the religious stores and shuls and same-sex parochial schools of Boro Park. The residents were also identical, down to the wigs and black-hat dress. It was hard to reconcile the two areas as a single town. Decker asked why the two populations chose to share, when each area had such a distinct identity.

'At this point, the municipality needs every single bit of property tax to keep Quinton going. If the Frummies seceded, there wouldn't be enough money to keep the services going.'

'Are there problems between the two halves?'

'Yes,' Jonathan said. 'But they need each other. There have been some compromises. But there have also been some nasty wars. At the moment, the Frummies want their own school district, but they want the city to pay for it. They don't understand the concept of separation of church and state. Even worse, they don't understand why it's good for them in the long run.'

'They have a point,' Decker said. 'They pay in taxes, but don't get anything back.'

'You've been talking to Rina. All the Orthodox like the voucher system.'

'Yes, she likes the voucher system, but she's come to realize that there's a point in maintaining a strong public-school system.'

'Well, then she's a first,' Jonathan said. 'The Frummies get the fire department, the garbage pickup, the police department. And lately, there's been some talk about their using the public schools in the morning, then going to the yeshivas in the afternoon so the yeshivas wouldn't have to hire teachers for secular studies.'

'That seems like a good idea,' Decker said.

'Unfortunately, the Frummies don't want the teachers teaching evolution, or sex education, or biology of any kind. Things that are mandatory in the Quinton school curriculum. Plus' – Jonathan sighed – 'the Frummies don't care about secular education. They were dragging down the standardized test scores. There was a big town meeting about it. It got ugly. Here we are.'

Jonathan parked the car.

Decker said, 'You don't approve.'

'I'm not saying you compromise your principles,' Jonathan said. 'But you don't have to create spectacles. Then when you throw in the embezzlement charges . . . It reflects poorly on all of us.'

'No group is perfect.'

'Of course not. And the vast majority here is wonderful. But when you choose to make yourself visible, you do have an obligation to be a *Kiddush Hashem*.'

Kiddush Hashem: it more or less meant to set a good example for God.

'Ready?' Jonathan asked.

'Sure.'

The rabbi opened the door to the van and got out. Decker followed him up the stone walkway to an unassuming two-story brick house similar to those in Boro Park. Jonathan didn't bother to knock. He opened the door and stepped inside.

'Chaim?' Jonathan turned to Decker. 'Come in. They're expecting us. Chaim?'

'Yonasan?' The voice was coming from upstairs.

'Yeah, it's me. I have Akiva.'

'I'll be right down.'

The living room was deceptively spacious. Or maybe it was just the lack of furniture. There was a small grouping around a fireplace – an upholstered couch facing a couple of chairs. But the rest had been formed into a dining room – a square table covered with a white cloth and surrounded by twelve chairs. The floor was tiled with limestone squares, no rug to soften the hard surface. There was a piano in the corner, sheet music on the stand. Decker wondered if Shaynda played.

The walls were painted off-white, freshly done, and bare except for several framed pictures of wizened, bearded rabbis. One was Menachem Mendel Schneershon – the Lubavitcher rebbe. Another was the Chofetz Chaim – a great Jewish scholar of the nineteenth century. Decker didn't recognize any of the other remaining portraits. Maybe the Liebers had other art and hadn't gotten around to hanging it up. Somehow Decker doubted that.

A gray-bearded man scrambled down the staircase. Around five-ten and lean, he appeared to be in his forties. He wore the usual Chasidic uniform – black suit, white shirt. No hat on his head; instead, he wore a big black velvet yarmulke. The hair that showed was very thin. Underneath the *kippah*, he was probably bald. He shook hands with Decker: the palms were calloused. Clearly, a man who did more than learn all day.

'Chaim Lieber.' He dropped Decker's hand. 'I can't thank you enough. I don't know what to say.'

'Please.'

His eyes watered. 'Please sit, Lieutenant.'

'Akiva's fine. Or Peter.' Decker sat down. 'I'm so sorry to meet you under these circumstances.'

'Actually, we met at happier times.'

'At my wedding,' Jonathan said.

'Oh yes, of course.'

'*Auf simchas*,' Lieber muttered. His hazel eyes were red rimmed. Then he rubbed his forehead. 'We've looked for her everywhere. So there's no need for you to . . .'

'I'm sure you have. Still, sometimes in a panic we overlook—'

'What I really need is for someone to talk to the police,' Lieber blurted out. 'Maybe they know something that can help us find her . . . find Shay—' His voice choked. 'Find Shayndie. If you could find out what the police know, that would help.'

'I agree.'

Lieber leaned forward. 'Do you think they'll talk to you?'

'I don't know, Mr Lieber—'

'Chaim, please! It's important that they talk to you. You know what questions to ask. We don't.' He rubbed his forehead. 'I want . . .' He broke into tears. 'I want my daughter back!'

'I'm so sorry —'

'Don't be sorry! Instead, do something!' He shook his head. 'I'm sorry—'

'Please,' Decker said. 'It's fine. Can I ask you a few questions, Chaim?'

'Anything at all.'

'I know your daughter was doing some . . . experimenting—'

'That's a dead end!' Lieber stated. 'We checked with those kids. The police checked with those kids. Nothing!'

'Do you have some names?'

'I don't remember . . . goyishe names. Ryan, Brian, Ian, Evan . . . You'll have to talk to the Quinton Police. But that's a dead end. You need to talk to the Manhattan Police. That's where she disappeared.'

'I have calls in to them.'

'Did they call you back?'

'Not yet.'

'New York Police is understaffed now. You'll have to keep at them.'

'I figured I'd just go down and show up in person. I'm a lieutenant. Sometimes that'll help. Sometimes not. Depends how cooperative they feel. I'd like to look at Shayndie's room.'

'Certain – oh no. You can't. My father's sleeping there. He was up all night.'

Decker was quiet.

'He's an old man,' Lieber said. 'Frail.'

'It's just the sooner I look, the more likely it is that I'll find—'

'Why don't you come back?' Lieber suggested. 'After you talk to the police. You can tell us what they say. And by then, I'm sure my father will be up. And my wife, too. You'd like to talk to her, I assume.'

'Of course.'

'She's out cold. Yonasan told me to give her pills, right?'

Jonathan nodded, but was clearly uncomfortable with the advice he had given.

Decker said, 'Can I just ask you about the other times Shaynda ran away?'

Lieber turned his head. 'Not *times*. A time. One time. She sneaked out and went to a party. The other kids started doing terrible things. She got scared and called us to pick her up. At least she had the sense to do that.'

'What happened?'

'I picked her up, what do you think?'

'Did you punish her?'

'Of course she was punished! She was lucky that the boys didn't try anything with her. Stupid child!' He winced. 'I was mad at her. Now I wish . . .'

Decker nodded.

'A rebellious child can take a lot from you.'

'I know, sir. One of my boys has a mind of his own.'

'It's different with boys! They can protect themselves! Girls can't. And girls get stupid when it comes to boys.'

'I'm sure you're right.'

'One time!' Lieber insisted. 'She promised that she'd do better after that. It really scared her.'

'What in specific?'

'I don't know! I wasn't there. I assume it was drugs and sex! All of those kids are wild animals. The parents have no control. They're no better than the kids – divorce, affairs, drugs, and alcohol – no wonder the children are beasts.'

Jonathan looked away, his jaw bulging under his cheek.

'She was doing better,' Lieber said. 'My brother . . . by no means a *tzaddick* . . . but he was . . . he had . . . She would talk to him. It was helping her. It was helping *him*. I thought he was doing *better*.'

'Maybe he was doing better, Chaim,' Jonathan offered.

'Yes, Yonasan, that's why they found him naked in a hotel room!'

Jonathan blew out air.

Chaim punched his right hand inside his left. 'Please, Akiva. Go down and talk to the police. If we find out what happened to Ephraim, then maybe we can find out what happened to Shayndie. Please. It's Friday. You don't have much time because of *Shabbos*. Go now!'

'I'd still like to see her room,' Decker said.

'Yes, yes. This afternoon. Come back and we'll talk then.'

'I could use a picture.'

'The police have one. Go talk to the police.' Chaim stood up and extended his hand. 'I can't thank you enough.'

Decker rose from the chair and shook the limp fingers. 'I haven't done anything yet.'

'Yes, you have. You're here and that's something.' He held up a finger. 'Like Moshe Rabainu and Avraham Avenu, you came when you heard the call.'

5

The number left on Decker's cell phone belonged to Detective Mick Novack of the two-eight – the 28th Precinct. The conversation consisted of a five-minute recap, Decker explaining who he was and why he was here.

Novack said, 'I just got all the paperwork I needed for searchin' the vic's apartment. Super's gonna meet me there with the key, along with someone from the six-three. Betcha they'll send Stan Gindi. The apartment's in Flatbush. Wanna meet me there?'

'Sounds good. Where's Flatbush?'

Dead space over the phone. Then Novack said, 'It's in Brooklyn. You heard of Brooklyn?'

'We have Brooklyn Bagel Company in Los Angeles.'

'Great. I'm working with a greener. Where are you calling from?'

'Quinton.'

'Quinton? What the hell you doing in Quinton?'

'I've just come from a visit with the vic's family – his brother.'

'That's right. So you're upstate. You'll still probably get there faster than me. I'm all the way uptown – Amsterdam and one sixty-two. Traffic's a killer. Freaky Friday.' He gave Decker the address. 'I don't

Faye Kellerman

suppose you know how to get there . . . to Flatbush.'

'Nope. But my brother's driving. He knows the place. He's the vic's brother-in-law.'

'The rabbi. Yeah, we talked to him yesterday. Seems like a nice guy. Except I heard he just hired a mouthpiece – Hershfield of all people.'

'That was on my advice. I told my brother to hire the best defense attorney around.'

'Your advice? What? You don't trust us out here? C'mon. All of America loves New York's finest.'

'Indeed they do. It's nothing like that. I don't know what's going on. The family needs to be protected.'

'Whose side are you on?'

'The side of truth, justice, and the American way.'

'Another one from L.A. who thinks he's Superman. I'll give you the address. Got pencil and paper?'

'Yep.'

'A *real* pencil and paper?'

Decker paused. There was hostility in the man's voice, but that was to be expected. They weren't exactly adversaries, but right now, they weren't colleagues, either. 'Last time I checked they weren't figments of my imagination.'

'It's not a stupid question even though it seems like a stupid question. All you jokers from L.A. got these PalmPilots. One day, you're gonna be caught in a thunderstorm and all your data's gonna be fried to a crisp.'

The first detective whom Decker met was five-ten, stick-skinny, and bald with round brown eyes and a big red mustache. He wore a gray suit with a white shirt and a black tie. That was Gindi. Novack was a bit taller – around six feet and completely square. He had a broken boxer's nose, wide, thick cheeks, and thick lips. His shoe-polish-black hair was combed straight back revealing a dune's worth of forehead, a deep brow, and hooded midnight blue eyes. His suit was dark blue, his shirt was white, and his tie was a dizzy pattern of thin red and blue stripes.

'I'm the resident Jewish detective for uptown,' Novack explained. 'Anytime one of the Chasids or Israelis or Jews gets whacked in Manhattanville or its environs, it's either me, or Marc Greenbaum, or Alan Josephs. They like a Jew for the Jews, just like they like a black to deal with the blacks, or a Puerto Rican with Puerto Ricans. Sometimes they might assign a Cuban to the Doms uptown. We have several Koreans with Koreans, and a couple of Taiwanese. We got a separate guy for Haitians. Over in Brooklyn, if it's a Jew, it's Steve Gold, or Ken Geraldnick, or Stan here. Am I right about this?'

'You are right,' Gindi concurred. 'Not that I think that's bad.'

'I didn't say it was bad.'

Gindi said, 'We got quite a few Jewish cops in Brooklyn. I think more in Brooklyn than in the city. Course we got a high concentration of Jews in Brooklyn. Not so many where you are, Mick.'

'No, not so many, although all the West Side Jews keep on pushing the limits farther north. Then you go *all the way* north, you got the ones in Wash Heights. That's why I was there this morning.'

'What happened this morning?' Gindi asked.

'Some discount-jewelry store in my area was hit. The owner was a Chasid – took some lead in the ass of all places. Guy lives in Wash Heights. He won't be making it to minyan tonight, but it coulda been lots worse.'

They were standing in front of a six-story flat-faced brick building that had been overlaid with soot. The sky's cloud cover had thinned, but the air was still cold and acrid. The side street that Ephraim had called home was narrow and filled with potholes. The sidewalks were cracked with a red, gritty slush leaking from the crevices. Next to the building was a small dirt lot containing lots of garbage and several bare-branched saplings.

'What kind of area is this?' Decker asked. 'Working class?'

'This particular area, yeah. Very Jewish, very religious. Not where *his* people live.' Novack cocked a finger in Gindi's direction. 'This guy here is Syrian. Flatbush has lots of Syrian Jews. They all got these strange names – Zolta, Dweck, Pardo, Bada, Adjini.'

'Flatbush has all sorts of Jews.'

'Yeah, but the Syrians . . . they know how to live, right?'

'You said it, Micky!'

Novack looked at his watch. 'Jeez. Twelve-thirty. Where's the super?'

'I have a key,' Jonathan announced.

'You've got a key?' Novack repeated.

'Yes, I have a key.'

'You mind opening up?' Gindi asked.

'Is that okay?' he asked Decker.

Decker said, 'He has all the paperwork, Jon. You're just speeding things along.'

'Then I'll open up.'

Jonathan brought them to the building's elevator, which barely contained the body mass let alone the weight. It moved in jerks and jumps, as slow as a slug. Ephraim lived down a dimly lit hallway, wafting with the faint odor of garbage and urine. His unit was number four, and the doorjamb had the requisite mezuzah. As the detectives pulled out their gloves, so did Decker, his still in the protective wrapping with the official LAPD seal.

'Whaddaya doing?' Novack asked. 'Lieutenant or no lieutenant, you're still a guest here. That means you and the rabbi *watch*.'

'I had no intention of touching anything,' Decker lied. 'I'm just a careful man. Last thing we want to do is screw something up accidentally. Let's go.'

'I sure hope you mean that,' Novack said.

'Detective, you're being nice to me,' Decker said. 'I appreciate it.'

Novack hesitated, then took the key from Jonathan and opened the door. As Jonathan walked across the threshold, he started to bring his fingers toward the mezuzah. Decker stopped him, and Novack caught it, nodding his thanks. Score a couple of brownie points for the greener from L.A.

Ephraim lived in a tiny one-bedroom, almost devoid of furniture. The living room area had a five-foot shopworn sofa, upholstered in faded green chenille. There was a small coffee table, its top made of plastic laminate designed to look like wood. It was peeling from age. On the table was a stack of magazines: *Time* on top, the others obscured. A mug sat to one side, the remaining coffee inside congealed and cold. Underneath the table was a shelf. There Decker saw a Jewish prayer book, a Jewish bible, and several works by Rav Menachem Kaplan. One was entitled *The Jewish Soul*, and the other was *Saving The Jewish Soul*. Across from the couch were two mismatched chairs pushed against the back wall, a pole lamp between them.

The dining area contained a square table with the top fashioned in ruby-colored linoleum that was meant to approximate marble; the legs were made from tubular steel. Four matching tubular steel chairs were placed around the table, the seats done in oxblood Naugahyde. It was probably an original 1950s table, and probably worth more than its original sales price.

Gindi was busy looking through the kitchen cabinets. Not too many of those, since the kitchen was the size of a closet. Decker could see a tiny refrigerator and a hot plate. Jonathan stood in the center of the living room, hands in pockets, a woebegone expression in his eyes. Decker walked over to him.

'I'm sorry.'

'It's so sad.'

'I know.'

'He was doing better, Akiva. He really was.'

'This was doing better?'

'A couple of years ago, he was almost living on the streets.'

'What saved him?'

'We gave him money, so did his father.'

'Chaim?'

'Chaim . . .' Jonathan shrugged. 'Chaim has seven kids. He keeps things afloat, but one can hardly be critical if he was a bit cautious with his money.'

'Of course.'

'Ephraim used to thank us profusely for not giving up on him. We took him in for more meals than I can remember. We tried to offer as much as we could while still maintaining some privacy. I know his father was always there.' He shook his head. 'God only knows what happened in that hotel room.'

'How did he kick his drug habit?'

'I don't know. He didn't talk about that aspect of his life.' Jonathan sighed. 'If you don't mind, I'm going to step out and grab a cup of coffee. I spotted a café down the block. This is just too depressing.'

Novack stepped in the room. 'Leaving, Rabbi?'

'Nothing for me to do. I feel like I'm in the way.'

'You look tired, Rabbi. I can cart this guy around.' A thumb crooked in Decker's direction. 'He's probably gonna want to see the crime scene, right?'

'That would be helpful,' Decker said.

'Why don't you go home and see your family – or your congregation.'

'Maybe the lieutenant needs me for something.' Jonathan's voice was so dispirited.

'I think Detective Novack is right,' Decker said. 'The only thing I'll need you to do is take me back to Quinton. I'd like to talk to Shayndie's mom.' He turned to Novack. 'Unless you want to come with me.'

'I would except I have some pressing business in the afternoon. Besides, I've already talked to her – to both the parents.' A meaningful pause. 'If you find out anything—'

'Absolutely. I'll tell you right away.'

'I feel bad about leaving you, Akiva,' Jonathan said.

'Tell you the truth, Jon, I think it would be easier.'

'And we're coming into the city anyway,' Novack said. 'You know where the crime scene is? A hundred thirty-four between Broadway and Amsterdam.'

'Yes, I know.' Jonathan wiped moisture from his eyes. 'It's not too far from my shul.'

'Where's your shul?'

'One hundred seventeen between Morningside and

St. Nick. Just across the park from Columbia.'

'You're a hop, skip, and a jump from the two-eight. I'll drop him off at your synagogue. It's not a problem.'

'You're being very kind.' Jonathan sounded so tired.

'Go rest, Rabbi,' Novack said. 'I'm sure a lot of people depend on you.'

'You're very right, Detective.'

Decker walked his brother to the door and let him out. 'I'll call you in a couple of hours.'

As soon as he left, Novack said, 'Poor guy. First, he's got a fuck-up brother-in-law. Then the relatives talked him into draggin' you into it. Now he's feelin' pretty bad about that.'

That about summed it up.

Novack said, 'The parents . . . they weren't too helpful. For now, I'm saying it's because they were overwrought. But I'm keeping my opinions open, know what I'm saying?'

'I hear you.'

'These kind of things. You always look to the family. I guess I don't have to tell you that.'

'That's why I told them to hire a lawyer.'

'Yeah, it was good advice.' He turned his head to the kitchen. 'Yo, Stan the Man! Wanna see what I found in the bedroom?'

The bald man closed the last of the kitchen cupboards. 'I hope it's more interesting than roaches. 'Cause I already seen a lot of those.'

'What did you find?' Decker asked.

'Magazines. And not the coffee-table kind.'

'Bad?'

'Legitimate stuff, at least. No kids or animals from what I could tell.'

'Male?' Gindi asked.

'No, female.'

Decker looked at Ephraim's coffee table. 'I'm going to move *Time* off the pile of magazines. All right?'

'Sure.'

Decker scooted the weekly periodical onto the tabletop, exposing a copy of *The New Yorker* and a stapled set of loose-leaf paper with EMEK REFA'IM on the blue cover page. He turned to Novack. 'Can I pick this up?'

Novack shrugged. 'You're gloved.'

Decker thumbed through the stapled papers.

'What is it?' Novack asked. 'Some homemade porno job?'

'Not with the words "*Emek Refa'im*" on it,' Gindi said.

Decker perused the printed words. 'What does it mean?'

'Emek Refa'im? "*Emek*" is a valley. I think "*refa'im*" is from "*refuah*"—'

'To heal,' Decker said.

'Yeah,' Gindi said. 'Valley of healing.'

'That would make sense,' Decker said. 'This looks like a handout for Jewish drug addicts.'

'Let me see that,' Novack said.

Decker gave him the packet. 'Looks to me like the organization has several chapters with their own kind of twelve-step programs. There are addresses in the back.'

Novack thumbed through the pages. 'I should pay these guys a visit. Wonder when they meet?'

'Today's Friday, so it's a safe bet they're not meeting tonight,' Decker said.

'That is true,' Novack said.

'How about tomorrow night?' Gindi said. '*Motzei Shabbos?* Everyone filled with spirituality from the holy day.'

'Or stress,' Decker said. 'When you're an addict and forced to interact with family, I bet you're pretty tense.'

'Now, that's a very good point.' Novack placed the magazine in an evidence bag. 'I'll give these jokers a call, see if Ephraim was associated with any of these chapters. If they meet tomorrow night, you want to come with me and pay them a visit?'

'That would be great,' Decker answered.

'Wanna see the X-rated stuff?' Novack called out.

'Twist my arm,' Gindi answered.

Decker's toolshed was bigger than the bedroom. The trio could barely fit without bodily contact. There was an unmade twin bed crammed against the wall and a single nightstand on which rested a phone, an alarm clock, and one framed picture – a Chasidic man standing next to, but not touching, a young girl of about fourteen. Decker stared at the picture.

'May I?'

Novack shrugged.

Decker picked up the framed picture, studying the faces. The girl was far from beautiful. Her nose was large and drooping, her cheeks still holding some baby fat. But her eyes – dark and round – shone with a mischievous gleam. She wore a long-sleeved pink shirt and a long denim skirt. Her hair was pulled back, probably braided. Her lips were shaped in a small, mysterious smile. The man seemed to be around forty, dressed in typical black-suited Chasidic garb. He was bearded with side locks, his head covered with the ubiquitous black hat. His smile was wide, the folds at the corners of his eyes crinkling with happiness. He showed the picture to Novack. 'Is that Shayndie?'

'Hard to tell from such a small image, but I think so.'

'They gave you a bigger image?'

'Yeah, a bat mitzvah photo. I had it photocopied yesterday evening, and this morning we've been passing it around the crime scene area. That's what I was doing when you called. She was wearing this pink fluffy dress. She looked like a tuft of cotton candy. She also looked way younger than thirteen.'

'She was probably twelve,' Decker said. 'Orthodox girls have their bat mitzvah ceremony at twelve, not thirteen.'

'Yeah, that's right.' Novack nodded.

Decker stared at the photo. 'She was older than twelve in this picture. Still fresh-faced. God, what a terrible thing! Can I keep this?'

'I'm bending rules.'

'That's why I'm asking.'

'Yeah, go ahead.'

Decker pocketed the picture. Again he scanned the room. A fourteen-inch TV sat on several cinder blocks at the foot of the bed. Novack told them that he had found the two boxes underneath the bed – one held dog-eared paperback fiction, the other held standard porno magazines.

Decker bent down and sniffed the sheets.

Novack said, 'I didn't smell any jizz, if that's what you're doing. But I don't need to bag the sheets. If we find the girl and she's' – he made circles with his hand – 'if she's got stuff in her, I got plenty of tubes of humors from the stiff to do DNA testing.'

Gindi was scanning the adult magazines. 'Nothing out of the ordinary. Except that this guy was supposedly a holy roller. But even them having stuff like this isn't out of the ordinary. You go talk to anyone in the nine-oh. Right as the Chasids cross the bridge from the city into Williamsburg, they've got these hookers lined up, waiting to ream out their pipes. Okay, so no one's perfect. But if that ain't bad enough, they have a real elitist attitude. If you're not one of them, you don't count. That's why it's okay to skirt the law, because anything but their laws don't apply to them.'

Novack held up his hands and dropped them to his sides. 'It's hard to believe that these are my people. Grandpa sacrificed everything just to make it over here, and these *yutzes* are too blind to notice what real freedom is.'

'Did you find anything to suggest that the vic was molesting the girl?' Decker asked.

'Not so far,' Novack said. 'No dirty pictures of the kid, if that's what you mean.'

Decker nodded. 'Any camera equipment or videos?'

'Nothing.'

'Did you have a look in her room yesterday?'

'No, haven't been out to the house,' Novack said. 'I only talked to the parents at the precinct. Like I told you before, I'm not *saying* they're hiding something. Maybe they just find it hard to relate to anyone outside their *chevrah*.'

Decker knew that *chevrah* meant their circle of friends. 'Could be.'

'That's why, you being here, it's a good thing for me if you're legit. You probably could get insider's info.'

'I'm probably closer than you are, but I'm far from one of them.' Again Decker regarded the picture. Just an uncle trying to do a good deed for a niece? Or a man obsessed with a young girl? 'Do you think he brought her here?'

Gindi broke in. 'You gotta know where you are, Lieutenant. This is a very religious neighborhood. People talk. How long before it would get around that a religious man is bringing a girl up to his apartment – let alone a girl child. Besides statutory rape being illegal, it's not *tzneosdik*.'

Tzneos meant modesty. Decker said, 'Maybe it did get back to the brother.'

'Nah.' Gindi shook his head. 'If he was doing something bad to her, it wouldn't be here in home territory.'

Novack came back from a closet holding a box. 'Lookie here.'

'Whaddaya got, Micky?'

'Looks like work-related stuff.' Novack plopped the box on the floor and picked up some random pages. 'Lists of items, prices, and bar codes from Lieber's Electronics.'

Decker said, 'Ephraim worked in the family business.'

'That's what they told me.' Novack shuffled through the pages. 'The old man told me Ephraim did whatever they needed him to do. And when he wasn't doing that, he worked inventory. And from the looks of it, he had a pretty good idea of what was going in and out of the stores.'

Gindi tapped his toe. 'Doesn't it strike you as odd that they'd put a man with a drug problem in charge of inventory? You know in business, there's always a certain amount of theft. It's like dangling a carrot.'

Novack said, 'Help yourself as long as you don't take too much?'

'Exactly.'

Decker broke in. 'If they thought he was really at risk, would they have trusted him in any facet of the business? Maybe the old man would, but a brother?' He shook his head. 'Betcha Chaim was watching him like a hawk.'

'Well, to me, it's still an angle,' Gindi said.

'Hey, this is what I do with my people in La-La Land. We throw out ideas and see what sticks.'

'Here too, and you made a good point.' Novack rummaged through the papers. 'Just more of the same. I'm gonna bag all this and go through this at my desk, slowly and methodically. Maybe there're other things that I'm missing.'

'Like what?' Gindi asked.

'Like a bankbook for starters. Guy musta had a checking account.'

Decker said, 'It could be that if he was part of one of those twelve-step programs, he didn't have a checkbook or credit cards. He might have dealt only with cash.'

'Yeah, that's a point,' Gindi stated. 'Lots of addicts have had credit problems and have been caught bouncing or kiting checks.'

'Then that would make our life a little harder,' Novack said. 'No paper trail.'

'Maybe he had some credit cards in the past,' Decker said.

Novack folded the ends of the box and began to tape the edges. 'I still think we should think about theft within the family business. Maybe Ephraim was paying off old drug debts. Maybe he didn't pay them off fast enough.'

'And the girl?' Gindi said.

Novack sighed. 'She's a big problem.'

'Poor parents,' Gindi said.

'Poor girl,' Decker said.

6

The crime took place in a dingy cell of a room
with a stunning view of a brick wall, although
Decker assumed that the killer – or killers – had
drawn the faded shade. The chalk marks were still in
place, the body positioned next to the bed. But
because there wasn't enough space on the floor,
Ephraim's left arm and leg had settled up on the wall.
The tech had extended the white figuration onto the
once-white painted surface now ambered to puke
yellow. Inside the outline of the head was a deep
brown stain – single amoeba-shaped sticky puddle of
dried and tacky blood about six to seven inches in
diameter. The rest of the wall was covered with print
powder, as were a lone nightstand, the phone, the
clock, and almost all the cracked white tiled floor.
There was a bathroom with a stained-gray porcelain
toilet streaked with dirt lines and an equally stained
porcelain sink.

Resisting the urge to rub his temples – his hands
were newly gloved – Decker felt an encroaching
headache. He hadn't had a decent meal in sixteen
hours and floating particles of fingerprint dust
weren't helping the situation. Plus, there was the odor
of waste: a strong stench of urine with the hint of

feces. Novack hadn't bothered with the Vicks; neither did Decker. He had seen and smelled worse.

Novack took out his notepad and an envelope filled with post-mortem photographs. 'Single shot through the temple area – close range judging by the entrance wound, but it was lacking the usual star-burst pattern.'

'Why's that?' Decker asked.

Novack shrugged.

Decker flipped through the snapshots. 'Exit wound?'

'No exit wound. So whatever it was, it's still in the skull. Probably a hollow point – something that exploded inside the poor bastard. We'll know more after Forensics pulls it out. The casing was a thirty-two caliber.'

'A hollow point . . .' Decker looked up from the pictures and back at the kill site. 'That would explain the lack of blood.' He went over and examined the chalk mark. 'We've got a solid mass of blood here. Which meant that the vic had to have fallen with the wound side down. Any ideas how it played?'

'Yeah, I was wondering about that, too. First off, I considered that he was shot on the bed and fell off. But then there would have been blood on the sheets where he rolled off. Problem is . . . no blood on the sheets. So next, we figure he was popped while he was cowered in the corner, or standing up in the corner.'

'Splatter?'

'No, no splatter on the walls there. Not that we could find.'

'That's impossible.'

'Them's the facts.'

Decker said, 'Unless he was lying left side down,

and shot through the floor, there has to be some amount of splatter from the entrance wound.'

'So we're figuring maybe this wasn't the kill spot.'

'So where was the kill spot?'

'Not in this room.'

Decker said. 'But that would mean taking a body up the stairs . . . what? Ten flights?'

'There's an elevator. They could have stuffed him in a duffel.'

'We rode up that elevator. It took about twenty minutes. Not to mention that it would have been one heck of a big duffel.'

'It's been done before,' Novack said.

'Let's suppose . . . for a moment . . . that the guy got here on his own two feet.'

'You mean he took the girl up here?'

Decker thought about that. 'You find any evidence that the girl was up here?'

'Nothing. No sperm-stained sheets, no dress, no purse, nothing to suggest any kind of sexual activity whatsoever.'

'Okay, for the moment, let's assume that the girl wasn't up here.' Decker raised his eyebrows. 'We'll worry about her later. Anyway, Ephraim was kidnapped and taken up here – maybe in a duffel, maybe by his own two feet . . . somehow he got up here.'

'That we know. What we don't know is if he was dead or alive.'

'Assume that he was alive when they took him up here.'

Novack laughed. 'You're from L.A. Write the script, and I'll play along.'

Decker smiled. 'Suppose somebody brought Ephraim here on his own two feet.'

'Probably more than one person,' Novack said.

Decker nodded. 'Yeah, probably to get him upstairs without his breaking away, there had to be two people – dragging him upstairs with a gun pointed at his head. Maybe they duct-taped his mouth.'

'Not when we found him.'

'Ask the coroner to check for glue around his mouth.'

Novack nodded, but he didn't write it down.

Decker went on. 'They lead him to this room . . . pull the shades—'

'By the way, I had some people canvass the next building over for witnesses.'

'The one out the window?'

'Yeah, that one. Nothing.'

'Okay, okay.' Decker's brain was reeling. 'They pull the shades and pop him somewhere up here that's not going to leave any splatter.' He looked at Novack. 'Was his hair wet?'

'Not when I got here,' Novack said. 'But I will say this. His hair was short . . . almost shaved to the scalp. It woulda dried in a few minutes. You can see that in the post-mortem pics.'

Decker looked at the photos. Ephraim had had a very close-cropped haircut. 'How about his clothes? You don't have his clothes?'

'No, we found him buck naked. What are you thinking?'

'The toilet,' Decker said. 'They drag him into the bathroom, dunk him into the bowl, and popped him. The water washed away most of the blood. It also probably muffled the sound.'

'Makes one hell of a splash.'

'Was the floor wet?'

Novack checked his notes. He shook his head. 'No . . . I didn't mention it. I think someone woulda noticed pink water on the floor.'

'Towels in the bathroom?'

Again Novack checked his notes. 'No. It's a crummy hotel.'

'It still might provide towels in the bathroom. Someone should ask.'

Novack was quiet. Then he said, 'We should check underneath the toilet-bowl rim for splatter.'

'Yeah. If you don't find anything, you might want to Luminal it. Also, tell Forensics to check the vic's lungs. He may have taken some water into his lungs before he died.'

Novack scratched his neck and cleared his throat. 'That can be arranged.'

'Do you mind if I look around?'

'Not too long.'

'Ten minutes?'

'Knock yourself out.' But after five minutes, Novack seemed annoyed. 'What are you looking for, Decker?'

'Just trying to figure out . . . how he got here.'

'The room was registered to John Smith,' Novack said. 'Paid for in cash. The receipts had already been taken to the bank and deposited, so we couldn't pull prints off the bills even if we knew what we were looking for.'

Decker gave the place a final scan. 'And you found nothing at the scene?'

'Only thing we found of any significance was a single pill.'

'A pill?'

'Yeah, like an aspirin pill. But it wasn't aspirin. No imprint on it. Even generic drugs are imprinted.'

'Ecstasy?'

'Yeah, of course. But even those pills are usually imprinted with something – a 'toon or a heart. The guy had a drug problem; the pill may have come from his pocket. We sent it to Forensics. It's being tested. If it's a known drug like ecstasy, results shouldn't take long.'

'My brother said he used coke,' Decker remarked. 'Do they make cocaine in tablets?'

Novack shrugged. 'I'm not an expert in these things. We don't even got Vice in our hub, let alone Narc.'

Decker held up the photos. 'Can I keep these over the weekend or are these your only copies?'

'Those *are* copies. Originals are in my file back at the two-eight.'

'So I can keep these?'

'What do you want them for?'

'I just want to . . . stare at them. See if something jumps out at me. I'll give them back before I leave.'

Novack ran his tongue over his teeth. 'I suppose you look honorable enough. Sure, take them.'

'Thanks, Novack.' Decker pocketed the photos.

Rather than take a chance with the moribund elevator, they elected to walk down the ten flights of steps. The stairwells were dark, lit by a bare bulb on each floor, and rank with odors and bacteria. Decker was happy his hands were gloved. He wished his lungs had equal protection. As they stepped outside onto the sidewalk, a heavy gust of wind nearly knocked them over. Immediately, Decker's ears were assaulted by the honking of horns and traffic. He took off his latex gloves. 'You know, I can catch a cab to my brother's shul.'

'I can drop you off—'

'Nah, it's out of the way.'

'It's no problem for me to take you, Lieutenant.'

'Thanks, Detective, but I'll be fine.' Decker paused. 'So you're going to check out those twelve-step chapters—'

'Yeah, Decker, I had intentions of doing that.'

Novack was irked. Decker said, 'I'm a pain in the ass, and an older one at that. That means I'm not only obsessive, but I keep asking the same questions because I'm forgetful. Be happy you're not my wife.'

Novack smiled. 'I'll check out the chapters.'

'What about dealers? Where would a religious guy like Ephraim buy his blow?'

'Probably from the same pushers that sell to the regular crowd. Way too many dealers out there for me to narrow down.'

'Any known dealer that specifically caters to the Orthodox crowd?'

Novack thought a moment. 'Okay, Decker, this is what I'm gonna do for you. I'm gonna ask Vice. I'll translate the New York part, and you can help me out with the family part and all their religious stuff.'

'I'll do the best I can,' Decker said. 'But I'll tell you this much. I'm not *that kind* of religious. Furthermore, the Chasids up in Quinton are probably biased against me because I didn't start out religious.'

'Aha!' Novack's eyes narrowed. 'What brought about the transformation?'

'My wife.'

A smile. 'Was it worth it?'

'Absolutely.'

Novack laughed. 'I thought of something. It's gross.'

'I'm not sensitive,' Decker said.

'You gave up ham to get to the pork.'

'Yeah, that's gross,' Decker said. 'Can you call me on my cell *Motzei Shabbos* – Saturday evening.'

'You got it.' Novack shook his hand. '*Shabbat shalom.*'

'*Shabbat shalom,*' Decker answered.

Only in New York.

7

The ride back to Quinton was a killer. Traffic out of the city was a parking lot of red taillights, wind blowing dirt and debris onto the cars and roadways. Stoically, lifelessly, Jonathan sat at the helm; eyes fixed ahead – an inert driving machine. Decker hadn't meant to, but he found his eyes closing. When he opened them next, the van was pulling off the highway. His mouth tasted like sawdust, his stomach long past hungry. He just felt empty.

Jonathan handed him a bottle of water. Decker drank voraciously.

'Thanks.'

'I've got some fruit in the back. Apples, pears, oranges.'

Decker reached over and devoured an apple in four bites. He then went to work on a pear.

'I should have bought you a sandwich,' Jonathan remarked. 'I'm sorry.'

'No, this is fine.' Decker finished the bottle. 'I'll be hungry for Shabbat. I'm sure the Lazaruses will have plenty of food to help me out.'

'That's true.'

They zipped past Liberty Field.

Decker started peeling an orange. 'Are you coming into Brooklyn?'

'For *Shabbos*? Yes. Mrs Lazarus invited my parents. I told Raisie we needed to be there for you.'

'That's all right, Jon. I'm used to it—'

'Actually, that's a lie. It isn't for you; it's for me, Akiva. I need to see you in a different context, in a family context. I have real misgivings about this whole thing . . . dragging you into it. I don't know what I was thinking. I called in a moment of weakness.'

'That's what family's for.'

'So far, it's been very one-sided. You've never once called me for a favor.'

'That's because I'm an oldest child. I dispense; I don't take.'

'But we're all adults.'

'It's ingrained patterns, Jon, and I'm okay with it. My boys are coming in for the weekend. If they weren't here, I might not have come. But they are coming, and I'm here, and lets all make the most of it.'

'You're being charitable. That's my job, not yours.'

Within minutes, they made the transition to the poorer side of the tracks. The van cut through the near-empty roadways. Decker's wristwatch read two-thirty. 'When does *Shabbos* start?'

'Five-thirty.'

'And how long will it take us to get back to Brooklyn?'

'At least an hour, maybe longer. Why?'

'If we have time, I'd like to stop by the Quinton Police . . . ask a few questions.'

'That'll be tight, although we've been making record

time.' Jonathan turned onto the Liebers' house, then pulled the van curbside. 'You've never met Minda. She's difficult under the best of circumstances.'

'I'll tread lightly.'

'It won't matter,' Jonathan stated flatly. 'She's just who she is.' He got out and slammed the car door. Decker winced at the noise, then opened the passenger door and stepped out. He had to fast-walk to keep up with his brother. Jon was resentful. So that made two of them.

Chaim opened the door even before Jonathan knocked. 'She's awake, but it isn't good, Yonasan. I think we should call the doctor.'

'Can we come in first?' Jonathan asked.

'Oh, sure, sure.' Chaim had put on a freshly starched shirt. He had bathed, too. Even though he was technically in mourning for his brother, the official period usually didn't start until after the funeral. Plus, it was permissible to bathe before the Sabbath. Lieber stepped away from the threshold. Everyone went inside.

Chaim said, 'What did you find out?'

Decker sat down on one of the twelve dining-room chairs. 'Are you talking to me?'

'Yes, of course. Weren't you with the police all this time?'

'For most of the time, yes.'

'So what did you find out?'

Decker rubbed his forehead, 'Mr Lieber—'

'Chaim.' He began to pace. 'What is this? We're family. Why are you calling me Mr Lieber? Is it bad news?'

'Right now, it's no news,' Decker said.

'But you were there for four hours.'

'Three,' Jonathan said. 'There was a lot of travel time—'

'Three, four . . . you must have learned something!' Lieber spun around and faced Decker with fiery eyes. 'What did the police tell you? Anything at all?'

'It's at the very early stages of the investigation—'

'Ach!' Lieber waved him off. 'C'mon, c'mon. Now you're stalling—'

'Chaim!' Jonathan broke in. 'If he knew something, don't you think he'd tell you?'

'I'll tell you one thing,' Decker said. 'I saw the crime scene. I can't swear to it, but, personally, I don't think Shaynda was in the hotel room with your brother.'

'So where was she? Where is she?'

'That I don't know.'

'C'mon! She's an innocent! Where would she go?'

'I don't know, Chaim,' Decker said. 'I'm from L.A., not New York. I guarantee you the police are looking for her.'

'Ach!'

Decker's head pounded. He tried a different approach. 'Chaim, can I take a look at Shaynda's room, please?'

'Why?'

'Just to get a feel for the girl.'

A shrill voice barked out Chaim's name. He looked up at the staircase. 'I'll be right up, Minda.'

'I'm coming down. Who are you talking to?'

'The detective.'

'What does he want?' A woman materialized on the staircase. Her head was wrapped in a towel; her body was covered head to toe in a black caftan. Her eyes were swollen pink and raw, her skin red and blotchy. Her fingers played with one another – constant motion.

Chaim bounded up the stairs and offered the woman his arm. She shook it off. 'I'm not an invalid!' She stared at Decker with feral eyes. 'Did you find her?'

Chaim said, 'This is my wife, Minda—'

'He knows who I am. Who else would I be? Did you find her?'

'No, Mrs Lieber, not yet.'

'So what are you doing here?' She glared at him. 'If you didn't find her, *why are you here*?'

'I wanted to look in Shaynda's room, Mrs Lieber. It will give me a better understanding of who she was.'

'I don't have *time* for this kind of nonsense.' Once she reached the ground floor, she began to pace like a caged feline. 'Just get out there and *find* her.'

'Going through her room might help me find her, Mrs Lieber.'

'No, it *won't* help you find her because she shares a room and I've already cleaned it and it's right before *Shabbos* and I've got a lot on my mind. I don't need another person under this roof! Chaim, why are you still here? You're going to be late for *Mincha*!'

'I'm trying to get ready, Minda.' Abruptly, Lieber turned to Decker. 'Will you please leave?'

Jonathan's face was beyond shocked. He was clearly appalled. 'Chaim, don't speak to him like that. You asked me to bring him out here!'

'Then maybe I made a mistake.'

'Maybe you did,' Decker said quietly.

Suddenly, Minda broke into tears. She screamed,

'Just get out of my way. That's what I need. I need everyone to get *out of my way*!'

Decker sighed and tried to think like a professional. A girl's life was at stake. 'Just let me have a quick look—'

'There's nothing in the house!' Minda insisted. 'Don't you think I'd tell you if I found *something*.'

'I'm not saying you overlooked anything on purpose.'

'She's out there!' Minda's voice was high and squeaky. 'Why are you here? Go look out there and do some good! Search the streets!' Her eyes became globes of fire. 'Why can't you find her?'

'I'm doing what I can—'

'No, you're not. You're here instead of out there!'

'Because of the lateness of the hour, Mrs Lieber, I think my time would be better spent here.'

'What do you care about the lateness of the hour? *Shabbos* isn't your problem.'

That sure put Decker in *his* place. 'What does *that* mean?'

She glared at him. 'Don't play stupid with me! You *know* what it means.'

Decker was so angry he could barely focus. He willed himself to keep his voice under control. 'Yes, Mrs Lieber, I suppose I do know what it means. *Shabbat shalom*.'

He stormed out of the house. His fury was so all-consuming that it took a moment before he realized that his brother was talking to him.

'. . . doesn't mean anything, Akiva. She's beside herself.'

'I realize that.' Decker's voice was a growl. He opened the van door and sat inside, arms folded in front. His stomach was a tight knot of acid.

Jonathan got behind the wheel. 'Akiva—'

'Funny. As a goy, I was certainly good enough to drag out here to settle things down. Now, when I actually try to work, they're putting up fences. You're damn lucky I'm not that sensitive. More important, you're damn lucky I really want to find this poor girl.'

Jonathan said, 'You're not a goy.'

'No, I'm not. But she doesn't know that, does she? As far as she's concerned, I'm this big, dumb lug of a cop from hick town L.A. who converted just to please Rina.' Decker caught his breath. 'Look. I feel for the woman. I really do, Jonathan. But it still pisses me off.' He leaned his head back and stared at the van's ceiling. 'I'm out of my element here. They're right. It was a mistake for me to come out.'

'I am so sorry!'

For the first time, Decker heard the pain in his brother's voice. 'God, I'm taking it out on you.'

'You have every right to be angry.'

Decker smiled. 'Spoken like a true pastor.' He checked his watch. 'Well, the good news is we'll have time to visit the Quinton Police.'

Suburban police departments had a distinct advantage over their city rivals – a large homeowner tax base. A case could be made that the richer WASPs on the north side were supporting the poorer Jews on the south side because their houses were bigger and the lots were expansive. But an equal case could be made in the opposite direction – that the Jews were contributing more than their fair share because for every one Gentile manse, there were three Jewish houses. What the Jews lacked in quality, they made up in quantity.

The primary police station was located in Liberty

Park, with a half-dozen, drop-in station storefronts –
manned by two officers – scattered among the three
commercial areas. The station's construction was
new: a square edifice of steel and one-way mirrored
glass that was well lit and well ventilated. The detectives' squad room was spacious with approximately
the same square footage as Decker's squad room back
in L.A. The difference was that Devonshire hosted
seating for forty-three gold-shield carriers, whereas
Quinton had twelve full-time detectives, each with his
or her own phone, answering machine, voice mail,
and computer.

The Homicide/Robbery division was 99.9 percent
robbery, and .1 percent homicide. Of the three
homicides that Quinton had last year, one was a
suicide – a ninety-six-year-old man with late-stage
prostate cancer – and two were reckless homicides –
Man I – from the same vehicular accident. For a
fleeting moment, Decker entertained thoughts about
retiring to a pastoral suburb like Quinton. The idea
left his cerebral cortex as soon as it entered.

Because he was a lieutenant from a big city,
Decker was awarded a meeting with Virgil Merrin,
the chief of the Quinton Police. Merrin was six-one,
one step shy of fat, with that wet-shave pink skin,
and hair so blond and thin that his scalp showed
through. He had light blue eyes that sparkled when
Decker told him he was originally from Gainesville,
Florida. Merrin was from West Virginia, so that
meant they were both good old boys. After several
minutes of batting around bass-fishing trivia, Merrin
got down to substance.

'A cryin' shame about the girl.' Merrin wore a blue
suit with a light blue shirt, the buttons stretched by

the man's gut. He gave a soulful glance to Jonathan. 'A damn shame! We went house to house – all of the girl's friends. Nothing!'

They were in Merrin's office on the third floor. It had a generous view of the park – of the wind-bent tulips shimmering like waves of colored banners. The lake was also visible from the window, the surface steely with tiny whitecap ripples. From where Merrin sat, he could see it all. In another context, it could be considered cozy. All that was lacking was a fireplace, a newspaper, and a cup of coffee.

'What about the other side?' Decker asked him. 'The public-school kids.'

Merrin chuckled. 'Let me explain. The two sides . . . no interaction. Even the Jews who *live* in the north side . . . no interaction with the Jews in the south.'

'One of the father's complaints—'

'That'd be Chaim Lieber.'

'Yes, sir,' Decker answered. 'One of Rabbi Lieber's beefs with Shayndie was that she was hanging with some of the public-school kids. Wild kids.'

'See, that's another problem,' Merrin stated. 'That's his definition . . . the wild kids. What may be wild to him is harmless to us. He sees a girl in shorts during the summertime; to him, that's a wild whore of a girl. What do you and me see? A girl that's dressed for summer. If Shaynda Lieber was really hanging with some wild kids . . . then I could do something for him. 'Cause there is a certain element – not a bad element, per se – but a certain element. You know the story – loud, unsupervised parties, fast driving, binge drinking . . . and yeah, probably a toke or two. See, if I knew for certain that it was those kids, then I could maybe pay them a visit. But I think that to Rabbi Lieber, any kid on the north side is a wild kid.' His eyes went to Jonathan's face. 'See what I'm saying here, Rabbi?'

'We understand.' Decker turned to Jonathan. 'Didn't you say that Shayndie used to hang out at the mall?'

'Yes,' Jonathan answered. 'The one in Bainberry.'

'All the kids on the north side hang out at the mall in Bainberry. That's neither here nor there. Correct me if I'm wrong, but didn't all this hullabaloo take place in the city?'

'Yes, of course,' Decker said. 'But I'm just wondering if she's maybe hiding out with one of the north-side kids.'

'Why would she do that?'

'I don't know,' Decker said. 'Maybe she saw something. Maybe she's afraid to come home.'

'Only reason she'd be afraid to come home is if one of her own kind was implicated. Now, you know as well as I know, Rabbi, I could ask those folks questions from today till tomorrow. They're not going to talk to *me*. But maybe they'll talk to you.'

Punting the responsibility back to him – back to the Jews.

Decker said, 'You're probably right. But if you do hear of something—'

Merrin spread out his hands in generosity. 'Of course, if I hear of something, I'll go straight to the parents. I've got people on this, Lieutenant. We did search the south side, door-to-door. And maybe you have a point there . . . her hiding in the north side. You know what I'll do for you? I'll have my men ask around.'

Decker knew what that meant. A cursory walk to a couple of houses, maybe passing out a few flyers.

Merrin said, 'I'll have my men *and women* ask around.' He smiled. 'I hope you're not one of those sensitive types. There are no biases in this department, but old habits . . .'

Decker nodded. 'Thanks for seeing us.'

Merrin gave out a heavy sigh. 'I'm not giving up on her. You know that. If she's around, we'll find her.'

Decker hoped he was right. Because the Stones notwithstanding, time wasn't on their side.

8

'I t's my Johns Hopkins ID.'

Decker glanced at his stepson, then studied the picture. Jacob, with his smoldering light eyes and a chip of inky hair over his brow. The teen exuded appeal – matinee-idol looks with that perfect sexy sneer. 'This was before you cut your hair.'

'More like before the yeshiva made me cut my hair.' Jacob straightened his tie. 'I was doing my James Dean persona.'

Sammy took a peek over his stepfather's shoulder, then regarded his brother. 'Don't flatter yourself.'

'C'mon,' Jacob protested. 'Don't I have that sultry Tennessee Williams bad-boy stare?'

Again Sammy studied the photo. 'Maybe then you did.' A grin. 'Now you don't.'

Jacob punched his older brother's shoulder. Sammy was about an inch taller than Jacob, about six feet even barefoot. There was very little physical resemblance between the two boys. Sammy took after his father – sandy-colored hair, impish brown eyes, regular features, and a wise-guy smile. He was good-looking, but not pretty. Jacob was a clone of Rina: he had 'the face'. However, the two boys had nearly identical voices and speech inflections. Decker couldn't tell them apart over the phone.

Jacob said, 'The picture's for you, Dad. When I graduate from Ner Yisroel, looking gaunt and pale, remember what you and Eema did to me.'

'A little academic pallor never hurt anyone.'

Jacob frowned. Then abruptly, his face lit up. 'Zeyde, Zeyde, don't you look handsome!'

Rav Lazarus had walked into the living room with cane in hand, although he wasn't visibly using it for support. His smile was blinding, even though the teeth had browned from years of tea drinking. He went over to his grandson, looped his arm around Jacob's neck, pulling him down so he could plant a kiss on the forehead. He stood no taller than five-five, with a flowing white beard. In honor of *Shabbat*, he wore a long black coat, a wide black waist sash known as a *gartl*, and a beautiful black hat. His voice was raspy and high, almost as if he were choking. 'Yonkeleh.'

'Zeydeleh.' Jacob kissed his grandfather's cheek. 'You can be proud of me. I now have my own black hat.' He showed him his Borsolino, then put it on his head. 'What do you think?'

Rabbi Lazarus patted his cheek. 'I think you're a good boy!'

'Like my *abba*?' Jacob said.

'Like your *abba*.' The old man smiled at Decker. 'Like both your abbas.'

'*Shabbat shalom*, Zeyde.' Sammy kissed his grandfather. 'Are you ready?'

'*Cain, cain*,' he said, answering yes in Hebrew. 'Of course, I'm ready.' He walked over to Decker. 'Thank you for coming. You made my wife very happy.'

Decker smiled. Of course it was *only* Sora Lazarus who was happy about hosting the two grandsons who carried the Lazarus name. 'I'm very glad to be here.' He ran his fingers through slightly damp hair. The shower had felt good, but by the time Jonathan had made it back to Brooklyn, Decker had been the sixth in line to step into the bathroom. The water had turned tepid. At least it wasn't cold.

The dining table had extended into the living room: the table set for twenty-six. Decker's family was five; then the two elder Lazaruses and their daughter's family brought it up to thirteen. Jonathan's wife and kids along with his parents who lived just a few blocks away added another six for a total of nineteen. Then, at the last minute, Mrs Lazarus invited Jonathan's brother Shimon, who also resided in the neighborhood. Shimon, of course, was also Decker's half brother and the oldest of the five Levine children. He was outgoing and funny, and Decker liked him a lot. Over the years, Decker had kept in touch only with Shimon and Jonathan . . . not counting the yearly *shanah tovah* card to Frieda Levine. As far as the rest of the Levine clan, there hadn't been contact past that initial burst of brotherhood.

Twenty-six bodies in total.

Decker's half relations were kept a secret out of respect for Jonathan's father. Alter Levine had never known that Frieda, his devoted wife of forty-seven years, had given birth to an illegitimate child fifty years ago. He could have never imagined the anguish that Frieda had suffered when she put the baby boy up for adoption. But that hadn't been the final chapter. Ten years ago, while Decker and Rina were in Boro Park visiting the Lazaruses, he had run full force into the poor woman by chance, turning her life upside down.

Decker's life as well.

He was still sorting things out. The volume of blood relationships was simply overwhelming. When Decker was at home, in L.A., he often felt like a lone ship out on a vast sea of emptiness. Here, it was as if his boat were moored in a marina – safe but crowded.

Smothering was the operative word.

Yet, there was something about family . . . for better or worse . . .

Seeing the elongated table reminded Decker of the Lieber house, and for a brief moment, he felt a twinge of the hell they must be going through. So painful, yet Decker refused to let the poison inject and take hold. It had been thirteen years since the Lazaruses had lost their only son, yet tonight their hearts were filled with *simcha* – joy – as they *shep nachas* – or took pride – over their grandsons and nine-year-old Hannah. Decker owed it to the Lazaruses to be grateful for life. He bent down and kissed the small man's hat. '*Shabbat shalom*, Zeyde.'

The old man smiled with thin, pale lips. He threw the cane on the couch and took Decker's arm. 'You're a strong boy. I can lean on you, yes?'

'Any time. That's what muscles are for.'

It was wonderful, it was beautiful, it was spiritual, but it was also exhausting!

By the time Rina made it to bed, it was after one. Sora Lazarus didn't wash dishes on *Shabbat*, so there would be a ton of cleanup Saturday night, *Motzei Shabbat*. But it was truly astounding how much work went on even without washing dishes. The serving, the clearing, the scraping of the plates, the food storage, the piling of dishes, the counting of the silver

– plus the kitchen was so small!

And then there was the initial tension when Frieda arrived. However, Peter never failed to amaze her. He was a different man than he had been ten years ago, so much more comfortable with Jewish religious customs and with himself. He actually seemed relaxed – joking and smiling with the boys, with everyone. It had been Jonathan who was tense – nervous and fidgety – but he was dealing with so much right now. She also couldn't help but wonder what had gone on between Peter and him.

Crawling into bed, she scrunched up her pillow, then curled into the covers. A moment later, she felt Peter kiss the iota of face that wasn't obliterated by the blanket.

'You're still up?' she whispered.

'Waiting for you.'

She rolled over and faced him. 'I love you madly. But I'm very tired.'

'I don't mean that, darlin'!' He kissed her nose. 'I'm tired, too. I just wanted to say I love you. That's all.'

She pulled off her covers and snuggled against him. 'That's so sweet. If I had a speck of energy, I would definitely make that compliment worth your while.'

Decker paused a moment. 'You know, there's no harm in trying . . .'

She whacked his shoulder. 'You were wonderful tonight. Considering all that's going on, you were nothing short of a miracle.'

'It's called compartmentalization. Can't let the bastards get me down.'

'Should I ask how it went with you and Jonathan?'

A sigh. 'Well, let me put it this way,' Decker said.

'Remember when we were out here ten years ago, and Frieda Levine suddenly realized that I was her long-lost son. And how she fainted when she saw me. And then the entire evening turned into a big fiasco with your running in and out to bring her food. And me food? And Rosh Hashanah was a total mess. And *then*, the crowning glory, the very next day, Noam disappeared?'

'That bad, huh?'

'No, that was a cakewalk compared to this. At least, Ezra and Briena were on my side. They *wanted* me to find Noam. They actually *helped* me.'

'Chaim and Minda aren't helping you?'

'Minda is a difficult woman. She doesn't like me. She just about called me a goy to my face.'

'Oh my!'

'I'm sure part of it was hysteria. But there was a part of her that meant it, too.'

'What about Chaim?'

'The first time I saw him, he was all gratitude. Four hours later – the second time I saw him – he asked me to leave the house.'

'That's bizarre. Why the sudden shift?'

'I don't know. Either he was displeased by my lack of progress, or my charm isn't what it used to be.' He sighed. 'I know I told you that some cases can be solved in a half hour. This isn't one of them. There is *no way* I am going to be able to do anything. I am totally useless.'

'I'm sure that's not true.'

'I'm sure it is true. I was only able to find Noam because Hersh the psycho took him to L.A. That made all the difference in the world. In L.A., I have resources. It's my home territory. I'm lost here. I need an insider to show me the ropes. And from the looks of it, it ain't gonna be Chaim or Minda. I can't even get them to let me search Shaynda's room. I can only imagine what they would say if I asked to talk to some of Shayndie's friends or her siblings. Even if I were the type to go around them, I know that the community would close ranks.'

'You're trapped.'

'Like spider's prey. If they really cared about their daughter, they'd give me more information. This wall of silence makes them look complicit . . . like they've stashed her away and they're pretending that she's missing. I don't know. Maybe she's pregnant, and they shipped her off somewhere, using Ephraim's death as an excuse. Who knows? Maybe they set the entire thing up—'

'Peter, that's a horrible thing to say.'

'It's not nice, but it could be true.'

'I'm sure it's like you said. Minda is just distraught!'

'Well, she certainly doesn't trust me.' Decker's good nature suddenly snapped. 'Jonathan calls me up . . . asks me to come out. So I come out. Within twenty-four hours, I think I've outlived my usefulness.'

Rina said, 'You're frustrated—'

'Correction. They're frustrating me! Just like when we first met. I was the evil cop. Well, you know what, Rina? I'm tired of playing that role.'

'I don't blame you. What I can't figure out is why they're so hostile toward you. Jonathan made it sound as if they begged him to ask you to come.'

'Things have obviously changed.'

'What about the cops? The ones you met with today? I guess it's technically yesterday.'

'Micky Novack. He's a good guy. Very sympatico,

but he's also a busy man with more important things to do. He can only tote me around for so long; then it's every man for himself.'

'So what's next?'

'Not much as far as I'm concerned. I say we weather out the weekend here, then cut short our stay in New York. That'll let us spend more time in Florida with my folks. We can take Hannah to Epcot and Disney World. I can take her horseback riding or for a boat ride out on the lake. We can visit the Everglades. I really *need* a vacation.'

Rina was silent.

Decker tried to hide his irritation. 'What's the objection?'

'No objection. You're right.'

'You feel bad about leaving the Lazaruses.'

'Actually, it's okay with me. Tonight's dinner was a little intense in the emotional department.'

'Then what is it? My mother?'

'Your mother and I get along fabulously. She respects me because I know Old Testament better than she does. And your father's downright adorable.' Rina stroked his face. 'It's not your parents at all. And it's not leaving the Lazaruses. It's you. You hate it when you have to give up. You think you're okay. Then it eats away at you.'

'Not this time.'

'Famous last words!' She looked at him intently. 'You promise to forget about this as soon as we leave?'

'I promise.'

'And you really can just forget it that easily?'

'You bet. How about this? We take the boys out to dinner Sunday evening; then you and I go to a Broadway show—'

'Broadway's dark on Sunday night.'

'Really?'

'I would not lie to you, Peter.' She noted disappointment in his voice. 'How about a jazz club? More your style anyway. I'm sure the Lazaruses will baby-sit Hannah.'

'Fabulous.' Decker smiled in the dark. 'That's the spirit! Let's opt for fun while our hearts are still beating.' He kissed Rina long and slow, feeling a tightening below the waist. But he decided to move on. 'Good night, darling. I love you.'

'Love you, too.' Rina closed her eyes, was just about to drift off when she heard him speak.

'. . . off chance that Micky Novack will call tomorrow night.'

'Huh?' She was groggy. 'Who's Mick – oh, the cop. What did you just say?'

'I said, that there was a teeny, tiny off chance that Novack might call me tomorrow night. When I left him, he was investigating the possibility that Ephraim might have attended some twelve-step program meetings for Jewish addicts. If he gets a tip on that, he said he'd call me. Then maybe we'd go out together and interview the members of Ephraim's chapter . . . if Novack gets a lead.'

'I just thought you washed your hands of the entire thing.'

'Only if he gets a lead, Rina.'

'But you're not obsessed.'

'No, I'm not. Obsessed would be if I went out to the meetings without a lead and started asking questions myself. That would be obsessed. Do you see the difference?'

'Yes.'

'Are you just agreeing with me to shut me up?'

'Yes . . . I mean, no.' Rina lifted her head and kissed her husband's lips. 'Good night, Peter.'

She pulled the cover over her face. She fell asleep to the background noise of his muted grumbling.

9

A *teeny, tiny off-chance call, huh?*

Not that Rina had actually *said* anything. She hadn't needed to *say* anything. She had simply given him one of *those* looks. The actual verbalized question had been: 'Do I change the airline tickets?' Decker answered with an offended 'No, of course not,' and left before she could see him blush.

They were walking on Broadway – Novack and he – passing the upper Seventies. The street was wide, but even so, cars were backed up from traffic light to traffic light, the area teeming with life and all the young people who frequented what the Upper West Side had to offer. There were scores of cafés and restaurants, lots of bars, and lots of stores – not the outrageously priced boutiques on Fifth or Madison, but drugstores and bookstores and liquor stores and grocery markets. The night was cold and damp, but Decker had brought along gloves and an overcoat – an old heavy wool thing that he had purchased twenty-five years ago when he and his first wife went to London on vacation in the wintertime: Off-season prices were all he could afford. The trip had been miserable, but he had been warm.

Novack was wearing a black ski parka. 'While you

were praising God at *Shabbat* services, I was working. Course that's my job. I just wanted to assure you that we're not all *yutzes* out here.'

Decker's expression was surprised. 'Why would I think that?'

'The toilet-bowl thing,' Novack said. 'I had it checked out. There was recent splatter on the rim. I shoulda thought of it myself. Course it's a lot easier to be smart when you're working on one case as opposed to twenty, and your city ain't under siege.'

'Absolutely,' Decker said.

'Still, it made me feel bad, you know. Got my ass in gear, and that's not a bad thing. So I started calling some of the phone numbers on the pamphlet on the dead guy's coffee table. The Emek Refa'im handout. Except no one was answering the phone. And then it dawns on me . . .' He knocked his head with his fist. 'It's *Shabbos*. They're not using the phone. So I tried the good old-fashioned phone book . . . looked up the names.'

'That's a lot of leg work.'

'Damn right! But the Knicks are playing again Sunday, so what the hell. I'll watch tomorrow's game. Now, it was very confusing because the chapters meet in the city, but none of the names have city listings. Then it hits me. They're Chasids, probably live in Brooklyn like Ephraim did, but they *meet* in the city, because they don't want anyone from home base knowing that they have a problem. Anonymity, you know. So I start looking up things in the Brooklyn directory, and I got lucky. Since they're not answering the phones, I figured I take a drive south.'

Decker nodded. 'What happened when you showed up at their doors?'

'They weren't pleased, but I was discreet. I musta visited three, four men . . . one woman also. When this guy Ari told me he knew Ephraim, you coulda knocked me over with a spoon.'

'Did he know that Ephraim had been murdered?'

'Yeah, he knew. He was agitated about it. I don't know who was asking more questions, him or me. Anyway, he was talking to me on the sly – can't let the nice little Jewish wife know what's going on – so he asked if I could meet him at some kosher restaurant around here.'

'He's not afraid of being recognized at a kosher restaurant?'

'He says it's not a problem. Nobody'll know him because he'll be wearing civilian garb. I take that to mean not Chasidic dress.'

'Civilian garb?' Decker asked. 'He said that?'

'He did indeed. This whole thing about them being in the army of *Hashem* . . . I guess these guys take it literally.'

Marvad Haksamim meant Magic Carpet in Hebrew. The place had carpets all over the walls, carpets on the floor, and a big carpet tacked onto the ceiling, draping the eatery like a tent. Tivoli lights twinkled from the windows, and a couple of framed pictures of Jerusalem framed the doorway. But the restaurant did have linen napkins and tablecloths, and candles and a vase with a fresh flower decorated every tabletop. There was also a pretty decent wine list. Decker treated himself to a glass of Cabernet. Novack opted for a beer.

Ari Schnitman – whose civilian dress consisted of a black polo shirt, jeans, and sneakers – played with a glass of soda water. On his head was a knitted *kippah* instead of the usual velvet yarmulke or a black hat. But because his hair was so short, the *kippah* could not be bobby-pinned on. It kept threatening to topple over any moment. Schnitman was in his early thirties, with a well-trimmed beard, an ashen pallor, and pale green eyes hidden behind wire-rimmed glasses. His features were small, as were his hands. Decker had met him while he was seated. He knew he was going to tower over Schnitman when they both stood up to say good-bye.

In the middle of the table sat a plate filled with appetizers – spiced carrots, potatoes with scallions and vinegar, olives, pickles, hummus, eggplant salad, and merguez – a spicy sausage that was dripping with oil.

Nobody was eating.

Schnitman was nervous. His voice was barely above a whisper. Decker had to strain to hear him over the background noise. 'It's not that I think this tragedy has anything to do with Emek Refa'im. I know it doesn't. It's just that this kind of thing . . . on top of it being horrible. I liked Ephraim; I really did. It's just so devastating to the morale.'

'Devastating how?' Novack asked.

'You know . . . to think that he might have slipped up. Ephraim had just celebrated two years of being sober. It's terrible to think that a relapse not only ruined two years of hard work, but had cost him his life.'

'You think it was a drug thing gone bad?' Novack asked.

'That's what it sounded like. I heard that the police found him naked in a hotel room, shot execution style.'

Neither Novack nor Decker said anything.

Schnitman dropped his head in his hands. Then he looked up. 'If you've never been chemically addicted, you don't know how hard it is for those of us who are. I say are, because even though we are no longer addicted physically, we will always be addicted mentally. It's a personality type. It really is a disease. It's like AIDS in a way. It's always there. But you learn how to live with it. And if you don't treat it respectfully, it will kill you.'

'How long has Ephraim been coming into your chapter?' Decker asked.

'Three and a half years. The last two, like I said, he has been sober.'

'When was the last time you saw him?'

'At the last meeting – Tuesday night.'

'And everything was fine?' Novack asked.

'Yes, yes, of course.'

But Schnitman had become defensive.

'Are you sure about that?' Decker pressed. 'Nothing on his mind?'

'Something is always on your mind when you're an addict—'

'Nothing out of the ordinary?'

'He was . . . antsy.' The young man sighed. 'But that's not unusual. The first couple of years being drug-free . . . you're always antsy.'

'Nobody is saying you were negligent or did anything wrong,' Decker assured him. 'We're asking you questions only because we need information. You tell us he was antsy. We're going to ask you what was wrong with him.'

'I don't know. But I did ask him about it . . . if he was nervous about something. Did he need help? He said it wasn't about drugs at all. It was personal. I asked if he wanted to talk about it, and he said no, everything would be okay. He had it under control.' Schnitman's eyes watered. 'I guess he didn't have it under control. But how was I to know?'

Decker said, 'No way for you to know except in retrospect.'

Novack said, 'No idea what these personal problems were?'

'No.'

'Money, possibly?'

'I don't know. One of the things we teach is not to push confession too early. It can have serious consequences. This is a stepped program. People go at their own speed and their own pace. And there was nothing to suggest that his problems were anything unusual.'

No one spoke.

'Well, obviously, they had to have been unusual for this to happen.' Schnitman wiped his eyes. 'I'm going to go wash.'

'I'll come with you,' Decker said.

'Anybody know where the facilities are?' Novack asked.

'In the back.'

Schnitman and Decker got up to go to the sink. As expected, Decker did tower over him, and Schnitman seemed to shrink even further, noticing the size difference. They ritually washed their hands, then said the blessing while eating warm pita bread. In silence, they went back to the table and sat back down. Novack excused himself.

Taking pita from a basket, Schnitman dipped a piece in the hummus and snagged a thick glob of the paste. 'I had no idea that he had real problems, Lieutenant. He just wasn't . . . that open. More than that he seemed to be doing okay. I just didn't know!'

'You couldn't have known.'

'This is terrible.'

'Yes, it is,' Decker said. 'Did Ephraim ever talk about his niece?'

'Shayndie? Yes, all the time.' Schnitman went in for second helpings, then thirds. His appetite seemed to pick up. He spooned carrots, olives, and eggplant salad onto his plate. 'She was a good point in his life, someone to be a role model to. He even brought her to a meeting once because he wanted her to see where drugs would lead her. I think it had a profound effect on her – some of the stories that we told her. She was very quiet, but you could tell that she was taking it all in.'

Novack sat down. 'What'd I miss?'

'Ephraim brought Shayndie to an Emek Refa'im meeting once,' Decker said.

'He did?' Novack took a couple of pieces of sausage. 'Wow, this is good! Hot!' He fanned his mouth. 'What was the girl's reaction at the meeting?'

'I just told the lieutenant here.' More carrots onto the plate, followed by several spoons of potatoes. 'She was quiet but affected by it all.'

'Did she talk to any of the members?' Decker asked.

'Not that I can recall. Like I said, she was quiet.'

'Maybe one of the women?' Decker tried again.

'I don't remember.'

'Can you ask?' Novack said.

'Sure, of course.' Schnitman broke off another piece of pita and smothered it with eggplant salad.

'Ephraim . . .' He chewed his food. 'The way he explained it . . . he was taking her under his wing because nobody else in the family wanted to address her problems.' He popped an olive into his mouth. 'My people . . . I love them. But there is a certain tunnel vision that the *Haredi* have. To some of them – the very, very narrow-minded – listening to a woman sing – *kol esha* – is as bad as shooting smack because both are sins. Of course, we know that you can't compare the two acts either physically or morally, but unless you're familiar with that environment, you can't possibly understand it.'

Decker said, 'My wife covers her hair.'

Schnitman looked surprised. 'Oh. But you're not *Haredi*, though.'

'No, and neither is my wife. But I know what you're talking about.'

A waiter came to the table. 'Anything else?'

All three men shook their heads.

He placed the bill on the table and left.

Schnitman looked at the carpet on the ceiling. 'You're modern Orthodox.'

'That's what my wife says,' Decker answered. 'To me, it's still pretty fanatical. I'm a recent convert – a *baal teshuvah*.'

'How recent is recent?'

'Ten years. Believe me, that's still recent.'

Schnitman bit his fingernail. 'The modern Orthodox don't like us.'

'Why do you say that?'

'Because they don't. They think we're loafers and freeloaders and lazy bums. But it's not true! Some people are raised to be doctors, others lawyers. Most of the *Haredi* have been raised to be scholars. That is what we consider worthwhile – the study of Torah. Nothing else matters.'

Decker nodded.

Schnitman looked away. 'You're probably thinking that it's working people like you who support people like me who learn all day. But that's how you get your *schar* mitzvah – your place in heaven.'

'No, Mr Schnitman, I get my own place in heaven – if it exists – by doing my own good deeds. I don't depend on people to do it for me.' Decker focused in on the man's green eyes. 'Look, Ari, let's try to forget about the minuscule differences right now. Because compared to the world out there, all of us – you, me, Detective Novack – we're all lumped together as those pesky Jews who are always causing problems.'

'That is the truth,' Novack said. 'Just look at how the news portrays Israel.'

'Exactly. So let's all of us do a mitzvah and try to figure out what happened to Ephraim. Because maybe that will tell us what happened to Shaynda.'

'I'm sorry. I just don't know what happened to either of them!' His voice was thick with depression. 'I've told you everything I could think of.'

'I dunno,' Novack said. 'Maybe you haven't told us everything because maybe you feel like you're breaking a confidence or something.'

'Not with a young girl missing. And besides, there are no more confidences because Ephraim is dead.'

'So you can answer me if I ask you what was Ephraim's addiction?'

'His addiction?'

'Was it pot, booze, coke—'

'It was cocaine. Ephraim was a cocaine abuser.'

'And . . .'

'That's it. Just cocaine.'

'Crack or blow?'

'Blow.'

'You're sure that was his only chemical bad habit?' Novack said.

'Addiction, Detective.'

'Addiction, then. He ever mention experimenting with other drugs?'

'No. Only coke. But he had it bad. He was, at one point, going through several hundred dollars a day.'

Novack whistled. 'Enough to get him into some pretty heavy debt.'

'He was in debt,' Schnitman said. 'But, as I understand it, he was in the process of paying everyone off. He claimed to be making great progress.'

'Maybe it was great progress for him,' Novack said. 'Maybe it wasn't so great for the people he owed money to.'

'Possibly. I don't know.'

'Could that have been what he meant by personal problems?' Decker asked. 'He was in deep debt, maybe?'

'Your guess is as good as mine.'

'Sure he wasn't taking anything else?' Novack asked. 'Like ecstasy, for instance?'

Suddenly, Decker knew what Novack was doing. The pill found in the hotel room: the analytic results must have come in. Imprinted or not, it must have been ecstasy.

'Only cocaine and only through his nose,' Schnitman insisted. 'How do I know this? Ephraim wouldn't take anything into his stomach that didn't have a *hechsher* on it.'

A *hechsher* was kosher certification. Abruptly,

Decker laughed. 'I didn't know that there was rabbinically supervised cocaine.'

'No, of course there isn't.' Schnitman was offended. 'I know it sounds crazy, but some of the most religious abusers won't take drugs orally. Instead, they shoot poison into the blood or sniff toxins up their noses. Just so the object doesn't pass through their lips. I know it's a ridiculous point of law, but the Bible says *lo toechlu*; that you can't *eat* nonkosher food.'

'It also says you can't touch it,' Decker said.

'Well, that's why they have straws to blow the stuff up your nose!' Schnitman was angry. 'You can make fun of us, Lieutenant, or you can try to understand us. Yes, we have inconsistencies. I'm sure you have them as well.'

'Indeed, I do, Mr Schnitman. I'm sorry if I offended you.'

'Yeah, you've been real helpful,' Novack said. 'Here. Try a sausage. Real spicy, so watch out.'

'Thanks, but I'll pass.' Schnitman pushed away his plate. 'I should be getting back. I have to *bentsh*.'

'That makes two of us,' Decker said.

After they were done saying the Grace after Meals, Novack handed Schnitman his card. 'And if you hear anything—'

'I'll call you, yes.' Schnitman took out his wallet, placed the card inside, then took out a ten-dollar bill.

Decker held him back. 'I'll take care of it.'

Schnitman said, 'One of the things we learn to do when we face our problems head on is to pay our own way. So I'll take care of it.'

'That's ridiculous,' Decker said. 'We asked you out. It's our treat.'

Novack took the check. 'This is a Homicide investigation. You're a witness. As far as I'm concerned, let the city of New York pay for my heartburn.'

Decker buttoned his coat and rubbed his gloved hands together. He had forgotten a scarf, and his face felt the bite of the wind as he walked down Broadway. 'The pill was ecstasy.'

'Yes, it was.'

'So if Schnitman is to be believed, it couldn't have come from Ephraim.'

'Do you honestly believe that a blowhead would stop himself because the high wasn't blessed by the rabbis?'

'As strange as it may seem, Micky, I can see that.'

'Well, you're a step closer to it than I am, Pete.'

They walked a few moments in silence. Then Decker said, 'Where would a kid like Shayndie hide in this town?'

'You kidding?' Novack said. 'I wouldn't even begin to guess. Look around. A million cracks in the naked city for kids to fall through.' He walked a few more steps. 'I'll ask Vice. And Juvie. Don't expect too much.'

'It would probably be too early for her to hit the streets,' Decker said.

'Nah, a pimp wouldn't turn her out just yet.' Novack shrugged. 'If she don't show up back at home or if she don't show up under a rock, maybe she'll show up on the streets. All we can do is wait. Time to call it an evening. Where are you going?'

'Back to Brooklyn. How about yourself?'

'Queens, but I got someone waiting for me back at the two-eight.' They stopped walking. 'We don't get half a chance with the young ones, Pete. The locations are always changing. By the time we figure out where the kids might be hiding, the bad boys got 'em stashed away.'

'If you have a snitch, maybe we can talk to him.'

'Nobody's gonna admit to having a fifteen-year-old. The jail time for that kind of shit is very bad. The young ones need someone with real clout who can hide them from the cops *and* protect them from the johns. Not a lot of pimps want to be bothered with the hassle with so many eighteen-year-olds willing to do the job. Plus, you add that the kid may be running from a murder ... who wants that kinda heat?'

Decker nodded.

'It must be the same in L.A.'

'Yeah, although I'm not a Vice cop. Never have been. Did Juvenile for six years. Lots of sad cases.'

'Then you probably know more about it than me. Where'd you find the kids?'

'The patrol officers were the ones who usually found them. Lots of time the kids were starving and diseased. Sometimes they came into the police stations on their own, asking for protection or asking us to act as an agent between their parents and them. You know, help them get rid of the abusive boyfriend or stepfather.'

'Yeah, it's the same all over.'

'I know some spots in L.A. And if I don't know the spots directly, I have people I can talk to. Here, in Manhattan, I'm in the dark.'

It was close to eleven with the mercury dropping by the moment. Still, the sidewalks held hives of people marching at a clipped pace, the mist of warm breath producing as much cloud cover as the skies. About half the shops were still open, and those that were closed stood locked but not caged in by metal bars and grates – a change from the last time Decker was here. In the street, headlights and taillights were haloed circles of red and white.

Novack said, 'I don't know much about the pimp scene here. But I do know someone who does. If you really think that maybe Shayndie went that route, lemme call him up.'

'I don't know what route she took,' Decker said. 'I'm grasping at straws because I'm running out of time.'

'When are you leaving?'

'Monday . . . or maybe even Tuesday.' Rina was going to make fun of him. He could hear her in his head. *Should I change the tickets now, Peter?* 'But only if we're getting somewhere.'

'*We're* getting somewhere?'

Decker smiled. 'Only if I think I might be able to help you, Detective Novack.'

'Ah, much better.' Novack smiled. 'All right. Since you're under a time crunch, I'll see if we can meet with him tomorrow morning.'

'That would be great. Because otherwise . . .' Decker threw up his hands. 'It could be she left the city . . . that she's in Quinton. Cops over there said they'd look again, but the chief of the Quinton Police didn't sound too hopeful. Actually, he wasn't at all *helpful*.'

'Who'd you talk to?'

'Virgil Merrin.'

Novack shrugged. 'Don't know him. We're our own country out here.'

'I'm beginning to realize that. Do you think we can meet with your guy early tomorrow morning?'

'Early? Like how early?'

'Eight, nine.'

'Now, that I don't know. He's Irish. Saturday night is pub night.'

'Tell him if he meets me at eight, I'll buy him a case of his favorite beer.'

Novack nodded. 'Lieutenant Decker, that just may be the right incentive.'

10

Ephraim Lieber had met his end just blocks away from the 28th hub precinct, in a blighted tenement to the west of Harlem. It was a neighborhood of elevated train tracks and chain-link fences that surrounded weed-choked lots, a vicinity with enough space to hold auto-repair shops, car washes, and a slew of one-story fast-food joints that could have easily been transplanted into Decker's native L.A. turf. Exterior fire escapes hugged grime-coated brick buildings like scaffolding. Still, as Decker drove through the streets, he saw the possibilities. Old, wonderful – albeit graffitied – brownstones with great bone structure. And there was Riverside Park, a stretch of trees, foliage, and gardens that snuggled against the Hudson, an oasis replete with benches and jogging pathways. It came in around 72nd and continued uptown until about 120th, ending several blocks away from the two-eight. The park, developed in the 1940s and 1950s atop railroad tracks, served as a botanical reminder of what had probably flourished before Manhattan became the isle of asphalt and skyscrapers.

The precinct was two stories of raw concrete that must have been raked with combs while the cement was drying. Entrance inside was through steel double doors that looked not only solid but also bulletproof. Decker took three steps down, and stood in front of a bright blue horseshoe-shaped desk manned by a black woman in uniform. To Decker's right was a glass case filled with the precinct's sports trophies; to his left were a couple of offices and a row of bolted lime green plastic chairs, the sole occupant being a sleeping homeless person of indeterminate gender curled up as tightly as a potato bug.

As Decker approached the desk, Novack was bounding down a set of steps.

'Hey. Right on time. Up here.'

Decker followed Novack upstairs.

'How you doin'?' Micky asked.

'Fine.'

'Good. I got him to come, but it wasn't easy.'

'I owe you.'

'Yeah. Right.' Novack led him past a cubby used as the squad-room secretary's office. 'Welcome to the two-eight. It ain't an architectural showpiece, but we do have a nice view of the gas station.'

Except for one other man, the place was empty – one of the advantages of working Sunday morning. The area given over to the gold shields was cramped, a maze of waist-high cubicles stuffed with standard-issue metal desks, functional chairs, and basic computers. The walls were whitewashed cinder block, the water-streaked ceiling held dim fluorescent lighting, and the flooring was composed of white crushed rock tile scuffed dirt gray. There were a few stabs of humanity, courtesy of several desktops holding wilting potted plants or an occasional homemade child's ceramic mug or paperweight, some scattered personal pictures. The majority of the domain, of course, was given over to business.

Papers abounded.

Loose-leaf sheaves were piled high on any flat surface that would hold them, or posted chockablock on bulletin boards. They spilled out of file cabinets and from plastic bins that also contained thick wads of forms and reports. Street maps were taped to the wall, dotted with crimes that had been coded by different colored pins. There were two interview rooms and between their peacock blue doors was a bulletin board overlaid with police sketches of felons at large.

One specific printed poster caught Decker's eye. It showed the American flag, the caption reading: THESE COLORS DON'T RUN. Below the poster was another bulletin board filled with snapshots of bleeding, ash-covered officers from September 11.

Novack caught him staring. 'You know, being in the Job, you think you've seen it all.'

Decker let out a wry laugh. 'Guess what?'

'Ain't that the truth.' Novack pointed to the room's other occupant. 'That's Brian Cork from Vice standing over my desk. Hey, Bri, say hello to Lieutenant Decker.'

Cork looked up. 'Mornin'.'

'Mornin'.'

They gathered at Novack's desk. Cork appeared to be in his forties around five-ten, with big shoulders and a growing beer gut. Around the chest and arms, he was a mound of muscle. If the precinct had a football team, these guys would have been perfect ends. Cork had a round, ruddy face, with thin, almost bloodless lips and pug features. He also had a broken nose perched on his face like a patty-pan squash. He was scanning through the post-mortem pictures of Ephraim.

He said, 'So you're a lieutenant in L.A?'

'Yep.'

'What are you doing out here, messing with this trash?'

'I was wangled into coming out here to be the translator for the cops. The vic was a brother-in-law to my brother. I told him I'd poke around. I was just telling Micky that I think I've outlived my usefulness. Even the family is sick of my face. Pretty good trick since I've only been here for two days.'

'Family . . .' Cork made a face. 'I've got six brothers and sisters. Three of them are cops, so you know it's gotta be bad news right away. We get together every Christmas. It always starts off full of good cheer, but by the end of the evening, more punches are thrown than at a boxing match. Sheez, I'll take the street over pissed-off siblings any day of the year.'

'What can you do?' Decker said.

'What can you do is right.' Cork sighed. 'So you're bowing out?'

'Since I'm not adding anything, I think that's the smartest thing to do.'

'So for what it's worth, I'll put my two cents in. This is just observation.' Cork was still staring at the pictures. 'You know what it looks like to me?'

'What?' Novack asked.

'It looks like Family—'

'I don't think it's Family, Bri.'

'I didn't say it was Family, Mick, I said it *looks* like Family. Not current Family. Back four, five years when C.D. was still in the business and still aligned with the old man. It's not one of his, though. First off, C.D. don't do nothing unless it's big money, and this guy is obviously low level. Second, C.D. would never, *ever* clean a mark in a hotel. Too many people, and C.D. don't attract attention to himself. And third, and this may be rumor, but last I heard, C.D. was out of the business. I'm just saying it looks like one of his. A single shot. Not much blood. No extraneous shit. Clean and simple.'

'C.D.?' Decker asked.

'Christopher Donatti,' Novack answered him.

It took Decker a moment to absorb the words. Only then did a flood of images hit him like an overexuberant wave. Very few of Decker's murder cases were committed to instant memory: Chris's was one of them. Eight years had passed since Decker's last contact with the younger Donatti, yet the details were still as fresh as a brisk wind. The murder of a high-school prom queen, Donatti the lead suspect. He'd been Whitman back then, and though the last name had changed, Decker was sure that the kid had not. Once a psycho . . .

'The hit looks like it was done by Chris Donatti?'

'It *looks* like it – that's all. C.D. hasn't been tied to anything since the old man had a massive coronary.'

'Joseph Donatti had a heart attack?' Decker asked.

'Yeah, Joey had a bad one.' Cork stared at him.

'Must have missed that one.' Decker swallowed. 'When did this happen?'

'About four, five years ago,' Novack said.

'I'm slipping,' Decker said. 'So does Chris Donatti run the Family?'

'You mean the Donatti Family? There is no Donatti Family. It dissolved.'

'What happened? Did a rival boot Chris out?'

'No, C.D.'s the one that dissolved it.' Cork stared at Decker. 'You keep calling Donatti Chris? Are you on a first-name basis with the guy?'

Decker shrugged. 'So what's he doing? C.D.?'

'We got a problem with him. The problem is he's a cipher. He don't talk.'

'What do you mean, he doesn't talk?'

'Just that. He don't talk. Complete opposite of the old man. Old man ordered a hit, half the world knew about it. Not C.D. You know after the old man was retired, everyone was waiting to see what would happen. How C.D. would flex his muscle. Then it came – two hits of top dealers in Washington Heights. Bam, bam. Clean as a whistle. In-and-out jobs. Donatti's M.O. to a tee. So we're thinking, oh boy, C.D.'s moving in on Dominican territory. Watch out for the war. Then you know what happened?'

'What?'

'Nothing, that's what happened. While the Doms are scrambling around, trying to reorganize after losing two bosses, someone moves in and pays them all off. I'm not talking about chump change here; I'm talking big bucks. Next thing we know, half of Wash Heights is suddenly Benedetto territory.'

'Chr—C.D.'s father-in-law.'

'You know more about this than you're letting on.'

'No, I don't know anything about these events. That's why I'm asking you.'

'Yeah, Benedetto was C.D.'s father-in-law. So we figured that C.D. went in and divided up the spoils between him and his father-in-law. You know, as a gift to the old man. Except three months later, C.D. and Benedetto's cow of a daughter are no longer wedded in holy matrimony, and suddenly C.D. is gone. Like vanished off the face of the earth. The old man – Benedetto – he's got all the territory. So we figured that Benedetto muscled out Donatti, that the kid was either lying six feet under with dirt in his eyes or implanted in a foundation of one of the Camden, New Jersey, rejuvenation projects. The other possibility, of course, was that the guy was in hiding, deciding on his next move. If he's laying low, we figured – oh boy, another war. So you know what happened?'

'What happened?'

'Nothing, that's what happened. So we think he's dead. Then maybe twelve months later – this was about three or four years ago – C.D. pops up out of nowhere. He's livin' uptown not too far from here, taking beaver shots of teenage girls—'

'Kiddie porn?'

'Nah, they're all over eighteen. How do I know this? I've tried to bust the guy no less than ten times. His girls are all righteous – for now. He's got some Supreme Court decisions pending that may put him down for a while, but the guy is a weed. He'll pop back with something new. For the time being, we know he's pimping his girls, but we can't find the chink in the armor. You know why?'

'Why?'

'Because C.D. don't talk.'

'He and the old man still in contact?'

'Yeah, sure. Since he's surfaced, we see him visiting Joey every now and then. Nothing too heavy. Outta obligation, I think. Joey adopted C.D. They're not related. You probably know that.'

'I know that.'

'C.D.'s got no blood family, no friends, no nothing in the way of social connections. What he does have is one of the seediest rags in the business. A twenty- to thirty-page glossy pictorial of young girls – all of them barely eighteen – dressed up as even younger girls who play out every middle-aged guy fantasy known to mankind. You know – teacher/student, patient/candy striper, making it with your daughter's best friend—'

'Lovely.'

'I don't know who the fuck he's selling this shit to, but he must have some kind of market. What started as a cheap, homemade job has blossomed into something with high-quality photographs and advertising. I'm not saying he's ready for prime-time magazine space, but there are buyers out there.'

'American enterprise.'

'Wanna know what I think?'

'What?' Decker asked.

'I think Donatti gave Benedetto Wash Heights as payment to get out of the Family. The guy is too much of a loner to take orders from higher-ups. Not that he's exactly come up in the world. If he's living the good life, he's hiding it well.'

'Don't he own the building, Bri?' Novack popped in.

'This is true. He owns quite a bit of real estate around a hundred thirty-fifth in what's called the Shona Bailey area. The neighborhood has all these brownstones – nice babies, but in serious disrepair. The Bailey was doing real well for a while. It was the darling of the dotcoms. Then the economy tanked and September eleventh hit. Last I heard he's been picking up the buildings for a song.'

Novack shook his head. 'No one ever accused the kid of being brainless.'

'So if I were to look for him, I'd find him uptown around a hundred thirty-fifth?' Decker asked.

'Yes, I suppose, although I don't know if he'd be in at nine forty-five, Sunday morning. Why would you want to look for him?'

'Because you said the hit looks like one of his. And if he preys on young girls, a desperate fifteen-year-old may be just his kind of meat.'

'I don't know why he'd mess with underage girls when he has lots of legit babes doing his bidding. Guy's a pussy magnet – always has been. The kind of bad boy that stupid girls love.'

Not just stupid girls. Decker thought for a moment. 'You have his address?'

Cork eyed him. 'What are you going to do, Decker? Go over and ask him about it? If you want to go after Donatti, you don't just pop in and announce yourself. You go over there with warrants. Otherwise, he don't talk to you.'

'I don't have time for subtlety,' Decker said. 'I just want to ask him a couple of questions.'

'Want me to come with you?' Novack offered.

Decker's heart sank. He wanted to talk to Donatti alone. 'Sure.'

'You gonna be a party to this nonsense, Mick?' Cork made a face.

Decker said breezily, 'You know, Novack, he's probably not even in. I've got your cell. If I get anywhere, I'll call you. Unless you *want* to come.'

Novack shook his head. 'Not with the Knicks playing this afternoon. I promised the missus I'd clean out the garage. I'd like to get it done so I can watch the game in peace.'

'Go home, Mick. I'll be fine.' To Cork, Decker said, 'The address?'

'You really want to do this?'

Decker nodded.

'I'll look it up for you,' Cork said. 'My notebook's in my car. Hold on.'

Cork disappeared. Novack regarded Decker, staring at him before he spoke. 'Where are you going with this, Pete?'

'Beats me. But I'm not having luck going the traditional route.'

'It's not wise to get too involved in other people's business.'

Don't tread on me. Decker said, 'Hey, if you object, I won't go.'

'Just don't mess up anything, all right? Vice don't like to look stupid.'

'I hear you.'

But the tension held fast. Neither spoke until Cork came back several minutes later holding a piece of paper. 'It's not too far from here, 'bout fifteen blocks uptown. I forget if it's between Riverside Drive and Broadway. Or just right east of Broadway.'

'I'll find it.'

Cork handed Decker the numbers. 'Something's not computing. You know more about Donatti than you're letting on.'

'C.D. spent some time in California. We crossed paths.'

'Ah!' Cork said. 'History or no history, you're wasting your time. Even if he's there, he won't talk to you.'

That very well could be the case. Except that

Decker had a weapon that obviously the cops didn't know about. 'Maybe one of his girls will talk.'

'Pshhh.' The detective waved him off. 'Nah, they don't talk. I know 'cause I've tried. Whatever hold Donatti's got on 'em is a choke hold.'

11

Rina would have killed him; Novack – if he had known the entire story – would have blasted him for going it solo. It was irresponsible; it was dangerous; it was just plain stupid. It was all those things because C.D. was a stone-cold psycho, C.D. was a killer, and C.D. hated his guts. Yet, Decker gave himself a pat on the back for being a trusting soul, facing the kid without so much as a nail file for defense. But it was more than trust. After seven years of serving as a lieutenant, directing his charges, and pushing paper rather than solving crimes, Decker was buzzed with the thrill of action. Except for several exceptional cases, he had been a prisoner of his own success, trapped behind a desk, his reflexes slowed with age and atrophy.

What kind of reception he would get, Decker didn't bother to contemplate. As long as Chris didn't shoot him on the spot, anything else would be okay.

Going by foot, he discovered that the area looked closer on the map than it did in person. By the time he found the place, it was ten-thirty in the morning. C.D.'s building was uptown, six stories of dilapidated brick material several blocks away from potentially lovely brownstones. But it had a lobby with the entrance door locked tight. There were buttons that corresponded to the various units – twenty in all. The fifth and sixth floors were taken up by one tenant: MMO enterprises. Since C.D. supposedly owned the building and used it as his studio, Decker tried that button first. It rang several times; then to his surprise, a woman responded over the intercom, 'MMO.'

'Police,' Decker said.

A momentary delay, and then a loud buzz, one that allowed him to come into the building. He took the stairs up five flights and stepped out into the corridor. There was a single door to the left, marked with the number 13. He pushed another button, and again was buzzed in. He immediately stepped through a metal detector. Of course he set it off.

In front of him was a girl who couldn't have been over fifteen.

'There's a bucket for your keys and wallet and anything else you might have that would cause it to go off. Could you please step back and try it again?'

Decker followed her instructions, picking up his personal effects on the other side. There was a lad sitting by the girl's side, reading a magazine. He was of slight build, but maybe he only appeared that way because he was wearing an oversize Hawaiian shirt. Decker couldn't see the outline of a gun, but he was sure it was there. The boy/man's eyes traveled to Decker's.

The girl said, 'Can I help you, Officer?'

She was dressed for efficiency – a black suit, with her hair tied back in a ponytail. No makeup. Her hands were as smooth as a baby's, nails clipped short and no polish.

'I'd like to speak to Mr Donatti, please.'

'Do you have an appointment?'

Her eyes never wavered from his.

'No, but it's important.' He showed her his gold shield and ID.

The guard put down the magazine and gave Decker a hard stare, Decker answered him back with a smile. The girl exchanged glances with the guard. He nodded.

She said, 'Hold on a moment, sir.' She picked up a phone and punched in several numbers.

'Mr Donatti, I'm very sorry to disturb you, but there's a policeman here.'

She stopped talking. Decker couldn't hear Donatti's response.

The girl said, 'May I see your identification and badge again?'

'Certainly.'

'It's Lieutenant Peter Deck—'

'Son of a bitch!'

That, Decker heard. He staved off a smile. The girl hung up the phone, with a slightly bemused look on her face. 'He's in the middle of a shoot. You must really rate.'

'I don't know about that.'

'He'll be with you in a few minutes.'

'Thank you.' Decker smiled, realizing that there wasn't as much as a stool for him to sit on. Not much space for excess furniture anyway. It was a nondescript area with cream-colored blank walls with barely enough room for the receptionist and guard. Chris probably didn't get much company.

With Donatti, a few minutes actually meant a few minutes. The interior door opened, and there he was. No longer the lanky heartthrob of a teen, Christopher Whitman Donatti, at twenty-six, now cut a big swath. He was broad across the chest, with massive arms and developed biceps. His left hand gripped a Hasselblad that looked like a toy in his fingers. He was clean shaven, his abundant blond locks shorn just a step away from a buzz cut. A lean, long face contained high cheekbones and a wide forehead, with ruddy skin that wasn't weathered but did hold some seams. He had a strong jawline, not chiseled but more manly than boyish. Generous lips that protected straight white teeth. Noticeable large blue eyes: ice-colored with no reflective quality whatsoever. What was the opposite of luminous?

Decker and his six-foot-four frame had always faced Chris eye-to-eye. For the first time, he sensed his line of vision moving upward.

'You grew.'

'I always was a late bloomer.' Donatti wore loose clothing – a black T-shirt over khaki cargo pants, the pockets bulging – probably filled with photographic paraphernalia and, no doubt, a state-of-the-art piece. His feet were housed in black suede running shoes. He was still blocking the door, staring at Decker. 'I need to pat you down.'

'I made it through security.'

'I need to pat you down,' Donatti repeated.

The child/guard was on his feet, his right hand on his hip. His face may have looked young, but his eyes reflected pure business. 'Can I be of assistance, Mr Donatti?'

'Thanks, Justin, but this one's mine.' Donatti gave the girl his camera, then turned to Decker. 'The position?'

Without protest, Decker faced the wall, leaning forward on his arms. It was natural for Donatti to assume that Decker was wearing a wire or carrying a gun – something for defense. As it were, Decker was putty, nothing but his brain for protection. Donatti was thorough with the frisk – front and back, up and down, inside and out. He went through Decker's pockets, sorted through his credit cards and personal identification. From his wallet, the kid pulled out the one lone photograph Decker was carrying – the recent snapshot of Jacob.

Donatti showed him the photo. 'This is the only picture you carry?'

'My son gave it to me a couple of days ago. Normally, I don't carry any pictures of my family.'

'Protective?'

'A lot of people resent me.' Decker smiled.

Donatti's face was flat. He stared at the snapshot. 'He's the image of your wife.'

Decker's stomach did a little dance. He didn't respond and tried to look unimpressed.

'Am I wrong?' Donatti said.

'No, not at all.'

Donatti returned the picture to Decker's wallet, placed it back into the jacket pocket. He rummaged through the rest of Decker's jacket, fishing out the envelope that held the crime-scene photos.

It gave him pause.

Carefully, he scrutinized them, studying them one by one. Again he stopped when he got to the photo of Ephraim with Shaynda. Though his eyes were fixed on the faces, his expression was completely blank. Abruptly, he placed the snapshots back in the envelope and slipped the whole package back into Decker's pocket. Then stepped away from the door. 'Okay. You can come in.'

The loft was enormous, with vaulted high ceilings, and large, dusty windows letting in filtered light. Each window had a shade on it – some were rolled up, some drawn. The floor was made from old planks of cherry wood, scuffed but still intact. Most of the studio was empty space, except for a bank of built-in cabinets underneath the windows, a weight rack, a cello case next to a backless chair, and the actual shooting area. Here was the place of action: a jumble of prop boxes, numerous hanging backdrops, several differently colored carpets, chairs, tables, and lighting accessories. There were umbrellas, tripods, reflectors, and spots – all of them positioned around the main stage

There was music in the background – something classical but atonal and avant-garde which Decker didn't recognize. It was very low-pitched like whispered conversation. Two young boys – probably teenagers – were rearranging props and photographic equipment, pulling things in and out of boxes and bags. They were flitting around the center stage and its main occupant – a naked girl wearing spiked heels on her feet and a boa around her neck. Her blond hair was pinned, but in disarray. She wore little makeup – lipstick, a spot of blush. Big blue eyes were taking him in.

Decker averted his gaze, electing to look at his shoes.

All his girls were legit.

She was probably eighteen, but she was made up to look around fourteen.

Wordlessly, Donatti started fiddling with the background tripod that held an electronic flash. 'Go on.'

'Are you talking to me?' Decker asked.

'Yes, I am.'

'Do you mind if we talk in private?'

'Getting distracted, Lieutenant?'

'Distracted is a good word.'

'Hey, you said it was important. I figured we can talk while I work.' He regarded Decker's eyes, his face cold and expressionless. 'But if you want to talk to me alone, you'll have to wait.'

'How long?'

'Beats me. But you can sit if you want. You can even take a cup of coffee.'

Decker's eyes swept across the room. There was a coffeepot resting on top of one of the cabinets. He walked over, poured himself a Styrofoam cup of black coffee, and looked around for a chair.

Donatti said, 'Matt, get the lieutenant a box to sit on.'

One of the young boys snapped to it, bringing Decker a wooden crate. Decker thanked him, then watched Donatti pose the girl while trying not to stare too hard. Donatti positioned her, head back and legs apart. Then he nudged a reflector upward with his toe. 'Up . . . up. Like this, okay?'

Matt nodded, gripping the silver surface.

Donatti took a lens out of his pants pocket and switched it with the one in his camera. 'Keep the damn thing up!' Again he kicked the reflector. 'Like that! Jesus! Reading?'

The other young boy held up an exposure meter. A flash went off and the boy gave Donatti some numbers.

The two assistants appeared almost prepubescent – narrow-hipped and narrow-shouldered, without any signs of facial hair. One was of dark skin – Latino or Puerto Rican – the other was Anglo. Both had long, silken hair – perfect chicken-hawk material. Decker wondered if Chris was swinging both ways, or at the very least pimping both ways. The boys were all work and showed no interest in the young girl, who was the center of attention – licking her lips provocatively as she parted her legs, her eyes on Decker.

Again Decker looked at his feet. 'Nice place,' he said, absently.

'Like it? I own the building.'

'Very entrepreneurial, Chris.'

'I like business. It suits me.' Donatti did a slow turn and faced Decker with lightless eyes. 'By the way, I called you Lieutenant. That means you call me Mr Donatti.'

'I stand corrected.'

Donatti went over to the center and peered through the camera. 'Matt, you got to lift up the reflector around an inch . . . yeah, there. Richie, you want to kick up that back light, I'm getting a nasty shadow . . . to the left. That's good. Hold out the meter.'

A flash went off.

'Reading?'

Richie gave him the numbers. Donatti was not happy. He played with the lights, the umbrella, and the reflectors. As his frustration increased, Donatti's assistants seemed to grow more and more anxious, exhibiting nervous twitches. There was no attempt at camaraderie. It was Mr Donatti this, and Mr Donatti that. Finally, the conditions met with Chris's approval, and Donatti started snapping, talking the girl through it as he worked. He was fast and furious, dripping with sweat under the hot lights. The model was also sweating profusely. He worked continually for about five minutes; then without warning, Donatti stopped, swore, picked up a spray bottle of iced water, and blasted it over the young girl's chest and vagina.

The model shrieked. 'God—'

'I know it's cold,' Donatti told her. 'It can't be helped.' He tossed her a cold pack. 'Put it over your hot spot.'

'Huh?'

Donatti marched over to her and slapped the cold pack on her vagina. 'Hold it. And stop looking angry. You're supposed to be a fantasy, and fantasies don't look like they sucked on lemons. If the men I sell to wanted that expression, they'd fuck their wives.'

'It's freezing,' she whined.

'Just hold it and stop bitching.' He turned to Decker. 'Ice shrinks the membranes down. It makes for a prettier picture. I gotta get air-conditioning in this place. Not only would I be more comfortable, but it would also keep the nipples erect.'

'It's cold outside,' Decker commented.

'The windows don't open. Security.' He turned back to the model. 'Okay, you can take it away . . . good. Now give it to me, Tina. C'mon, baby, make your moves.'

She began to pose in a provocative manner while Donatti snapped away, then stopped again. He growled, 'You keep sweating.'

'I can't help it!'

He sighed. 'If you can't beat 'em . . .' He went over to one of the cardboard boxes and started pulling out props. He chose a sweatband, a pair of sneakers, socks with pom-poms, and a calculator. He tossed her the accessories. 'Put those on. We'll go for the fucked cheerleader look, all right?'

She took off the black spiked heels, put on the socks, then tried to put on the sneakers. 'They're too small.'

'So cram your foot into it, Cinderella. Don't lace it up, all right. You know what? I got an idea. Put one on, let the other one dangle. Yeah . . . like that. Now put on the sweatband . . . Wow, that's good!' He placed the calculator at her feet, then squirted another round of ice water on her. Waiting a few moments, he opened the girl's legs and fluffed up her pubic hair. 'Throw your head back, but keep your eyes fucking the lens. Good girl. Now put your finger in your spot, but not all the way . . . just the nail. Good . . . real good.'

She whined as she talked. 'Like *why* do you want a calculator?'

'*Because* you're supposed to be a schoolgirl. You remember school, don't you?'

'Like ha-ha, I'm laughing.'

'You be polite,' Donatti growled. 'We have company.'

His voice was menacing, putting fear in the girl's eyes. In a toe tap, she was all business.

'That's good,' Donatti complimented. 'That's really good, Tina. C'mon, give me those luscious lips, baby!'

The girl gave him a wide smile that made her look around twelve. Donatti was pleased. 'You got it, baby.' Snap, snap. 'Do the camera, honey, do it hard and nasty. Man, you are fucking good.' Snap, snap, snap. 'You got the look, sugar, the perfect wet dream for all old farts who can't get it up.'

She leered at Decker. 'Old farts like him.'

Donatti stopped and followed her gaze. He had been so distracted, he'd forgotten about Decker's presence. His eyes went dead. 'Yeah, old farts like him.' Snap, snap. 'Not him specifically.' Back at the model. 'I've seen his wife.' Snap, snap, snap. 'Getting it up probably isn't one of his more significant problems.'

After fifteen minutes, he stood up straight and shook out his shoulders.

'That's the roll.' He took several fifties out of his wallet and gave them to Richie. 'Take an hour break. Bring Amber and Justin with you. Be back by noon. If you're late, I'll be pissed.'

Richie nodded.

'I expect change.'

'Yes, sir.'

Donatti grinned, then tousled the young Latino's hair. The boy smiled shyly. The girl slipped on a pair of sloppy sweats and threw a knapsack over her back, making her appear even younger.

'Tina,' Donatti called out.

She turned around.

Donatti gave her a thumbs-up. Her face instantly lit up . . . like turning on a switch. After everyone left, Donatti said, 'I've got to look at the rolls. Help yourself to some more coffee. I'll be out in about a half hour.'

The loft held four interior doors. He walked through one of them and was gone from sight. Thirty-two minutes later, he reappeared, a timer in his hands.

'This way.' He motioned to Decker, taking him through a different door. As soon as Decker stepped across the threshold, Donatti flipped several switches – including the light – then locked the door with two solid dead bolts. The office was spacious but held no windows. The illumination was muted, the ventilation provided by an overhead fan. Again there was very little furniture. A thirty-by-sixty table surrounded by four chairs probably served as a desk. Donatti had a lamp, a phone, and a fax machine, but nothing else sat on the table's surface. There was a single file cabinet against the wall, a clock above it. The wall also had a half-dozen video monitors that gave Donatti a view of the lobby, his own front door, and several other sites around the building's exterior. Next to the monitors was a wall panel containing ten lights – some were green, some red. Decker figured that they represented various security zones.

Donatti sat on one side of the table; Decker took a seat opposite him. No one spoke. Then Decker laid the crime-scene photos on Donatti's desk, along with the picture of Ephraim and Shaynda.

Donatti didn't look at them. 'Why in the world do you think *I* would talk to you? You ruined my life.'

'That's a very negative spin on it, Chris. I think of it as saving Terry's life instead.'

'Did she give you my address?'

'No, the cops did.'

'The cops?'

'Yeah, the cops.'

Donatti let out a laugh. 'It's nice to be thought of as the bullet behind every single whack in this city.' His eyes darkened. 'You know, after I found out that Terry was pregnant, I kept waiting for her to tell me. Six months after the kid was born, I finally figured out that she had other things in mind . . . things like denying me my son. And that angered me. I decided to give Terry a little time to get it together. If I didn't hear boo from her by the time the kid was a year old, she was going to meet with a very unfortunate accident. Three weeks before the target date, I get a letter from her. It starts off like this.

' "Dear Chris, I wasn't going to tell you, but Lieutenant Decker prevailed upon me." '

He paused.

' "I wasn't going to tell you, but *Lieutenant* Decker prevailed upon me." '

'Now that really angered me. It angered me that she wasn't going to tell me. It angered me that she only told me because you told her to do it, and it really *pissed me off* that you made lieutenant.'

'Sounds like you were angry, Chris.'

'Yes, I was, and it's *Mr Donatti* to you.'

'You already told me that.'

'Well, you seem to have forgotten. I'll chalk it up to old age.'

'Fair enough.' Decker rubbed his eyes. They felt hot and itchy. 'Terry tells me you two have been in contact for several years now.'

'Minimal contact.'

'What does that mean?'

'Ask her.'

'She says you come out to see her and your son a half-dozen times a year.'

'So she still writes to you.'

'Occasionally.'

Chris rolled his eyes.

Decker said, 'Yeah, she told me you don't approve.'

'No, that's not what I said. I told her that she shouldn't put anything down in writing. If she wants to talk to you, she should call you. I know that Terry has some kind of father fixation with you. It's harmless. It's probably healthy in light of the fact that her old man is a raging alcoholic. I just don't want any connection to me in writing. It's not healthy for her or the kid.'

Decker thought a moment. 'Cops don't know about Terry or the kid, do they, Chris?'

Donatti gave Decker a hard stare.

'I'll take that as a no,' Decker answered. 'So who does know about them other than me? Joey?'

Donatti closed his eyes, then opened them. A harmless gesture, except it was one that Decker knew very well. It meant that Decker had touched on something. It meant that Chris was edgy.

Decker smiled. 'Joey has no idea that you're in contact with Terry. He thinks you broke it off with her eight years ago, and that was that.' The smile widened. 'Joey doesn't know dick about her or the kid, does he?'

'Am I reading this right, Decker?' Donatti's nostrils flared. 'Are you actually *using* Terry as a bargaining chip?'

'God forbid! You know I don't work that way.' He exhaled. 'Be hell of a lot easier if I did.' He pointed to the pictures. This time, Chris finally looked at them. 'I'm a stranger here, Mr Donatti. I need help. I'm interested in any information about the hit and what this guy did to get bumped. But more important, he was with a fifteen-year-old girl. This girl, here.' Decker pointed to the one picture he had of Shaynda. 'She's gone, and the parents are frantic. Any ideas?'

Donatti answered with another shrug.

'Is that a yes or a no?'

Donatti didn't answer. A timer dinged. 'Excuse me, I have work to do.' He stood up and waited for Decker to do the same.

Decker paused.

'That means you've gotta go,' Donatti said.

Reluctantly, Decker got up and left the room. Chris locked the door and put the keys in his pants. 'You can let yourself out the same way you came in.'

Again Donatti disappeared behind one of the doors. Decker waited, deciding what to do. He knew if he left now, he'd never get another chance. Donatti would think him a gutless jerk. Yet if he pushed Donatti, that wouldn't work, either.

C.D. don't talk.

But back then – eight years ago – Chris did talk, having told Decker lots of things in his time of need. In some perverse way, Decker had been a kind of father figure to Donatti as well as Terry. While Chris was serving time, Decker had been his link to Terry. More important, Decker had been C.D.'s passkey out of prison. Yes, it was Decker who had put him in the hole, but when certain forensic irregularities came to light, it had been Decker who had bought Donatti his freedom. If anything were to work with the kid, it would be the old roles, not the new ones.

There was no way Decker could convince Chris that he had his interest at heart. But he could convince Donatti that he cared about Terry – because that was true. Decker had given the girl money when she had been desperate – abandoned by everyone, including her parents. One thousand dollars that Decker could ill afford went to support Donatti's son when Chris wouldn't have anything to do with her. Now that they had resumed a relationship, Terry had probably told him about it: Chris was no doubt resentful. Still, Decker had come through for Terry, and Donatti placed a huge premium on loyalty.

Decker sat back down on the wooden crate and rested his elbows on his knees. If he were to get anywhere with this homicide, he needed an insider and who better than Donatti?

Provided that Donatti had nothing to do with the murder.

Sure it was a risk, but what was life without that occasional adrenaline rush?

Decker waited patiently, happy to just sit and do nothing. When Donatti finally emerged, he stopped in his tracks, seeing Decker. 'You're still here.'

'Yep.'

'Why?'

As Decker stood, Donatti tensed up every muscle every sinew as if expecting Decker to pounce. Instead, Decker dropped his voice to a soothing whisper. 'You have a beautiful son, Donatti, because you chose his mother well. That much we agree on. As far as Terry goes, I die with your secret, guy. You know me well enough to realize that my word is not only gold but also noncontingent. If you can help me out, fine. If not, it's no hard feelings. I walk away and you never hear from me again.'

With that, Decker turned and left.

12

I f Donatti had something to do with the hit, he
didn't give off any telltale vibes. But then again
Chris had always been good at hiding things, so
Decker didn't dare rule him out. Clearly, Donatti
favored youth – teenagers he could control and
manipulate. He had to recruit his girls from somewhere, and as long as Shaynda was still missing, any
predator of young girls was suspect. Decker had
stirred up the muck. Now it remained to be seen
what would surface.

Walking along Riverside Drive, he bundled up in
his coat and stuck his hands in his pockets. The sky
was all pewter and charcoals, enclosing the Hudson
River like dented armor. A pungent wind was roughing up the water's surface. Decker felt the sting in his
cheeks and on the tip of his nose. Brisk in step, he
spotted a taxi and flagged it down. As soon as he did
it, he realized he didn't know where he wanted to go.

With the case stalling and no new leads, there
wasn't any reason to stay in Manhattan. Yet, just as
Rina had predicted, he was reluctant to let go. Why
had the Liebers turned hostile? Stress manifesting
itself or the sinking realization that Decker would not
be able to work miracles? A true professional would

have returned to Quinton and bullied the family into cooperation. But that was the problem: the Liebers were family. His relationship with his half brother Jonathan wasn't fixed in concrete, and Decker didn't want to jeopardize a tenuous bond that took ten years to build.

His options were dwindling, but he still had some recourse left. Since he was in Manhattan anyway, he could pay a visit to Leon Hershfield. The attorney was working on a high-profile case, and because Hershfield wouldn't work on Saturday, logic dictated that the lawyer was probably in his office on Sunday.

He gave the driver the Fifth Avenue address, calling Hershfield on his cell phone. The lawyer didn't sound thrilled to hear from him, but he was smart enough to invite Decker over. Twenty minutes later, Hershfield met him at the door to his office. He was impeccably dressed in sporty attire – a camel-hair jacket over gray slacks, a white shirt, and red tie. Not the usual Brioni or Kiton suit, but still appropriate for a seven-figure, high-powered attorney. Hershfield's shoes looked to be boots – elephant hide.

'No rest for the weary,' he told Decker as he closed the door behind him. 'Sit down. Would you like a cup of coffee?'

'No, I'm all right.'

A glance at his wrist revealed a thick gold watchband. Hershfield said, 'It's noon. How about some lunch? I was going to order in. The Broughder case has been incredibly time-consuming. Who has time to go out? But I'd be happy to order you a sandwich or bagel.'

Decker smiled. Hershfield had just related a

page's worth of hidden messages: *I'm a busy man, I've got commitments, and I've got time restraints. You're imposing on them. I've looked at my watch. I'm clocking you.*

'No, thank you, Counselor. I shouldn't be here more than a few minutes. Thank you for your time.'

Message received loud and clear.

Hershfield sat back in his desk chair. 'So how are you feeling?'

'I've been better.'

'Jet lag.'

'I'm sure that's part of it.'

Silence.

'Are you making progress to your satisfaction?'

'No.'

'That's too bad.'

'Part of it is I'm working blind.' Decker licked his lips. 'I'm getting this strange feeling that I'm not wanted.'

'Cops are territorial.'

'Not the cops, Counselor, the clients. I have this notion that certain people are sorry they got me involved. Lord only knows why they called me.'

'Initial panic, maybe?'

'Probably.'

'Then maybe it's time to say good-bye.'

The speed with which Hershfield answered gave Decker second thoughts. It seemed likely that the Liebers had contacted Hershfield, maybe even asked him how to get Decker off their backs. 'Although, I've got to tell you,' Decker answered, 'I'm having a hard time letting go. I have this thing . . . my daughter says it's called the zygarnic effect. It's this pathological need for closure. At least, that's what my daughter says.'

'Children love to categorize their parents.'

'My wife says the same thing about me. Must be a kernel of truth in there.'

'I'm sure you're right. But if the need is pathological, maybe such doggedness is not such a good thing.'

'It works well in my field.'

'I suppose it does.' Hershfield smiled. 'And what about the cops? When we last spoke, you said you were going to contact them, ask them questions.'

'They've been very cooperative.'

'That's good to hear. Do you think that they're competent?'

'They're fine. Good actually. Motivated.'

'So why not leave the case to them? Unlike you, they're not working blind. They have the resources and the connections. Why visit trouble? The family won't appreciate it anyway.'

'Why do you say that?'

'Because that's the way we Jews are, *nu?*'

Now he was being folksy as well as conspiratorial.

'Maybe it's time to close up shop before you get in over your head.'

Decker eyed him. 'Over my head?'

'It's just like you said, Lieutenant, if I may be blunt. New York is a behemoth. If you're not a local, you don't stand a chance. Even if you were a local, you'd be in thick gravy. Plus, you've got this subset called Chasidim. If you think the cops are doing a good job, I would strongly suggest that you bow out before you get sucked into something you can't handle.'

Decker stared at him. 'I'm not wanted.'

'Don't take it personally.'

'Who am I pissing off? Obviously, Minda doesn't like me, but I think it's more.'

Hershfield shrugged, offering Decker a palm-up gesture. 'I like you. In some ways, I identify with you. We're both *frum yiddim*, trying to negotiate the world for a bunch of black-hatters who think we're goyim. Why stick your nose into dung if people are only going to tell you that you stink?'

'That's what I do for a living, Counselor. Stick my nose where it doesn't belong.'

'But you're not getting paid for this, Lieutenant. You're taking precious vacation time to get spit at. And if you think you're going to redeem yourself with these people, even after this is over, think again. You've been with the tribe long enough to know that working for Jews is nothing but problems. I'm getting paid for it. But what do you need it for?'

The anonymous complainer could have been anyone from Chaim to the cops, even Donatti, who used Hershfield as his lawyer. And if it were Chris, maybe Hershfield was using the Liebers to deflect the heat off him. Decker said nothing.

'Anything else?' Hershfield asked.

'Yes, actually there is something else. First time we met, you asked my brother about Mr Lieber's stores as a pass-through for money-laundering drug dollars. Do you know something that I don't?'

'Lieutenant, if you want to work from that angle, it's fine with me.'

'I don't need your permission.'

'No, Decker, you don't.' Hershfield's face had tightened, the skin over his bony cheeks taut and dry.

'Look, murder is a terrible thing. And I'm devastated about the young girl. Really, I am. But until she's found – one way or another – the Lieber family has to be protected. That's why you hired me. And that's what I'm trying to do. Which is why I've instructed the family members not to talk to you until we know what's going on.'

Decker stared at him.

'It's for their own good,' Hershfield went on. 'I know that you've got a job to do, Lieutenant, but so do I.'

'You're shutting me down.'

'No, Lieutenant, I'm being a very good defense attorney.' Another flick of the wrist.

Decker stood. 'Don't bother. I'm going.'

'Lieutenant, don't be so bitter. I heard that you had a very nice *Shabbos*. That your sons came in to visit you for the weekend and your family was together. Think of that as the purpose of your trip.'

'Maybe you're right.' He smiled. 'Thanks for your time, Counselor.'

'It's no problem.'

Decker closed the door behind him, thinking there were only a select number of people who knew the specifics of his *Shabbos*, but only two of them who would have a reason to contact Hershfield. It was unlikely that Jonathan would have shut him down, so it was down to Raisie. The question was; did she call Hershfield on her own, or was she her brother's agent?

The larger question was, what did it matter?

He shouldn't be here. He should be where he was wanted, in Gainesville, doing something meaningful, like helping his old man rebuild the toolshed and fixing the plumbing for his aged mother. Instead, he was doing favors that no one appreciated.

No more Mr Nice Guy.

To hell with Quinton.

To hell with all of them.

13

His stomach was growling, matching his feral mood, but Decker had no one to blame but himself. If anything, Hershfield had been forthcoming. He was doing what he'd been hired to do. Getting representation had been Decker's idea. He'd been hoisted on his own petard.

Outside the building, he called the Lazaruses' number to speak with Rina, but she had gone out shopping. Just as well. He was too angry to be good company. Still, he missed her. He began to walk aimlessly, looking for a simple place to fight off hunger pangs. That was easier said than done. Lots of the restaurants in the area weren't open for lunch on Sunday, and those that were looked too ritzy for his blood. He finally settled on a small café on Third Avenue squashed between a flower shop and a Korean fruit vendor. The salad was mediocre – saturated with a garlicky dressing that had wilted the lettuce. Decker took a few bites, then gave up. There was a pastry shop a few doors down that looked pretty good. He tamed his groaning belly with an apple croissant and a double espresso.

Trying to make sense of it all, he was furious but, like Hershfield said, it wasn't all bad. Tonight the immediate family was going out to dinner at a steak house labeled by the boys as awesome. Then he and Rina would catch a little music, have a couple of drinks. Be *adults* for a change, and why the hell not. He took a final sip of coffee, then threw it in the trash.

It was a little after two. Decker was down to counting the hours until they left. He stopped at the corner of Fifty-third and Second Avenue and lifted his finger to signal a cab, hoping he'd find a driver willing to make the trek out to Brooklyn. Eventually, a bee-pollen yellow taxi pulled over, answering his signal. As Decker opened the back door to get in, a voice carried over his shoulder.

'Share it?'

Decker turned around. Donatti's face was placid.

'I'm always one for saving money.' Decker stepped aside. 'Beauty before age.'

Donatti slid in. Decker followed, giving the driver Donatti's uptown address. The young man slumped in his seat, his face as expressionless as plastic. The ride was silent until Chris's cell rang. He waited until it stopped ringing, then regarded the number, distaste flitting through his eyes. Then his face went slack.

The ride took over twenty minutes. Decker paid, and Donatti didn't argue. As soon as they entered the loft, Donatti said, 'I've gotta return a call from my office. Wait here. You can make some coffee if you want.'

Decker said, 'Want me to make enough for two?'

'Nah, I'm coffeed out. I've also got some Glenlivet single malt in the cupboard underneath the pot. Help yourself.'

Ordinarily, Decker wouldn't drink. But he poured two glasses of Scotch, trying to get some kind of camaraderie going. When Donatti returned, Decker gave him a glass. 'Was that Joey on the phone?'

'How'd you guess?' Donatti took a healthy swig.

'You made a face in the car.'

'Some things never change.'

'How's he feeling?'

'Terrible. He's working on fifty percent of his heart and that's after quadruple bypass. Actually, fifty percent is pretty good for a guy who never had a heart to begin with.'

Decker smiled and clinked his tumbler onto Donatti's glass.

Donatti said, 'What're we toasting to?'

'Whatever you want.'

'How about obscene financial success?'

'You've got it.'

Donatti picked up the scotch bottle, then took out a ring of keys. 'Let's go into my office.' He opened the door.

Decker said, 'After you.'

Donatti said, 'Age before beauty.'

Decker shrugged, then stepped inside the windowless chamber. The fan kicked in, so did the lights. The video monitors gave the decor a space-age module look. Decker stared at the TV screens. 'Good security.'

'It pays to be careful.' Donatti took another belt of Scotch. 'I've got it set up with every bug-blocking gadget on the market. I'm not saying I can't be had, but currently this is as good as it gets. Besides, after September eleventh, Feds got more important things to do.' He downed his drink, then poured himself another. 'After you left this morning, I got curious.' His eyes met Decker's. 'What's your interest in the whack? It's a local matter.'

Decker said, 'Doing a favor for a friend.'

'You take your hard-earned vacation time to spin your wheels in the shit holes of New York to solve a low-level pop. Must be some good friend.'

Decker analyzed Donatti's words. He had called the pop low level – a dodge or was it truly something beneath him? Of course, Donatti wanted information, but what exactly was he asking? How much did Decker know so he could figure out how to cover his ass? Some kind of truce, maybe? That was probably wishful thinking. In the end, Decker went with the truth because it was the easiest.

'I'm doing a favor for my brother.'

Donatti's eyes never wavered. 'Your brother?'

'Yeah, my brother. I'm helping him out. The victim was a relative of my brother.'

'The vic was your relative?'

'No, my brother's relative. He was my brother's brother-in-law.'

'So you're telling me that you're doing this to help out your brother.'

'Exactly.'

'Your *brother*?'

'Donatti, I know you're an only child, but there are those of us who – for better or worse – have siblings.'

'You're telling me that your brother needs *your* help?'

Decker scratched his head. 'Why is this a problem for you?'

'Your brother has been in Vice for over twenty-five

years in Miami. I would think he has his own connections on the East Coast.'

'Oh!' Decker sat back. 'Now I understand. That's Randy – my full brother – although he's not my blood brother. We're both adopted. I met my birth mother about ten years ago. Her youngest son – my half brother – he's the one I'm helping. He's a rabbi.'

'You were adopted?'

'Yes.'

'So you're a bastard.'

'Are you telling me something you didn't already know?'

Despite himself, Donatti smiled.

Decker said, 'How do you know Randy?'

'Florida is New York South. Things that happen up here often affect things down there and vice versa. My family's always had a vested interest in knowing who does Vice. So this guy who was cleaned . . . he's your brother-in-law?'

'No. He's my half brother's brother-in-law. My half brother's wife's brother.'

'Got it. And you're that close to him that you come out and eat your free time for him?'

Decker thought about it. 'I like him. I wouldn't want anything bad to happen to him or his family because of his association with the vic. Is that a possibility?'

'How the hell should I know?' Donatti drained his second Scotch.

'It's just that you're a knowledgeable guy, Donatti.'

'You've got a bridge to sell me, Lieutenant?'

'So scornful at such a young age.'

'I've lived a hard life. Neglected and abused. You should know the story.'

Decker took up the Scotch bottle and poured Chris another drink. 'Did you happen to mention me to your lawyer, Donatti?'

'My *lawyer*?'

The surprise seemed genuine. Decker affected insouciance. 'Maybe not.'

'You mean Hershfield?'

'Yes, Hershfield. I went to see him because he's being retained for the family. I didn't want the police questioning them without representation.'

Donatti laughed. 'There's a switch.'

'Hershfield told me that certain parties resented my nosing around Ephraim's death. I was wondering if that was you?'

Donatti glared. 'Do I seem like the type who'd whine to my lawyer? Christ, Decker, I gave you more credit than that.'

'Well, someone isn't happy.'

'Then I would suggest you find out who's doing the bitching. It may help solve your problem.' Donatti frowned. 'You didn't mention *me* to Hershfield, did you?'

'No, I did not. Although if he's your lawyer, I think he'd know that we have a history together.'

'He knows about your putting me in prison. He also knows that you reopened the case and got me out of jail. But he doesn't know about Teresa McLaughlin. And he certainly doesn't know about the kid. I'd like to keep it that way.' Donatti swirled amber liquid around his glass. 'Being as you do know about them, I want you to promise me something. I want you to promise me that if anything ever happens to me and Terry's left out in the cold, that you'll take care of her and the kid.'

'You mean your son, Chris.'

'That's subject to debate.'

Decker fixed his eyes on Donatti's face. 'You've got to be kidding!'

'No, I'm not kidding.'

'Well, you should be kidding.'

'Let me tell you something, Decker. I was married for three years and never came close to knocking up my wife.'

'That's because you have to bed her to get her pregnant.'

Donatti laughed. 'Man, ain't that the truth. Being married to my ex-wife says a lot about the state of my hard-on. I can literally fuck anything. Problem is, I shoot blanks. I took tests. If there was one healthy little motherfucker swimming in my gonads, the doctor didn't find it. Needless to say, I'm skeptical about the kid.'

'We're talking about Terry, Donatti.'

'All it takes is one little motherfucker from one other cock, Decker.'

'The boy is yours.'

'So she says.'

'C'mon! You've *seen* Gabriel, haven't you, Donatti?'

'Of *course*, I've seen him.' Donatti scowled. 'All that says to me is she probably fucked some guy who looks like me.'

'Take a paternity test. I guarantee you she won't object.'

'True. She says anytime, and that's worth something. She knows what would happen if I caught her lying.' Donatti looked up at the ceiling. 'Gabe's a smart little motherfucker. Gifted too. He's already playing several of Mozart's piano concertos. How do

I know this? Because I not only paid for the piano, but also for the bastard's lessons.'

'Good for you.'

Donatti looked up. 'He has an ear, I'll give him that much. So maybe he is mine. He certainly didn't get that kind of talent from his mother. Brains, yes, looks, yes, but not the gift. All that means is she fucked somebody who looked like me *and* who was musically tapped.'

'Now you're being ridiculous. Take the test, Chris. Then you won't have to think about it.'

'But what if she's lying?' He made a face. 'Then I'd have to pop her. I don't want to pop Terry. I *love* her.'

'You don't have to pop her. And she's not lying.'

Donatti kept his eyes on his drink. 'This morning, you asked about my contact with Terry. It consists of my going out to Chicago for a couple of days every other month. I spend time with the kid – pick him up from school, help him with his homework, sit with him while he practices the piano, take him out to dinner, then tuck him into bed. It gives Terry some extra time for her studies. Then after Gabe goes to sleep, I fuck Terry's brains out. After we're done, I give her money.' He shook his head. 'There are blue laws on the books against things like that.'

'It's called supporting your child.'

'It's called being a sucker.' Donatti plunked the glass down on the table. 'I want to know that she'll be taken care of in case I get whacked.'

'I'd help her out even if you didn't get whacked.'

'I know. You sent her money in the past.'

'She's paid me back—'

'*I* paid you back.' He sat back in his chair. 'After I reestablished contact with her, I paid off all her debts.

They weren't extravagant, but they were sizable.'

'She wasn't living the good life.'

'Actually, she was living in a slum, working two jobs, and trying to support Gabe and go to school at the same time. The girl is industrious by nature. But I still rescued her even after she dumped me like garbage. I'm putting her through medical school; I'm paying for the kid's private education. I pay her rent, give her money for food and clothing and utilities and insurance and books and whatever the hell else she needs. I've turned her life around, Decker. I've taken it from hell and morphed it into something livable, and all I ask for in return is sporadic sex and an occasional "I love you, Chris." She fakes it well, tries real hard to make me happy. And she does make me happy. She's the only thing in the world that I've got – her and the kid – and I'm totally obsessed with her. Look, Decker, I don't want you to help her out of the goodness of your heart. I want you to feel *obliged* to help her. That way, it'll get done.'

'She's on her way to becoming a doctor. Why all the concern?'

'We're both orphans. I'm an actual orphan, and she's got a useless father, a bitch of a stepmother, and two nice grandparents who are now too old to help her out. I need to know she'll have somebody out there – for her and my son.'

There was that real possibility that she would marry another man who could take very good care of her. Decker didn't dare bring it up. 'No problem. If she needs me, I'll be there for her.'

'Good.' Donatti stood up. 'Good. I appreciate it. Thanks.'

'That's it?'

'That's it.'

Offering nothing in return for Decker's promise, Donatti stood. So did Decker. 'So maybe we'll talk again soon, Chris.'

'Maybe.' He shrugged. 'Maybe not.'

C.D. don't talk.

It didn't matter. Decker had done the favor, and they both knew what that meant. The actual words were superfluous.

14

One good thing that came out of the discussion with Donatti: Decker had never even considered his brother as a source of information. Randy had been in Vice and on the East Coast for a very long time. If there had been rumors circulating about the Liebers laundering drug money, it was possible that Randy would have heard about it.

Decker called his brother on the cell. Randy picked up after the third ring. 'Decker.'

'It's Decker,' Decker answered.

'Peter, my man! When are you coming down? Dad just bought himself a set of new tools and a cooler of beer. He's got definite ideas, bro.'

'What kind of ideas? The toolshed.'

'The toolshed, sure. But the patio's all but gone. Crumbling stone, man. He's got this vision of a deck and a hot tub—'

Decker broke into laughter. 'Oh-man-oh-man!'

Randy was laughing, too. 'The two of them in the tub . . . is that an image or what?'

'More power to them,' Decker said. 'And Ma's agreeing to that?'

'As long as she gets her new plumbing in the bathroom, she's a happy camper.'

'It's a three-day stopover, Randy.'

'I'm bringing over four guys. You're the foreman, bro. What we've got is an old-fashioned barn-raising with a twist.'

'Swell.'

They both laughed, they both let it die down. Then Decker grew serious. 'I need to speak with you over a private line.'

'Are you talking from a land phone?'

'No, I'm on my cell. But I can find one.'

'Do that. Then call me back at this number. It'll take me about twenty minutes to get to the location.'

'It'll take me about thirty minutes,' Decker said.

'Then you'd better get started.'

Once Decker got a cab, the rest was easy. Luck was with him because Raisie was home. Jonathan's wife was petite with elfin features. She had Kewpie-doll lips, a pinched nose, and round electric eyes. Bright, red hair was clipped close to her face with feathered bangs falling over her forehead. A loose colorful caftan hung on her body. She put her finger to her lips. 'I just got the children down for a nap.'

'I'll be quiet.'

The Levines lived in a tiny apartment on the Upper West Side of Manhattan. The location came with two small bedrooms, two munchkin-size bathrooms, a closet for a kitchen, and cramped space that barely held a couple of couches and a dining room table. For the luxury of living in a thousand square feet, they paid something like four thousand a month rent. It boggled the mind, and Decker wondered why anyone would put up with such usury, especially after the terrorist attacks. But New Yorkers were a fanciful lot, constantly convincing themselves that less was more.

She let him inside but didn't look happy to see him. 'Jonathan's at the shul.'

'I need to use the phone, Raisie.'

'You don't have a cell?'

'I need a land phone.' He spoke softly. 'I know. I'm becoming a real pain in the ass.' She had told Hershfield as much. 'Look, I'll be out of your hair soon. You and your family don't have to worry about that.'

She lowered her head in shame. 'Akiva, I'm so sorry. This is all my fault. Jonathan didn't want to call you. I begged him to do it.'

'Be careful what you wish for,' Decker answered.

'It's just that Chaim thinks . . .' Raisie stopped talking.

Decker waited. 'Chaim thinks what?'

'He has this crazy idea that your investigation may be harming Shayndie's survival.'

'Okay.' He gathered his thoughts. 'And how does that work exactly?'

'He thinks she's holed up somewhere. He thinks that the closer you get . . . that it might scare her off. Or maybe tell the people who hurt Ephraim where she is.'

Decker's heart skipped a beat. 'She's contacted him?'

Tears formed in her eyes. 'No. I mean, not that I know of. Maybe. He talks crazy. So does Minda. At this point, they both might be delusional.'

'I don't know, Raisie. It sounds to me like the ideas are coming from somewhere. Has he talked to you about Ephraim's death, confided any suspicions to you?'

'The answer is no. But I must be honest, Akiva. If

he confided something in me, I wouldn't tell you. I have to respect the family's wishes.'

Hence talking to Hershfield, trying to shut him down. 'Even if it meant compromising Shayndie's welfare?'

She bristled, her visage hard and angry. 'None of us would ever do something to compromise her welfare.'

Decker was quiet.

'Do you have any idea when Ephraim might be released?' Her voice was very cold. 'We'd like to give our brother a proper burial.'

'I don't know, but I'll call up Novack and ask him for you.'

Raisie put her fist to her forehead. Then she looked up. 'Thank you.'

'No problem.' Decker tried to hide his anger. 'I have to use your phone. I need some privacy.'

'In the back bed—' She sighed with a heavy heart. 'Akiva, don't be upset with me. Don't be mad. Please. If Jonathan knew that I've upset you, he'd be very angry. He adores you . . . absolutely worships the ground you walk on.' Tears fell down her cheek. 'I've lost my brother. Please be patient.'

Decker ran his hand down his face. The woman was in mourning for a dead brother, had two small children, and was under terrible strain. 'Raisie, I'm sorry. I'm very pushy when I work. It's an occupational hazard. I'll call up Novack for you as soon as I make this other call.'

'Thank you so much.'

'You know what? How about if I use the phone in the kitchen, and you go lie down?'

She wiped her face. 'I need to get some things done.'

'You're in mourning. You're not supposed to be working at all.'

'We haven't started the shivah yet.'

'So get some rest while you can.'

'It's actually a good idea.' Tears in her eyes. 'I'm so *tired*!'

'Rest, Raisie.'

Finally, she agreed. Decker waited until she was out of sight. Then he dialed the number that Randy had given him.

'It's me,' Randy said. 'Go.'

Decker whispered, 'Money laundering. Emmanuel Lieber. He owns a chain of discount electronic-equipment stores. Cameras, computers, phones, radios, stereo . . . stuff like that. Business has been hard lately. Four days ago, one of his sons was murdered. Ephraim Lieber. He had a history of drug problems. He was with his niece. Now she's missing.'

'How old?'

'The niece is fifteen. Also, there's another brother I want you to check out. Chaim spelled Charles-Henry-Adam-Ida-Mary.'

'Last name is *L-E-I-B-E-R*?'

'*L-I-E-B-E-R*.'

'And the vic's first name?'

Decker spelled Ephraim, then Shaynda.

'Got it,' Randy said. 'Ephraim Lieber . . . Lieber . . .' A five-second pause. 'No, none of it rings a bell. I take it they all are Jewish?'

'Yep.'

'Chasidic?'

'Yes. Exactly. Why?'

Randy said, 'We've had a few cases where your religious brethren have done some naughty things

158

regarding illegal substances.'

'What kind of substances?'

'The gamut from what I remember. I'll look it up for you, Peter. Mostly, we get the Chasids on more typical charges – slum lording, rest-home fraud, tax evasion. And soliciting. You'd be surprised how many of these religious types pay for pussy. Born-again Christians as well as Jews. Course, we got a lot of pussy for sale in Miami. Anyway, I'll check around.'

'Thanks, Randy. So I'll see you when you get down to Gainesville.'

'You bet. I'll call you if I find out anything.'

'Thanks.'

'Pete, I know I'm your baby brother. And I always will be your baby bro. But let me give you a solid word of advice. 'Cause I know the East Coast, and you don't. Those guys, they're nothing but trouble. Don't put your balls on the line. They won't appreciate it.'

'You're not the first one who's told me that.' A pause. 'You're not the second one, either.'

'Then maybe you should listen.'

'Maybe I should.'

'But you won't.' Randy sighed. 'You're a stubborn guy. Not unlike the other Decker kinfolk I've known.'

'It runs in the family, Randy.'

'We're adopted, Peter.'

'Well, there you go, baby bro. Genes aren't everything.'

It was time to touch base with Novack. Their last interaction had left the New York detective testy, and

Decker didn't want to leave with a sour taste. And Raisie had asked about the release of her brother's body. He took out his cell and punched in the numbers. When he answered, Decker asked him how the game went.

'Like you don't know?' Exasperation. 'You know who they were playing against.'

'The Lakers.'

'More L.A. wise guys who think they're God.'

'Now you're being sore.'

'You see the game?'

'I heard the game,' Decker answered. 'Shaq fouled out in the fourth, but Kobe brought it home in overtime.'

'Yada, yada, yada,' Novack said. 'How'd it go?'

'How'd what go?'

'With C.D.?'

'Oh yeah, that. Nothing.'

'He wasn't in.'

'No, I saw him. He even offered me coffee. I drank it and am still alive to tell the tale. So I guess it wasn't laced with strychnine.'

'What'd you think of his place?'

'We talked in the reception area.' The truth, but not the whole truth. 'He has a metal detector right when you come in.'

'Probably has a lot more than that.'

'I'm sure he packs, but I didn't see it,' Decker said. 'Have you ever been inside the place?'

'Nope. Never had the occasion. You ask him about the murder?'

'Yeah.' Decker waited an appropriate amount of time. 'He didn't say anything, of course. I thought maybe I could read his face, but he's pretty stony.'

'It's his specialty.'

'I gave him my card. If I suddenly get whacked, you'll know who to interrogate.'

'That ain't funny, Decker.'

'I'm leaving tomorrow, Mick. I don't think C.D. will follow me to L.A. And if he does, there's nothing I can do about it.'

'You're sounding blasé about rather serious matters.'

'That's jet lag talking. There is a purpose to this call. My relatives want to know when Ephraim's body will be released for burial. No pressure: I just told them I'd make the call.'

'I think I heard something about releasing the body tomorrow. I'll get back to them.'

'Appreciate it. Anything new?'

'Wish I could tell you different, Pete, but no. Nothing's new. By the way, I put out a couple of feelers into what'shisface . . . Marino . . . the police chief in Quinton.'

'Virgil Merrin. Good idea. Anything?'

'Nothing so far, but I'm sure you expected that.'

'Why should anything be easy?' Decker told him.

'Hey, we'll solve it,' Novack insisted. 'But it ain't gonna be a slam dunk. You want that, talk to Shaq. Look, if I don't see you again, it was nice meeting you.'

'Likewise,' Decker answered. 'Thanks for everything, Novack. Maybe one day, I can reciprocate. You have my number. If you're ever in L.A., give me a call.'

'Thanks, Lieutenant, but I think I'll pass. You all are too tan and thin for my taste. And way too passive.'

'We call it "easygoing".'

'That's a buzzword for apathy. One thing New Yorkers aren't, and that's apathetic. Not your fault, Decker. It's all the sunshine out West. It cooks the brain.'

15

She was behind schedule. Rina knew she shouldn't have attempted shopping this late in the day, but the prices in Brooklyn were so much cheaper than in L.A., and if you knew where to look, you could find true one-of-a-kind things. Not that she was shopping for herself. Her bags were filled with dresses, coats, hats, shoes, and play outfits for Hannah – half the price of the department stores and some of the ensembles were imported from Europe. Hannah was such a pretty girl, and Rina loved to dress her up. Having a daughter, after two boys, was a new experience, and she savored every minute of it. She adored seeing Hannah preen in front of the mirror on *shabbat* morning. Rina knew that showering her with too much attention for superficialities wasn't a good thing, but what good are kids if you can't spoil them every now and then! Children were not toys – her teenagers had proven that with a sledgehammer – but sometimes it was fun to pretend.

At least, Rina had dressed for tonight before she went out, although she knew she'd have to reapply her makeup. Her skin just ate up the chemicals. Her clothes were comfortable but very nice – a black sweater set over an ankle-length black skirt that had a midcalf side slit. A little pizzazz, but still appropriate for a religious woman. Her oversweater was long and red and cashmere. It made her feel elegant and very posh. A spray of Chanel No. 19; hers and Peter's favorite perfume. After all, they were going out tonight after dinner. Her shoes didn't have particularly high heels, but they were still dressy.

Not sneakers, though. She had walked until her feet and legs were sore. She did have the good sense to send Hannah with Sammy and Jacob, knowing that the little girl couldn't possibly keep up with her. Her children went into town to see the Museum of Natural History. They'd meet her at the steak house.

Peter's whereabouts were a mystery.

She checked her watch, swearing that this was the last store. It was getting dark, and her arms couldn't carry any more packages anyway. She was next in line, but the woman in front of her kept arguing over the price of a sale item. Rina tried clearing her throat, she tried tapping her foot, but nothing seemed to work. The woman was determined to get a further reduction on a reduced price.

Rina looked around, arms folded across her chest, her bags dangling from her hands. Scanning the area, checking out the crowd because it was better than being aggravated.

The first time around, she barely glanced at him.

The second time around, she realized he was looking at her . . . *staring* at her. Hard, penetrating blows that were so unnerving, she almost dropped her bags.

He was tall and muscular, exuding strength. Dressed in black jeans and a black ribbed crewneck sweater under a brown cord jacket and combat boots, he kept leering at her with cold blue eyes.

Who on earth?

And then sudden recognition sparked in her brain.

What on earth?

She should have felt immediate intimidation because he was so big and powerful. But big and powerful didn't scare her. She'd been married to big and powerful for over ten years. She had dealt head-to-head with big and powerful. It was no big and powerful deal.

What she felt was fury. Who did he *think* he was!

She dropped out of her place in line, leaving behind an adorable navy dress with white trim *and* a matching coat and hat. It would have been a perfect Pesach outfit for Hannah if he hadn't come along!

She marched up to him and looked him square in the eye – the battle of baby blues. 'Care for some coffee? I'll buy. You carry the packages.' She shoved them into his chest and stomped out of the store. She could hear him chuckling with amusement while keeping pace behind her. She brought him into a nearby Starbucks, where she bought him a cup of plain coffee and bought herself a Caffè Latte. Then she took him to a local park – not much more than a patch with swings and slides – but it would serve the purpose. She chose a bench that was off the beaten track, but still visible enough to see people walk by.

She sat down first. He had the good sense to sit on the other side and place the packages in the middle. She watched his jacket fall open. She saw the gun, tucked into an internal pocket. She knew that he was very aware of her eyes on the piece. Something had clicked in those icy orbs.

They sipped coffee.

It was obvious that her edginess was pleasing him. Still, she waited for him to talk. She'd wait as long as he wanted. She was good at staring contests.

Finally, he spoke. 'Don't you Jewish women cover your hair in public?'

'I'm wearing a wig,' Rina answered.

'Really?'

'Yes.'

'It's a good one.'

'And an expensive one, too. It's made out of human hair.'

'Really?' He swallowed coffee. 'Now how does that work? Do they scalp someone for it?'

'No. They buy the hair from women who grow their own hair long and harvest it. It's a very time-consuming process. I think my wig probably comes from Asian women. It's very straight, and it doesn't frizz up in the fog.'

'What's your natural hair look like?'

'Mine?' Rina touched her bangs. 'This is my natural hair.'

'That dark?'

'Yes, it's almost black.'

'Wig's a good match.'

'Very good match.'

Silence.

'Doesn't it kind of defeat the purpose?' He gave her a hungry stare. 'If you're trying to be unattractive to other men, you're doing a poor job.'

Rina met his eyes with her own. 'The reasons for covering your hair go beyond physical attractiveness. I have some sweet rolls in the white waxed bag. Help yourself, Mr Donatti.'

'You can call me Chris.' He moved his eyes up and

down her body, slowly and with purpose. 'After all, I've called you Rina many times in my fantasies.'

'You may call me Rina in real life. I have no problem with that.'

Neither one talked.

Chris ran his tongue in his cheeks, his eyes never leaving her face. 'You know, I've had lots of girls, Rina. Lots and lots and lots of them. When girls literally fall in your lap, it gets a little old. It gets harder and harder – no pun intended – to get excited about someone. That means forbidden fruit begins to look *very* attractive.'

Silence.

Rina became aware of the children at play – such sweet, sweet sounds. Before she said anything, she made a point to formulate her thoughts. Then she spoke in a clear, steady voice. 'Were you raised with any organized religion, Mr Donatti?'

'Chris, please.' A slow smile. 'We're all friends here.'

'Certainly. Were you raised with any organized religion, Chris?'

Donatti continued to look her over. 'Catholic.'

'So you know a little bit of Bible, maybe?'

Chris smiled. 'I wasn't a very good Catholic, Rina.'

'Do you know about Yaakov and Aesav? Jacob and Esau in English.'

'It's been a while.' A predatory smirk. 'Why don't you fill me in?'

'Jacob and Esau were brothers . . . twins by birth, but that's as far as it went. They were very different. Jacob was a quiet, learned man – *ish tam* as we say in Hebrew. He studied; he behaved well; he did what his father instructed him to do; he didn't cause any problems. Esau was very different. He is described as an *ish sadde* – a man of the field. He was a superb hunter, a fine warrior, masculine, probably handsome, too. He was very charming, and his manners were beyond reproach.

'It has been said by the Jewish sages that Esau was born with a full set of teeth and a beard. It could be taken literally, but I choose to take it metaphorically, Mr Donatti. Teeth and a beard represent a mature man. What it says to me is that Esau was born as exactly the man he was destined to be. His entire childhood – all *the learning experiences and growth* that one gets from childhood mistakes – was irrelevant to him. He remained unchanged from infancy until the day he died.

'Now, the parents loved both of their children, but the father, Isaac, loved Esau more because he brought him fresh meat, and because Esau had excellent *derech eretz*. That means manners; that means he showed his father respect. Also, I believe that Isaac admired Esau's ability to hunt, so different from Isaac's own strengths. Sometimes you place a lot of value on tasks that are beyond your abilities. But the mother, Rebecca, who was more worldly, she loved Jacob more. She admired his quiet, pious demeanor.'

'Jacob sounds like a wimp.'

'No, he was not weak. His strengths were less overt.'

Donatti thought a moment. 'You know it's not good to play favorites with your kids.'

Rina smiled. 'You're absolutely right. That was part of the problem.'

He leered at her. 'Do you know that you've got a beautiful smile, Rina?'

Rina ignored him. 'There was lots of sibling rivalry. Eventually, it reached a flash point. There was a confrontation between the two brothers, and Jacob was forced to flee from Esau's wrath.'

'I told you Jacob was a wimp. What happened?'

'First Jacob tricked his brother out of his birthright. Then Jacob bamboozled his father into giving him the first blessing – the blessing that Isaac had planned for his elder son, Esau. Under the law of primogeniture, the older should have had dominion over the younger. But Rebecca, the mother, felt that the blessing should go to Jacob. Because of her wile and deception, Isaac wound up blessing Jacob first, giving the younger son, Jacob, dominion over Esau, the elder.'

'How'd she trick him?'

'Like any good mystery, it loses something in the translation. Read the book if you're curious. But there is a point to this story, like there is a point to everything in the Bible. Esau did not *deserve* the blessing. Not because he was a hunter, a *murderer* with bloodstains on his hands. Esau didn't *deserve* the blessing because Esau was an adulterer – a taker of other men's wives. Not that I speak for God, Mr Donatti, but in my religion, taking a married woman is a very odious thing.

'Now, I know how you feel about my husband. And you may want revenge. I hope not, but I can't stop you if you're set upon it. And, perhaps, you may succeed. But I will tell you this. If you ever, *ever* so much as lay a single finger on me in an inappropriate way, I guarantee that you – and everything you hold dear – will be cursed by God, by Satan, and by every living and dead creature in this universe. Not only in *this* lifetime, but in *all* lifetimes to come.' She glared at him. 'Eternally, Mr Donatti. In lay language, that means *for ever*!'

The silence hung in the air for several moments. Then Donatti forced out a laugh. 'Am I supposed to be nervous now?'

'It's fair warning. And you're blushing, by the way.'

Involuntarily, Donatti averted his eyes. As soon as he realized it, he stared at her again. 'So what happened to Jacob?'

'Happened to him?'

'You said he had to flee from Esau. If I were Esau and somebody stole something from me, I'd go after the son of a bitch with everything I had.'

'As a matter of fact, Mr Donatti, the two did meet up again. And Jacob was very afraid of his brother. Terrified that he'd not only steal his property but also his wives and children. Especially his wife, Rachel, because she was very beautiful. As I said before, Esau prided himself on stealing married women. When it was clear that the two men had to cross paths, Jacob made elaborate plans on how to deal with his vengeful brother. But in the end, it is written that Esau wept with emotions, threw his arms around his brother, and kissed him on the neck.'

'So Esau *forgave* Jacob?'

'Looks that way.'

'So Esau turned out to be a pussy, too!' Donatti sneered with contempt. 'Someone should rewrite the ending.'

Rina smiled. 'Perhaps then I should tell you this. While outwardly there was some kind of reconciliation, Jewish rabbis and sages have a different perspective on the reunion. They say that when Esau kissed

Jacob on the neck, he had actually tried to bite him. Not a little hickey, Mr Donatti. Esau had meant to kill his brother – cut the jugular vein with his teeth. But God had turned Jacob's neck to stone and instead Esau broke his teeth. Esau got the hint. Vengeance wasn't the answer.'

'I like that ending better.'

'I thought you might.'

Donatti sipped his coffee. 'Maybe vengeance isn't the answer as a permanent thing. But it does have a soothing temporary effect.'

'Possibly.' She folded her hands in her lap. 'Are you and my husband on opposite sides of the fence again?'

'Interesting question. What did your husband tell you?'

'Absolutely nothing! I had no idea you were even in New York. But by your being here, you must have known that *I* was in New York. This wasn't an accident. You had to have been following me. So somewhere along the line you must have met up with the lieutenant. Are you two at odds again?'

'Actually, he came to me for help.'

Rina paused. Her first thoughts were that somewhere during the course of Ephraim's homicide investigation, Peter must have suspected Donatti of being the hit man. But if that were the case – and Donatti knew that Peter was suspicious of him – why did Donatti approach her so brazenly?

Donatti seemed to read her mind. 'It's the truth. Ask the lieutenant if you don't believe me.'

'Are you going to help him?'

'I haven't decided.'

Rina felt the heat of his eyes. The warmth of embarrassment was flooding her own face, but she refused to back down. 'I'm sure you'll come to the correct decision.'

Donatti continued to study her face and body. 'God, you are beautiful!'

'Thank you.'

'I'd love to draw you, Mrs Decker. Or, at the very least, take your picture.'

'Neither is an option.'

'Must be hard being that good-looking. My son's mother is a stunning girl.' He rested his elbows on his knees and stared into the park. 'You must know Terry.'

'I don't actually know her, but I've heard that she's very beautiful.'

'She gets hit on all the time,' Donatti said. 'She's very serious – not unlike yourself – and all the male attention annoys her. Sometimes it even gets her into trouble. People make assumptions about her sexual habits just because she's single and has a kid. Even her professors. *Especially* her professors. Especially the *married* professors.'

'She gets harassed?'

'All the time. It got so bad with one of them that I had to go over there and prove a point.'

'I'm sure your sudden appearance cooled his ardor.'

Donatti laughed. 'Yeah. He calmed down pretty quickly after my visit. So what do *you* do when men get out of line? Do you sic the lieutenant on them?'

'No, Mr Donatti, I'm a grown woman, and I choose to take care of my own problems. I have found in the past that involving the lieutenant makes matters worse.'

He sat back and stared at her. 'Does your silence extend to this little tryst?'

She met his eyes. 'It isn't a tryst. On the off chance that you may actually help my husband out, perhaps it's best if I don't tell him. Because if I did tell him, he'd probably kill you.'

'If I didn't get to him first.'

'If you had wanted to do that, you would have done it a long time ago.'

'Revenge is a dish best served cold.'

'Still, I have no intention of telling my husband about our little chat, if that's what you're asking.'

'I'm not asking anything.'

'Okay. Then I'll ask something of you. It would make my life easier if you didn't tell him about it, either. Because if he hears about it from you, he'll not only be irate with you, he'll get mad at me for not telling him. Can you do me this favor?'

'I like doing favors.' Donatti smiled. 'We'll keep it our little secret.'

Turning everything into an act of intimacy. A prime-time manipulator. 'Thank you.'

'You're welcome.'

Donatti stood up and leered at her. 'Hey, why spoil what could be a beautiful relationship?'

'We have no relationship, Christopher.'

'Not you and me, Mrs Decker. The lieutenant and me.' Donatti handed her his empty coffee cup. 'There's a recycle bin over there. Toss that for me, please?'

'Not a problem.'

Again he gave her a hard, wolfish stare. 'Maybe we'll *chat* again someday.'

Rina raised her eyes to censure his. 'And maybe pigs will fly.'

Donatti broke into laughter. 'Mind if I give Terry your phone number, Mrs Decker. If she's gonna play chess with the big boys, she may as well learn from an expert.'

16

If anything seemed to fit, it would have been a drug deal that went sour. But then why would Ephraim take Shayndie with him, putting her in danger? Could the man have been that cowardly to use a little girl as a screen? And then there was Raisie, warning him that his investigation could be endangering Shayndie. That told Decker that Chaim was sitting on something. He considered calling up Novack, going over some ideas with the detective. But what if Raisie was right? If his probing lessened Shayndie's chances even fractionally – well, then, what choice did he really have?

Maybe the girl had gotten away and was in hiding. Maybe she had contacted her parents but was tentative about coming home. Or maybe there was another reason for her disappearance. Maybe she was pregnant and the whole thing about her being with her uncle was just an alibi. Maybe she was holed up in some home for wayward girls, and maybe Chaim didn't want Decker finding that out.

Maybe Decker's imagination was swirling out of control.

Drug dealers usually like to prove a point. Yet this time the kill was done at the hotel, with no evidence of torture.

Clean hit. Donatti's M.O.

The plane was due to take off tomorrow night at six. By then, it would no longer be Decker's business. Perhaps he should start having a good time right now. He was taking the entire family out to a very popular kosher steak house, and then afterward, he and Rina would go hear the Harley Mann Quintet at one of the hotels. Initially, Rina felt squeamish about going. How could she go out and have a good time when the Liebers were suffering?

'If by being miserable would help them, I'd agree with you. But right now, the best thing we can do for us – you and me – is to try to appreciate our own lives and have a little fun,' Decker argued.

Rina certainly had no comeback for that. Maybe a couple of glasses of wine would put her in a festive mood. At this point, he felt as if he could drink an entire bottle by himself.

He was supposed to meet the crew at six. He arrived twenty minutes early. At five to the hour, Decker spied three-quarters of his progeny – Sammy, Jacob and Hannah – walking up the street. Two good-looking young men and a squirt – all of them with their entire lives ahead of them. God, just let them be well. Decker felt that instant jolt of parental alarm but quelled it. Then he gave himself a psychic pat on the back for a job well done.

Hannah skipped over to him and took his hand. She was wearing a denim skirt and a green sweater, her red curls bouncing over her shoulders. 'Where's Eema?'

'She's meeting us here.' Decker bent down and kissed the top of her head. 'How was the museum?'

'Very good,' she replied. 'I liked the whale.'

'The whale was cool.' Jacob was rolling a carry-on bag. 'Very big.'

'We also took her to the Hayden Planetarium,' Sammy said.

'Sounds like a busy day,' Decker said.

'Yeah, my feet are tired,' Sammy complained. 'Can we sit down?'

'Let's give Eema a few more minutes, okay?' Decker suggested.

The kids weren't happy with the suggestion, but, for a change, no one argued. The boys were dressed similarly – dark sweaters and jeans. Jacob had on a thick denim jacket; Sammy wore a nappy, flannel plaid shirt that subbed as an overcoat.

'How's it going?' Sammy asked his father.

'Well, this is certainly the highlight of the trip,' Decker said.

'That good, huh?'

'It's good to see you guys.'

'There's Eema,' Jacob announced. 'At least, I think that's her. She's sort of buried underneath all that cargo.'

'What'd she do?' Sammy asked. 'Buy out the store?'

'Lord only knows.' Decker sighed. 'Why don't you two go help her?'

'I don't know, Dad,' Sammy said. 'I think she has a certain balance. Lo be it me to disrupt what might have taken five hours to build.'

Decker glared at him. The boys hurried over to their mother and relieved her of the packages. She gave half to Jacob, half to Sammy. 'You'll take these back for me?'

'I'm not going back to Brooklyn,' Jacob said. 'I've got a train to catch, Eema.'

'I'll take them back,' Sammy said.

'The good son,' Jacob countered.

They stopped at the entrance to the restaurant. Jacob smiled at his mother. 'Buy anything for me?'

'A couple of shirts,' Rina said. 'Most of it is for Hannah.'

'Great.' Jacob pouted. 'First you send me to a school that locks me up in a cell and scalps me. Then all I get is a couple of shirts.'

'Such neglect.' Rina threw her arm around her younger son and kissed him ten times on the cheek.

'How about me?' Sammy asked.

Rina kissed him as well. When she reached over for Hannah, the girl pulled away. 'Not in public.'

Both she and Decker laughed. It was hard to tell the babies from the adults without a scorecard. Rina said, 'I think you both grew.'

'You just saw me yesterday,' Jacob said.

'You grew from yesterday,' Rina said. 'Shall we go inside and eat?'

'Yeah, it's better than being dysfunctional out here for the whole world to see,' Sammy said.

Jacob added, 'Besides, this is the best food we're going to have in the next six months.'

Sammy said, 'Ain't that the truth.'

'Go in and get our table, boys,' Decker said. 'Take Hannah with you. I need to talk to your mother for a moment.'

'Do I really have to carry all this stuff?' Sammy held the bags aloft. 'Can't we just check it in at a bank vault or something?'

'Go now, please!' Decker toughened his voice.

'Uh-oh . . .' Jacob took his sister's hand. 'We don't want to hear this.'

Decker waited until the two of them were alone. He said, 'You're going to make fun of me, but I'd like to stay another day. They're releasing the body tomorrow, which means the funeral would be on Tuesday. I think we should go.'

And Decker's last conversation with Donatti had been promising. He was hoping that Chris might come through with something.

Rina said, 'Far from making fun of you – although it is tempting – I admire your flexibility and your compassion. It shows what a true man you are. I will, once again, change the tickets.' She threw her arms around Decker's neck and kissed him hard on the mouth. 'It's not religiously modest, but it is heartfelt.'

'I like that!' Decker said. 'To what do I owe the honor?'

'Just for being you. Now, we should go inside so the kids don't think we're fighting.'

It took them ten minutes to be seated. The tables were so close to one another that Decker could have lap-danced with his neighbor's Cornish hen. With all the packages and Jacob's valise, they were as tight as pack animals. The tables were covered with red-checkered paper and there was sawdust on the floor. It was loud and noisy and smoky, but boy did it smell good.

It took another five minutes to get menus from a waiter wearing a blue denim shirt, white jeans, and sneakers. All the servers were dressed alike. They scuttled and scurried as if their job consisted of aerobic exercise. Another five minutes produced five glasses of iced water and bread and margarine.

Next everyone got up to ritually wash so they could break bread.

The bread was gone five minutes later.

They had been in the restaurant for a half hour, and all they had to show for it were crumbs and ice cubes. Prison could have done just as well.

'Hey, Sammy,' someone called out.

Sammy turned around. 'Ari!' He got up and talked to Ari for five minutes. He made introductions. Rina and Decker smiled. Hello, hello. Ari left; then a busboy came, holding more bread. He took orders for drinks, then left.

Rina asked Decker, 'How hungry are you?'

'I was hungry when I started out. Now I'm ravenous. And *no*, I don't want to split anything.'

'Boy, someone's blood sugar has taken a nosedive,' Sammy said.

'Eat the bread,' Rina offered.

'I don't want bread!' Decker groused. 'I want meat!'

The waiter finally came back, pad in hand. 'Are you ready?'

'I've been ready for forty minutes—'

'Peter—'

'Chateaubriand for two for one,' Decker ordered.

'It's big,' the waiter remarked.

'So am I.' He handed the waiter the menu.

The boys decided to split the Chateaubriand. Rina chose the rib steak. Hannah ordered a hot dog and fries. Jacob heard his name called out, then turned around.

'Reuven! What are you doing here?'

'Probably the same thing you're doing here,' Reuven answered. 'Bumming a meal off my parents. These are your parents?'

Jacob said, 'These are my parents.'

Reuven smiled. 'Pleased to meet you, Mr and Mrs Lazarus.'

'Actually, it's Mr Decker,' Decker answered. 'I'm his stepfather.'

'Yeah, but he pays all the college tuition, so that qualifies him as a dad,' Sammy answered.

Reuven's father broke into laughter. He offered his hand to Decker. 'Shragy Miller.'

'It's Rav Miller,' Jacob told him.

Decker shook his hand. 'Pleased to meet you, Rav Miller.'

'Shragy, please! This is my wife, Rivka, my daughter, Rachel.'

Miller was squat, dressed in rabbinic black. His wife was tall and bone thin, and was wearing a *shaytl*. Her features were as pinched as her husband's were round. The daughter's face had combined the best of her parents – regular features, sparkling hazel eyes, and hair the color of chestnuts. She was very pretty, and Decker wasn't the only one who had noticed. Sammy had made eye contact with her. Now he was looking at his napkin.

The adjacent table had just opened up. The obvious thing to do was invite them to sit down. Rina did exactly that. She introduced herself to Rivka, and after a few disorganized minutes, everyone was seated. The girl actually managed to speak with Sammy without looking at him. A pretty neat trick; Decker supposed that she had learned it in Being *Frum* 101.

She asked, 'So where do you go to school?'

'One guess.'

'YU.'

'So what else is new?'

'YU and Columbia,' Jacob added.

'Ah,' Rachel said. 'One step above the riffraff.'

'I am the riffraff,' Sammy said. 'YU was a little weak in my major, so they let me do a joint program.'

'What's your major?'

'Neuropsychophysiology . . . premed. But I didn't want to take the YU premed major. I actually wanted a real major.'

'Yeah, I'm trying to do that with Stern, but I'm getting a little resistance.' There was tightness in her voice. 'I don't suppose you had problems, being *male* and all.'

Sammy was quick with the comeback. 'I'm sure some of the older rabbis at Stern have some antiquated notions of what girls can and can't do.'

'If you come from a black-hat religious family, they have definite ideas.'

'You have to know where to finagle.'

'Any pointers?'

'A few if you want them.'

'That would be nice.'

Rina said, 'You know, kids, why don't you all sit on one side, and let us sit on the other side?'

Another several minutes of reorganization; this time, Rachel and Sammy sat next to one another.

'Lucky me,' Rav Miller announced. 'I get to sit next to this *motek*.'

'Say hello, Hannah,' Decker said.

'Hello.'

'And what are you learning in school?' the rabbi asked.

'Right now, the *dinim* of Pesach. And the Haggadah of course.'

'And what can you tell me about the Haggadah?'

'I know that *Hashem* had to take the Jews out of Egypt very fast.'

'Yes, and why is that?'

'Because the Jews were so bad that if *Hashem* didn't take them out real fast, they would have been stuck in the lowest level of *Tumah* – sin. That's why *Hashem* took them out after two hundred ten years and not four hundred years.'

Everyone burst into laughter. Rina blushed. 'I think the *rav* was referring to taking the Jews out quickly before *Paroah* changed his mind about letting the Jews go.'

'Oh,' Hannah said. 'Yeah, that too.'

'You've got a real thinker,' Miller told Rina.

'She's . . . unique.'

Decker succumbed and devoured another piece of bread. Rivka stared at the kids. To Rina, she whispered, 'If the body language was any closer, they'd be nose-to-nose.'

Rina said, 'Wonder when they'll work up the courage for eye contact.'

Rivka sighed. 'I suppose it's better than the Shidduch Directory. I'm surprised. Rachel is usually very reserved.' She looked at Rina. 'How old's your boy?'

'Almost twenty.' Rina looked at the girl. 'She's eighteen, nineteen?'

'Just turned nineteen. What yeshiva did he go to in Israel?'

'Gush.'

The mother nodded.

'And your daughter?'

'Midrashet Lindenbaum.'

'Oh. Bravenders,' Rina answered. 'Very progressive.'

'She's got a mind of her own.'

'That's good.'

Rivka asked, 'How old were you when you got married?'

'Seventeen. And you?'

'Eighteen.'

Silence.

Rivka turned to her husband. 'Shragy, enough with the questions. You're driving the poor little girl crazy.'

'She's very bright. She doesn't mind.'

'How do you know?' She waved him off.

Finally, finally, the food came. By the time everyone had finished, they had twenty minutes to catch the first set. Rina regarded Sammy. There was still a blush in his cheeks. His food was barely touched. She elbowed Decker and whispered, 'You look a little tired, Peter. How about we give the tickets away, and you and I take a nice romantic walk instead?'

Decker's face registered surprise. 'Are you sure?'

'If you don't mind.'

'I don't mind at all.' He was thrilled with the idea. He had just demolished half a cow. A walk sounded good for the soul, good for the waistline. And there was this part of him, this obsessive little voice that kept telling him to take one more crack at finding Shayndie. Rina was giving him an out, and he took it.

'It's absolutely fine with me, darling.' Decker took his wife's hand. 'We can make our own music.'

Rina offered the tickets to the parents. The rabbi said, 'I'm not much for jazz – too many notes. How about if you give the tickets to the boys?'

Jacob said, 'I've got a train to catch.'

'I'll go,' Reuven said.

Jacob kicked him under the table.

'On second thoughts, I've got to go pack.'

Sammy said, 'I'll take them if no one else wants it.' To Rachel, 'Do you want to go?'

'Yeah, I'll go.' Rachel blushed. 'Why let the tickets go to waste?'

'You two better *bentsh* and get going,' Rina told them. 'It's late.'

'We have *mezumin*,' Rav Miller stated.

The three men were necessary to say extra prayers before the Grace after Meals. Decker said, 'Then let's all *bentsh* and get going. Rav Miller, would you like to do the honors?'

'You do the honors.' Miller punted back to Decker.

'No, I insist.'

'But you provided the tickets for the children.'

Rachel was exasperated. 'Somebody please start or we're going to be late.'

Rav Miller led the group in the Grace after Meals. Afterward Decker turned to Jacob. 'Do you mind taking Hannah and the packages back to Brooklyn?'

Jacob held up his carry-on.

'Oh, that's right. You're leaving.' So much for his hunting down Shayndie. 'Okay. So we'll see Jacob off and go back to Brooklyn.'

Rina stepped in. 'You look like you have a few pickup items to do here in Manhattan before you go back. I'll take Hannah and the packages back.'

'What about our walk?'

'Don't worry about it.' Then she whispered, 'We have our exercise later on tonight.' She turned to her daughter. 'Come, Chanalah, let's say good-bye to your brother.'

Everyone took turns saying good-bye to Jacob. By the time her younger son left, there were tears in

Rina's eyes. Then she said, 'Now the hard part. Finding a cab that's willing to take us across the bridge.'

Rivka spoke up. 'Nonsense. We've got a car. We'll take you. Where are you going?'

'Boro Park. Where do you live?'

'Englewood.'

'It's way out of your way.'

'It's fine. Shragy's parents live there. We should stop by so Reuven can say hello. Shragy, help her with the bags.' Rivka said to Rina, 'We'll go bring the car around.'

'Thank you,' Rina answered.

After the Millers left with Reuven, Decker held his daughter's hand and smiled at his wife. 'I'm not really doing anything in the city. Just bumming around.'

'You want to try one more time,' Rina said.

'You know me too well.'

He seemed so demoralized. Rina squeezed his hand. 'You're not responsible for saving the world, Peter.'

'Yes, I know. It only seems that way.'

17

Heading downtown from Forty-eighth street, Decker started walking, hands in his pockets, coat wrapped tight around his chest. Twenty blocks later, he was in front of the address of Ephraim Lieber's chapter of Emek Refa'im. It corresponded to a basement somewhere in the Garment District. During daylight hours, the area was teeming with people, many of them pushing steel racks of clothing from one location to another. Blocks of stores and marts, showcasing one line after another, the rag reps promising their buyers exclusives on the newest items in the fickle world of fashion. At this time of night, the streets were dark and quiet, its huge monolithic structures casting shadows over the pavement, filmy moonlight breaking through the steel clouds. Artificial lights illuminated an occasional window: Someone was working overtime, getting the jump.

With nothing to keep him in the area, he retraced his steps uptown. Maybe he could reach Sammy and accompany him back to Washington Heights in a cab. Then, because he wasn't too far away, he could swing by Donatti's on the way back. He got to the hotel a little after nine, but the jazz set still had forty minutes to go. Since there was a nearby café, Decker stopped in and ordered a pot of herbal tea. He might as well keep warm.

Five minutes into his Lemon Zinger, he realized how ludicrous his idea had been. Sammy was on a date, for goodness' sake! Decker's was the last face he'd probably want to see. He took a final sip, then put down a fiver and left. At Forty-fifth and Eighth, he hailed a cab.

'Share a ride?'

Decker whipped around.

The man was truly a phantom.

This time, Donatti was with a young girl. She appeared around fifteen, but knowing how careful Chris was, she was probably eighteen. Donatti opened the door, and Decker went inside. The girl slid in next. Last came Chris.

Her pixie face was painted with very little makeup and framed with dark hair. Innocent face, but the dress was anything but. She had on a red tank top, a leather miniskirt, and fishnets. Around her shoulders was a feathered boa. No bra, her nipples were big and erect. She must have been freezing in the getup.

Donatti gave the driver an address. No one spoke.

As the blocks sped by, Decker felt something against his leg. He moved closer to the door, but the child was persistent, nuzzling her limb against his. It was only after her hand had brushed against his thigh and had come to rest on his knee that he had had enough.

Fury welled inside of him. He shot Donatti a hateful look so filled with venom that even Chris's stone demeanor cracked around the eyes. He pulled his charge's hand off Decker's thigh.

Donatti said, 'Switch places with me, honey. You're bothering him.'

With one swift motion, he lifted her across his lap, swatting her fanny as he put her on his right side.

'Ooh, do it again,' she purred.

'Behave yourself,' Donatti told her. 'We're in public.'

'Never stopped you before.'

This time, he gave her the force of his eyes, and she slumped back in the seat, hands in her lap.

'Pull over here,' Donatti told the cabbie. 'Keep the meter running. Wait for me.'

The driver nodded.

Donatti said, 'Get out. I'll walk you to the door.'

The girl said, 'He's not coming up?'

'No, he's not coming up.'

'Why not?'

'Because he's not.'

'Well, maybe he'd like to come up.'

'No, he wouldn't.'

'Are you coming up?'

'No. Get out.'

'Why not?'

'*Out.*' This time, Donatti didn't wait. With his long arms, he reached over and opened the passenger door, then pushed her out of the hack. She fell on the sidewalk, but before she could get up, Chris was on her, yanking her to her feet, then dragging her to the front door of an apartment building.

Decker swallowed his wrath as he watched the abuse. Shaynda was still missing. As soon as Donatti and the girl were out of earshot, the cabbie said, 'The company don't like us waiting for fares.'

'If you want to take off, it's fine with me,' Decker said.

189

The driver chuckled. 'No, I don't think that would be a good idea. You know who that is, don't you?'

'Yes,' Decker said.

'You sure you know?'

'Christopher Donatti.'

'Just thought I'd say something, in case you didn't know. 'Cause I heard him ask for you twose to share the cab. So maybe you didn't know.'

'I know. Thanks.'

Decker peeked out the window. The girl had thrown her arms around Donatti, was in the process of trying to kiss him. He recoiled from her face and shoved her away. To mollify his rough behavior, he gave her another playful swat on the butt. Then he walked back and gave the cab his loft address.

Donatti threw his head back and closed his eyes. Acting so casual while Decker was still nursing resentment. The more he thought about it, the angrier he became. Just what was Donatti trying to pull? He couldn't have been that moronic as to give that girl – that *child* – an order to seduce him. So what was the point? Just a little head trip to see Decker squirm?

Enough was enough. Donatti might have had information, but right now, Decker was too damn furious to be with the bastard. To deal with Chris, Decker needed to be calm and nonjudgmental. He had to walk it off.

He blurted out to the driver, 'Just pull over here.' A good two-dozen blocks shy of Donatti's digs.

Chris opened his eyes, looked at him.

'This is my stop,' Decker insisted.

'Here?' the driver asked.

'Here. Pull over now!'

The cabbie did as told.

Decker threw half the fare in Donatti's lap. 'Hey, thanks a lot, buddy.' He threw open the door and stormed out.

It took over twenty minutes of marching uptown on Riverside Drive for Decker to steady his rapid heartbeat. As he trod down the near-empty street, the Hudson River looking black and endless, he couldn't erase the image of that pathetic little girl, shoved and demeaned, yet she was trying so hard. It saddened him – all these broken souls – but what was the sense of bleeding? Even if Decker had had the capacity to redeem her, there were hundreds of others waiting to take her place.

It was cruel outside, a hard, malodorous mist pricking his face. He was fast approaching 135th, and was at a juncture. Jump or cut bait.

Shaynda was still missing.

Like a cat to his piss, he navigated his way toward Donatti's building, reaching it, but hesitating before pressing the bell. There was a better than good chance that by now Donatti was equally as pissed, meaning that Decker had blown his one chance. Just terrific!

Suddenly, the buzzer sounded without Decker's finger on the button.

The video monitor in the office: Donatti had been watching for him, *Waiting* for him.

Decker went inside the lobby, and this time took the elevator up. The cage was slow and bumpy. He was buzzed into the anteroom and went through the metal detector, but he didn't set it off probably because Chris had turned it off. The door to the loft was open. Chris greeted him with two glasses of Scotch, holding one out to Decker.

'Pass.'

Donatti didn't move, his arm still extending the crystal cut glass. Their eyes locked. Decker knew that if he didn't take the booze, he might as well pack it up. If Donatti was sitting on something, Decker might as well find out what it was. Give the bastard this little victory. He took the glass.

Chris clinked it with his own, then took up the bottle and opened up his office. Without a word, Decker went inside. Chris followed, locked the door, and flipped the antibug switch. He sipped the booze while he and Decker did a staring contest. This time, Decker wasn't going to give ground.

Donatti went first. 'She improvised. You've gotta know that wasn't my idea.'

Decker continued to make eye contact. 'Then what was she doing with you in the first place?'

'I was helping her out of a jam.'

'Which you put her into by pimping her.'

Donatti seemed amused. 'If I were pimping her, she wouldn't have been in a jam.' He drained the Scotch. 'Can I help it if she's a bad judge of character?'

Decker didn't answer.

Donatti said, 'I usually make it a point to stay in good standing with my former models.'

'Former?'

'Yeah, she's nineteen now. Can't use her anymore. Too exposed and too old.'

'At nineteen, she's too old.'

'One year, Decker,' Donatti said. 'Eighteen to nineteen. Men have an infinite appetite for pussy as long as the flesh is fresh. We're talking a high-turnover business.'

'Where do you get them from?'

'That's my specialty. Which leads us to the point of this meeting. What I say can't go beyond these four walls. Not to your wife, to your lawyer, to your rabbi, even to yourself when you sing in the shower. The results of a slipup can be very deleterious.'

Decker didn't answer.

'Silence isn't good enough. I've got to have your word.'

'You put an awful lot of trust in my word, Donatti.'

'Is it unfounded?'

Decker hid his expression behind the glass.

'If I don't have your word, there's no point to any of this.'

'Don't confess a murder to me, Chris.'

'Who me?' He grinned. 'Your word?'

Decker nodded.

Donatti said, 'I'm only doing this so you won't yank your chain. I've got the girl. That means you can concentrate on the whack. If the cops told you that I did it, they're lying. I don't know anything about it. If I find something out, I'll pass it along.'

He stood up, but Decker didn't. 'What do you mean, you've *got* the girl?'

'Just that. I've got the girl. I've had her since Friday. She's safe. That's all you have to know.'

'What about her parents—'

'When I say you can't tell anyone, I mean you can't tell anyone. I thought that was understood.'

'They're frantic with worry.'

'I'm sure they are. But they're still included under *no one*, Decker!'

Silence.

Decker's head was awhirl with options. 'She's fifteen, Donatti.'

'I know that.' He smiled. 'That's why you can't tell anyone. I could go to prison. Having been in prison, I know that I don't like it. It's getting late—'

'You have other girls?'

Donatti stared at him. 'You're asking a lot of questions, Decker. The answers may put you in conflict. That won't do either of us any good.'

'How many girls do you have, Donatti?'

Chris didn't answer.

Decker needed Donatti's trust to get information. He made a calculated choice. 'It stays between you and me, I swear.'

Donatti sat back down and poured himself another drink. 'Twenty at the moment. If I wanted, I could have a hundred. Most of them are sixteen plus, but I have a few who are younger.'

'Boys?'

'Yeah, I got some faggots, too. Like the birdies you saw helping me out. Those two were over eighteen, but not when I first met them. No straight boys: I used to take them in . . . nothing but problems. They'd pester the girls and get into dogfights with me over the alpha spot. You can imagine who won out. Pains in the ass – all of them.'

'You pimp them.'

Donatti looked up at the ceiling. 'Pimp is a very loaded word, Decker. I do them favors. In return, they do me favors. Matter of fact, they're *so* grateful to me that they can't *wait* to do me favors. The way I look at it, I'm the final railway stop, a last-ditch effort to save their asses from the real cold characters. Sometimes I even buy them from the bad boys if they look good enough. I have places where I let them dry out. I give them food, a roof over their heads, clothes on their backs, and drugs if they need it. About twenty-five percent leave after a few days, another twenty-five leave after a week. Usually, if they stay more than two weeks, I've got 'em hooked.'

'Hooked?'

'No, not on drugs . . . on *me*. I've got them convinced that they can't survive without my protection.' Donatti spoke patiently. 'I'm practical, Decker. I don't overwork the racehorse. The last thing I want is for them to be wasted sexually. I want them fresh and sassy-looking. A healthy-looking young nasty girl spreading her legs is a turn-on. A sexually abused waif cowering in the corner isn't.'

'You use them for your magazine.'

'That's the whole purpose, Decker. To get young pussy for my various enterprises. But to do that, I first gotta get them to eighteen. Ideally, I'd like to keep them without having to farm out their services, but right now I have a cash-flow problem because I'm on my own. See, with the Family, if you want something, there's always money, but no savings plan. When Joey ran out, he simply took what he needed from whoever had it. Me? I'm looking for the long term.'

'Lots of adult magazines in the racks, Donatti.'

'Not to mention the videos and the interactive displays on the Internet. Which is why I'm going for the niche market. Not the hipsters, Decker, like in *GQ* or *Esquire*. Or the losers who gawk at silicone boobs in *Playboy* or *Penthouse*. Can *you* – as an older married straight male – relate to any of that shit?'

'I don't buy those magazines, Donatti.'

'Because they don't talk to you, Lieutenant. Who do I talk to? Committed married men in complacent but dull marriages. Those who don't want to throw away everything by having a sleazy affair, but their sex lives have gone to seed. They're a beleaguered lot. Maybe not in your case, Decker, but lots of middle-class guys can use a little empowering. Having been trapped in a hideous marriage for three and a half years, I know what I'm doing. I know all about the Internet and the Web pages and the self-directed on-line porno sites – I've got plans for those, too – but in the end, it's inconvenient to take a laptop into the can to whack off. The wife might suspect something.'

Decker looked away and shook his head. 'You've done some marketing research, Chris?'

'We're living in sophisticated times. I'm in experimental stages right now, from the advice columns to impregnating the pages with the right aromas. There is a load of money to be made doing young meat legally. By the time I reach thirty, I want to own half of Harlem. So yeah, my girls do me favors, but I'm not ruthless. And that's the God's honest truth because if I wanted to, I could work my bitches day in and day out, twenty-four/seven. After September eleventh, more than a few New Yorkers had midlife crises: guys who saw those motherfuckers crash into the WTC and felt that the end was at hand. But they survived along with their cocks, and getting pussy, especially fresh young twat, placed high on the to-do list.'

'Funny, Donatti,' Decker snarled. 'I saw heroes, not degenerates.'

'We all see what we're searching for,' Donatti countered. 'And what I know is demand is high right now. In this economy, a quick lay is still a cheap thrill.

So maybe my girls are doing me a few more favors than usual, but slavery is illegal in this country. None of my girls are forced.'

'That depends on your definition of forced.'

'The kids are free to leave. But if they leave, they can't come back. If they feel equipped to take on that big bad world out there . . . well, more power to them.'

'Nothing a little intimidation won't take care of.'

'It is a scary world out there, Decker. If some of my stories make them a little cautious, I can live with that.'

Decker smoothed his mustache. 'And you're not worried about loose lips?'

'My kids don't talk. So far, I've got a one-hundred-percent compliance rate because I'm very persuasive.'

'And if they did talk?'

Donatti shook his head ever so slightly. 'Don't go there.'

Decker exhaled heavily and turned away. Abruptly, he slammed his fist down on the table.

'I know,' Donatti said. 'You want to beat the shit out of me. You want to pound my good-looking, arrogant, motherfucking head into a bloody pulp, and lop my oversize cock off because I'm in the driver's seat. There was a time when the tables were turned, and I felt the way you're feeling now. But we're both adults now. You've got to swallow, Decker, just like I swallowed for eight years. If you were honest with yourself, you'd realize that I'm being big about this. You ruined my life.'

Decker's laugh was mirthless. 'You recovered pretty quickly, Chris.'

'You don't know *dick*.' Donatti turned ugly. 'I had

my *uncle* convinced. I had *her* convinced. I could have *owned* her – body and soul – if you hadn't fucked it up.'

'Women aren't chattel anymore, Donatti.'

'That's what you think,' Donatti spat back. 'I was this close!' He pinched off an area between his index finger and his thumb. Then he sat back and sighed. 'You know how it is . . . always obsessed with the one who got away. And I was obsessed with her to begin with.'

'You're better off,' Decker said.

'You mean, *she's* better off.' Donatti took a gulp of Scotch. 'Fuck the past. I'm a big boy. So I don't own her. But I'm sure as hell *renting* her. And believe me, I've got her on a long-term lease. Besides, Terry isn't the issue here. So forget about Terry. You've got other problems. At the moment, *your* problem is camped out with me and very happy to be there.'

Decker felt his blood pressure rise, and that wasn't doing anyone any good. 'She's in one piece?'

'Absolutely.'

'What's her mental condition?'

'Very agitated. I found her that way. Right now, she won't talk about it. That's okay. I don't need to know details.'

'What are you doing with her?'

'Just letting her chill. I don't pimp, but if I did, I wouldn't ever send anyone out like that. Way too unstable.'

'So you're just letting her have free room and board, and asking nothing in return?'

'That about sums it up. Could be she'll chill for a day or two, and I'll never see her again. That's a chance I always take. The other possibility is, she'll want to do me favors. I stay in touch with all my girls, Decker. They're out there on the streets – some selling their butts at their own risks, some are even working legit jobs. They're my eyes and ears. They keep me connected to what's going on because they're very grateful to me.'

'Scared of you?'

'Same thing.'

'She's safe?'

'Yes, Shayndie is safe.'

Saying her name. Showing Decker that he was legit. His eyes bore into Donatti's. 'You screwing her, Donatti?'

'Nah . . . not yet. But if she stays with me long enough, I will.' Donatti stared back. 'Sex promotes loyalty.'

'What do you do with the boys?'

'Like I said . . . sex promotes loyalty.' A sly smile played on Donatti's lips. 'Nervous about being around me, Lieutenant?'

Decker wagged his finger at Chris's face.

Donatti laughed. 'I do whatever I have to do to get the job done. None of it is thrilling. To my kids – girls and boys – sex is lying on your back, squeezing your eyes shut, being real still, and letting Uncle George or Daddy do his thing. Between you and these four walls, I'd much rather fuck your wife—'

Decker was on him before the kid knew what hit him. He slammed Donatti against the wall, using all his weight to keep him pinned and helpless while he clamped his hands around his throat. He hissed out, 'We need to establish some ground rules, Chris.'

Then Decker heard the click, felt something hard pressed between his legs.

Donatti choked out, 'Let . . . go . . . of . . . me!'

Decker tightened his hands around Chris's throat. 'So shoot me, you son of a bitch! Then what'll you have? A big bloody mess on your hands.' But he loosened his grip. 'My wife is off-limits! Understand?'

The gun pressed harder against Decker's groin. Donatti's face was red from anger and lack of oxygen. 'Let! Go!'

'*Understand?*'

Silence. The moments ticked away. Finally, Chris raised his hands up in the air, a double-action automatic in his left hand; probably a Walther TPH.

Decker released him. 'We're doing business.' He backed away and sat back down. 'Let's not get personal.'

Donatti shook himself off, then rested the gun on Decker's forehead. 'Some men might consider that a compliment.'

'I don't.' Decker was trying hard not to flinch. 'We need to respect each other's privacy.'

Donatti held the gun on him for another minute – a very long time for a loaded barrel to be pressed to your brain, but Decker took comfort in knowing that a Walther has reliable safety features.

Eventually, Chris lowered the piece. He cleared his throat and downed some Scotch. Then he began to pace like an animal – flushed and red, his breathing rapid and punctuated. Decker felt his heart pounding against his chest, but he attempted to mask his fury by clutching his hands and keeping his expression flat. The both of them: two adrenalized bulls. The office stank like a gym.

Finally, Donatti placed the semiautomatic down on the tabletop and spoke in a guttural voice. 'Don't do that again. After my father and Joey, I have no more tolerance for abuse.'

Decker held out his hands. 'You behave, so will I.'

'Fuck only knows why I took that shit from you.'

'Because I'm not only Terry's father figure, I'm yours as well. Sit down, Chris. It's over. We'll call it a draw.'

Chris tapped his foot, then sat back down. 'Okay. You did your dance: I did mine. You should still thank me for sparing your nuts.'

'Thank you.' It took Decker a few moments to catch his breath. 'I'd like to see her. Shayndie.'

'You think I'm holding her against her will?'

That's exactly what he'd been thinking. He didn't trust Donatti, but he was all Decker had. 'No, I believe you. But I'd still like to see her.'

Donatti looked at him.

'No setup, Donatti. Just something to ease my worried head. Just you, the girl, and me. You have my word on that, too.'

'You want to ask her questions.'

'She's a material witness to a murder. I could use a little help.'

Donatti said, 'If you upset her, she'll bolt. That won't do either one of us any good.'

'Can we just play it by ear?'

'As long as I direct.'

'Whatever you want, big guy.'

Donatti ran his hands across the top of his shorn blond locks. 'I suppose I could set it up.' He thought for a long time. Then he took out a piece of paper, wrote something down, and gave it to Decker. 'Meet me there tomorrow night, around eleven, eleven-thirty. If I don't show, I'm not jerking you around. It means I couldn't risk it. Cops are all over the place now. It's hard to move without a cruiser on your ass.'

Decker looked at the address. 'Where the hell is this?'

'You're a detective. Figure it out! And don't even think of putting a tail on me. The girl is safe right now. But if you make her a liability, I'll do what I need to do.' Donatti scratched his head. 'Want a piece?'

Decker blinked. 'You mean a gun?'

'Of course I mean a gun.' He slid the Walther over to Decker's side of the table. 'What did you think I meant? A piece of ass? I can get you that, too, if you want.'

'I don't want either.'

'Do you have one – a piece?'

'No, but I don't intend on getting jammed, Chris. I'm better off being clean.'

'Think so?'

'Yes, I think so. A gun might give me a false sense of security.'

'Suit yourself, Lieutenant.'

This time, Decker stood up. 'I've got to go. See you tomorrow. You will be there with Shayndie?'

'If possible, I'll be there. And if Shayndie's still around, she'll be there, too. I told you I have an open-door policy. One never knows.'

'Where she is . . . are there phones?'

'No.'

'So if she . . . contacted someone, she would have had to leave the building.'

'She wouldn't leave without my permission. Not if she wanted to come back.'

'You have guards posted, Donatti?'

'You make it sound like a prison. It's not that way. Yeah, I have people who help me out because I can't be there all the time. I got business to take care of. Your little excursion has already put me back in terms of man-hours.'

'Where'd you find her?'

'Trade secret. Aren't you going?'

Decker didn't move. 'I know this is an odd question . . . If you could find out if she's a virgin . . . it might help me out.'

Donatti laughed. 'Are you putting me on?'

'Good Lord, I don't mean for you to *fuck* her. *Please* don't do that. I mean, if you could ask her or . . . I don't know.'

'I can find out if she's been busted.' He shrugged. 'You suspect the uncle?'

'I can't rule it out.'

'It would fit. They've all been sexually abused. That's why my tea-and-sympathy routine rings true. I've been there. I know their pain firsthand. That's why they trust me. You know the saying: You can always catch more flies with honey than with vinegar.'

'And if the honey doesn't work, Chris?'

'That's why God invented firearms.'

18

'**Y**ou were restless last night.' Rina buttered her toast. 'I didn't give you enough of a workout?'

Decker lifted his eyes from the paper. 'If my heart had been beating any faster, I would have had a coronary.' He rolled his shoulders. 'It's the darn bed. It's the size of a matchbox with hay for mattress stuffing.'

'You know, Peter, I have the plane reservations on hold. Ephraim's funeral is scheduled for three in the afternoon.'

'Today?'

'Yes, today. Apparently, the body was released last night. We could pay a shiva call afterward and be out on a flight to your parents by ten tonight if we start packing now.'

Decker dropped his voice. 'I need to stick around for another day.'

Rina was holding toast. Her hand froze somewhere between the table and her mouth. 'You're on to something.'

'Could be.'

'It has to be strong to keep you here. You couldn't wait to go.'

'You're right.'

'Can I ask what it is?'

'Not yet.'

It was Donatti, of course. But Rina couldn't say anything. She sipped coffee and picked up a copy of *Agudath Yisroel's Guide to Kashruth*.

Decker put down the newspaper. 'I'm not cutting you short. I'm just trying to be cautious.'

'Of course.'

He took her hand. 'Look, darling, why don't you and Hannah leave for Florida tonight—'

'No.'

'My mother would be thrilled. We both know she likes you better than she likes me. And she likes Hannah better than both of us.'

'Peter, I'm not leaving without you. We all leave tomorrow morning. One more day won't hurt. As a matter of fact, why don't you call up the station house and just take the whole week off. We can spend more time with your parents. We won't have to rush things. Rush, rush, rush. And what is the hurry? To solve one more case that's going to be processed through the overloaded justice system? We're not getting younger.'

'You mean *I'm* not getting younger. You're still young.'

'I'm almost forty—'

'Oh please!' Decker glared at her. 'You're thirty-eight and you look twenty-two. I'm fifty and look every inch of it.'

'Well, I think you're very handsome.'

Decker smiled. 'That was sweet. Thank you.'

Rina said, 'There are loads of things to do in this city. I can take Hannah to the zoo or the Botanical Garden or the Met. I can go over to YU and bug

Sammy. I can shop. Things are much cheaper here. Just tell me for what time should I rebook the flight. Tuesday morning? How about Tuesday night – just in case?'

'Tuesday night is fine. And you're right. I'll call up the station and take the entire week off. It'll make my parents happy, and we'll be able to relax. We'll fly back from the Gold Coast on Sunday.'

'Wonderful!'

'I'm glad you're happy.' Decker picked up the paper.

Rina said, 'I can't believe you're actually listening to me.'

'I throw you a bone every once in a while. Keeps you grateful.'

Decker had learned that many Jews held their funerals in two stages. First there was the *hespid*, or memorial, where the closed casket was brought into a hall or synagogue and eulogies were given. Then the coffin was transferred to grave site and buried by friends and family. Since there was no synagogue in Quinton big enough to hold all the mourners, the *hespid* was done in the Community Hall in Liberty Park. But even that building couldn't contain the thick black swarm of people that spilled out the door and into the parkway lawns.

Rina had gone into Quinton earlier with Jonathan and Raisie. They had asked Decker to come along, but he had declined because of obligations: He was still trying to locate the address that Donatti had given him. He had told his wife and his brother that he'd meet up with them later. He'd drive to Quinton in his own car. (Sora Lazarus's car, but who's counting?) Decker hadn't figured in 'heavy, heavy traffic and getting lost' time. He was a half hour late, and not only couldn't he find a seat, he couldn't even get into the structure. Because he was technically 'family,' he could have muscled his way inside, but he decided not to bother. He and the Liebers weren't on solid territory. He'd stay in the background.

The outside air held imminent frost, the ground beneath Decker's feet cold and hard. The skies were a lighter gray than yesterday, the tufts of clay-colored cotton drifting through the ether, muting glare from the sun. All day, blue was on the verge of breaking through but never made it past the cloudy barrier. He rocked on his toes, trying to get circulation into his bones. His shoes had worn soles, and his dress socks were California thin. Hands crammed into his pockets, he gave a quick glimpse to his surroundings.

In the distance was a playground with toddlers climbing on gym equipment or running in bulky sweaters and coats, frantic nannies and housekeepers jogging to keep pace with the rambunctious youngsters. There were more nannies and housekeepers pushing strollers along the undulating paths that cut through the parkway. Children were trekking through the park on their way home from school. The baseball field was empty. The basketball courts held a couple of lively games.

Idyllic in a way, except Decker knew teenagers: For them, peace and quiet were code names for mind-numbingly boring. Adolescents needed action, excitement, and stimulation. When the hometown didn't provide it, kids went elsewhere. Even a parochial kid like Shayndie found herself sneaking out at night to attend 'forbidden' parties.

Not that it was relevant now. From the closed religious community of Quinton to the predatory claws of Donatti, it had been one hell of a downhill ride for the little girl.

Decker's chest was still tight from last night's confrontation with the Young Turk. But even the gun to the head was easier to deal with than Jacob on a bad day. His stepson, several months shy of eighteen, had given him excellent training in self-control. All Decker wanted was to bring the girl back and get the hell out of here. What started out as excitement had quickly turned to a gladiator fight of wits and wiles with a psycho. It would be round three tonight . . . another round or two before he could secure the girl.

What would he have to give Donatti to get Shaynda?

Standing fifty feet to his left was a trio of Hispanics. There were two somber, dark-eyed women, their faces slathered with makeup, their hair coiffed with lots of air and teasing. Both of them were garbed in black pantsuits and overcoats. With the two ladies was a mustachioed man with slicked-back hair. The gent was about fifty and had donned an out-of-date black suit, a white shirt, and a narrow black tie. Clearly, they had come for Ephraim's funeral, but who were they?

Decker went over to find out. As he approached, the buzz of undertone Spanish disappeared until he was left with intruded-upon silence. He thought about speaking in their native tongue, but nixed the idea. He didn't want to appear like the know-it-all, condescending Anglo.

'I'm from out of town,' Decker tried out. 'Are you friends of Mr Lieber?'

'I work for him,' answered the older man. He was heavyset, his black hair streaked with gray. His accent was thick.

'Ah,' Decker said. 'You work for Mr Lieber. The older man? Or the son?'

An indeterminate shrug. 'For the family.'

'You all work at the stores?' Decker said.

'Why you ask so many questions?' one of the women wanted to know. She appeared middle-aged with thick hips, a broad behind, and a generous bosom – all stuffed into a package less than five feet tall. And that was with heels.

'Just trying to make conversation.' Decker smiled. 'I'm from out of town.'

'So what you doing here?' the miniature woman asked.

'I'm a relative of a relative,' Decker explained. '*Mi hermano es el esposo de la hija de Señor Lieber.*'

They looked at him with suspicious eyes. '*¿Que hija?*' the older man asked him.

'Raisie,' Decker said. 'Jonathan . . . the rabbi. He's my brother. My half brother, actually. It's a long story.'

Silence.

'So why you out here?' the short woman demanded. 'Why you not with your brother?'

'Good question.' Decker appeared to give it some thought. 'I don't know the Liebers really. I don't want to violate their privacy, even though my brother asked me to come. Heck, you all probably know way more about the family than I do. You work with them every day, right?'

No argument there.

'Darn shame,' Decker said. '*Que dolor.* To lose your

209

son so terribly. I heard that they were very close – father and son.'

Silence.

Decker shrugged. 'Maybe not.' He looked away.

The short woman said, 'Mr Lieber loves all his children.'

'Of course.' Decker smiled at her. 'He was very happy when Ephraim came to work for him at the stores.'

No response.

Decker said, 'Well, that's what my brother said.'

'He was a good man, Mr Ephraim,' the short woman answered. 'Always *feliz* . . . happy, happy, happy. Big smile on his face.'

'Big smile,' echoed the second female. She was younger, thinner, and taller, but not by much. 'He likes to joke – Mr Ephraim. Always with the jokes.'

'Different from his brother, no?' Decker added.

'Psss . . .' Munchkin woman wrinkled her nose. 'He's good man, Mr Jaime, but not with the jokes. *Muy grave*. And he watch you like you're a *bandido*, he *es* so afraid you steal. I don' steal nothing. It *es* *estúpido* to have big TV set in my apartment. If the others on the street find out I have big TV set, they break into my apartment and steal it. Then they steal other things because they *es* there. I only have *lee*-tle TV set in my bedroom. Mr Lieber, he give it to me for Christmas two years ago. It has remote control and cable. I happy.'

'You no need nothing else, sister,' the other woman spoke up. 'TV is better than the mens.'

Both the women laughed. The man shook his head in disgust.

'Mr Lieber gave you a TV?' Decker said. 'That was very nice.'

'He is a berry nice man; I am very good worker. Seven a.m., I am there. One hour lunch. Then I come back, I work till six. Every day for five days. The store no open on Saturday, and I don' work on Sunday. I go to church. Then I get my nails done.' She showed him red talons. 'Acrylic. Berry hard.'

'Very pretty,' Decker complimented.

The woman actually blushed. 'He berry good to me, Mr Lieber.'

'What *trabajo* do you do?' Decker asked.

'I do everythin'. I do the register. I stock the shelves. Berry, berry tall shelves. The store *es* berry big with tall shelves.' She held her hand way up in the air. 'They have big ladder. At first, Mr Lieber don' wants me to climb, but I wear berry good shoes. Is no problem. I am very strong.' She made a muscle.

A smile crept into the man's lips. He fired off Spanish that intimated that she had gotten her muscle from jerking private things up and down. She glowered at him in return, then blushed when she realized that Decker understood him. They were about to exchange words, but Decker broke in.

'What about Mr Jaime? Is he a nice man, too?'

'Berry nice,' the shorter woman said. 'But not with the jokes. Not like Mr Ephraim. He's with the jokes. And Mr Ephraim always gives me *mucho ayuda*.'

Ayuda meant help. Decker felt the air turning even colder, his breath a wisp of mist in front of his nose. Daylight was receding quickly. Within a couple of hours, it would be dark. 'You two work together.'

'*Sí, sí*. We stock the shelves together. Sometimes I go on top, sometimes he go on top.'

The man said, 'You can go on top of me, Luisa.'

Luisa shot back a gesture that was less than kind. Then her face saddened. 'He talk to me, Mr Ephraim. He ask about my children. He once give me money for a parking ticket. Fifty dollars. I pay him back, but he don' ask me for the money.' Her eyes watered. '*Es* berry sad.'

Decker nodded his agreement.

Luisa rubbed her hands together. '*Es* cold, no?'

'You want to borrow my gloves?' Decker asked. 'I have pockets.'

She looked at the leather accoutrements enviously.

'Honestly, I'm fine.' He gave them to the woman.

Reluctantly, she put them on. '*Gracias*.'

'*Por favor*.' Decker stuck his hands in his overcoat. 'That was Mr Ephraim's job? To stock the shelves?'

The man spoke up. 'Mr Ephraim? He do everything. He stock the shelves, he work at the cash register, he sweep the floors. I see him two, three times cleaning the toilets. Nothing is too small for him. He is berry nice man. He never complains. He don' yell. Every time I see him, he *es* happy. Big smile.' He looked down. 'I will miss him. It is terrible.'

'Yes, it is terrible,' Decker said. 'Was Ephraim resentful to be doing all the small stuff?'

All of them shook their heads no.

'Ephraim was happy for any job,' the man said. 'He *es* lucky the old man loved him so much.'

Marta burst into tears. 'It is berry bad! Poor Mr Lieber.'

'It is terrible!' Luisa concurred.

Decker nodded, then waited before he spoke again. 'Did Ephraim seem preoccupied lately? *Preocupado?*'

The trio exchanged innocent glances.

'No' to me,' Marta said. 'He same to me.'

But the man was looking somewhere over Decker's shoulder. '*Señor?*'

Luisa said, 'Teddy, he is talking to you.'

'Me?' Teddy answered.

'Did Mr Ephraim seem preoccupied?'

'He is beeg man with *responsabilidad*.' Teddy pulled a cigarette pack out of his pocket. He lit up. 'I thin' maybe he worried that Mr Jaime don' think he's doing a good job.'

'Did they fight?' Decker inquired.

'No' too much. No' too loud. Sometimes he don' like Mr Ephraim talking to the womens.'

'Mr Ephraim likes all the womens,' Luisa stated. 'He nice to the girls, but he was berry nice to the old womens. He makes jokes with them, and they laugh. He *es* berry nice to everybody. Always with a smile . . . big smiles.'

'Did he have a girlfriend?' Decker asked. 'Ephraim?'

Luisa thought for a moment, then shrugged ignorance. She turned to the other woman. '*¿Que piensas, Marta?*' You see Mr Ephraim with a girlfriend?'

'No, never. I don't see him with a girl. *Es* berry sad that he don't have a wife. Mr Ephraim loved the kids.'

'Yes, I heard he was close to Shaynda – his niece,' Decker said. '*La hija de Señor Jaime.*'

'He nice to all de kids from Mr Jaime,' Marta answered. 'If Mr Jaime . . . If he bring the kids to the stores, Mr Ephraim plays the games with him. He likes Street Fighter Two.'

'It sounded like he was a nice man,' Decker said.

'Berry nice.' Luisa's voice cracked. 'It is no good

for the father. My heart is very heavy for him – Mr Lieber. Ten years ago, his wife . . . she died.' She leaned over and whispered, 'Cancer.'

'Oh, he cry and cry,' Marta answered.

'Berry sad,' Luisa concurred.

Decker turned to Luisa. 'You said that Mr Jaime watches you like a hawk.'

'He don' mean nothing bad.' She furrowed her brow. 'There *es* lots of stealing in the stores. We have alarm . . . a sensor with de bars that you stick on the packages. Then you swipe the bars at the cash register, and that turns off de sensor. But bad people don't care. They run into the streets. It is berry bad.'

'Very bad,' Decker agreed. 'But why would Mr Jaime watch you, Luisa? You've worked for Mr Lieber, how long?'

'Twelve years.'

'Exactly. Why would he think that you would steal from the store?'

'I don' think he *think* I steal,' Luisa clarified. 'He is just a careful man.'

Or the store was having a big theft problem, Decker thought. Maybe that's what the fights were about.

Teddy was talking '. . . worked for Mr Lieber for seven years. I never take nothin'. Not even a battery.'

'No one say you steal,' Marta said. 'Why you get so excited?'

Teddy took a deep breath. 'Mr Jaime talk about inventory to Mr Ephraim. I hear them say that someone was stealing. It's not me.'

'Not me, either,' Marta said.

Decker remembered the boxes of inventory lists found in Ephraim's apartment. Was Ephraim checking up on someone, or was he covering his tracks? Decker said, 'Any idea who was stealing?'

Teddy shook his head vehemently. 'Mr Lieber gave Mr Ephraim the inventory because Mr Jaime hated to do it. It is boring, counting this and that. Ephraim don't mind it. That was Mr Jaime. He always gave Ephraim the long and boring jobs.'

'Why not?' Marta questioned. 'Mr Ephraim only work mebbe two years. Mr Jaime worked years and years when Mr Ephraim was . . . well, you know.'

'He do de drugs,' Luisa whispered to Decker.

Decker nodded. 'Was Mr Ephraim angry about doing inventory?'

Just then, the Community Hall doors opened, the black glob of human mass splitting like a dividing microbe. From the opening yawn came the pallbearers, lumbering through the crowd, hoisting a pine casket on their shoulders.

Decker pointed to Jonathan. 'That's my brother. The one in the far left corner.'

'*Vaya con Dios.*' Luisa whispered. Then she started crying. '*Vaya con Dios.*' She found Marta, and the two of them hugged each other as they wept together.

Decker spotted his wife, sobbing into a handkerchief. 'I'd better go to my family.'

'Your gloves, *señor.*' Luisa began to peel them off her hands.

Decker stopped her. 'You can send them back to me when you get home. Mr Lieber will send them to my brother. He knows my address.'

'You are berry nice.'

He thanked her, then thanked them all. He pushed his way through the thickness and went over to comfort Rina.

19

It was after five by the time Ephraim was laid to rest, the sunlight withering like yesterday's prom corsage. The experience was emotionally wrenching, and Decker needed a good stiff Scotch before meeting with Donatti. Plus, he had yet to find the exact location of the meeting spot because all Donatti had given him was an address. It took him over an hour just to deduce that the place was in New Jersey.

Decker had suggested a quick dinner before he went out, but Rina had other things in mind. The proper thing to do was to make a shiva call, to personally express condolences to Emmanuel Lieber and his four remaining children, one of them Decker's sister-in-law. As much as Decker wanted to talk to the old man – he wanted to get the father's perspective on his son's new life as a sober man – he couldn't deal with Chaim and Minda Lieber *and* Christopher Donatti in the same evening. Because Shayndie's welfare outweighed protocol, he told Rina to go without him.

'But Jonathan's expecting you.' They were outside the cemetery gates, at the ritual washing fountain. The sky had turned from ashen gray to deep charcoal, and the temperature had dropped even further.

As Rina poured ice-cold water over her hands, her fingers turned ketchup red. Silently, she recited the traditional prayer made upon exiting a graveyard.

'It can't be helped.' Decker took the washing cup from her. 'With the new scheduling, I'll have time to pay a shiva call to the family tomorrow. Can you bum a ride from Jonathan?'

'That's not a problem.' Rina dried her stiff hands with a damp paper towel. 'If I can find him.'

'We were among the first to leave. He has to stop here first, right?'

Rina nodded.

'So you'll be able to find him.' Decker rinsed his hands and muttered the Hebrew words. 'Just tell him that I'll see him tomorrow.'

'That's his van. It might be nice if you told him yourself—'

'For goodness' sake!' Decker grumbled. 'All right, *I'll* tell him!'

Red-eyed, Jonathan got out of the vehicle and shuffled, stoop-shouldered, over to the washing area, his arm linked about his wife's arm, both of them weathered by the tragedies of the past few days. Raisie had fresh tear marks on her cheeks, her nose pinkened by cold and sorrow. Decker tapped his brother on his shoulder. Jonathan pivoted and looked up, a stunned expression on his face. Decker crooked a finger, and Jonathan broke away from Raisie.

'Can you take Rina to your in-laws, then back to Brooklyn?'

'You're *not* coming?'

'I can't, Jon. Something came up—'

'What?' The Rabbi's pale face instantly filled with color. 'Are you on to something?'

217

'No, not at all,' Decker lied. 'Just tying up loose ends with the detective.'

'You wouldn't miss shiva for that,' Jonathan snapped back. 'You've got a lead.'

Decker pulled him aside, away from the open ears. 'Jonathan, listen up, because this is important. I'm going to make myself very clear. This stays between you and me.'

The rabbi nodded eagerly.

'No, I have nothing to tell you,' Decker insisted. 'You'll have to trust me. Still, you can't talk about me to anyone – not your brother-in-law, not your father-in-law. If they ask where I am, tell them I'm not feeling well.'

'Yes, yes, I understand!' He grabbed Decker's jacket. 'I'm your clergyman, Akiva. Just tell me! You'll have confidentiality. I can't and won't breathe a word of it to anyone. It's not fair to shut me out! Please! Now more than ever, I need to know.'

'Stop right there!' Decker tried to control his temper. 'Let me try again.' He looked at his brother with stern eyes. 'I'm not telling you anything, and you don't say a thing to anyone! If you shoot off your mouth, if even you give someone the wrong impression with a little, tiny look, you're going to *fuck* everything up! Is that *clear* enough?'

The rabbi recoiled at the obscenity.

Decker ran his hand over his face. Dealing with Donatti was turning him into a bastard. 'I'm sorry.'

'I understand.' Jonathan put his hand on his brother's shoulder. 'I have no idea what you're dealing with, Akiva, but obviously it's something or somebody dangerous. Don't give it another moment's thought. I know how to make excuses and make them believable. They'll never suspect a thing.'

Decker exhaled out loud. 'Jon, you've just got to trust me.'

'Of course, I trust you. I'm very sorry to intrude.'

Decker tried to calm his rapid breathing. 'I'll go get Rina.'

'Akiva.'

Decker waited.

'Thank you.' He reached out toward his brother. 'Thank you for everything.'

Sealing the deal with a bear hug.

It took Decker over three hours to find *a* place, and after so many twists and turns and dead ends, he wasn't even sure it was *the* place. It was underneath deserted elevated train tracks, a few blocks from the numbers that Donatti had given him. He had followed instructions, but Chris had given him right and left, instead of east and west. Decker was somewhere out in Jersey, that much he knew, away from anything populated, away from anything civilized. The last city that he remembered driving through was Camden – a poverty-stricken, blighted, poorly lit area of deteriorating brick tenements and boarded-up, abandoned buildings. Sometime ago, Decker recalled reading an article about urban renewal in the city. From what he had seen, it wasn't evident.

It was almost eleven. Standing in dirty, damp mist that chilled him down to the marrow, with only a tire jack at his feet for protection, he rocked on his soles and rubbed his bare hands constantly to keep sensation in his fingertips. Why the hell did he give his gloves to Luisa? Ah well, maybe he'd pump her later on and she'd remember his act of chivalry . . . give him something juicy to work with.

His car was parked fifty yards away – as close as he could get to the spot. Distant highway sounds could be heard – a roar of a motorcycle, the rumble of big rig, an occasional honk. Beyond manufactured noise, the area was eerily silent.

New Jersey, home to 'Born in the USA' Bruce Springsteen. Decker knew there were gorgeous and wealthy neighborhoods in the state, but this wasn't one of them. Didn't TV always put the mobster's dump spot somewhere in the Garden State? Was that why Donatti had chosen it? Had he dumped bodies here before?

A blare sounded in the distance: something that was traveling because of the Doppler effect – the wave of noise advancing, then receding. A series of hoots. Owls, possibly? Then once again there was nothing, a creepy stillness that was worse than the creaks and the cracks.

And what if Donatti didn't show?

Then that would be that.

At the moment, the option sounded all right to Decker, much better than freezing his nuts off in the middle of nowhere. Breathing in soot and grime, continuously looking over his shoulder or behind his back because any second he might get sliced up by some fifteen-year-old psycho punk with nothing better to do. One side of Decker was almost hoping that C.D. would revert to his pathological lying self and pull a tilt. Donatti was a funny bastard. He wasn't evil for evil's sake, but he was self-serving and amoral – an unscrupulous son of a bitch who did evil things, and that made his moves even harder to figure out. An evil man will kill and rob and rape for the thrill, for the fun and games. An amoral man like Donatti had no problems with killing and robbing, but he didn't do it for kicks. He did the deeds, sure, but only if they were in his best interest.

Just what was in Donatti's best interest?

Decker took out a small bottle of Chivas and took a stiff drink. For dinner, he had eaten a tasteless vegetarian sandwich made with stale bread. It was atonement for eating so much meat yesterday night. He was trying to help his stomach out. Instead, the 'supposedly' light food was sitting like stone in his gut.

Another drink just to soothe the nerves.

He was completely disoriented: a friggin' sitting duck. Why the hell hadn't he taken the piece that Donatti had offered him? But even that could have been a setup.

You take the piece, and then I'll have a reason to shoot you.

With C.D., Decker just didn't know. Donatti had talked about Decker swallowing, just as he had for eight years. Was this meeting staged? Was it masking a final act of revenge that had lain dormant for years, turning over in a cold, cruel mind?

Eleven-fifteen.

Decker took another swig of booze.

Fifteen minutes passed, producing nothing but hard shivers down his spine and numbness to his toes.

He'd wait until the witching hour. Then . . . that was it.

Five minutes before midnight, Decker saw it – an approaching, silent shadow. No car in his view; Decker hadn't even heard any faraway engine sounds.

He wondered how the shadow had gotten here so quietly. Did it walk on tiptoes, or had Decker's mind wandered so he hadn't noticed obvious noise?

His nerves shot into overdrive as he bent down to pick up the tire jack – heavy and cold in his grip. Slowly, the shadow took shape, Donatti materializing through the mist. He was dressed in a woolen overcoat, with gloves on his hands. He was literally dragging a package behind him – a small, frail thing swathed in a baggy coat. Her hands were wrapped in knitted mittens, but there were holes at the fingertips. She appeared like a toddler next to Donatti's massive frame. Even at a distance, Decker could tell that she was crying, sobbing to him, *begging* him.

'Please don't make me go back.'

'No one is making you go back.'

'Please don't make me talk—'

'He just wants to see you—'

'No, please, no!' She was clutching Chris's arm, her nails digging into his coat. Strands of long, matted hair stuck to her wet face. He continued to lug her closer, and Decker took a few steps out to meet them. At that point, Decker saw that she was shaking harder, absolutely trembling with dread, barely able to support her own weight under bent knees.

Decker stopped advancing. 'It's okay. It's okay. Stay where you are.' He studied the girl. It appeared to be Shayndie, but with it being so dark and with her face obscured, Decker just wasn't sure. Donatti halted his footsteps and the girl immediately buried her face into Donatti's ribs, just under his armpit.

'She's obviously comfortable with you,' Decker remarked.

'What can I say?' Donatti answered. 'Natural charm. Shayndie, just answer this man's questions and we'll go back—'

'He'll tell my father.'

'I won't tell your father,' Decker answered.

'Don't believe him, Mr Donatti. He's one of them.'

'Nah.' Chris blew her off. 'He couldn't care less about Jews. He has to pretend to be Jewish, or else his wife will get mad. C'mon, Shayndie. I'm cold and I'm grumpy. Let's get this over with.' He grabbed her by her arm and pulled her away from his body. Then he bent down and looked in her eyes. Instantly, Shayndie covered her face with her palms.

'He won't hurt you.' Donatti pulled her hands down. 'He's actually an okay guy, all right. I promise he won't hurt you. And if he does, I'll kill him, all right?' A gun was pulled from his coat. It was a big one, possibly a Magnum. Donatti stood up and pointed the weapon at Decker. 'See this? I have the weapon; he doesn't. That means he's screwed if he tries anything.'

'Please don't make me talk to him.'

'Shayndie, answer his questions, or I'm gonna get *pissed*! I'm tired. I want to go home. Just do it, okay?'

She nodded, but then slapped her hands over her face again.

'And take your damn hands off your face! C'mon, girl! I'm willing to help you, but you gotta pull yourself together.' Again he bent down. He lowered his voice. 'C'mon, sugar. Can you do that for me?'

She didn't answer, but Decker noticed that the shaking was subsiding.

He kissed her forehead and pulled loose hair from

her face. 'Please, sugar? You want to make me happy, don't you?'

She nodded.

'This would make me happy. Can you do it? Can you talk to him?'

Again she nodded.

'Yeah, I know you can. You're a strong girl.' Donatti kissed her cheek, then stood up, his eyes fixed on Decker's face. 'Make it quick or we're both gonna have problems.'

'Can you tell me what happened to your uncle, Shaynda?'

She muttered something, but Decker couldn't make it out.

'I can't hear her.'

Chris sighed with exasperation. He bent down a third time. 'C'mon, honey. Whisper it in my ear.'

She did as told. Donatti nodded as she spoke behind a cupped hand. He said, 'Someone grabbed him as they were walking to the museum. She got away.' To Shayndie, he said, 'Did you see who did it?'

'Men,' she muttered.

'How many?' Decker asked.

'Two . . . three. They were *frum*. They wore *kapatas*.'

'Lubavitch?' Decker said.

A shake of the head told him no.

'Satmir?'

Again the answer was negative.

'Breslav.'

'No. I mean I don't know. They wore . . . *shtreimels*.'

'*Shtreimels?* In the middle of the work week?'

She nodded yes.

'And they were dressed up in silk *kapatas* or something?'

She nodded.

Donatti said, 'Can you translate this for me?'

'The men who took her uncle wore Chasidic Jewish garb. There are many different Chasidic sects. The Liebers are a certain sect, and I'm trying to find out if one of his own whacked him. She thinks it might be another sect because they wore Sabbath dress in the middle of the week. A *shtreimel* is a unique broad-rimmed fur hat worn only on Sabbath and special occasions.' Decker made a face. 'Something's off, Donatti. Sounds like someone was playing dress-up.'

'Any idea who?'

'I wish.' To Shayndie, Decker said, ' Did you recognize *any* of the men?'

A quick shake of the head.

'You're sure about that?'

'It happened very fast,' she mumbled. 'I was scared.'

But Decker felt certain that the girl was holding back. 'Have you talked to your parents since it happened?'

Wide-eyed, she shook her head furiously. Then she grabbed on to Chris. 'Can we please leave, Mr Donatti. I'll do *anything* you want. I swear I will. Anything! Just don't make me go back with him.'

At that moment, the little girl meant her every word. For Donatti, she would have spread her legs in an eye wink. It made Decker sick to the core.

'Please, Mr Donatti?' Shayndie begged.

'Sure. You did a good job.'

'Thank you!' She burst into tears.

'Wait here a moment, Shayndie. I want to talk—'

'Don't leave me!' She glommed on to his body. 'Please, don't—'

'*Stop it!*' Donatti plucked her off his body, as if he were dusting off a piece of lint. He spoke low and menacing. 'You wait here, understand?'

'Don't make me go with him.'

'Did I say that?' He took her by the shoulders and shook her hard. 'Did I *say* that?'

'No.'

'You shut up, you stay put, and let me get rid of him! Then we can both go back.'

Tears were pouring down her cheek. But she nodded okay.

Donatti took several large strides forward, looped his arm around Decker's back, and drew him out of Shayndie's earshot. With her protector at a distance, Shayndie started to move toward him. Immediately, Donatti warned her back with a look. To Decker, he said, 'She's a virgin.'

Decker regarded Donatti's face. 'How do you know?'

'Because I asked her.'

'And you think she's telling the truth?'

'I know she is. Before I nailed her, I asked her. I told her it was very, very important that she tell me the truth. I told her I didn't care a rat's ass one way or the other, but it had to be the truth. Because the one thing I hated was being lied to. She swore. She wasn't lying. She was a virgin.'

Decker took in his eyes. 'A few seconds ago, you said she *is* a virgin. Present tense.'

Donatti looked at him in mock confusion. 'Did I say that?'

'Yes, you did.'

Chris smiled enigmatically.

Bastard. Decker said, 'Okay, Donatti, where do we go from here?'

'I'll contact you.'

'What about her parents?'

'Nothing until I contact you. You tell her parents, all bets are off. You tell her parents, that also means you broke your word. That means you're a dead man.'

'Then it's a good thing my will's in order. When will you contact me?'

'I don't know. You'll have to be patient.'

'Patience is my middle name. Right now, I'm inclined to poke around closer to home. See if I can find out who these religious guys are, now that I know she's safe with you. I'm assuming that my nosing about won't step on your toes?'

'Not at all. I don't know anything about the hit. More important, I don't care. If all the Jews in the world suddenly dropped dead, I'd be happy. More money for me.'

'You're a hopeless sentimentalist, Donatti, just like the Nazis.'

'You know I'm not a big Wagner fan.'

Decker said, 'If I come up with some faces, I'll want to talk to her again. What do I do?'

Donatti said, 'I'll call you.'

'And I can show her the faces?'

'If you play by my rules, it can be arranged.'

'Thanks.' Decker rested his hand on the young man's shoulder. 'I suppose I shouldn't tell you this, Donatti, but you've been helpful.'

'Good.' Donatti grinned. 'I like doing favors.'

'I'll bet.' Decker started to walk away. Donatti caught him by the arm. 'I fooled around with her,

Decker, but she's still whole. Out of respect for you, I didn't fuck her.'

Decker nodded. 'I appreciate it.' He waited a moment. 'Did she know anything sexually?'

Donatti's lips curled upward. 'I usually charge money for details, Lieutenant.'

Decker kept his anger inside. He spoke deliberately. 'Should I be concerned about a *molestation* angle?'

'You know, I don't think I've been with someone that innocent since Terry.' Donatti let out a soft laugh. 'Jesus, even Terry knew what a hard-on was. I'm sure last night was the first time that Shayndie had ever *seen* a cock, let alone *touched* one. That girl is from another century.'

Decker was quiet.

'She wasn't being diddled,' Donatti said. 'I'd stake my life on it.'

'All right. That's helpful.'

Donatti looked upward. 'Do you have any idea how much I could get for her in the white-slave trade? I have at least three Middle Eastern clients who'd give a fortune to rape a Jewish virgin. They'd whisk her out in a private plane, take her to their country, pass her around, then sell her to a brothel.'

Decker blurted, 'Whatever you'd charge, I'll pay it.'

'You couldn't afford it.' Donatti bit his lip. 'Maybe we can arrange a trade with your wife.' Immediately, he backed away, holding out his palms for a shield. 'I'm kidding! Don't worry. I'll keep Shayndie safe. After you find out what happened, and it's okay for her to go home, I'll return her to you – unharmed and intact.'

Decker was still breathing hard. 'Thanks. Thanks a lot, Chris.'

'That makes another favor you owe me.'

'You're keeping score.'

'You bet your Jewish ass I'm keeping score.'

20

Decker awoke with a jolt, drenched in sweat and shaking. It was eight in the morning – Rina had already left the bed – and since sleep was out of the question, he decided to grab the day. Knowing that Shayndie was alive and relatively safe, he could concentrate on the murder. Since Chaim had shown only scant interest in his brother's homicide, Decker was forced to interview the only person who had truly felt every inch of the loss. Emmanuel Lieber was sitting shiva at his house in Quinton. The idea of intruding upon an old man's sorrow made Decker feel queasy, but if it brought results, perhaps it would be worth it. After a quick recitation of the morning prayers, he mentally planned his day. First he'd pay the shiva call, then he'd contact Micky Novack, hoping that the detective had made headway on the case. By then, maybe he'd hear from Donatti.

Maybe.

Decker didn't want to change his ticket a third time. But if Donatti didn't deliver the girl today, Decker would be forced to rearrange his flight. His conscience wouldn't let him do anything less. Shaynda's safety was paramount.

The trick was how to explain it to Rina.

His wife was sitting with Hannah at the breakfast table, the little girl garbed in a new red-black-and-white houndstooth sweater and pleated red wool skirt. There were sneakers on her feet, and her nose was buried in a book. Decker kissed his wife, then his daughter.

'You look like you're ready to play the bagpipes,' he quipped.

Hannah didn't answer him. Absorbed in her book, she didn't even hear him.

Rina smiled. 'I like bagpipes.' She looked her husband up and down. 'I've got a brilliant idea, Peter. I'll play the bagpipes if you wear a kilt.'

'My legs are private property.' He poured a big bowl of Cheerios and put two pieces of bread in the toaster. 'Where are you and the little colleen off to today?'

'Hannah's going to play with her new New York best friend. I'm going shopping.'

'What a shock!'

'Make fun all you want. The bargains are too good to resist.'

'I begrudge you nothing. Are you taking the car?'

'No, I have a ride into the city. I figured that you'd need the car.'

'You're right. I'm going over to Quinton.' He filled a mug with coffee, then buttered his toast. 'How was the family last night?'

'As expected.' Rina sighed. 'How was it for you?'

'As expected.' He turned to his daughter. 'Hi, Hannah. Remember me? Your father? The tall one?'

She looked up and smiled. 'Hi, Daddy.'

'Hi, Hannah. I love you.'

'I love you, too.' She put down her book. 'Do you like my sweater?'

'It's a beautiful sweater.'

'Eema bought it for me.'

'Eema has good taste.'

'I'm going to play today with Leah Sora Estee Beryl. She should be in school, but she has the chicken pox. But I don't have to worry about the chicken pox because I already had the shot.'

'That's good.'

'Kenny Talbot, a boy at my school, he had the chicken pox. After he came back to school, he brought a picture with his face all full of poxes. It was yucky. I hope Leah Sora Estee Beryl is not that bad.'

'Is that one person? Leah Sarah—'

'Sora,' Hannah corrected.

'Is that one girl?'

'Yes, she's one girl with lots of names,' Rina said. 'Are you ready, Chanaleh?'

Hannah nodded, got up, and kissed her father's cheek. 'I'm glad you didn't name me four names. It wouldn't fit on my math sheets at school.'

Rina took her daughter's hand and helped her on with her coat. 'You like the coat?'

'The coat is lovely.'

'Thirty dollars.'

'That's a good price.'

'No, it's a steal. Learn your shopping lexicon. Come along, sweetheart. Let your father eat breakfast in peace.'

Decker bid them good-bye. Fortified with Cheerios, two pieces of toast, a large glass of orange juice, and four cups of coffee, he felt ready to fulfill a mission.

Emmanuel Lieber lived in a one-story white clapboard house with a wraparound porch, and a wood-shingled roof. The front lawn was dead from winter fallout, but several large trees hinted green-bud wood teasing of spring renewal. A stone walk-way led up to an old oak door coated with peeling varnish. As Decker climbed the three steps up, he could hear the clatter of conversation – low, deep voices. Standing on the porch, he peeked through the window and saw swarms of men dressed in black Chasidic garb. No *shtreimels* however. That could be significant.

He was about to lift the knocker, but then the door opened and three Chasids flew out, eyes turned downward, hands behind their backs, their *payot* flying as they fast-walked past him.

Decker went inside.

The crowd was so thick, so without light and air, that he felt as if he were in the middle of a twister. The sheer density made it hard to move. Eventually, he was swept toward the front, into the grief-stricken family that included three sisters, one brother and a father steeped in abject tragedy. They were seated on pillows that rested on the floor, their eyes saturated with deep despair. Mr Lieber and Chaim wore black pants, black shoes, and white shirts that had been intentionally ripped directly under the collar: the indication of mourning. Atop their heads were large black yarmulkes. The three sisters wore somber-colored skirts and blouses also torn near the collar. Two of the three women had on wigs; Raisie had elected to wear a scarf.

Jonathan was at his elbow. He guided him into a corner and offered Decker some coffee.

'I'm fine.'

'Soda, water?'

'Nothing. I'm fine.'

'Thanks for coming down,' Jonathan told him. 'Especially since you must be on a very tight schedule.'

'Not too bad, actually. The plane doesn't leave until nine tonight.'

'Oh . . .' An uncomfortable pause. 'I thought you were leaving this afternoon.'

Decker regarded his half brother. 'Tonight.'

Jonathan nodded. 'Good. I mean, not good. I mean . . . I'm sure you'll be thrilled to leave.'

'You're looking tense, Jon. Anything wrong?'

Jonathan hesitated. 'No . . . just. What can I say, Akiva? What can I say?'

'You can tell me what's on your mind.'

'Me, I just can't . . . stop thinking about Shayndie.'

Guilt tugged at Decker's heart. 'It's terrible.'

Jonathan nodded but didn't add anything. His gaze wandered over the crowd, resting on Chaim's face. The two of them locked eyes, but then Chaim turned away.

Jonathan said, 'Let me introduce you to my father-in-law.'

'It's all right.'

'No, no. I insist.'

Although Decker didn't know Jonathan that well, he knew when someone was unsettled. Unsettled was the euphemism. If Decker were objective, he'd bet that Jonathan was sitting on something. But this was not the time for confrontation, especially since Decker hadn't owned up to the truth last night. Maybe he could pull it out of Jonathan later on.

A moment later, Decker was standing in front of a beaten old man. Mr Lieber's eyes went to Decker's face and failed to register any recognition. But then he noticed Jonathan . . . standing next to this strange large man in a brown suit. Quickly, the old man put two and two together. He acknowledged him with a nod.

Decker nodded back.

Lieber was a much bigger man than Decker had expected – wide across the chest and face, with a large, drooping nose and thick, prominent lips. Once he might have had a solid square jaw, but his jowls covered the bone structure. His eyes were hooded and multicolored, changing tint depending on the light and atmosphere – anatomical mood rings.

Chaim stood up, his eyes having darkened into black orbs of fury. Decker wondered what he had done to make this man hate him so much. It wasn't as if Decker had hurt his daughter. On the contrary, he had actually found a link to the missing girl. He felt terrible about keeping the secret, and for one brief all-too-human moment, he thought about relating the wonderful news to Chaim. But if it got back to Donatti and if she was harmed because of his indiscretion, then who would be at fault?

No, it was better to be overcautious.

'I had thought that you had left,' Chaim told him.

'Tonight,' Jonathan said.

'Why tonight? What business do you have here?'

Decker threw his head back. 'Rina wanted to stay for the funeral. And I had things to wrap up, Rabbi Lieber. You don't involve people in your affairs and then suddenly leave without saying thanks.'

'Are you admonishing my behavior because I didn't thank you?'

'Chaim,' Jonathan started out.

But Decker held up his palm to silence him. 'No,

Rabbi Lieber, not at all. I meant the cops who had helped me. I'd like to remain on good terms with them.'

'Well, you don't have to worry about New York's finest because they certainly haven't helped much, have they?'

'I'm so sorry, sir. This must be so agonizing for you.'

'Terribly agonizing.'

But he sounded more angry than despairing. His eyes narrowed, his body thrust toward Decker in an antagonistic pose. 'You don't know anything, Lieutenant. Go home.'

'Chaim!' a raspy voice chided. '*Es pass nisht. Vus machst-du? Setze dich!*'

'But Papa—'

'*Nisht gebest mir de Papa. Setze dich non! Nisht dray mir a kop.*'

Reluctantly, Chaim returned to his pillow. Mr Lieber motioned Decker to a chair. 'Sit down, Lieutenant. Do you want some tea?'

'No, thank you, Mr Lieber. Do you want some tea?'

'No, I don't want anything right now.' He looked at his son-in-law. 'Jonathan, get the man some tea.'

'Really, I'm—' Decker stopped himself. 'Yes, of course. Thank you.'

'While you're up, get some for Papa,' Raisie chimed in.

'I don't want any—'

'Papa, you must drink!'

'I'll have only if you'll have,' Decker proposed.

The old man nodded.

Jonathan sighed heavily and went to the kitchen for tea.

The old man leaned forward. 'You will forgive Chaim's manners. He is under terrible, terrible stress.'

'Of course, Mr Lieber. I'm sure my presence has added to it. I just wanted to pay my respects to you. Then I'll go.'

'He expects miracles. For that, he must pray to the *Abishter*.'

' "It is better to take refuge in *Hashem* than to rely on man",' Decker quoted from the Hallel service.

'Yes, exactly.' Lieber's eyes watered. 'It's so terrible.'

'Yes, it is. I'm so sorry.'

'Horrible.' Lieber wiped his eyes. 'And you are leaving tomorrow?'

'Maybe tonight. Maybe tomorrow. We'll see how it goes.'

Donatti had told him to wait for his call, but how long could Decker be patient?

'At the *hespid* yesterday, I spoke to people who worked with Ephraim. I also spoke with others who knew your son. Ephraim seemed like a man who was full of heart.'

'Who did you speak to?' Chaim challenged.

'A woman named Luisa—'

'Ephraim gave her money,' Chaim sneered. 'Of course she liked him.'

'And since when is *tzedaka* considered a bad thing?' Raisie asked him.

'Charity begins at home,' Chaim said.

'Don't fight,' another sister castigated. 'Don't we have enough to deal with?'

Raisie regarded Decker, then pointed to her sisters. 'This is Esther; this is Malka.'

Decker offered his condolences to them.

'And who were the others who knew Ephraim?' Mr Lieber wanted to know.

'I spoke to a man who met Ephraim in an organization called Emek Refa'im.'

'Yes, yes,' Mr Lieber said. 'The counseling place.'

'A place for drug addicts, Papa,' Chaim stated.

'A place to *help* them,' Mr Lieber insisted. 'He was doing so well, Lieutenant. Ephraim was.'

'So I understand.'

The old man sighed. 'So well.' Tears in his eyes. 'In the business, too.'

'How long had he been working with you and Chaim?'

Lieber didn't answer.

'Two years,' Chaim said dully.

'Two years,' the old man repeated. 'He enjoyed it. I could tell he liked the business.'

Chaim rolled his eyes, but the old man didn't see it.

'I'm sure he loved being part of the business,' Decker said. 'What was his job there?'

'What difference does it make now?' Chaim snapped.

'The man wants to know,' Mr Lieber said. 'He was a jack of all boxes—'

'Jack of all trades,' Chaim corrected.

'He'd work the register, stock the shelves, take inventory in the stores and in the warehouse, fill in if people didn't show up.'

'Assuming he'd show up,' Chaim said.

'Chaim!' Raisie chastised. 'Please!'

Chaim rubbed his face. 'I'm sorry.'

Jonathan returned with the tea. He handed a glass to his father, then to Decker. 'Thanks, Jon.'

Chaim said, 'I'm going upstairs for a moment, Papa. I'll be back.'

'I'll go with you,' Jonathan said.

'Sure. Come on.'

The two men trudged through the crowds, standing close to each other, an unspoken message between them.

Sitting on something.

Did the girl bolt? Had she made contact with them? Last night, she had been petrified to have anything to do with any of her kinsmen, but a new dawn often brought a new perspective. Maybe she had decided that the safest place was home.

Or maybe he was reading too much into the camaraderie. Maybe they both wanted to get away from the crowd – which was certainly legitimate.

Mr Lieber sipped his tea. 'I thought things were working out.'

Decker returned his concentration to the old man. 'I'm sure they were working out.'

'Then *why*? *Why*?' Watery, rainbow-colored eyes took in Decker's face. 'The police said that it was drugs. Why was he with the drugs?'

Decker didn't answer, masking his silence by drinking the diluted brew.

Mr Lieber shook his head. 'The flesh is weak.'

'Mr Lieber,' Decker whispered, 'maybe it wasn't drugs. Can you think of anyone who might want to hurt him?'

'No! No one!'

'I hate to ask you this, sir. But maybe you or your son have made someone angry?'

'Me?' The old man shrugged. 'I make all my

customers angry. Jews are impossible people to work with. Everyone wants a bargain. You don't give them what they want, they complain. But no one would get mad enough to hurt me.'

'Can I ask you another personal—'

'Ask, ask.' Lieber put the tea glass down on the floor and took Decker's free hand. 'Ask.'

'Did you owe anyone money?'

'Just the bank . . . business loans. Nothing that would require Citibank to strong-arm me or my sons.'

'No individual loans?'

'No one. I have money in a business account, money in a savings account. Nothing too big: Business hasn't been so hot lately. My sources go under, lots of theft . . . always happens when times are tough. But not tough enough that I have to borrow from the loan sharks, if that's what you're asking.'

'Yes.' Decker placed his empty mug by his chair. 'That's what I was asking.' He formulated his thoughts. 'What about employees? Any problems with any specific individual?'

'Not that I know of. Most have been with me for ever. The part-timers . . . that's Chaim's job. Hiring and firing. We get some turnover with the shleppers, the men who load and unload the heavy boxes at the warehouse. You hire who you can get at minimum wage. Sometimes it's recent aliens with green cards, sometimes it's high-school dropouts, sometimes students looking for a summer job.'

'Whoever's available.'

'Yes. If you have some questions about them, ask Chaim.'

'I would if he'd talk to me. And if he doesn't want to, it's understandable.'

'Yes, it is,' the old man agreed. 'Maybe another time.'

'Maybe.'

Decker could see that others wanted to draw close to Mr Lieber, to participate in the mitzvah of comforting the mourner – *menachem avel*. He got up and uttered the customary Hebrew words of comfort to Raisie and her sisters, then to Mr Lieber. He nudged his way through the crowd to the back of the room.

Chaim and Jonathan weren't visible anywhere. So be it. Without fanfare, Decker left. As soon as he was outside, he let go with a deep exhalation. It had been so stifling in there, he hadn't realized how much his chest had been hurting. Walking down the pathway, breathing a bit easier, he heard a car screech as it pulled up to the curb.

Minda Lieber rushed out of the dented van, slamming the door behind her. Completely disheveled, she had improperly paired the buttons of her dress with the corresponding buttonholes. Her wig was messy and askew. She was flapping her hands and weeping hysterically. Decker grabbed her.

'What's wrong?'

She tried to break free of his hold, screaming how dare he touch her – a married woman. But Decker only held on tighter.

'Minda. What . . . is . . . *wrong?*'

The woman broke into high-pitched screams. 'They found her! She's *dead*! Oh God, she's *dead. She's dead*—'

'*What!*' Decker's heart was hammering against his chest.

'She's dead! Can't you hear! She's dead! She's dead! She's dead!'

The woman's knees buckled. Decker caught her as she passed out.

21

He was operating on overdrive, pure speed and adrenaline tearing out of upstate and hitting the city by eleven, and getting off the Parkway at 132nd. He found parking a block away, then ran over to the building. Punching the button. This time, it was Donatti on the intercom, annoyance in the bastard's voice. Breathing hard, Decker announced his name and was buzzed in. The reception area was empty – no guard, no secretary – and that made sense because it was lunchtime. Decker marched through the metal detector, setting it off with his keys. He didn't bother to retrace his steps because Donatti had opened the inner door. The kid was wearing jeans over a loose Hawaiian shirt. Decker stomped past him, into the studio.

Donatti's irritation turned to anger. 'What the hell do you think you're doing?'

Dozens of pornographic photos were spread out over a large conference table – snapshots of teenage girls with pursed lips and bedroom eyes doing things to gray-haired, potbellied men. Obscene pictures made even more outrageous because Donatti was a hell of a photographer. Rage boiled over in Decker's gut, turning his face into something feral. Donatti caught the look, his eyes equally furious.

'Who the *fuck* are you to judge me?! Get the fuck out—'

Decker caught him by the throat and threw him against the wall. Using his body weight, he leaned his knee hard against Donatti's groin, tightening the fingers around the son of a bitch's throat, trying to pin his hands with his shoulders. The harder Donatti struggled, the more pressure Decker applied to the windpipe. He pressed his kneecap harder against the kid's crotch.

'What did you *do* to her?' Decker growled out.

Red-faced and flushed, Chris managed to shake his head.

'*Talk to me, dammit!*' He gripped harder and spoke louder. '*What did you do to her?*'

'Who?' he whispered hoarsely.

'*Shayndie! She's dead!* What did you do—'

'Noth—'

'*STOP LYING, YOU MOTHERFUCKING PIECE OF SHIT! WHAT DID YOU DO TO HER?*'

'I can't talk . . .'

His eyes rolled back in his head. Decker loosened his fingers, giving him enough air to breathe and speak. 'Answer my question, or I'll kill you.'

'Jesus, Mary, and Joseph, I just saw her *six hours* ago,' he choked out in a whisper. 'She was *fine*. Let me *go!*'

Decker gave a final squeeze, then abruptly pushed him away. Donatti fell down to his knees, holding his throat, gasping for breath. Decker paced with hard clomps against the wooden floor.

'You said she was *safe* with you! You said she'd be *okay*! You told me you'd take care of it, and I trusted you, Donatti. Either you were lying or you fucked up. And by fucked up, I mean fucked up, *big time*!'

Still red from oxygen buildup, Donatti could only stare at him. He panted like an overworked bulldog, then abruptly broke out in a ripe, rich sweat, drenching his face, shirt, and pants. His mouth began to spew froth, and for a brief moment, Decker thought he was going to have a seizure. Instead, Donatti got wide-eyed, stood up and kicked the underside of a conference table so hard that the pictures flew up, wafted in the air, then rained down. Another kick and the table fell over.

From that moment on, every item in the room became a projectile – articles from his prop box, his tripod, stands, chairs, lamps, the coffeemaker, the mugs, his booze, his glasses, whatever Chris could lay his hands on – except his cello. Objects whizzed by at Mach speed – the kid had an arm – and although nothing was deliberately directed toward Decker, it didn't matter. So many things were flying rapidly and with such force. Solid objects hurtled across the room, crashing and smashing, splattering shards and blades of ceramic and glass. Decker couldn't step or move anywhere. He balled himself up in a corner.

'*Donatti, stop!*' he ordered.

But Donatti didn't stop. A decanter was pitched in Decker's direction, missing his head by inches. A quick sidestep had saved his skull from massive injury.

'*Donatti—*'

CRASH!

'Chris . . .' Decker inched his way over to him, using his arms and jacket for protection. '*Stop it, dammit! Chris!*'

He touched Donatti's shoulder. He should have known better. Even so, he would have successfully evaded the blow.

Except he had forgotten that Chris was left-handed.

Decker took the clip full-faced, staggering three steps backward before he hit the wall and collapsed. His vision was starry; his head seemed as if broken into a million pieces. When he could see again, he realized – with some minor satisfaction – that his jaw was whole. His nose might be another story. It was bleeding profusely, as was his lip. He could see and hear, at least well enough to realize that Donatti had moved on – from throwing to ranting.

' . . *know* what this is going to do to my reputation? Do you *know* what this is going to do to my bitches? If I don't find this motherfucker and fast, you might as well put a *fucking bullet* through my *fucking head* because I'm as good as *fucking dead*!'

Donatti was frothing at the mouth. He was shaking so hard his teeth were clattering. His face was dripping like a window in a rainstorm, sweat just pouring off his forehead. He was stomping back and forth, heels of his boots stamping dents into the floor. Muttering, swearing, sweating, spewing. Then he punched the wall, knocking a hole in the drywall.

Still winded from the slam in the face, Decker continued to sit, hunched up on the ground. He wiped his nose on his shirt. 'Help me up.'

Donatti whipped around and glowered in the direction of the voice, his eyes searching the room. When they found Decker, they regarded him as if he were a stranger.

'I *said*, help me up, dammit!' Decker ordered.

Donatti stopped pacing, still staring at Decker's face. But he extended a hand and hoisted Decker back on his feet. Then he took two giant steps backward, shaking with rage and neurotransmitters. 'Are you going to coldcock me if I turn my back?'

'Don't tempt me!' Decker growled. He smoothed out his clothing and gingerly touched his face. 'You need a drink. I'm going to get you some booze. Keep your friggin' hands in your pockets!'

Donatti's voice was still hoarse from being choked. He cleared his throat. 'Get your face some ice while you're at it.'

Pulling out a single bottle of Scotch that had managed to survive the onslaught, Decker gave it to the kid. Then he took out an ice tray and liberated the frozen cubes. He wrapped them up in a paper towel and placed it against his rapidly swelling face.

Donatti offered the bottle to Decker, who grabbed it and took a healthy swig. Then he returned it. Chris took another drink.

Passing the bottle back and forth for another fifteen minutes, neither talking, but both of them snorting and swearing. The room was a disaster area – hot and stale and reeking of male stink. Decker felt his stomach lurch, but refused to show weakness by sitting down.

Minutes passed – five of them, then ten. Finally, Donatti took out his keys and opened the door to his private, bug-free office. As soon as they were both inside – the door locked and the switches on – they both collapsed into chairs. Donatti draped his upper body down on the table, cradling his head in his arms. His eyes were closed. He was still breathing hard, still sweating, although not nearly as copiously.

'I gotta think.'

'You didn't clean her—'

'No, I didn't *clean her*. Why would I *clean* her?'

'Money.'

'If I wanted money, I would have *sold* her.'

Silence. Decker nursed his very sore face. The ice had turned to cold water, the towel clammy in his hands. 'Any ideas?'

'Shut up and let me think.'

'Is it possible that someone found out—'

'No.' Donatti lifted his head, then sat up. '*No!* I've got people watching—'

'They were bought off.'

'It's impossible. They would know what I'd do.' He shook his head with despair. 'She must have left on her own.'

'After last night, I find that hard to believe.'

'After this morning, I find it *impossible* to believe!' Donatti reached into his file cabinet and pulled out a pack of cigarettes. 'I gave it up for Terry.' He liberated a smoke. 'Filthy habit.' He lit one up and exhaled a gush of tar and nicotine. 'But right now, my nerves are shot.'

'Give me one.'

Donatti lit another smoke and passed it to Decker. Within moments, the room took on a chemical haze. 'When I left this morning, that little girl was so clingy, I had nicknamed her Saran Wrap.'

'So what happened?' Decker took in deep puffs. He'd forgotten how wonderful a nicotine rush was.

'I don't know.'

'Someone took her—'

'Impossible!'

'No, Chris. Nothing's impossible!'

Donatti exhaled a plume of sour, booze-laden breath. 'She left on her own.' He stubbed out his cigarette and pulled out two water bottles, tossing one to Decker. 'Something changed her mind.'

Decker drank greedily. 'Any ideas what?'

'No.' Donatti looked at him. 'I told you she was unstable. She was even more freaked after she met with you. *You* probably scared her away.'

'Me?' Decker answered.

'Yeah, you! You freaked her out.'

'Then it was up to you to calm her back down—'

'*Fuck you, Decker!*'

Neither one spoke as they gulped down water. Decker touched his nose. It was throbbing with pain. 'Assuming she left on her own, where could she have gone?'

'I don't know. There's no place as safe as mine.' Donatti gritted his teeth. 'I can't imagine why she bolted! It doesn't make sense. You gotta leave now. I gotta make some calls.'

Decker said, 'You want to do me a big favor?'

'No. Get the *fuck* out of here!'

'Stop being so vile!' Decker finished the smoke and the water. 'You want to make some headway, do yourself a favor and stay out of it. At least, for now.'

Donatti jerked his head up. 'I think my fist scrambled your brains. Get out of here!' He pulled out a gun. 'OUT!'

'Yeah, yeah, yeah.' Decker felt his lip. That throbbed, too. 'What is that? A Walther double automatic? Twenty-four rounds, right? It's a nice one.'

Donatti squinted at him, then erupted into laughter. 'I'm glad you approve.'

'Put it down, Chris . . . please.'

'Since you said please.' He placed it on the table and picked up the booze.

'Donatti, let's think this out logically,' Decker began. 'I came to New York as this big-cop lieutenant to help out with a homicide. What happened? I fanned, kiddo. Zilch as far as Lieber's murder, and now Shayndie's dead. The local heat have got to be thinking that I'm a bust – this big, dumb lug from hick town L.A. who couldn't detect his way out of a paper bag.'

He dabbed his face and nose with the wet towel.

'It's not far from the truth.'

Donatti regarded the lieutenant's face, then passed him the bottle.

Decker took a drink. 'Right now, I'm a washout. No one's afraid of me. Not the Liebers, not the cops, not you, and not the bastards who whacked Shaynda and Ephraim. I'm a steaming turd, my man. No one wants to get *near* me. But you . . . you're different, Donatti. You've got the rep as a real nasty dude. If you start nosing around and the perps get wind of your involvement, they're going to rabbit. Even worse, if you screw up, you're dead meat. Me, on the other hand, I screw up, it's par for the course. For the time being, it's in both of our best interests to keep you a guarded secret.'

The room was quiet.

Donatti banged his fist on the table, wincing in pain. The gun jumped up and down, landing with the barrel pointed at Decker's stomach.

'Get that thing out of here,' Decker groaned.

'Shit!' Donatti picked up the Walther and stowed it underneath his shirt. Rage invaded his face. 'They got one of my *girls*, Decker. It's *personal*!'

'But if she bolted, and they didn't take her from under your nose, it isn't personal. Think about it for a moment, Chris. Say I did scare her into bolting. Then whoever popped Shaynda didn't even know she had an association with you. If that's the case, you sure don't want it advertised that she was one of yours, right?'

Donatti was silent.

'Talk to your people, Chris. Maybe they'll tell you she simply rabbited.'

'Is it possible you were followed last night?' Donatti said.

'I don't see how!' Decker said. 'I took so many twists and turns, it would have been impossible to tail me. Not because I was so clever, but because I was lost.'

'Did you check for a tail?'

'Christopher, that's offensive.'

He threw his head back and looked at the ceiling.

Decker said, 'Talk to your girls.'

'Of course I'll *talk to* my girls.' He ran his fingers atop his stubble of hair. 'Man, there goes that trust. I was invincible to them. They'll never feel the same way again.'

'I would think just the opposite, Donatti. *If* Shayndie ran away on her own accord, it'll make you look stronger in their eyes. They'll have to be thinking, "See what happens when someone tries to make it on her own. See what happens when I don't have Mr Donatti's protection." That's what I'd be thinking.'

Decker raised a brow.

'Am I right about this?'

Donatti didn't answer. He picked up the bottle,

then put it down, his face restored to its former expressionless self.

'You'll have to trust me on this one.' Decker took the wet towel off his face. Now his nose was frozen as well as sore. 'As tempted as you are, you've got to stay out of it. You're an excellent hunter, Donatti, when you know who your prey is. But in this case, we don't know the prey. That's my specialty. Finding the bastards. Let me handle it.'

Again Donatti looked at him.

'Yeah? I'm right? You know that.' Decker nodded. 'You back off and you won't be sorry. Because I'm going to find this son of a bitch and put him in deep freeze. Don't worry. He'll be taken care of.'

'Not the way I had in mind.'

'It's true we have different styles,' Decker said. 'This entire mess has to do with my business – my family. You owe it to me so I can redeem myself. Give me this one or we'll both end up in deep shit.' He touched his nose and lip. 'How the hell am I going to explain this to my wife?'

'Just tell her some random nutcase came up and slugged you. It's New York. She'll believe you.' Donatti rubbed his head and pushed the bottle over to him. 'I don't see what I missed . . . There must be something else going on.'

'Maybe there is.' Decker inhaled. It hurt to breathe. 'If you give me a chance to figure this out, then maybe we'll both know what happened.'

Silence.

Decker needed Donatti's cooperation; he didn't want to get in Chris's way. Mistakes could be lethal. 'So you'll back off, right?'

'No, I won't back off,' Donatti snapped back. 'But

since it's your family, I'll give you a twenty-four-hour head start. Then it's everyone for himself.'

'Even I can't work that fast. Seventy-two hours, Chris. At the end of three days – solve or no solve – I'm out of here.'

'Right.'

'Donatti, I'm not jerking my chain over this. No one has a one-hundred-percent solve rate.'

'What's yours?'

'High enough. But it's not one hundred percent.'

'Forty-eight hours.'

'Sixty hours, starting now. You broke my nose, you bastard. You owe it to me.'

Chris leaned over the desk and examined Decker's features. 'No, I didn't break your nose. I just clipped it. I got you on the cheek – bone's swollen, but not too bad. It wasn't full force, Decker. If I had meant business, your face would have been a Cubist study.'

'If you're asking me to thank you, forget it. Sixty hours.'

'This is *stupid*! You want me to back off until you leave town, I'll do it. But I'm not paying for your funeral.'

'I'll keep that in mind.'

'I'm serious, Lieutenant. You may be a good cop in L.A., but out here you don't know horseshit.'

'So fill me in.'

'That's impossible. Could you fill me in on what makes a good Homicide cop in Los Angeles? These kinds of things are intuitive. I've lived on these streets and with these people all my life. It's just this . . . feel – this sixth sense. Here I can do in a day what you couldn't do in a year. I'd actually be an asset to you.'

'I don't think a partnership would enhance either

one of us in the reputation department.'

'I've worked with cops before.'

'Not honest ones.'

'No such animal.'

Decker didn't argue. What was the point?

'I could turn you into a homicidal maniac in a minute because I know your weakness. But why bother? Cleaning your family isn't gonna solve my problems.'

'That is very true. Give me sixty hours solo, Donatti. I need to know I won't be stepping on your toes.'

'All right.' Donatti threw up his hands. 'I'll give you till Friday, if you last that long. If you land on your ass, I finish up my business my way. Deal?'

Decker said. 'You stay out of my hair—'

'I said, "Deal." Abruptly, Donatti jumped over the desk and planted his mouth on Decker's bloody lip. 'There. Signed, sealed, and delivered with a kiss.'

Decker grimaced as he wiped his mouth. 'What the hell was that for?'

'I dunno.' Donatti was amused by Decker's repugnance. 'I'm used to kissing authority figures. I used to kiss my uncle on the lips all the time.'

'I'm not your friggin' uncle, Chris.'

'You said you were my father figure. In therapy, they call that transference.'

'Then I take it all back.'

'You're squirming, Decker.' Donatti licked his lips and wiggled a pierced tongue. 'Could that be . . . *panic* raising its ugly head?'

'Christopher, for heaven's sake, grow up! I don't give a damn where you park it, as long as you keep your hands off my family and me. Why the hell should I care who you fornicate with?'

'You cared about Shayndie. You asked me not to bust her, and I didn't.' Donatti was wistful. 'Now I'm sorry I didn't. She wanted me to do it, and I said no. I was wrong. I should have fucked her. No one should die a virgin.'

22

Not a whit.

That was how much Decker believed Donatti. Walking back to the car via Riverside Drive, Decker kept his hands in his pockets as he stared over the parkway. The sun had burned several holes in the cloud cover, casting an intermittent glare over the sluggish Hudson. The streets were a traction nightmare, a mixture of motor oil and ice-chunked water. Cars were splashing sludge and mud curbside, causing Decker to do a two-step to avoid the mess. He touched his swollen face, biting back the pain with stoicism and Advil. He concentrated on his choices, the two very different paths he could take.

The first was to follow the bastard: to find out what was on Chris's dance card. Five seconds later, Decker nixed the idea. The man was savvy and would pick up a shadow as easy as a firearm. Plus, Donatti knew the city streets, and Decker did not. A tail would not only be useless, but would also alert Donatti to the already known – but as yet unstated – fact that Decker didn't trust him.

Give the man a round of applause. Donatti had put on a good exhibition. But the shock and outrage meant nothing. Chris was a pathological liar, having stalemated several lie-detector tests given by veterans in the field. He hadn't been perfect, but good enough to make the experts wonder. The most convincing piece of evidence that Chris had going for him was the 'Why bother?' What would he have gained by having Shayndie murdered? No real money in it, and now he had Decker bird-dogging his ass.

C.D. don't do nothing unless there's something in it for him.

For right now, it was handy to put Donatti on hold, not to discount him, but to direct the efforts elsewhere. Decker's second and slightly more viable option was to go back to square one and try to figure out what the hell went wrong. That required another look inside the Lieber family. Help from Chaim and Minda was a lost cause. They hated him with an irrational passion, having converted him into a convenient scapegoat – *azazel* in Hebrew, the symbolic sheep thrown off the cliff on Yom Kippur that atoned for the community's past sins. Tackling Minda and Chaim, in such horrendous times, was absolutely out.

But Jonathan was another matter.

Decker thought about Jonathan's reaction to the news of Shayndie's death. The surprise and shock were real enough, no debate there, but something about Jonathan's incredulous response was off, as if he hadn't even *considered* Shaynda's death a possibility. It had been out of character because Jon had been so skeptical during the five days prior to her death. He should have anticipated murder as a possibility, readying himself to help out his in-laws should things go bad. Jon was a clergyman; that was his job. Yet when the news hit, it seemed as if Jon were knocked down even harder than Chaim.

And then there was that irksome suspicion, the tweak in the gut that Decker had had during his shiva call just before his literal run-in with Minda.

Chaim and Jonathan are sitting on something.

Combining their secretive stance with the knowledge that Shaynda had either bolted or disappeared from Donatti, Decker concluded that the girl must have contacted Jon or Chaim somewhere between six in the morning – when Donatti last saw her – until her death roughly four hours later.

So it really wasn't a matter of going back to square one. What he needed to do was retrace those crucial four hours. Of course, what had occurred during those four hours were probably by-products of the murder five days ago.

He decided to start with the easiest chore: to change the plane tickets.

Decker had to remain in the city, but there was no earthly reason for Rina and Hannah to stay with him. That meant he'd have to convince his wife to go on to Florida *with* his daughter, and *without* him. Dealing with Donatti was a cakewalk compared to dealing with Rina. She seemed in constant denial of danger. But while she didn't have much regard for her own safety, she did care about Hannah. He'd use that angle – that too many deaths were traumatizing, and it was abusive to keep Hannah in such a morbid atmosphere.

He arrived at his car, but before going in, he placed a call to the Lazaruses on his cell. As expected, no one answered. Rina wasn't carrying a cell phone, and he had no idea where she was. Presumably, she hadn't heard the news, because if she had, she would have called him. He had no choice but to wait to hear from her.

The second call was to Jonathan's cell. The voice on the other end was a mixture of anger and fear. 'I can't talk right now, Akiva. As you know, things are a mess. Getting messier by the moment.'

'Fine. I'll come out to Quinton. I'll see you there in an hour—'

'No, *don't* do that!'

'Then where—'

'Akiva, I *can't* meet you right now. I have Chaim and Minda to deal with.'

'Jonathan, listen to me.' Decker spoke with purpose. 'Something was going on this morning before we all heard the terrible news. You *know* something. Or at the very least, you thought you knew something. Now, you can either deal with me, or I'll call in the police, and you can sort it out with them. Take your pick.'

Silence over the phone.

Jonathan said, 'You're blackmailing me.'

'That's not fair. But I'll let it slide because you're under duress.'

'I didn't mean . . . What do you *want* from me?'

Now it was pure anger.

Decker said, 'I'll meet you in Quinton – at Liberty Park right outside the Community Hall.'

'Not in public.'

Decker held back his own anger. 'Ashamed to be seen with me?'

'Akiva, *please!*'

It was a low blow. Decker apologized, but he didn't back down. 'Jon, you don't know me all that well, so let me clue you in. You brought me out. Now I'm involved. I don't get uninvolved just because you and your brother-in-law decide to scrap me. As a matter of fact, that kind of about-face makes me very curious.'

'It's not what you think.'

'So let's meet and you can explain it to me.'

Again no one spoke.

Decker said, 'Where'd they find her?'

'Fort Lee Park.'

'Where's that?'

'Jersey.'

Decker's heart started hammering. '*Where?* Like the middle of the state?'

'No, Fort Lee is right over the George Washington Bridge . . . five minutes out of the city. The park is commemorative grounds.'

'Big?'

'Yes.'

'Populated?'

'During the day, yes. It's a big place.'

Decker didn't know where he was last night, but he knew he had been more than five minutes out of the city. More like an hour from Manhattan. One possible scenario: Chris had murdered Shaynda after Decker had seen her, then dumped her on his way back to his place. But why would Donatti make the drop somewhere so visible and so close to his digs? He was a pro; he didn't like to advertise. Unless he was the type who'd do it for kicks – which really gave Decker something to worry about.

Jonathan cleared his throat over the line. 'Cops were thinking that maybe' – he cleared his throat again – 'maybe she's been hiding out there. Lots of spaces to hide because it's so big. Historical . . . goes back to revolutionary days. That's why it's so close to the bridge. Actually, they named the bridge after

George Washington because it's so close to Fort Lee.'

Jonathan was rambling. Decker interrupted him. 'I'd like to talk to the Quinton Police again. It's no problem for me to travel back upstate. If you don't want to meet with me in public, give me a private place.'

'We could meet in the city. They want me to go to Jersey . . . to identify the body . . .' There was a deep, depressed sigh over the line. 'Akiva, I don't know if I'm up for it.'

'Would you like me to come with you?'

'They need a relative to identify—'

'I know, Jon. I've never met the girl.' The lie came out as smooth as tanning oil. 'I just meant I'd accompany you for moral support.'

'That's very generous of you.' An exhalation. 'Thank you.'

'It's fine, Jon. When do you want to go?'

'Someone was going to meet me at the . . . the morgue at about five.'

Four hours from now. Decker said, 'That gives me enough time to come out to your neck of the woods. If you want to meet with me, fine. If not, we'll talk later. I'll go see the police. When you're ready to leave upstate, let me know and I'll follow you into New Jersey.'

Jonathan's voice dropped to a whisper. There were tears in his words. 'I think I might have messed up.'

Decker said, 'I'm sure you didn't. I'm sure you did what you thought you had to do. Let's meet in Quinton and talk about it.'

'Yes, that probably would be a good idea.' Now the anger was directed at himself. 'It's what I *should* have done this morning.'

'Wouldn't it be nice if we all had hindsight,' Decker consoled him. 'I know I'm persona non grata at the Liebers'. Tell me where we should meet.'

'I don't know . . . my mind's a blank.'

'Is there a Starbucks somewhere?'

'No, that wouldn't be good. Someone might see us.'

'How about we just talk in the car?' Decker suggested. 'With the windows fogged up, no one will be able to see inside.'

'No, that's . . .' Another clearing of the throat. 'The only thing that comes to mind is a Tattlers between Quinton and Bainberry.'

'Sounds good.'

No one spoke.

Jonathan said, 'Are you familiar with the chain?'

'Nope.'

'It's like a raunchy Hooters.'

'*This* is where you want to meet?'

'I've never been there, Akiva. It's the sole place I can think of where it's unlikely we'll meet anyone from the community. And if by chance we do see someone there, believe me, he'll pretend we don't exist.'

Dividing Quinton and Bainberry were six miles of untamed woods holding hundreds of bare trees and scores of tangled brush. The border between the two townships was demarcated by the Bainberry mall, a series of connected brick buildings sitting in a slick pool of asphalt parking. Like an errant child, Tattlers sat by itself, unattached and off to the left. Jonathan was waiting for him, his eyes jumping behind his glasses when he saw Decker's face.

The hostess, whose nametag said BUFFY, offered them a wide smile of capped teeth and a chest of cleavage and silicone. After seeing Donatti's pieces of work, Decker delighted in seeing a healthy, clothed – albeit scantily – woman who was clearly out of her teens. Because the uniforms lacked a lot of fabric, the temperature inside 'the gentlemen's club' was turned up to sauna level, encouraging the patrons to remove jackets and ties. Someone wanted the guys to feel comfortable. It probably made for better tips.

Decker slipped the hostess a twenty. 'A private booth in back.'

She averted her eyes – probably because he looked so messed up – but still managed a sly smile. 'Anyone in particular, sir?'

While he had out his wallet, he showed her his gold shield. 'Anyone who can bring me a large pot of strong coffee and make herself scarce.'

Immediately, the woman was all business. 'I think we can help you out, Detective. This way.'

She led them past the stage spectacle: three topless women in thongs gyrating under multicolored klieg lights. Men were hooting and catcalling, egging the girls to do lewder and lewder things. They were prevented from doing even ruder things by a sign that stated ABSOLUTELY, POSITIVELY NO TOUCHING!

Jonathan looked away, but Decker took them in, his eyes moving up and down their perfect bodies. They were young, beautiful, and energetic. They probably made good money, more bucks than working on circuit boards or changing hospital bedpans. Not to mention all the attention they got. The scene was pure circus, lacking only the big top.

Not that Decker was offended or surprised. In a

Donatti society that emphasized outcome rather than process, and stardom was worshiped above all, in a country where porn stars were trophies for rock stars, and people confessed to adultery and incest on national TV, well, then, why the hell not?

Except that Rina still ascribed to this outmoded concept of modesty as dated as Mayberry, USA. Over the last ten years, he guessed he had become an old-fashioned guy, and outmoded was just fine by him.

As requested, Buffy gave them a hidden booth in the corner, away from the flesh display, more like a peep show from where they were sitting.

'I'll get you the coffee, Detective.'

And she did . . . right away. 'Anything else?'

'Jon?'

The rabbi shook his head, keeping his eyes off Buffy's ample bosom.

'A bagel if you have it,' Decker answered.

'We have a bagel, lox, and cream cheese platter.'

'That's fine. And I'd also like a cup of ice and a napkin.'

Buffy nodded. 'Does it hurt?'

'Not too bad.'

'I'll place the order and get you the ice,' Buffy said. 'Ambrosia will be your server.'

'Thank you.' When she was gone, Decker said, 'Where do they come up with these names?'

Jonathan attempted a smile, but his eyes were glued to Decker's bruises.

Decker ignored the unstated question mark. 'When I worked Sex Crimes, I used to come to places like this all the time. Sleazier places, actually. Real down-and-dirty stuff. The girls were older, much more shopworn, perfect fodder for psycho bullies who liked to punch and rape. It was very sad.'

Jonathan nodded.

'These girls look healthier.'

'But for how long?' Jonathan asked. 'They're all under twenty-five, wouldn't you say?'

'Yeah, that's about right.'

'It's only a matter of time before their looks go. Then what?'

'Well, if they haven't sucked it up their veins or blown it up their noses, they might be okay. There's money to be made here. It's not as if they lost their opportunities to become rocket scientists.'

Buffy came back with the ice and napkin. 'I have some aspirin.'

Decker reached into his pocket and pulled out a bottle of Advil. 'Thank you, but I'm fine.' He poured the cubes into the napkin and placed them on his face.

'What happened?' Jonathan finally asked.

'Some street psycho took an instant dislike to me.'

'That's awful!' A hesitation. 'He just *punched* you?'

'I probably shouldn't have made eye contact. At least, he didn't jab any lethal bacteria up my veins.'

'Good Lord, don't say that!' Jonathan shook his head, rubbed his eyes under his glasses. 'I am so sorry. Are you in pain? I could probably get you a prescription for something stronger.'

'I'm fine. How bad is it?'

'You haven't looked in a mirror?'

'I've avoided it.'

'The entire right side of your face is reddish purple.'

'I'll just tell people I got hit in the face with a blueberry pie.'

'This is all so horribly depressing!'

'We've both had better days . . . better years.' Decker poured two cups of coffee. 'Anyone say how she died?'

'She was shot.' Tears in his eyes.

'Where?'

He shuddered. 'Why?'

'I'm just curious to see if there are any similarities to Ephraim's murder.'

'I would think it's a given – the same people who murdered Ephraim, murdered Shayndie.'

'That's logical, but you can't assume anything.' The ice felt soothing. 'Are you ready to tell me what you were holding back this morning?'

The rabbi fiddled with his napkin and doused his coffee with cream and sugar.

Decker said, 'Just start talking, Jon. It's easier after you get the first few words out.'

'Chaim called me around seven, seven-thirty. He told me he needed to talk to me in person.'

'You came out to Quinton?'

'Immediately,' Jonathan answered. 'His voice sounded agitated, but at least it was animated. As soon as I got there, he brought me into the basement so we could talk alone. He swore me to confidence. And that is why I didn't tell you, why I *couldn't* tell you.'

'I understand.'

'I'm only telling you now because you've threatened to go to the police. Not that I'd tell them anything – I'm entitled to claim pastoral confidentiality – but it would open up wounds. I thought it might be easier to deal with you than the police.' He lifted his eyebrows. 'Maybe not.'

'Believe it or not, my purpose is not to give people a hard time.'

'I know that.' Jonathan sighed. 'Now that she's gone, I suppose it's all irrelevant anyway.'

'Talk to me, Rabbi.'

'Chaim told me he had reason to believe that Shaynda was still alive. He said he had heard from certain people that she was okay.' He blinked back tears. 'Obviously, someone was mistaken. Perhaps Chaim misunderstood or it was wishful thinking on his part.'

'Or whoever Chaim talked to was lying. Who are these people?'

'At the time, Chaim couldn't or wouldn't say. He said he only confided in me because he knew I'd keep a secret. And secrecy was very important. If word got out, bad things could happen.'

'Did word get out?'

'I don't know, Akiva. I know that Chaim told me, but I don't know who else he told. At some point, when things are quieter, I'll ask him.'

'And that's all Chaim told you. That he had reason to believe that Shaynda was alive.'

'No. He also hinted that maybe there was some kind of ransom demand in the works. And if things went as planned, and someone needed to do an actual exchange of money for Shaynda, would I be willing to help?'

'What did you say?'

'I said of course I'd help. Anything.'

'And Chaim gave you no hints about Shaynda's location?'

'No.'

'So let me make sure I understand.' Decker took

267

the ice off. 'Chaim heard from some anonymous source that Shayndie was okay.'

'Yes.'

'And he thought that there might be a ransom demand. And if that happened, he asked you to be a go-between.'

'Yes.'

'Did Chaim actually talk to Shayndie?'

'I don't think so, no.'

'So the source could have been lying or mistaken, or Chaim could have misunderstood.'

'Yes.'

'Is exchanging the money for Shaynda the only favor that Chaim wanted you to do for him?'

'No.' Jonathan rubbed his eyes underneath his glasses. 'No, there was more.' Tension had crept into his voice. 'It seems that you've become an obstacle – a sticking point.'

'How so?'

'I don't know, Akiva. I do know that Chaim said that the kidnapper or ransom demander or whatever . . . that he wanted you out of the picture. As soon as possible.'

Decker raised his brow. 'Out of the picture in what way?'

'That you should leave the city, of course.' Jonathan's eyes got wide. 'That's what it means, right?'

Ambrosia – a robust blonde wearing a bikini top and broad shorts – served Decker a bagel and lox platter. He gave her a twenty. 'More coffee; then we're fine.'

'That's it?'

'That's it.'

Ambrosia frowned.

'It's nothing personal,' Decker said.

'Hey, you think I'm complaining?' Her accent was as broad as a flatiron. She stuffed the twenty into her shorts' pocket. 'So far today, this is my best tip for the least work. 'Bout a half hour ago, another gentleman tipped me a fifty. But I had to bend over a lot and pretend I didn't know he was copping a feel.' She looked at Decker. 'You're a cop. Why do they call it "copping a feel"?'

Jonathan said, ' "To cop" means to steal.'

'Heh-heh, that's funny.' Ambrosia tittered. 'That "cop" means to steal.'

Decker and Jonathan sat stone-faced.

'You don't see the humor in that?'

'You keep talking, I'm going to take back the twenty,' Decker said.

'Gotcha.' She came back with a new coffeepot, then left.

Decker said, 'Any idea who Chaim talked to?'

'No. Since Shayndie was fine, I felt it wasn't my place to ask questions.' Jonathan looked down. 'I'm sure they just meant for you to leave the city.'

'A strange way of putting it, then.' Decker shrugged. ' "Out of the picture". Has kind of a permanent ring, don't you think?'

Jonathan broke out in a sweat. 'I didn't take it *that* way at all.'

'Maybe you're right.' Decker smeared cream cheese on his bagel. 'I don't suppose this place has a *becher* for washing hands.'

A fleeting smile. Jonathan hid his shaking hands by clasping the coffee mug.

Decker felt sorry for him. 'I've been threatened more times than I care to remember. I take them all seriously, but so far, it's all been talk.' He plopped a sheet of lox over the bagel bottom, then put the top on. He bit into his sandwich. His lip and jaw hurt as he chewed, but not as bad as he thought. 'You should eat.'

'The way Chaim said it . . . it sounded like that's all they wanted. For you to leave the city.'

'Then maybe you're right. Calm down.'

'Chaim asked me if I could get you to leave.'

'Get *me* to leave?'

'He wasn't having much success.'

'He was that eager?'

'Yes, he was, Akiva. Why? I don't know. Anyway, I told him it wasn't necessary, that you were leaving in the afternoon anyway. He seemed satisfied with the answer.'

'Did he ask you for my flight number or anything like that?'

'No. Why would he—' Jonathan blanched. 'What are you thinking? That he wanted to check up on you to make sure you left?'

'Maybe.' *Or maybe Chaim was thinking about seeing me off in a more permanent fashion.* Decker kept his thoughts to himself.

Jonathan dabbed his sweaty forehead. 'This psychotic who punched you . . . Was it a warning from someone?'

'Nah, that was pure bad luck,' Decker assured him. 'It's okay, Jon. I'm fine. Did Chaim ask any other favors from you?'

'Actually, he asked me to keep an eye on you,' Jonathan admitted.

'You mean to spy on me.' Decker took another bite. 'What'd you tell him?'

'I told him it wasn't necessary. It's a complete mystery to me, Akiva. Why would Chaim *ask me* to *ask you* to come out – just to push you away?'

'Because I didn't do what he wanted me to do. I didn't do *anything*. He and Minda wouldn't let me do anything. And maybe that was the whole point. To make a show of wanting something done, but not really wanting something done.'

'I don't follow you,' Jonathan said.

'I was the poster boy, my man, something Chaim could point to and say he tried. But in fact, he didn't try at all. And before you get all offended, I'm not saying that's the case. I'm just making suggestions. That's what I do. Suggest some theories and see which ones make sense after the dust clears.'

Jonathan was quiet. 'I wish I had a response. Because it is strange, Akiva. Even in his grief, Chaim made it a point to ask me where had you gone after you heard the news. He seemed obsessed by your actions.'

'What did you tell him?'

'I told him I didn't know. Where, *did* you go, Akiva? You left very suddenly.'

'I wasn't wanted, Jon. It would have been inappropriate for me to intrude on their grief.'

'So where *did* you go?'

'Back into the city.'

'Why?'

'I figured maybe Detective Novack could fill me in on some crime details. He wasn't in. I took a walk and got punched out for my efforts.'

Jonathan was satisfied with the explanation.

Decker said, 'It might have helped me out if you had told me everything this morning, although I understand why you didn't. You didn't want to jeopardize anyone.'

'That, and I couldn't break a confidentiality.'

'I wonder why the "source" was so anxious for me to be out of the picture.'

'I can only assume that you were close to something, even if you didn't know it.'

'So then I have to go back and figure out what I was close to.'

'No, what you have to do is leave, Akiva. Tonight. As scheduled.'

'What difference does it make now, Jon? She's dead.'

'But you're still alive. Now that I think about it, "out of the picture" doesn't sound promising. And I'm not sure if your punch wasn't a warning, despite what you say. If something were to happen to you, I'd never forgive myself. I think we should leave it up to the local police.'

'You're right, but I'm not ready to let go. I'm sending Rina out, but I'm staying until Friday.'

'Akiva—'

'It's decided, Jon. Don't argue. You won't win. You want to help me or not?'

'Of course, I'll help you. What do you need?'

'I need your wheels. As soon as Rina leaves, I'm going to find a cheap place in the city. Which means I'm going to have to give back Sora Lazarus's car.'

'You will not find a cheap place anywhere in the city. You'll stay with me. Don't argue. It's a done deal; I can be stubborn, too. And yes, you can have my car. But now you let me speak my mind. What you're doing isn't fair to Rina.'

Decker put another twenty down on the table. 'Let

me be the judge of that.' He got up. 'Let's go get the morgue out of the way.'

Jonathan arose from the table. 'I suppose we should.'

'I'll be with you the whole time.' Decker put his hand on his brother's shoulder. 'We'll get through it.'

'What choice do we have?'

Together they walked out, passing the stage production as they left. Same show, but different girls, shaking tassels that hung from their nipples. Decker's eyes went to the patrons, flushed from sexual arousal and drinking, shaking hands and sweating palms stuffing twenties into the dancers' thongs. Cheering the girls with each bump and grind, making kissy noises and obscene gestures.

Decker walked a few more paces, then did a double take. Sitting at a front table, drinking and hollering like an ace, was Quinton Police chief Virgil Merrin. His ultrablond hair was plastered wet against his pink scalp, his belly jiggling as he laughed and whooped.

Decker stopped moving. 'Wait a sec, Jon.'

'What?'

'Just wait here for a sec.' Decker went over to Merrin. 'Hi, Merrin, remember me?'

Merrin turned and looked up. He was in civilian clothing, his face and armpits wet, his body reeking of musty sweat. He stared at Decker, his pale eyes without recognition. It could have been the bruises.

'Lieutenant Peter Decker . . . LAPD. I asked you some questions about Shaynda Lieber.'

'Ah! Yeah, sure, I remember you, young man.' A stare. 'What happened to your face?'

'Gotta watch those baseball bats.' He smiled. 'I'm kidding.'

'I hope so.' A smile, but something behind it. 'Have a seat.'

'No thanks. I was on my way out.'

The chief winked at him. 'I won't tell if you won't tell.'

Decker winked back. 'How about this? You can tell – and I can tell.'

Merrin's expression turned chilly. Decker continued to smile.

Locking eyes, but only for a few moments.

Then Decker left.

He glanced over his shoulders just the one time.

23

'I know you're upset—'

'Of course I'm upset! I'm very upset! This is horrible!'

Decker took a deep breath and let it out. 'I'm sorry, honey.'

Rina wiped her eyes, then transferred the phone receiver to the other ear. 'I suppose I shouldn't be surprised. But still, I kept hoping . . .'

'I know, honey, I know.'

'I don't want to go to Florida without you, Peter. Why do you have to stay here? Can't the police handle it?'

'Sure they can handle it.'

Silence.

Rina placed the receiver back on the original ear. Both ears were now hot. 'You promise you'll come out on Friday?'

Her disappointment was audible. Decker said, 'I promise.'

'And you'll be careful?'

'Absolutely.'

'If you truly love your daughter, you'll take extra precautions.'

'I will.'

'Am I going to see you before Hannah and I leave?'

'Yes, of course. I just have to finish up this business in Fort Lee; then I'll come back to Brooklyn and take you two to the airport.'

'Are you in New Jersey now?'

'No, Jonathan and I are just leaving Quinton. I'm sorry you had to find out like this. I'm sorry I couldn't be the one to tell you.'

'It's all right.'

'Was Chaim rude to you?'

'I didn't speak to Chaim; I spoke to Raisie. She was wondering where you were. She told me that all of them were wondering where you were. If you're in Quinton, why don't they know where you are?'

'Because I'm not with them. I'm with Jonathan. We had to speak in private.'

'They said you left in a huff.'

'No.' Decker kept his patience. 'Not in a huff, in a hurry. I thought it would be kinder to the family to let them grieve alone.'

But Rina was skeptical. He left because he had somewhere to go. But she didn't push it.

Decker said, 'Can you change my plane ticket or should I do it?'

'I can do it. I really wish you'd reconsider.'

'Maybe I will. Maybe I won't last until Friday. But I'd like the option. Should I call up the airlines?'

'I'll do it, Peter.' She blew her nose. 'All this arranging and rearranging. I should become a travel agent.'

'I'm sure you'd be the best.'

Rina smiled despite herself. 'As long as you're in Quinton, you should drop by Mr Lieber's house. I have a feeling the family would like to see you.'

'Why do you say that? Chaim practically kicked me out this morning.'

'Well, maybe Raisie would like to see you.'

'I can't see anyone right now.' Two thirty-seven on his watch. 'If we're going to make it to the morgue in Jersey, we're going to have to hustle. Jonathan has already spoken to Raisie, although she doesn't know I'm in Quinton. Nobody does. Like I told you, Jon and I had to talk in private. Don't mention my presence to anyone.'

'I won't.'

'I don't think I'm well regarded by anyone over there,' Decker said.

'What does that mean?'

'I'll tell you when I see you. I've got to go. See you in a couple of hours.'

He hung up before she could tell him to take care.

Rina picked up the packages from the floor of the phone booth and tried to regain her composure. She had been stunned by the news, by the way she had found out. Calling up Raisie just to find out if Peter was there. Hearing all the weeping in the background. It broke her inside and out.

Leaving the city earlier than planned, Rina knew that her ride back to Brooklyn wouldn't be ready for a couple of hours, so she told her that she'd find her own way home. She had completely lost her desire to shop or eat or do anything other than mope. Her bags were as heavy as her heart, her entire body zapped of its vital juices. All she wanted to do was go into a private corner and weep.

She went through her wallet. There was enough for a cab, but what a waste of money. Instead, she consulted a bus schedule. It was a short hop, but with all the downtown traffic, who knew how long it would take her? She began a slow trudge over to the stop. Her *shaytl* felt like a helmet on her head, her shoulders aching from toting around pounds of outfits. Why did she always go so overboard? As if L.A. didn't have children's clothing? She was a hog, just buying because it was there and because it was cheap.

Where was her restraint?

Lugging her bags as she tried to negotiate a crowded sidewalk, evading the masses of human flesh, trying to pass without bumping into people who were bumping into her. If she were honest, she'd admit that she was thrilled to be leaving. How she wished that Peter would come with Hannah and her. She hoped he would be okay. She truly hop—

Without warning, she was thrust forward with such impetus that she tripped over her feet, her head abuzz from several loud background pings and pops. She found herself flattened against the hood of a parked car, her face smashed against the hard metal, pushed down by an arm. The motion was so sudden and carried out with so much intensity, she had bitten into her lip. Blood filled her mouth. Scarcely able to breathe because something or someone was pressing down on her, covering her, smothering her with horrible, heavy weight. The force of the crash had winded her, sending a deep, searing cramp into her belly. She was gasping for air.

Then, as quickly as she was crushed, she was liberated. Pulled upward and onto her feet – dazed and confused.

'I tripped,' Donatti was telling a crowd of onlookers. He looped his right arm around Rina and drew her against his chest. 'Are you okay, darling?'

One second more and she would have yelled for help. Except a sensation stopped her . . . something warm and wet seeping into her clothing. When she looked down, she saw his left hand gripping his jacket as blood was squirting out from a tear in his clothing. Her eyes grew several diameters as her brain integrated what those pings and pops had been. Her lips parted as she opened her mouth to scream.

Donatti grabbed her neck and kissed her hard on the mouth for what seemed like minutes. In fact, it was only a few seconds. But it did the trick. It shut her up.

'Thank God, you're okay!' He liberated a handful of Hannah's clothing from one of Rina's packages and wedged it between his jacket and shirt. Kissing her again before turning to the stragglers still gawking at Rina. 'Do you fucking *mind*?'

Quickly, they dispersed, embarrassed by their own curiosity. Donatti pulled her closer, snaking his hand around her shoulder. 'Let's get a cab.'

It was clear to Rina that he was using her for support. She put her arm around his waist and hailed a cab, helping him in first. Then she went in beside him, handing him another handful of clothing. Donatti acknowledged the gesture with a nod, stuffing the clothes against his wound.

'I'll pay you back—'

'Please.' She leaned over to the driver. 'Where's the nearest hospit—'

Donatti yanked her back in the seat, then gave the cabbie his home address. Rina was about to protest, but his eyes, reptilian and venomous, warned her off. Instead, she took out a red T-shirt and dabbed his wet forehead. He took hold of the cloth and wiped his entire face. Then he sat back and closed his eyes, keeping his breathing as rhythmic and smooth as possible.

The ride seemed interminably long. Traffic was heavy and not a word was uttered between them. As they rode through the city, she noticed that he was inching farther and farther away from her until his head was plastered against the window. His bleeding seemed to have slowed. Or maybe he was just bleeding into the blob of clothing pressed against the wound.

Rina closed her own eyes.

Inevitably, this, too, would end.

All things end.

But nowadays, the endings hadn't been too good.

The coming of *Mashiach*? Better to have faith, then to lose it.

Forty minutes later, the cab slowed as it pulled curbside. She opened her eyes, then reached into her purse. Donatti placed his hand over hers. With effort, he slipped his hand into his jacket, parting it just enough for Rina to see the gun. He pulled out his wallet, extracting from it two one-hundred-dollar bills. He leaned forward and snapped them in the driver's face. When he spoke, his voice was as cold as a bullet.

'You take her to whatever address she gives you.'

'But—'

Donatti slapped a bloody hand over Rina's mouth, then slowly brought it back to his side. 'You take her to whatever address she gives you; then you forget you ever saw us. Do you know what I'm saying?'

'Yes, sir.' The man's voice was a tremor of terror.

'You know who I am?'

'Yes, sir, I know.'

'Who?'

'That man with that older man, the one with the trial . . . with the fancy lawyer . . .' His head was bobbing like a buoy. 'I know, I know.'

'It's good you know who I am,' Donatti said. 'Because now I know who you are. You're Faroom Narzerian. I bet you have a family, right?'

The head bouncing up and down as if on a spring.

'That's good. It's nice to have family.' Donatti picked up the cabbie's hand and crushed the bills in his palms. 'Now if you *really* forget who I am, then I will *really* forget who you are. But if you don't forget, I have a very . . . long . . . memory. Know what I'm saying?'

'Yes, sir.'

He glanced at Rina, his eyes rolling in their sockets. He reached out to open the door. His hand was painted with blood. 'Take care.'

Again she started to speak. Again Donatti smacked a hand over her lips. Hard. Her lip was already sore from where she had bitten into it. It hurt. She hurt. He spoke in low, deliberate tones. 'Remember what you said about what would happen to me if I laid a finger on you?'

She removed his hand from her mouth and wiped her lips with the tips of her fingers. 'Yes.'

'Take it *back*.'

'I take it back.'

'You can do that, right?'

'Yes, I can do that.'

He stared at her.

'It's okay.' She nodded. 'I understand what you did and why you did it. It didn't count.'

'You're right. None of that counted.' In a flash, he was on her, his mouth kissing her hard on her swollen lower lip, sucking up her blood. 'Now that one . . . that did count.' He managed a devil's smile. 'Get out of the city. Go home. Take care of yourself. I mean that. I like you.'

He opened the door and limped out. She watched him unlock a glass door and slip inside a foyer. Within moments, he was out of sight.

24

Jonathan had gone beyond pale, his complexion having turned chalky – dry and gray. After finishing with mounds of paperwork, Decker took his brother's arm – an act of physical as well as emotional support – and the two of them trudged outside to the parking lot to retrieve the van. Seeing Jon's shaking hands, Decker offered to drive. Jonathan told him no, then opened the car doors, taking up the driver's seat. They sat for several minutes in silence, staring out the windshield.

Jonathan's eyes were moist and red. He whispered, 'What kind of monster does things like that?'

Decker didn't have an answer. Guilt was still pouring into his conscience. He should have taken Shayndie forcibly, brought a gun and shot Donatti. If he had planned it more carefully, had trusted his own instincts instead of that bastard—

'What kind of *God* creates such monsters?' Jonathan said.

'I'll drive,' Decker offered once again.

'I'm all right,' Jonathan answered. 'Thanks for coming.'

'I just wish . . .' Decker started to pound the dashboard but wound up tapping it instead. 'I'm sorry I failed you. I failed the whole family.'

'You didn't fail, Akiva. That's ridiculous.'

'You don't know.'

Jonathan turned to him, waiting for an explanation.

'I could have done better.' Decker was abashed. 'I should have done better.'

'I don't believe that for a minute. If anyone failed, it was God. We're nothing but his pawns – little pieces He moves around His board called the universe.' His lip trembled. 'It's not that I doubt His wisdom. That's why we say *Baruch Dayan Emes*. I believe every word theoretically. But I am human . . . fallible . . . emotional. Right now, I'm very angry at Him.'

Tears marked paths down his cheek.

'You and me both, buddy.' Decker slumped in the chair. 'You and me both.'

More seconds passed, then a minute. Finally, Jonathan started the van and put it into reverse. 'Where to?'

'While you were signing papers, I got hold of Micky Novack. I'm supposed to meet him at a restaurant at . . .' Decker looked at the paper. 'Broadway between one hundred fourteen and one hundred fifteen . . . or maybe one fifteen and one sixteen.' He gave him the exact address. 'It shouldn't take longer than an hour. Then I was supposed to meet Rina and Hannah at your apartment and take them to the airport.'

'When's the flight?'

'Nine . . . something. It's a commuter flight. It leaves out of La Guardia.' Decker's watch read six. 'Am I cutting it close?'

'Say you're done at seven. At least, forty-five

minutes to get to La Guardia if traffic isn't heavy.' A sigh. 'Yes, you are cutting it close.'

'Give me a half hour with the guy.'

'Tell you what,' Jonathan said. 'I'll drop you off, run down to my shul, pick up my messages and mail, then come back and fetch you. That should eat up the thirty minutes.'

'Sounds perfect.'

'Yes, things always sound perfect in the abstract.'

Novack stood up when Decker walked into the deli. The place was as small as a kiosk, crammed with a half-dozen linoleum-topped tables and chairs with cracked Naugahyde cushions. There was also a counter and stools, the seats filled to capacity. It was after work hours, so the detective had donned a flannel shirt and jeans instead of a suit. His fingers were greasy from the homemade French fries that he was munching. A half-eaten corned-beef sandwich was on the plate, as were two pickles. Decker sat opposite him, squeezing his body into nonexistent space. A wash of warmth swept through him and he began to sweat. He loosened his tie and unfastened the top buttons of his shirt.

Novack continued to stare, even after he sat down. 'You're sweatin'. You feeling okay?'

'I think my blood sugar's low.' He eyed Novack's remaining half sandwich. 'This isn't a kosher place, is it?'

'Kosher style. That don't count, I know. They got some vegetarian stuff. I think the mushroom barley soup is vegetarian.'

'That'll do.'

'Coffee?'

'Great.'

Novack hailed a waitress – a geriatric, bony woman whose name was Alma. Five minutes later, a steaming bowl of thick soup was placed in front of his nose. Even with his swollen membranes, the mixture smelled good. It tasted even better. Served with fresh rye bread surrounded by a thick seed crust, Decker was in heaven, though he had to eat slowly.

Novack had finished his sandwich and decided to top off his meal by ordering a cup of coffee and a healthy wedge of apple pie. 'What the hell happened to your face?'

Decker gave him the standard line about being punched. Novack looked dubious. 'You report this guy?'

'He ran off. I could have chased after him, but my head was spinning.'

'It looks like it hurts.'

'It does, but not that bad. My wife hasn't seen it yet.'

Novack scratched his cheek. 'She ain't gonna be pleased. Matter of fact, if I was her, I'd be thinking that *maybe* you weren't being too truthful. That someone attacked you and you're trying to protect her – or maybe trying to *hide* something from her. Or maybe *hiding* something from everybody, including me?'

An admonishing look.

Decker was casual. 'If someone was out to get me, Novack, I would have had a bullet in my head.'

Novack thought about that. It was probably true. 'We gotta be honest with each other, Pete.'

'Absolutely,' Decker lied.

'Yeah, absolutely.' Novack's expression was cynical,

but he didn't persist. 'So you just come from the Fort Lee Police?'

'From the Bergen County Morgue actually.' Decker chewed the bread slowly, then swallowed. 'Do they know what they're doing?'

'Yeah, Bergen gets its share of bodies from us 'cause it's right over the bridge. I'm not saying the park's a dumping ground – they got the area under constant patrol 'cause it's a popular spot – but it's a big place, and this ain't the first time a corpse has shown up.'

'Is there interdepartmental cooperation?'

'In the ideal, yeah. Practicality wise, it depends on who's leading the investigation.'

'A guy named Martin Fiorelli.'

'I heard the name, but I've never worked with him. I haven't worked all that much with Jersey Police, but I know a couple of people who have. Now I'm not saying this to sound like sour grapes or nothin' like that. Just that some of those smaller departments have this complex about NYPD comin' in and takin' over. And maybe it's justified, 'cause we got some pushy people. But that's still no excuse for not sharing information. 'Cause it'll be of real interest to me to see if Ballistics turns up a match, being as it looks like the same M.O.'

Decker said, 'The single shot to the head was visible on the ID, but they also got her in the chest.'

'Really. You saw that?'

'No, I skimmed the M.E.'s report at the scene. I wish I had more time to study it, but I was too busy taking care of my brother.'

'How's he doing?'

'Not too well.' Decker finished the last spoonful of

287

soup. He felt better. 'No one's doing too well.'

'I can imagine. Losin' a fifteen-year-old period, but especially like that.' Novack shook his head. 'I don't know how long the body's been sitting there. I'm wondering if maybe she was popped right at the beginning, at the same time Ephraim was taken in.'

'I believe the report said time of death was somewhere between two hours to four hours before they found her.'

'She was fresh, then?'

'Yes.'

'What a shame. No rigor—'

'Not even close,' Decker said. 'No discernible lividity.'

Most of the shock had leeched from Decker's system; guilt had taken its place. Why the hell had he trusted that scumbag motherfucker! Maybe he could get the guy arrested? But on what grounds?

'. . . natural that the girl had witnessed something, maybe escaped. Then she was tracked down and murdered.'

Focus, Decker! 'Or maybe she was in on it in the beginning.'

'She set up her uncle?' Novack's face said he wasn't buying.

'Or maybe she was the target,' Decker tried out. 'The uncle was in the wrong place at the wrong time.'

'He was the drug addict,' Novack said.

'He'd been sober for more than two years.' Decker finished his coffee, signaled the waitress for another cup. 'The thing is we don't know.'

'*We* don't know?' Novack gave him a calculated stare. 'So now you're an honorary member of the two-eight homicide division? I thought you was leaving. Matter of fact, I thought you already said good-bye.'

'Look, I don't mean to step on anyone's toes, but I figured as long as I flew out all this distance, maybe I'll stick around for a bit.'

'How long?'

'I'll be out by Friday.'

The two men eyed each other.

Decker said, 'Honestly, Mick. By Friday, I'm gone. I have to visit my parents. As it is, they're going to be pissed that I've delayed it for two days.'

'So why do it?' Novack scratched his head. 'What are you after, Pete?'

'I failed. I want to go back to the beginning and start over now that I know a little bit more about the family dynamics.'

'Share the details with me, Pete,' Novack said. 'That kinda thing makes a primary investigating detective very happy.'

'For what it's worth, here it is. I know that Chaim resented his brother's presence in the business. But maybe Chaim had a reason for being hostile.'

'First off, how do you know he was resentful?'

'When the news came down about Shayndie, I was in the middle of paying a shiva call to the old man. I was talking to the father about his son. Trying to be nice. Ephraim was *dead*, Micky, and Chaim still couldn't think of anything nice to say about him. Also, Chaim was very concerned about people stealing from him.'

'How do you know that?'

'Talking to store workers at Ephraim's funeral. They told me that Chaim had concerns about theft. Ephraim was in charge of inventory. Maybe Ephraim was stealing. Have you had a chance to look over the papers you took from Ephraim's apartment?'

'I skimmed through around half of them. Just lists of items. Don't mean nothin' to me 'cause I have nothin' to compare it to. I don't know if the inventory's being monkeyed with or not. You think Chaim hired someone to off the brother because Ephraim was stealing?'

Decker thought about the question.

It wouldn't be the first time in Jewish history that brother had been pitted against brother. The Bible was rife with attempted fratricide: Cain and Abel. Isaac and Yishmael. Yaakov and Aesav. Joseph and his brothers. In the book of Genesis, hatred between siblings was more the norm than the exception.

'Sure, why not?'

'Because it would be easier to fire him, Decker.'

'So maybe it was the other way around. Maybe Chaim was stealing from the store, and Ephraim caught him because the old man had put his younger son in charge of inventory. Maybe Chaim resented Ephraim's do-gooder stance, especially since he's been working in the stores for years and Ephraim was a late comer. Besides, Chaim could rationalize the stealing by convincing himself that the store belonged to him anyway. If he was stealing from anyone, it was insurance.'

Novack said, 'Chaim was putting in false claims?'

Decker said, 'It's easy to check out.'

'True,' Novack said. 'If any of the past news items are to be believed, there are certain Jews who have no problems committing fraud. But if Chaim was going to pop his brother, why put his daughter at risk? Why not catch Ephraim at his apartment or as he's leavin'' his drug-addict place or when the man's alone? Why do it when he knew that Ephraim was going to take Shayndie out for the day?'

Decker said, 'I've been thinking about that very question. The only answer I can come up with is putting your daughter at risk deflects suspicion away from you. If your brother's a victim, police will investigate you *especially* if you two work together. But if your teenage daughter is also a victim, well, they're going to tread lightly.'

'You're telling me that Chaim set up his own daughter to prevent Ephraim from telling his old man that Chaim was stealing from his own store?'

'I'm not saying I have it down or I have it right. I'm just suggesting possibilities.'

'Don't get frustrated, Lieutenant.' Novack finished his coffee. 'We're on the same side. Maybe you're still hungry.' Again he flagged down the waitress. 'He needs another bowl of soup, Alma.'

'I've got to leave in ten minutes,' Decker said.

To the waitress, Novack said, 'Make it quick.'

Alma growled, 'There's a McDonald's two blocks away for quick.' She gave them her back and huffed away.

Decker leaned over the table and spoke softly. 'Maybe Chaim paid the cleaners to pop the brother but to let the girl go. Maybe that's why there's no evidence that Shayndie was at the hotel. They let her get away. But something got fouled up.'

'Like what?'

'I don't know. Maybe she was supposed to come home to her dad in a panic and tell him all about it. Then they'd go to the police together . . . Chaim doing the talking. Maybe Chaim had concocted a story that would have explained what happened but also would have drawn attention away from him. Instead, Shayndie freaked out and went into hiding. And that made the cleaners real nervous. Maybe they figured she wasn't trustworthy, so they hunted her down and popped her, too. But that wasn't part of the original plan.'

Novack didn't respond right away. 'She'd witnessed the kidnapping. So she had to be dealt with.'

'Exactly.'

'Then why did your brother bring you out?' Novack asked.

'I was talking to my brother about this. Maybe I was just a showpiece, something that Chaim put on display to convince everyone that he really cared. In fact, both Chaim and Minda hate my guts and have done nothing but put up obstacles.'

'Interesting.'

The second bowl was plopped onto the table, soup spilling over the rim. Decker tried to thank her, but Alma was gone before he could get the words out.

'Eat,' Novack said. 'You can use nutrition.'

As Decker spooned soup into his mouth, he thought about Donatti. The hit seemed too careless for the bastard's signature. And why admit to Decker that he had her? Why did he let him *see and talk* to her, for God's sake, only to pop her?

To throw him off track?

If Donatti did it, he had become boastful and reckless, and that wasn't him. The man was nothing if not calculated.

Novack said, 'Maybe Chaim brought you out because he wanted a couple of things from you. One, he figured you, better than him, could find out what the police knew. You'd report back to him, and then he could figure out his next options. Or two, Shayndie was gone, and he needed you to find her.'

'Seems logical to me.' Decker checked his watch. He had two minutes before he was to meet with Jonathan. 'Anything turn up on Virgil Merrin?'

'He worked Charleston PD as a lieutenant for eight years. Before that, he jumped around quite a bit . . . mostly police departments in Texas. That's always a little weird, except if you're a real political type. You know, constantly upgrading until you get the number one spot somewhere. Looks like he met with success.'

'I saw him in a Tattlers today, Mike.'

'Interesting.' Novack raised his brow. 'What were *you* doing in Tattlers?'

'It's a long story. I was with Jonathan—'

'The rabbi?'

'Yes.'

'Go figure.'

'He wanted to meet at a place where he was sure that no one else from Quinton's Jewish community would be.'

'That's what they all say.'

'Or maybe my brother's a horny guy. That's not the point. Virgil Merrin is the point. He looked to be a steady customer.'

'I'll keep digging.'

'Thank you. You're being more than generous.'

'Yeah, I am. I'm being stupid, if you want to know the truth.'

Decker said, 'I think I alienated him. Merrin. I know I did . . . alienated Merrin.'

'How?'

Decker told him how.

'That wasn't smart. Whaddya do that for?'

'It bugged the hell out of me . . . the way he was acting. It also pissed me off that he implied that I was like him.'

'Decker, if you want to get help, you gotta make him think that you twose have something in common.'

'Yeah, I know. It wasn't smart. I've been doing lots of stupid things lately.'

'Then maybe you should quit before you have a bigger problem than a black eye.' Novack's warning was veiled in kindness. 'Especially when you lay shit on me, saying that some anonymous phone caller tells your brother that he wants you "out of the picture". That don't sound too good.'

'He didn't tell Jonathan; he told Chaim. Jonathan never spoke to this guy.'

'So Chaim could be lying.'

'Definitely.' Decker frowned. 'If some lunatic thinks he's going to scare me away, he's sadly mistaken.'

'What would scare you off?' Novack asked.

'A gun to the head, maybe.' Decker shrugged. 'Not even that. Now, a gun to my wife's head, that would scare me.' He felt a chill run down his spine. 'I will be very happy when she's out of here.'

'When's she leaving?'

Decker checked his watch. 'I'm taking her to the airport right now. I've got to go.' He pulled out two twenties. 'Enough?'

'Way, way over. The bills only eighteen-fifty.'

'Leave the rest for a tip.'

'Twenty-one fifty?' Novack laughed. 'That's more than the going rate for a blow job.'

'Alma looks around eighty,' Decker said. 'But if she's willing, Novack, be my guest.'

'Eighty's a little old,' Novack said, 'but there are advantages. I think Alma wears dentures. Ever get sucked by someone with no teeth?'

'Never had the pleasure.'

'It's smooth sailing all the way.' Novack smiled and nodded. 'Yeah, no teeth ain't such a bad thing.'

Silence.

Then Novack broke into gales of laughter. So did Decker.

Novack chortled and pointed a finger at him. 'I had you going.'

'Fuck you, Novack!'

Decker spoke a little too loud. Alma came over. 'Problems, Detective Novack.'

'Alma, this man just left you a twenty-one fifty tip.'

The old woman gave a wide smile, showing her full set of plates. 'Thank you. You made my day. Next time you come in, I'll give you a little extra treat.'

Decker knew she was trying to be nice, but it came out wrong. He thanked her and left, hoping she didn't notice that he had wrinkled up his swollen nose.

25

She didn't want to be angry, not in front of Jonathan, but her stomach was swirling with anxiety. It was completely irresponsible of him to stay in New York when clearly someone wanted him to leave.

Someone wanted *both* of them to leave.

Maybe that wasn't *quite* true, because analyzing what had happened to her this afternoon, Rina concluded that it was just as likely – no, it was *more* likely – that the shooter had been after Donatti, not her. She had just been in the wrong place . . . or maybe – yes, likely – he had been following her like he had before, and that had put her in the wrong place. Or maybe he knew something she didn't know and he had been watching her . . .

Maybe she shouldn't try to sort it out because her thoughts were a jumbled mess. She sat back in the seat and heaved a big sigh.

'I know, I know,' Decker said. 'I cut it too close.'

'What took you so long?' Rina couldn't hide her irritation. It wasn't good to be peeved with Peter in front of Hannah, either.

'Just stupid stuff,' Decker admitted. 'I'm very sorry.'

'I'm fifteen minutes away,' Jonathan said, 'You should be all right.'

'When are you coming, Daddy?'

Hannah had asked the same question five minutes ago. Decker said, 'On Friday, pumpkin.'

'You promise?'

'I promise.'

The girl nodded, but she was clearly upset.

'I *promise*, Hannah Rosie,' Decker emphasized. 'I'll be there. You can sit on my lap when I make *Kiddush*.'

'You stand when you make *Kiddush*,' Hannah pointed out.

'Afterward,' Decker assured her. 'When I eat.'

'I can sit on your lap the whole meal?'

'Most of the meal.'

The child stared at her mother. Rina took her hand. 'He'll come, Hannah. He just has a few details—'

'I know, I know,' she interrupted. 'I hope Grandma will bake with me.'

'I'm sure Grandma will bake with you.'

'I like her cookies.'

'She makes very good cookies.'

'We're here.' Jonathan scanned the various areas to park. Most of the signs registered full. 'It's going to be tough finding a space.'

'Just drop us off,' Rina told him. 'We'll be fine.'

Decker said, 'You've got a heavy suitcase.'

'I'll manage,' Rina answered. 'There's a spot right over there, Jonathan. Pull over and drop us off.'

Decker knew she was upset. 'I'll help—'

'I don't need help.' Rina tried to keep the tension out of her voice. It wasn't working. 'I need you to be okay.'

'I'm okay.'

'You don't look okay.' Then she silenced herself. Jonathan eased the van curbside. Rina bounded out and lifted open the hatch.

Decker was at her side. 'I'll get it.'

'I can get it—'

He held her arm. 'Rina, please, don't be this way. I love you. Please!'

Her heart relented. Gently, she touched his eye. 'Does it hurt a lot?'

'Not nearly as much as your anger.'

She kissed him softly. 'I love you. So do your children. And your parents. And your sibling . . . siblings. You have lots of people who love you.'

'I know that.' He grabbed the suitcase handle and hefted the valise out of the van. 'I'm not going to do anything stupid.'

'I hope you mean that. I'm skeptical of your story about being punched.'

'You think I'm lying?'

'The verdict's still out.' Rina yanked up the handle and wheeled the suitcase over to the entrance, show-ing the security guard the tickets.

Decker picked up his daughter and gave her a big hug. 'I love you, muffin.'

'I love you, too.' She kissed his cheek. 'I'll miss you.'

'Take care of your mother.'

'I think she's 'posed to take care of me.'

'How about if you take care of each other? Sound good?'

'I guess.'

Decker lowered his daughter to the sidewalk. Rina hugged Jonathan, then kissed her husband. 'We've got to go.'

Jonathan offered Rina ten dollars. '*Tzedaka* money.'

Rina took the bill. 'Next time, Jonathan, it will be under better circumstances. '*Auf simchas.*'

'Amen!'

Decker kissed his daughter, then his wife. ' I love my girls. Take care.'

Rina took Hannah's hand in her right, the luggage in her left, and fast-walked through the glass doors. After standing in a line for check-in, she made it through security with time to spare.

The flight had been delayed.

But in this case, the respite was welcome. She took a hard bench seat in the terminal. Hannah unleashed her backpack from her shoulders, took out a book, and began to read.

'Do you want something to eat?' Rina asked her.

'No, Eema, I'm fine.'

Rina sat back and closed her eyes. Then they sprang open, and she bolted upright.

'Are you okay?' Hannah asked her.

'Uh . . .' *Think of something quick.* 'I forgot something. Not important. I'll get it at Grandma's.'

Hannah shrugged and went back to her book. Rina chided herself. How could she possibly relax? This afternoon, someone had fired bullets in her direction – although the shots were clearly meant for Donatti . . . most likely meant for Donatti. Or . . .

A warning for Peter?

The problem was that she just didn't know!

If she wanted resolution, she was going to have to out-Peter Peter in the legwork department, because there was only one way to find out.

'I have to make a private call, Hannalah.'

The little girl looked up.

'I'm going to move a couple of seats away.'

'I won't listen, Eema.'

'I know, sweetheart. But it's better if you don't hear.' Rina took an empty seat across from her, then fished the cell phone from her purse. Randy answered right away.

'Hey, Sis. You're delayed. Big surprise, huh.'

'An hour so far. Is this going to be stressful on Mom? We're not getting in until nearly one.'

'No, because I'm going to pick you up. I already sent Mom and Dad to bed.'

Silence.

Randy said, 'What is it, Rina? Is he all right?'

'Someone punched his face, Randy.'

More silence.

'He insists on staying. I'm worried.'

'Want me to come to New York?'

'It may come to that. We'll talk when I get there.'

'Don't worry, Rina. He's been around long enough to know his limits. He's not a reckless man.'

'I hope you're right.' She summoned up her courage. 'Randy, I'm very tired. Since the flight is delayed for who knows how long, I was thinking that maybe . . . could you maybe just pick us up in the morning?'

Silence.

'Would that be possible?'

'Anything's possible.'

'I figured I'll go back to Brooklyn—'

'Rina, you're bluffin' me. What are you up to?'

'Randy, I need to talk to someone—'

'Who?'

She didn't answer him. 'It shouldn't take more

than a couple of hours. I'll catch an early-morning flight. Get into Orlando around nine. Will that work?'

'Yeah, it'll work. But I don't like it.'

'Then you won't like the next part, either. I don't want Peter to know about it. I'll call him tonight. But if he calls tomorrow to check up on things, or to talk to Hannah, can you cover for me?'

No response over the line.

'Randy—'

'I heard you. Rina, letting Pete poke around is one thing. You're a completely different story. What in heaven's name are you thinking?'

'Please, Randy! It's just until tomorrow morning.' A pause. '*Please?*'

'You two deserve each other.' Displeasure in his voice. 'What are you going to do with Hannah?'

'I'll take her back to Brooklyn. That's a given—'

'You and me need to have a good, long talk when you get in tomorrow.'

'I'll tell you everything I know. Start to finish, Randy, I promise.'

'I love that guy. He's the only brother I got. And I'm rather fond of you.'

'I won't do anything stupid.'

'I wish I believed that.' A pause. 'Okay.' More resolute this time. 'Okay, I'll cover for you. I have to talk to Pete anyway. He asked for some information, and I may have something for him tomorrow morning.'

'He called you?'

'A couple of days ago, yeah.'

'What did he ask you about?'

'That's not for me to say. Rina, I swear to God, you better know what you're doing, because I'm

Hannah's legal guardian. If something happens to both of you, do you want me raising your daughter?'

Randy was on wife number four. He was making a very strong point.

'I think you're a fine man.'

'That may be, Sis, but we have differing styles. I'm bringing it down to a level you can understand.'

'I hear you. Thank you very much.'

'I'll feel a lot better when you thank me in person.'

By the time she made it back to Manhattan, it was almost midnight. To her surprise, she made it uptown in twenty minutes, amazed at how fast she could cross the city without traffic as an impediment. Still, she didn't get out right away, sitting in Sora Lazarus's old Honda, staring at the building. She was on a tight schedule. It was do or die. Finally, she pulled the door handle and made the plunge, locking the car with the remote. A quick glance around, then she ran over to the building's lobby.

No listing for Donatti.

Either he was unlisted or she had received the wrong numbers. By now, it was way too late to start pushing random buzzers, but having come this far, she wasn't quite ready to admit defeat. Noting that the fifth and sixth floors were taken up by one tenant, MMO, she figured that maybe that was her best bet. But before she could depress the corresponding white button, the door barked out an irritating drone.

She went in, stopping in front of the elevator.

Where to?

No idea.

He'd come get her.

And he did – sunken eyes, pale lips, and a complexion that was florid and pallid at the same time. He wore black sweatpants and a loose white T-shirt. His feet were bare. He crooked a finger and she followed. The silent ride up was incredibly slow. As they got out, he put his finger to his lips, then took her through an anteroom with a metal detector. When Rina set it off, he shushed her silently and waved her forward, through a door and into a spacious loft filled with windows that framed city lights. A pile of broken glass and tangled metal took up most of the center area. To the right was a zone devoted to photography equipment; three doors took up the left-hand wall. He opened one of them, then stepped aside, indicating that she should go in first.

She did.

The room was spacious enough, but claustrophobic simply because it lacked the tall windows of the studio. No windows *period*. He bolted the door shut, then turned on a series of switches that illuminated a panel in Christmas-tree colors, and started the whirling of an overhead fan. Monitors from video cameras showed different positions around the building. The man wasn't taking chances.

He sat down, and so did she. She was much more nervous than she thought she would be. She allowed herself a minute of thinking time, then spoke.

'I just have one question.'

Donatti waited.

'Do you know who hurt Peter?'

He took in her clear aqua eyes and said nothing.

'Was it you?'

Still, no response.

'Did you punch my husband?' Rina demanded to know.

He smiled, but it was a weak one. 'Mea culpa.'

Rina slumped back in her chair and placed her hands over her mouth. Tears dropped down from her eyes. 'Thank you, God!' She exhaled exhilaration. 'I thought someone was trying to *kill* him.'

'Maybe someone is.' His voice was a whisper. 'Maybe that someone is me.'

'Nonsense!' Rina dismissed him. 'Why would you let him go? Why would you have let *me* go?'

'I like playing head games.' His eyes locked onto her face.

Abruptly, she felt herself go hot. She said, 'I woke you up.'

'No, I was awake.'

For the first time, she realized how compromised he was. His face was sopping wet. He dabbed his brow with a damp towel that had been on his desk. She felt ashamed of herself.

'You're ill. How can I help you?'

'Interesting question.' A look. 'You can start by taking off my shirt.'

She got up, and so did he, towering over her. That was okay. She was used to that. With steady hands, she lifted the cotton Tee over his gun, over his bandaged ribs, then over his head. Her nose was hit with a strong stench – sweat, decay, and infection – made even more intense because the room wasn't well ventilated. The gauze was saturated and had turned rusty brown. 'Let me take a look—'

'Leave me alone.' He sat back down. 'I haven't had a mother in over a decade and I don't want one now. You have to get out of this city, Mrs Decker. The lieutenant would be wise to leave, but he probably won't because he's a stubborn man. Besides, he can take care of himself.'

'Was . . . you know . . . was it for you or for me?'

'This?' He pointed to his ribs.

Rina nodded. 'Yes, that.'

'I have some ideas. Don't worry. I'll find out. I *have* to find out. Something like this can ruin a hard-earned reputation like that!' He snapped his fingers. 'Whoever it is . . . whoever he was after . . . he's not too good at what he does. Because we're both still alive.'

Rina shuddered. 'Why would he be after me?'

'I'm not saying he is. But if he is, you can probably answer that question better than I can.'

'I didn't think Peter was even close.'

'Then maybe it's time to stop and take stock.' He closed his eyes and tried to breathe away the pain. 'Whoever this was meant for is irrelevant. Outcome is outcome. You owe me.'

'You saw the person?'

'I saw enough glint of metal to know what was coming. I'm attuned to that kind of thing . . . very . . . detail oriented.'

Again she heard him gasping for air. 'Let me see the wound.'

'It's nothing. Strictly superficial. It nicked a few ribs. Listen, Mrs Decker, if you get out now, no one has to know. Especially your husband.'

'I plan to do just that. Originally I was supposed to go out tonight. As a matter of fact, the lieutenant thinks we've gone out tonight.' She took out her cell phone. 'Can I make a call?'

Donatti pushed his phone over the desktop. 'Your

cell won't register in here.'

Reluctantly, she picked up the phone and called Peter, pretending that they had landed and everything was fine. He kept asking her if she was okay. He could hear the anxiety in her voice. Somehow she managed to convince him that Hannah was too cranky to talk to him, and Randy had to concentrate on his driving. He believed her. Why should he not believe her? She knew she should feel guilty, but she didn't. The subterfuge was worth everything. That his swollen face had come from Donatti's fist was a big relief. A known quantity – albeit evil – was still better than the unknown.

When she hung up, Donatti was looking at her, an amused smile on his face. 'Very sneaky, Mrs Decker. And not very religious, if you ask me.'

'On the contrary, it's called keeping the peace in the home front. *Shalom bayit.*' She clasped her hands together. 'How did you know I was in danger?'

Donatti slumped back in the chair. 'I could give you a line. Tell you lies and you'd believe every one of them. About how I was being chivalrous and trying to protect you. I *didn't* know you were in danger until I saw the piece. The truth is, I was stalking you, Mrs Decker. I get a real sexual buzz by spying on women who are unavailable to me. After Terry broke with me – before we reestablished contact – I used to spy on her all the time. I still do. It really excites me.'

Rina couldn't hold his eyes. A warm blush swept through her face.

'You're nervous. That also gives me a buzz. Don't worry. I'm not going to touch you. I don't believe in taking women by force. However, if you're interested, all you gotta do is wink. I'm not as sick as I look.'

'Remember what I told you that day at the park?' Rina said. 'I've reinstated every single word.'

Donatti managed a fleeting smile. 'Well, then, since sex is out and your plane isn't scheduled to leave for four hours, do you want to crash here?'

Rina's eyes went back to his bandage. 'Your wound is oozing, Mr Donatti. Please let me take a look at it.'

'I'm fine.'

'No, you're not. You're in pain. If it's only pain, then you're fine. But if your wound is festering, you've got a serious problem. Just stand up and let me take a peek. Even if you're fine, your bandage needs to be changed.'

Donatti stalled, then got up from his chair. A moment later, she was close to him, her eyes level with his waist. He could feel her breath on his oversensitive skin. She began to peel back the layers of bandage. As she worked, he focused in on her face, a mask of concentration. Instantly, he was aware of her fingertips brushing against, him. Not even a smidgen of sexual overtone.

Rina regarded his wound – red and swollen and oozing. A brownish raised ring sat on the left side of his rib cage. Next to it, the skin was torn and shredded. It was especially jarring because the bullet holes sat on his otherwise perfect body. 'You got hit twice. First one's just a graze wound. Second one went in and out.'

'I'm all right.'

'That may be, but it's more than superficial. What do you have by way of medicines?'

He reached into his file cabinet and handed her a large plastic shopping bag filled with dozens of vials of pills, creams, ointments, and medical supplies –

bandages, tape, clips, cotton balls, cotton swabs, and even a suture needle. The pills were prescription drugs that had been tagged but were without proper labels. No dosage, no Rx, no instructions whatsoever. There were antibiotics, anti-inflammatory medication, anabolic steroids, including a full course of prednisone, and at least ten different types of pain medication, including codeine and morphine.

'Did you get these on the black market or something?'

'I don't believe in paying retail.'

Rina dispensed with the lecture. She began to sort through the various medications. 'What are you taking?'

Donatti sorted through the bottles. 'I think I'm taking this one.'

'Amoxicillin?'

'Yeah. Isn't that an antibiotic? I took it when I had a sore throat.'

'Except you don't have a sore throat, Mr Donatti. You have a bullet wound.' Rina studied the medicines. 'This will do – Keflex. It might upset your stomach. Take it anyway. You have enough for ten days. You'll probably need more. What you *really* need is a doc—'

'Are you done?'

'No, Christopher, I am *not* done. I haven't even started. I want to clean this up. To do it properly, it'll take a while.'

'I'm tired.'

'So am I. The sooner we start, the faster it'll be done.'

'Then you'll leave?'

'Yes.'

'Anything to get rid of you.'

Rina told herself to start with the basic. 'I need to wash my hands.'

He thought a moment, then reached in his file cabinet and took out several shrink-wrapped packages of latex surgical gloves. Good ones – strong and thin. Rina stared at them, then at him. Then snapped them over her hands.

'Even better.' She sat on a chair while he stood. She took a cotton swab and began to clean the suppurated area.

He winced and jumped.

'Sorry, I know it stings.'

He wrinkled his nose. 'It stings and it *stinks*.'

'It's infected.'

She worked in silence. A minute passed, then another.

Donatti said, 'You have a light touch.'

'Good.'

'You're not very squeamish for a religious woman.'

'That's a non sequitur.'

'You've done this before.'

A statement, not a question. 'Yes.'

'Nursing the lieutenant's gunshot wounds?'

'Actually, yes, I've done that. But my experience goes beyond that. When I first got married, I lived in Israel . . . during the Lebanon invasion, about eighteen years ago. I lived in what you people in America call a settlement way back when it really *was* a settlement—'

She stopped talking, needing to concentrate for a moment.

'Today these settlements are actually towns. Besides, I prefer to think of it as resettlement, but that's my bias talking. Anyway, a group of us pioneer women decided to do our bit for our soldiers on the front lines. Six of us went up North to help out. I was all of twenty. There was this medical camp at the border – makeshift of course, but it had good equipment. There were around . . . oh, fifty beds maybe. The first day there was awful – the moaning, the groaning, the wounds, the smells, the injuries. The second wasn't any better. But by the end of a week, you either leave, or you do something useful. Once you've learned, you never forget.'

Donatti was stunned. 'So what did the lieutenant do while you were nursing soldiers?'

'I suppose he was doing police work in Los Angeles.' She threw pus-filled swabs into the garbage and regarded his eyes. 'I wasn't married to Lieutenant Decker back then, Christopher. I lived in Israel with my first husband.'

Donatti was silent. Then he said, 'You're divorced?'

'Married at seventeen, two baby boys by twenty, a widow at twenty-four.'

Donatti raised his eyebrows, then stifled a yelp.

'Sorry. I need to clean out this fold. It's a little deep.'

The room fell quiet.

Donatti said, 'So Decker's not the father of your sons.'

'Not the biological father, no.'

'Does he get along with them?'

'Very well actually.'

'How'd you meet him? Decker?'

'My first husband and I eventually moved back to the States. We lived in an insulated, religious community. My husband died there, but I stayed on. A crime occurred and the lieutenant was in charge of the investigation. I, being unattached and tremendously attracted to the man, acted as a go-between for the police.'

'What kind of a crime?'

'Rape. Back then, the lieutenant was a Sex Crimes detective.'

'Someone try to rape you?'

She stopped. 'I didn't say anything about my being the victim.'

'I just assumed.'

Rina didn't answer. But Donatti saw her jaw tighten. 'I've upset you. I'll shut up.'

'You didn't upset me.' But she fell into silence, chewing on her swollen lip as she tried to keep her composure.

Donatti felt for her. He said, 'My old man was an Irish two-fisted drunk. Used to pummel me all the time. Just beat the *crap* out of me. When I was seven, he got drunk and repeatedly kicked me between the legs. I lost a testicle.'

Rina froze. 'That's absolutely horrible!'

'It wasn't pretty, especially because I didn't get proper cosmetic surgery right away. I used to hide underneath a towel at gym.' His laugh was bitter. 'Guys used to think it was because I was a big guy with a small you know what.'

'That's terrible. I'm so sorry.' Rina bit hard on her lip. The scab opened up and bled into her mouth, but she continued dressing the shot wounds.

Donatti went on. 'He beat my mother, too.' His face darkened. 'Cops were called in at least a dozen times. Didn't do shit . . . Bastards didn't give a damn. They'd haul him in, put him in jail to sleep it off overnight, give him breakfast in the morning, and spring him. A couple days, maybe a week later, same thing, same routine. "Hey, Patty! Don't we always tell you to hit her where we can't see?" Just one big sick joke. Worst feeling in the world . . . being helpless.'

'That's terrible.'

Donatti grew black and silent.

'I can't fathom how someone could *repeatedly* beat up a child.' Rina's voice broke. 'You poor thing.'

'S'right.' Donatti was touched by her empathy. 'I survived. And I obviously don't have a hormone problem.'

'Obviously not.'

'Thank God for small favors.' Donatti wiped his perspiration-soaked face with a towel. 'It's not such a small favor. From two to one is livable. One to none is not. Eventually, I got cosmetic surgery. You couldn't tell anything just by looking.' A grin. 'Wanna see?'

'You must be feeling better,' Rina commented. 'You're making lewd remarks.'

'Just some harmless flirting.' His smile turned to a stony expression. 'I don't remember the last time I just flirted. I'm so used to using sex as a weapon. Comes from being molested, you know.'

She stopped cold. 'Your father molested you?'

Donatti noticed that she had gone pale. This time, he had hit something potent. 'No, my father used me for a punching bag. Joey Donatti – my adoptive father – he used me as his bitch.'

He looked away.

'My mother was Joey's mistress. He was crazy about her. After she died, I was an orphan and Joey took me in. Probably a deathbed promise he made to her. I was almost fourteen . . . at that weird in-between stage . . . not yet in full-blown puberty. Full of pimples, gawky. I was tall but skinny. Lithe, actually. Waiting for the muscles to come. I had long blond hair at the time . . . down to my shoulders.' He brushed his deltoid with his fingertips. 'The fashion of the day.'

He glanced down, into Rina's eyes.

'I looked like my mother. Joey used to take me into a room, make me kneel in front of him.' A pause. 'He had me perform oral sex on him while he ran his fingers through my hair.'

'Oh my God!'

'It went on for about a year, maybe a little longer. Then his wife finally caught on . . . gave him some choice words. Also, I became too much of a man for him to pretend. But even so, whenever he'd kiss me, he'd jam his tongue down my throat. I still kiss him that way. Only now, I jam *my* tongue down *his* throat. That's not sex, Mrs Decker; that's a power position. He's my bitch instead of the other way around.'

Rina's eyes moistened. 'The man who was responsible for the rape in my community . . . he molested my children . . . my younger son in particular. Ten years later and my son's still suffering. I only found out about it a year ago. You can imagine my guilt.'

'Does your son hold it against you?'

'No, not at all. Do you hold it against your mother?'

'No.'

'My son tries to protect me. My poor baby.'

'How is he suffering?'

She stared into space. 'Maybe suffering is too strong a word.'

But Donatti knew it wasn't.

Rina said, 'He's better now. But he had some drug problems, probably acted out sexually, although he'd never tell me that.' She stopped, trying to rein in her feelings. 'He's so *brilliant*, Christopher. Brilliant and popular with boys as well as girls. He's absolutely gorgeous. The girls *just love* him.' She studied Donatti's face. 'Maybe that's not such a good thing.'

'It's a double-edged sword.' Donatti paused. 'Your son . . . does he look like you?'

Rina didn't answer.

Donatti said, 'Could be it was like Joey. That the bastard wanted you, but he took your son instead.' He laughed. 'Bet you never thought we'd have *anything* in common, Mrs Decker. What happened to him? The unnamed molester.'

'He spent time in prison. He's been out on parole for three years.'

'Where is he now?'

'Somewhere in the Midwest.'

'Somewhere in the Midwest, huh?' Donatti laughed. 'You've probably memorized his address, his phone number, and everything about him, including how many times a day he pees.'

'Two-one-five Kingsley Avenue, Medford, Indiana. And yes, I do know his phone number, as well as where he works, and what car he drives, and which church he attends. However, I don't know how may times a day he goes to the bathroom.'

He smiled. 'Okay. Now I know you're for real. Has he bothered you?'

'No, he has not. But I don't think it's a coincidence that my son's problems came around the same time he was released. Hold still, please.'

Rina continued on, grateful for his silence as she cleansed, swabbed, and dressed his sores. He managed to keep from squirming, even though she knew the procedures had to hurt. His eyes were wet with pain, but she wondered how much of it was physical discomfort, how much was emotional remnants of what he had just confessed. When she was done, she stood up. 'You want me to put your shirt back on?'

'No thanks, Mrs Decker, the thought of anything touching my skin raises my hackles.'

'I suppose this is the part where I thank you for saving my life.'

'Want to pay me back?'

'No sexual comments, please.'

'None. I'd like to draw you.'

'No.'

'I'll behave both on the paper and off the paper. Nothing you wouldn't like to approve of. Nothing you couldn't show in public.'

'No.'

'You know, you're in my place. I was gracious enough to talk to you. Not to mention the fact that I prevented your children from being motherless.'

She met his eyes with her own. 'The last you drew someone, you ended up in prison. Learn from experience, Christopher. Besides, I have to get back to Brooklyn to pick up my daughter. That's your cue to let me out.'

'You mean, you don't like the stench of rotten meat?' He unlocked the door and she walked into the open space. It felt as if she'd been released from jail. Suddenly, her head began to spin.

'You look pale,' Donatti said. 'Maybe you should rest.'

Rina felt weak. 'Maybe for just a few moments.' She fell into a chair, her head having exploded into a million pinpricks. She propped her feet on a box. 'Gosh, I'm so dizzy!'

'It's breathing in all that alcohol in confined quarters.'

'It didn't bother you.'

'I've sucked up more chemicals than a laboratory hood. My brain's used to it.' Donatti regarded her. 'I could draw you just like that.'

Rina covered her face with the purse. 'Go away! Got to sleep. I'll let myself out.'

'Sure. In a minute.'

He waited a minute. In fact, he waited five minutes – the time it took for Rina to doze off. Fifteen minutes later, her sleep was deep. The purse, which had covered her face, had slid down to her chest and rested on her bosom, raising and falling with each breath she took. Donatti watched her slumber, his eyes studying her face and body. Even in repose, she maintained modesty, her legs crossed at the ankles, her dress pulled down to her knees.

He'd wake her in an hour. While he waited, he went to his art-supply cabinet and with great effort lugged out his charcoals and several pads of paper. Though he sketched Rina, his thoughts, as always, drifted to Terry. His longing for her was so all encompassing that his throat clogged. He wondered what she was doing, if she ever thought of him when they weren't together.

Terry had been right about one thing. He wasn't marriage material. Nor was he paternal material.

Though he loved Gabriel on some egotistical level – something that had emanated from his debilitated loins – he purposely kept his distance. Maybe Gabe could live the life that fates had prevented him from having. But it wasn't just karma that had turned him bad. Had Donatti been of stronger character, he could have pulled away. But he wasn't that strong – and he was *that* lazy. Equally as important, his current life was a rush – exciting, unpredictable, a chemical and sexual high. He was too entrenched to go back. He, like Esau, was a natural hunter.

His eyes drifted onto Rina's outline. He had told her he didn't force women. And that was true. He didn't force women – unless he wanted to. Rules were good until they weren't good. Then he broke them. There was a time – not long ago at all – when he had thought about fucking her in every orifice, using every position known in the *Kama Sutra* while she begged him not to. Yeah, he'd force her at first. That was the thrill. Then, of course, she'd get into it. She'd start moaning and groaning and plead with him not to stop. She would buck under his weight, writhing in pleasure until she'd ultimately give way to orgasm. And then after she had come, after every cell in her body had been spent from climax, he'd pop her: a quick shot to the chest, exploding her heart. His final revenge on Decker because the motherfucker had taken Terry away from him.

But now as he sketched her, witnessing her sleep so pure, so complete, Rina had transformed in his mind into all that was chaste and good. Any sexual fantasy with her would be totally obscene – an act of incest. Any thoughts of harming her had been erased from his mind.

His own mother had died when he was fourteen.
Maybe this one would stick around a little longer.
His own Madonna.
The image sat well with him.

26

I was dead to the world, deep in REM, but my brain must have registered some autonomic signal. As I groped for the phone, I felt my heart banging in my chest; my head dipped in foggy consciousness. I must have said hello because she spoke, saying words that I couldn't yet integrate. When I heard the word 'lieutenant,' I came alive. The clock on my nightstand told me it was three-fifteen in the morning.

'I know who you are,' I told her. 'Is your husband okay?'

'The lieutenant is fine,' she assured me. 'I'm terribly sorry to wake you up like this, but I just came from your boyfriend's place. He's not feeling well. I thought you'd like to know.'

'My boyfriend?' I was agitated, not fully awake. My voice was heavy; my speech was clipped and confused. 'I don't have a boyfriend. Who are you talking about?'

'I'm not making myself clear,' she explained. 'I'm not in Los Angeles, Terry. The lieutenant and I are in New York.'

New York.

Okay.

At least, I now knew whom she was talking about.

She had the good sense not to use names. I often heard unexplained clicks on my phone. Not surprising considering who had fathered my son. 'Is . . .' I was having trouble catching my breath. 'Is the lieutenant having some kind of problem with him?'

'No, the lieutenant is fine.'

'You're sure?'

'Positive. I only called because of your boyfriend. He really *isn't* feeling well.'

Again my heartbeat soared. My first thoughts were concern for his actual welfare. Almost simultaneously, those thoughts blurred into what would happen to my son and me if he were permanently compromised. Not very noble, but survival was a very strong instinct. I had a child to care for. I had two years of medical school remaining. I had a severely damaged credit history, a very humble savings account, and no other means of support. His well-being dictated my own.

I'd been silent for a long time. 'How sick is he?'

'He'll be fine, but you might want to pay a visit. I've booked you and your son on a ten o'clock from O'Hare to La Guardia. If you're not interested, I'll cancel it.'

My head was awhirl with the logistics of the visit. Could I afford the plane fare? Could I afford a baby-sitter? Could I afford to miss school? Silly musings. In the end, I had no choice. 'I'll keep the reservation. But it's better if I leave my son at home with a baby-sitter.'

'I'll cancel his reservation then.'

'I can do it if you give me the particulars.'

'Are you sure?'

'Of course. Let me get a pencil and paper.'

She gave me the flight number and the locator letters.

'This took some work,' I told her. 'Thank you very much.'

'You're welcome.'

'Who's paying for the ticket?'

'It's been taken care of.'

'Boy . . . if he asked you to call me, he must be really sick.'

'No, he's not *really* sick. I'm sure he'll be fine. But I think he'd appreciate a visit. Actually, he doesn't even know that I called you. That was my idea.'

'You aren't paying for the ticket, are you?'

'Don't worry about it.'

'I'll pay you back—'

'Please, I mean it,' she insisted. 'Not another moment's thought. This will be our secret.'

'All right.' I thanked her again. 'Please say hello to the lieutenant for me. Send him my fondest regards. Tell him things are going well.'

'I will. I'm glad to hear that.'

'Thank you.' The moments ticked on. 'You're a very lucky woman. Then again, I suppose the lieutenant's a very lucky man.' I heard myself chuckling over the phone. 'Of course, people do create their own luck, don't they?'

'Some people get the breaks.'

'That's nice of you to say, but I really do believe that people make choices. Of course, no one is *doomed* by one's past mistakes. Instead of drowning in the flood, you might as well build a swimming pool.'

The Levines' two-bedroom apartment was considered large by New York standards. Decker figured that 'large' must have referred to height. While it was true that the ceilings were ten-feet plus, all that air didn't add a toenail's worth of square footage to the floor space. Jon and Raisie had been kind enough to put him up in the kids' bedroom for privacy, moving their three small children to the living room on couches and futons. The kids' quarters was all beds – bunk beds and a second twin abutting the lower bunk. Decker had slept, sprawled out over the two lower twins, using the upper berth for his suitcase because there was no room in the closet for his clothes. There was a small desk jammed into a corner, but it was piled so high with papers and material that it was in danger of avalanching.

Somehow he managed to squeeze his six-foot-four frame into the bathroom to shower. Using only a modicum of contortion, he shaved, dressed, and said his morning prayers. By ten, he owned the place. Raisie had gone out, first to walk the kids to school, then back to shiva, but she had shown ample consideration by leaving him a full pot of brewed coffee and the *New York Times*. Jonathan had left early, had taken the subway to work, leaving him the van.

He was on his second cup when his cellular rang. Rina was on the other end of the line. 'How's your face?'

'It's still there.'

'Peter—'

'Swelling has gone down considerably. I feel a lot better.'

'That's the Darvocet talking.'

'Thank God for pharmaceuticals.' Decker put down the paper. 'You sound rested.'

In fact, Rina hadn't slept more than three hours in

the last thirty. By the time she had made it into Orlando, it had been close to nine. Then it took another hour by car to get to the Deckers', who lived outside of Gainesville. 'I'm very happy to be here. I wish you were with me.'

'Soon, darlin'. How's everybody treating you?'

'Wonderful. Hannah has already baked two batches of cookies.'

'Can I talk to her now?'

'She and your mother are out picking beets in the garden. Your mom is going to teach her how to pickle and can. Then they're moving on to pie baking. Later on, Hannah and I may take a bike ride.'

'Weather must be a pleasure after New York.'

'It's in the fifties right now, supposed to get up to the sixties. Full sun. Should be beautiful. Am I tempting you?'

'You jezebel.'

Rina stifled a yawn. 'I really should see what they're doing.' I *really need to go to sleep.* 'Randy has been standing over my shoulder. He's not pleased about your being there, either. He wants to talk to you.'

'What did you tell him?'

'Just a few salient details about the situation that you conveniently left out.'

'You're making my life difficult.'

'That's the idea. It'll motivate you to get the heck out of there.'

'Put my brother on.'

She gave the receiver to Randy and mouthed that she was going to bed.

Randy nodded. Into the phone, he said. 'How's your face?'

His voice was serious – all cop. Decker said, 'I'm

fine. I'm sure Rina exaggerated.'

'I'm sure she didn't. We've been talking, bro. I should get out the mustard 'cause someone's been hotdoggin'.'

'I'm sitting at a table, reading the *New York Times*, drinking coffee. Does that sound like any Sam Spade you're aware of?'

'We need to talk, Peter. Are you on a land phone?'

'I'll call you back in two.' And he did. 'I'm here. Are you calling just to blast me, or do you have actual information?'

'You can dish it out, but you can't take it.'

Randy was talking from concern, so Decker held his tongue. 'What do you have for me?'

'Okay, here we go,' Randy said. 'Okay. I ran Lieber through the channels in Miami-Dade County, and nothing pulled up. Nothing on Chaim Lieber, nothing on Ephraim Lieber, nothing on the old man. I keyworded Lieber on extended counties. Again zero. Ran them through NCIC. Zilch. There are other databases, but it'll take time. Since you're supposedly done with the case on Friday, I say why bother.'

'You're right. Don't bother.'

Randy hesitated. 'So you *really are* coming Friday?'

'Yes, I *really am* coming Friday. I promised Rina. I promised Hannah. And now I'm promising you.'

'Good. In that case, I'll tell you what I did find. I keyworded 'Quinton' into our local system, expecting to find nothing. Instead, I found out that some of the people from there own places in the Gold Coast – Miami-Dade, Boca, and Fort Lauderdale. I also pulled up information on some of the Chasidic Jews from Quinton, mostly having to do with them embezzling funds for the religious-school systems.

Do you know about this?'

'A little. Fill me in.'

'Several members of the Jewish community who were on the school board were indicted for commingling public-school funds with the bank accounts of their religious schools. There were also some allegations of inflated enrollments to get more money from the school district. Finally, something about welfare fraud and food stamps. You're working with some real fine fellows up there.'

'Not most of them.'

'Enough of them to make it look bad.'

'You said several members. What are you talking about? Two, maybe three people? I'd say that's *less* than par for the course in city politics.'

'Don't get defensive.' A long pause. 'You're probably right, Pete. It's just that they're visible and hold themselves up to something better. Makes you fair game for getting shot.'

Decker conceded the point. 'What can you do? People are people.'

'It feeds into the stereotype. If I didn't know Rina, I would think you are absolutely out of your friggin' mind to be associated with them. Even with Rina, I sometimes think you've gone overboard.'

'That's Mom talking.'

'No, Mom thinks you've gone overboard for different reasons. She's worried you're going to go to hell.'

'Tell her I'm used to warm climates. You know, Jews don't hold a monopoly on dishonesty. Some of the most religious Baptists have not been paragons of virtue, either.'

'That's true, but right now you're not involved with

sleazy Baptists. But you may be involved with sleazy Jews.'

'You just said that the Liebers didn't produce hits.'

'That doesn't mean they're clean. It could mean they haven't been caught. Anyway, let me finish, all right?'

'There's more?'

'Yes, there's more. Quinton produced a couple of hits in my district. For what it's worth, several teens who were vacationing in Miami with their parents were arrested during a rave raid. The kids were popping ecstasy. I believe they were originally slapped with drug possession, but the charges were knocked down to the lesser misdemeanor of disorderly conduct. Negotiations obviously. Someone got paid off.'

Decker's brain took off. *The lone pill in Ephraim's hotel room.*

'Bro, are you with me?' Randy said into the receiver.

'Yeah, yeah, I'm here. Ecstasy, huh?'

'Yeah, ecstasy. That's usually the drug of choice at the raves.'

'What happened to them?'

'They were juveniles. The records are sealed.'

'When was this?'

'Recent. Six months ago.'

Around the time Shayndie was hanging out at the mall.

'Sealed, huh?' Decker questioned.

'Like a drum. I have no idea who they are. However, if Ryan Anderson and Philip Caldwell turn up as problem children in Quinton, well, no one would be surprised. Helpful?'

'Very. Thank you, Randal.'

'You can thank me by keeping your promise.'

'I swear—'

'Yeah, yeah. By the way, you must know that ecstasy is a vice of your brethren.'

'What are you talking about?' Decker asked.

'Israeli Mafia. The Oded Tuito case up in New York? You do know about that, don't you?'

Decker didn't. Even as a lieutenant in charge of the detectives' squad, he had little if nothing to do with either Vice or Narcotics. They were in separate divisions. Plus, he had lived almost all his police life three thousand miles away from the East Coast. 'Tell me about it.'

Randy said, 'Oded Tuito was a drug courier, finally arrested in Spain after outrunning authorities in New York for about nine months. He used erotic dancers to smuggle in Ecstasy from Europe into the U.S.—'

'*What?*'

'What's "what"?'

'Did you say he used *erotic* dancers?'

'Did I punch something meaningful?'

'Maybe.'

'You want to clue me in?'

'Finish up about Oded Tuto—'

'Tuito.'

'Spell it for me.'

Randy did. 'Where was I?'

'Oded Tuito was arrested in Spain.'

'Yeah, him and the other one . . . I forgot his name. Hold on, it'll come to me 'cause it's relevant.' Mentally, Randy thumbed through his notes. 'Anyway, the second dude also pleaded guilty to conspiracy to distribute – this was about a year ago. Both of them used erotic dancers, and both have ties to the Israeli

Mafia – Orgad . . . Jacob Orgad. That's the other guy. Anyway, before the dancers, guess who the dealers used for couriers?'

'Dare I hazard it?'

'Chasidic Jews,' Randy answered. 'They used couples, young married couples barely out of their teens. Some of the women were pregnant. The dealers stuffed the pills in socks and told them they were carrying diamonds. That went bust, too. But there is a point to all of this.'

'I'm listening.'

'This is still an ongoing case. When the cops took those two clowns outta the loop, other Israelis moved in and took over, but this time the ports changed – Miami-Dade. Narcotics has warrants out for several of them – Shalom Weiss, Ali Harabi, and Yusef Ibn Dod—'

'Last two sound Arabic, not Israeli.'

'They're Israeli Arabs. There is peace in the Middle East, but not the kind that the world has in mind. I found out from one of our Jewish Narcs that the Israelis and the Arabs do business together in three black markets: drugs, sex, and – I kid you not – watermelon.'

Decker laughed. 'Do you have any idea where these guys are hiding out?'

'No. We hauled some of the local dancers. One of them had a bad jones, and when she got desperate enough, she ratted out aforementioned names. But they rabbited as soon as they heard we had the girl in custody.'

'This is all very interesting.'

'Okay. It's your turn now, Pete. What in particular is interesting?'

'I'm wondering if Lieber knew Shalom Weiss.'

'Me too. You have some suspicions you want to share with me?'

'I found out something that didn't make much sense to me. Now maybe it does.'

'Go on.'

'Quinton Police chief Virgil Merrin. I met up with him at Tattlers—'

'What the fu— what were you doing there?'

'It's a long story. Why I was there is immaterial. I was wondering why Merrin was there. Why would he be in such a politically incorrect place right near his hometown?'

'Maybe he's a horny guy who doesn't like to travel too far.'

'Or maybe he was there for business, Randy. Think about the pieces of information you just gave me. Kids in Quinton arrested for possession of ecstasy in Miami. The Israeli Mafia using erotic dancers to smuggle in ecstasy. The Quinton Police chief in a restaurant specializing in erotic dancers. Three Israelis at large wanted for ecstasy imports. The girl who was murdered, Shaynda Lieber. She used to hang around some of the local Quinton kids . . . around six months ago, actually.'

'Interesting.'

'Too many connections to be coincidental,' Decker said. 'Or maybe that's wishful thinking. Randy, could you fax me a picture of Weiss? Actually, all three of them – what were the others' names?'

'Harabi and Ibn Dod.'

'Yeah, right. All three of them, if you have them.'

'Absolutely, I have something I could fax you. But first, you've got to level with me, Pete. If you have a fix on them, you have to tell me.'

'Of course I'd tell you, Randy. Do you honestly think I'd hold back?'

'No comment.'

'I'm wounded,' Decker answered. 'I don't have a fix, but I do have ideas. Because I'm asking myself where could these guys hide and not stick out.'

'In any Arab or Israeli community.'

'Or in any Chasidic community.'

'*Arabs?*' Randy was skeptical. 'Especially *now?*'

'If they're true Israeli Arabs, they probably speak Hebrew and have seen enough black-hatters to play the part. And if other New York Chasidim had done some transporting, maybe these jokers had made prior connections.'

'You're thinking Quinton.'

'If they were supplying the town, why not?'

'I'll come up—'

'Not yet, Randy. If they're here in Quinton and you come up, they might jump again. This time, who knows where? Sure, maybe it'll come to that, but first let me do some groundwork since I'm already a known quantity. Also, I'm still not sure how Merrin fits in, and *if* it has anything to do with the murders of Ephraim and Shaynda Lieber. Let me poke around a bit.'

'Just a little legwork, right?'

'Yeah, exactly.'

'Nothing confrontational, Peter, because these guys are dangerous fugitives. Weiss was in the Israeli army. He knows how to shoot a gun.'

'I hear you, Randal, and I thank you for helping me out. Also, I've got a pretty good working relationship with the detective in charge of the Lieber case. Mick

Novack of the two-eight in Manhattan. He's a capable guy. All I'm doing is maybe speeding things up a little because I'm working one file and he has fifty.'

Randy said, 'It's good to hear that you're not being stupid.'

Decker was offended. 'What the hell does that mean?'

'It means that you can't do this by yourself, Peter. There're too many people and too many possibilities. You need a partner – someone you can trust.'

'In theory, you're right. I could use you up here. But just as important – if not more important – I need someone in Gainesville to watch over the family. Who better than you?'

Randy thought about what Rina had told him this morning, about how she was sure that someone had been after her, after *both* of them. She had described Peter's face in detail, but was vague with the specifics about herself. Definitely holding back, probably because she was too confused or too scared to tell him what really happened. So maybe Peter's request about taking care of the family held some real weight. In the end, Randy acquiesced.

'You'll call me as soon as you start putting the pieces together.'

'Absolutely.'

'I'll keep researching from this end,' Randy said.

'Good idea.'

'Peter, please don't muscle it on your own. You know what we're working with.'

'Randy, I value my life.'

'That's very good, Bro. It's good to hear you say the words out loud.'

27

He insisted that he wasn't living like a king, and by his choice of lodging, I suspected that, for once, he was telling the truth. The building looked a hair-width short of dilapidated in an area gone of its glory days. But this was New York City, and I knew that here space was king: Real estate was judged by different standards. Columbia University was encroaching and, somewhere along the line, the land would be valuable. I rang the buzzer and a very sexy voice asked who I was. I gave her my name, which meant nothing to her. But she let me in anyway.

The place was on the fifth floor, number thirteen, and if that was significant of anything, I didn't know about it. I had to walk through a metal detector, and then a young guard checked my purse. The receptionist, a pretty girl who looked in her teens, asked if I had an appointment. When I told her that I didn't, she said I'd have to wait.

'He's in the middle of a shoot. It's going to be a while. Why don't you come back in an hour?'

'It's important,' I told her.

'It's always important.' A roll of the eyes. 'You'll have to wait, ma'am.'

'It's *very* important,' I insisted. 'I'm from out of

town. If Mr Donatti finds out that I was here and you didn't let me in – or even that you made me wait – I guarantee you he'll be very angry.'

She didn't answer right away. There must have been something in my voice – calmness and authority – a rarity for me.

'I'll take the heat,' I assured her. 'I know what he's like when he's angry. I'm not worried. Page him, please.'

She hesitated, but then she picked up the phone. I heard him screaming.

'*What!*'

'Sir, there's a woman—'

That was as far as she got. The slam of the receiver was so loud that even I recoiled. He flew out of the door, his face as red as the blood that had seeped into his cheeks. 'Who the fu—'

He stopped when he saw me. He was breathing hard, sweating hard as well. Mrs Decker had been right. He didn't look well. He spoke to me. 'Are you all right?'

'I'm fine. I need to talk to you.'

The room went quiet.

'You're sure everything's all right?'

I nodded.

He exhaled. 'Give me five minutes.'

I nodded again. 'Should I wait here?'

'Yeah.' He regarded his secretary. Her complexion had gone pale gray. 'It's okay, Amber. You did the right thing. Take the rest of the day off.' A glance over the guard. 'Both of you, take the day off. I'll see you tomorrow.'

The guard stood up. 'Are you sure, Mr Donatti?'

'Very sure. Here.' He gave them both a fifty. What I

could have done with that money. 'You can leave now. She's fine by herself. Have a good time.' To me. 'Five minutes.'

'Take your time.'

'Do you want anything? Are you hungry?'

'I'm fine.'

He held up his hands and disappeared behind the door.

Amber gathered up her belongings, giving me an expression that wavered between confusion and awe. I knew what she was thinking. *Who is this ponytailed bag lady with the strange feline yellow eyes, dressed in oversize chinos, a black ribbed crewneck sweater, worn sneakers, and a threadbare peacoat? Her clothes look like they came from a thrift shop.*

In fact, they did. Right now, Chris was paying tuition not only for my medical-school education but also for Gabriel's private schooling, as well as his piano lessons with a very sought-after maestro. Chris was paying my rent, my utilities, my child-care needs, and our health insurance. He paid off my under-graduate loans and gave me whatever spending money I asked for. He never questioned what I needed. His largesse allowed me to be job-free so I could concentrate on Gabe and my studies exclu-sively. I kept a microscopic watch on where each dime went.

I had known Chris for almost nine years. We met in high school back in my native Los Angeles. I had been incredibly naïve in every sense of the word, and I think that was why he was attracted to me. My face didn't hurt, either. Things progressed at a very messy pace and I thought I was in love. By the time I wanted to cut bait, it was too late. I was pregnant.

By now, I was aware of what Chris did, although we never discussed it. Donatti was a newsworthy name, and from time to time, I came across it in print. When Joseph Donatti had initially been indicted for murder six years ago, Chris had also been indicted as a coconspirator. Six months later, his charges were dropped for insufficient evidence. Eventually, Joey was acquitted. The picture of Chris and him hugging had made the front page of the *Trib*. I had seen several sidebar articles about Chris's magazine and the implications about his pimping and pandering. Nothing ever stuck.

No, we never talked about what he *did*, but we both knew what he *was*.

Ten minutes later, he accompanied two young boys and a girl out of his main digs, his arm around the girl, talking to all of them in whispered tones. The girl sneaked a sidelong glimpse at me. I smiled, but she did not. After everyone had left, he motioned me in but put his finger to his lips. He picked up his ubiquitous bottle of Scotch and we walked into a sizable but windowless office – neat as expected – with lots of security equipment. A ceiling fan added some air to the place, but the fluorescent overhead lighting was harsh. When he saw me squinting, he turned it off and elected to go with a soft pole lamp. I sat on one side of the square table; he lowered his body into a cushy chair on the other side. He gulped some booze, then followed it with an Evian chaser.

'Where were you hit?' I asked him.

His laugh was muted. 'She called you. Rina did.'

I cocked my head. 'You're on a first-name basis with her?'

'Actually not. That's her doing, not mine.'

'You like her?'

'She's very attractive.'

'She sounds very nice.'

'She is very nice.' More water. 'Where's the kid?'

'Your son,' I corrected him. 'I left him at home with a baby-sitter.'

'That's nice. I like being alone with you.'

'Your paternal devotion is touching.'

'That's assuming that I've acknowledged paternity.'

I gave a long, suffering sigh. 'Will you please take a simple blood test so we can be done with this? Why do you like to torture me? Why do you enjoy torturing yourself?'

His eyes narrowed. 'Don't yell at me. I hurt.'

I stood up and walked over to him. I put my hands on his strong, tight shoulders. 'Let me see.'

'You're not a doctor yet. Leave me alone—'

'Chris—'

'Leave me alone.'

'Please?'

He stood up and held my chin. He brought my face to his and kissed me hard. 'No.'

'You're being stubborn.'

'You look gorgeous, Terry. You always look great—'

'Let me see—'

'Jesus, you're impossible!'

He attempted to lift up his shirt. When I tried to help, he slapped my hand away. He showed me his wound.

'I'm not taking off the bandage.'

'You should,' I said. 'The wound is weeping through the gauze. Do you have any medication or replacement bandages or salves?'

He held out his hand in exasperation, then gave me

a bag filled with medical material – tape, bandages, medicines, salves, ointments. I went through the supplies, then wiped down my hands with a new bottle of beta-dyne. I started to take off the outer layer of adhesive. He winced.

'I'm sorry. Hopefully, it won't take long.'

'Do you know what you're doing?' he asked me.

'Yes.'

His expression was dubious, but he stood still. I peeled back the layers. 'Who dressed this? He did a good job.'

'She.'

I laughed. 'God, I can't believe what a sexist I am. Who's she? Mrs Decker?'

'Yeah.'

'Does Lieutenant Decker know about this?'

'Nope. Doesn't know about his wife being here, doesn't know that I've been shot. There's a lot that Lieutenant Decker doesn't know.'

'What's going on?'

'It's complicated.'

'My plane doesn't take off for a while.'

He talked to me while I worked. His sentences were terse. I was getting the encapsulated version. Probably the sanitized version as well. Twenty minutes later, I had patched him up. He sat down and took another swipe of booze.

'You shouldn't drink and take painkillers at the same time,' I told him.

'I gave up cigarettes for you. Leave me alone.'

'I care. It's not safe.'

'My system's impervious to drugs. It's a wonder I'm still alive.'

I took the bottle out of his hands, brushed my

fingers over his grizzled face. 'I'm glad you are.'

He regarded me, scrutinized me. A long time ago, his penetrating eyes made me nervous. Not anymore. Years of dealing with Chris's unpredictability had hardened me. I needed him – as my son's father, as my bank account. Initially, my grandparents had supported my son and me. They are lovely people, and I knew we were a burden. After eighteen months, I assured them that I would be fine and convinced them to move to a retirement community in Florida. Immediately, I was plunged into poverty. For almost two years, I put myself through college while trying to put bread on the table. Debt took on a life of its own. I was drowning, and Chris was watching. As I exhaled my last breath – a heartbeat away from eviction – Chris offered me a life preserver. I took it and haven't looked back, although someday I'm sure I will. It will not be a sterling moment in my moral history. Still, being his courtesan was better than choosing between quitting med school or suffering through another frigid Chicago winter without decent heat.

His hands went to my face. He kissed me . . . long and gentle. I could feel the ball of his tongue pierce as he swept through my mouth. He loosened my hair from the ponytail holder and ran his fingers through my long tresses. He kissed me again and again. 'I love you.'

'I love you, too.'

'No, you don't.'

'Not true,' I told him. 'Would I be here if I didn't?'

'Yeah, you'd do it out of obligation.'

'You sell my affections short,' I said. 'Don't be nasty.' I let my hand travel down to his inner thigh. 'Be nice.'

He placed it over his groin, and I felt him grow in my fingers. He closed his eyes, his breathing audible. He whispered, 'I keep forgetting what you do to me.' He gave me hungry eyes. 'This is the safest place, Teresa. The only place where I feel comfortable talking.'

'I didn't know you wanted to talk.' I stood on my tiptoes and kissed his lips, then bit them gently. 'Doesn't matter, Chris. Here's fine. Anywhere's fine.'

'You want a pillow or something?'

'Do you have something that's clean?'

He made a face. 'You're very funny.'

'I'm dead serious. I don't know who you bring in here.'

'No one. You know how meticulous I am.'

That he was.

'I have a stereo hooked up, too,' he said. 'Vivaldi's "Four Seasons"?' A rare sort of smile graced his lips, one that shot light into his eyes and showed how incredibly good-looking he could be. 'Gipsy Kings?'

'You beast you.' I answered his smile in kind.

'I'll be right back.'

His face had become suffused with little boy excitement, like the first time I had given him a birthday gift. He put on the music and brought in a big, fluffy pillow, placing it on top of the desk. I pushed it off, letting it fall to the ground.

I dropped to my knees.

A couple of hours later, I asked if there was a place where I could bathe. Though he claimed to use condoms assiduously, he refused to use them when he was with me, saying it was the one time he could let his guard down. But it was more than that. Anything less than full culmination implied my rejecting his basic being, so my pleas had fallen on deaf ears. I had had the good sense to get an IUD when we became intimate again, but it did nothing for disease. The last time I had begged him to wear protection, he became very angry – that silent, dreadful fury that sent waves of fear into my gut. He had this look – this deadly look. He used it whenever he meant business. I had been on the receiving end of his wrath and revenge. There were some things I just couldn't push him on.

'I have a unit upstairs. I'll come with you in a minute.' He took my hand and kissed my fingers one by one. Then he let go and got dressed. He was still breathing hard when he sat down. 'Let me rest for a moment. You gave me a workout, you animal.'

I got up from his desk and put on my clothes and clipped my hair back. I gulped down half the bottle of Evian, then gave it to him. He took a big swallow, then closed his eyes. He was drenched with perspiration. He didn't look well at all. I felt his forehead. 'You're very hot.'

'It's stuffy in here.'

'You've got a fever, Chris.'

'Any wonder after the calisthenics you put me through.'

'I'm concerned. Do you have a doctor I can talk to? You need Keflex.'

'I've got it.'

'Are you taking it?'

'No.'

'Why not?'

'It upsets my stomach.'

'Christopher—'

'I'll take it.' He finished up the bottle of water. 'I'm

probably just dehydrated. Stop nagging me.'

'I care.' I sat in his lap. 'Please?'

'Yes, I will take Keflex.' He nibbled my upper lip, then kissed me. 'Happy?'

'Yes.'

We began to kiss. Then he broke away.

'So who are you dating?' he asked me.

'No one.'

'Don't lie to me, angel. Who are you dati—'

'No one,' I insisted.

He pulled out a nutrition bar from a file cabinet, ate half, then offered it to me. I shook my head, so he finished it.

'Not dating anyone?'

'No, I am not dating anyone.'

'Then why'd you go to the Hilton with your classmate? What was his name? Michael Bonocelli? Did I pronounce it right?'

His eyes were dead, just waiting to pounce. I said, 'Your spy wasn't complete. If he would have been more watchful, he would have seen me walk out as well as walk in.'

His face told me he was unconvinced.

'They have a very good Italian restaurant, Chris. When Mike invited me to go to dinner, I had no idea he meant room service.'

'You still went out with him.'

'We were working on a paper together – "The Implications of Iatrogenic Causes in Radiation Deaths of Stage-Three Breast Cancer Patients" – a subject that interests me being as both of our mothers died from the disease. Thank God we had a son. The lead professor's name is Doctor Edwin Alvary. Mike offered me a dinner meeting, and I took him up on it.

Sue me. I get tired of mac and cheese or peanut butter every night.'

I pushed his face away from mine.

'I don't date, Chris. When would I have time? Besides, the last thing I want is a parade of men going in and out of the apartment. Gabe is *everything* to me. He is *not* going to grow up with a slut for a mother.'

'You wouldn't be a slut if you had a toss now and then.'

'But I *don't*! You know that 'cause you're watching me all the time. I only sleep with you, and that's different because you're Gabe's father. In fact, you're the only guy I've ever been with, period! For twenty-four years old, that is truly *pathetic*!'

'Not to me. I still get this incredible jolt every time I lay you down and spread your legs.'

Again I pushed him away. 'Stop being crude.'

'That was a compliment, angel.'

I scrunched up my face. 'That's such a male perspective. I want to have sex with you, ergo you should feel honored!'

'Men are dogs.'

Stated without expression. I quickly remembered whom I was talking to. I kissed his cheek. 'At least, you're a very generous dog.'

He took in my eyes. 'How much?'

'That wasn't a hint.'

He reached over to the second drawer of his file cabinet. Inside was a shoe box stacked with pictures of Ben Franklin. He pinched some bills off the top, then folded them into a wad and offered it to me. Longing in my heart, but I held my ground.

'I *said* that wasn't a hint.'

He counted them – eight hundred dollars. He added two more bills and then stuffed them in my hand. 'Buy something nice for yourself and the kid.'

'Thank you.' I kissed his cheek again. 'It won't go on for ever, Christopher. I'll be earning money in a few years.'

'I'm not complaining, Teresa.'

'You never do,' I told him. 'I should marry some sugar daddy just to give you a break.'

'I *am* your sugar daddy. What do you need someone else for?'

I shrugged.

He gave me a stare. 'Anyone specific in mind?'

'I'm talking theoretically.'

'You're pissing me off!'

'Some good-looking, much older man who'll baby me for the rest of my life. Someone who wouldn't be much competition for you.'

'He wouldn't be *any* competition for me because he'd be dead.'

'I mean much, much, *much* older, Chris. Like in his forties or fifties. That wouldn't bother you, right?'

'Forties maybe. Fifties, probably not.' He raised his eyebrows. 'Who would you go for, baby doll? Decker?'

'You're *sick*!'

'Yeah, you're right. No money.'

I faced him, suddenly turning serious. 'So you two are working together?'

'Beats me.'

I didn't like the attitude. I said, 'Christopher Sean Whitman Donatti, I swear if you hurt that man I will never ever, ever *forgive* you for the rest of my life!'

Rudely, he pushed me off his lap. 'What *is it* about

that guy that inspires such loyalty?'

'Besides the fact that he got you out of prison? Besides the fact that he sent me money when no one else would? Besides the fact that he is the only heterosexual male I've ever met who hasn't tried to sleep with me?'

'You forgot your father.'

'I stand by the original statement, Chris!'

He jerked his head up, taking in my eyes. 'What? *When?*'

I waved him off. 'Before I met you. He wasn't insistent. He wound up not doing anything.' My eyes watered. 'He couldn't. He was too drunk.'

'What else is new?'

'Jean caught us – him. To her credit, she didn't blame me. Didn't support me, but didn't . . .' I wiped the tears away. 'Melissa's that age now. I call her nearly every day. I tell her over and over that if he tries something . . .' I didn't dare finish my thought.

'You never told me.' He pulled me back onto his lap. 'You should have said something, angel. I could have sympathized. I was molested, you know. Joey, right after my mom died, he used to comb out my hair and make me give him blow jobs.'

'That's *horrible!*' I meant it. I touched his face and kissed his lips. 'Poor Chris.'

'Yeah, poor me.' He shook his head. 'You know, I keep my mouth shut for years. Then I wind up telling two people about it within twenty-four hours. What the hell is wrong with me?'

'Who was the other person?'

'Rina Decker. I don't know why I brought up my uncle. She has this way of getting stuff out of you. She and the lieutenant are suited for one another.'

'I'm sure that's true.'

'Jesus, I can't believe your old man actually—'

'It was over before it started.'

'I should pop him.'

'Chris—'

'I won't, but I should.'

'Can we switch the subject? It's so painful! Especially after making love.'

He brought me close to his chest. 'Is that what you consider it? Making love?'

'Yes, of course.' I looked at him. 'What do you consider it?'

'Making *beautiful* love.'

'So we're in agreement.' I leaned against him, my head to his heart. 'Does he know what he's doing? Lieutenant Decker?'

'He's no dummy, but New York's different from Los Angeles. He's in foreign territory, doesn't really know what or who he's dealing with. On top of that, he's not packing.'

I looked up. 'He doesn't have a gun?'

'I tried to give him one. He refused. The man is stubborn.'

'Who's he up against?'

'I've got some definite ideas – amateurs trying to look like some pros we both know. That means they're *stupid*. And stupid is dangerous. If I were his wife, I'd start looking at his life-insurance policy.' He took another gulp of water. 'It probably would be easier if someone popped him. More elbowroom for me. This problem has got to be taken care of.'

My heart started skipping. He must have picked up on it. He stroked my back. His voice was low and soothing. 'Baby doll, I tried. But he told me to butt out. So I'm out. Tell you the truth, I haven't been feeling well enough to do much of anything. If he wants to nuke it out solo, he can be my effing guest. I'm not the man's nanny.'

Gently, I put my arms around his waist, being careful to avoid his gunshot wound. I barely spoke above a whisper. 'Don't let him sink, Chris. Even if he doesn't want it, help him.'

He was silent.

'Please?'

Again he didn't answer me. But he didn't push me away. Instead, he drew me closer . . . nuzzling the top of my head with his lips . . . stroking my back . . . his fingers up and down my spine . . . playing me like an instrument. His touch could be so incredible. I gave off a little shudder.

'Cold?'

'No, just . . . mmm, feels good.'

'I know what my baby doll likes.'

'Yes, you do.' And by now, I could read him pretty well also. Affection meant he was listening. Affection meant he'd be cooperative. Affection was a very good sign.

28

If there were any answers, they'd lay in Quinton. Decker knew the Jewish sector of the town was a lost cause – he'd be as welcome as ham and Swiss on rye – but he held faint hopes that maybe he could salvage something with Virgil Merrin, ascribing his rude behavior to his own embarrassment at being seen at Tattlers. Then maybe he'd play out some of the ol'-boy routine, knowing he could make it work if he could just get the sneer out of his voice. With Merrin as an ally, he could possibly get names of some Quinton teens Shayndie might have known.

But he'd have to tread lightly.

Because there was this possible worst-case, politics-and-money-corrupts, trust-no-one scenario: Merrin was involved in ecstasy distribution, using erotic dancers as couriers for the Israeli Mafia members. There was also the unholy missing trio of Weiss, Harabi, and Ibn Dod. They could be back in Israel, camped out in a Jewish community incognito, or they could even be dead.

And even if this product of Decker's overactive imagination were somehow borne out, if the loose bits of facts that Randy had given him did weave into a fanciful cohesive story, how, if at all, would it relate to the Lieber murders?

Which brought him back to the original dilemma.

He needed to penetrate Quinton's Jewish side and that meant he needed someone trusted by the locals. More important, he needed someone *he* could trust. Decker required a mole with a firsthand knowledge of Jewish traditions, mores, and rituals – an insider who could point out the outsiders, but who would be loyal to him.

Since Rina was gone, there was only one person who could possibly pull that off.

How well did Decker know his half brother?

He supposed that he was about to find out.

It was a small but growing synagogue in the Morningside Heights district, within walking distance to Columbia University. The daily morning minyan, held at eight o'clock, often included college students, and because it was Conservative in denomination, the service included men and women in equal proportions doing equal duty. By the time Decker drove uptown and found a parking space, it was almost eleven, well past *Sha'chris*, and he figured maybe his brother could use a coffee break.

Jonathan's secretary, a twenty-something African American named Arista, informed him that Rabbi Levine was in conference with several of his parishioners and wouldn't be available until twelve-thirty. If it was a true emergency, she could intercom him, but short of that, he had asked not to be disturbed.

It wasn't a true emergency.

In that case, he was welcome to wait in the library if he wanted or perhaps he should go grab an early lunch. She'd tell the rabbi that he had come by. He thanked her and told her he'd be back at half past twelve and could she please ask the Rabbi to wait for him.

He went out of the shul and began walking down Broadway, a whiff of garlic hitting his face because the shul was next door to Tito's Pizza Joint. He turned up the collar of his overcoat and stuck his hands in his pockets. He should have called before he came. Cursing under his breath, Decker found a ubiquitous Starbucks and bought himself a large cup of black coffee. There wasn't anywhere to sit, so he leaned against a wall, looking like a dealer waiting to score. He thought about his options, mentally thumbing through his notepad, which, by now, was thick with his chicken scratches.

There were ways he could fill the time; people he could interview again. There was Luisa and Marta, the ladies he had met at the funeral. They worked inventory with Ephraim, maybe they had thought of something important since he had last seen them. And Luisa still had his gloves – a perfect excuse to call on her.

Except by now, she was at work at one of the Liebers' stores, and Decker's presence would be noticed. Maybe he'd try her tonight, in the privacy of her own residence.

There was Leon Hershfield. If anyone would know anything about hanky-panky within the religious Jewish Community, it would be him. The attorney was aware of lots of things, but asking him questions wouldn't help because of confidentiality. Usually, Decker could gauge reactions from his interviewees even as they pleaded the Fifth. A lot was conveyed through facial expressions and eye contact. But Hershfield was way too savvy to give *anything* away, even through nonverbal methods. Talking to him would not only be futile, but detrimental as well. It would give him Decker's insights with nothing in return.

Scratch the lawyer.

Finally, there was Ari Schnitman, the recovering addict who knew Ephraim from Emek Refa'im. Since Luisa and Leon weren't going to help, it was almost by default that the Chasid was elected. Schnitman dealt in wholesale diamonds on the East Side. Since Decker didn't want to lose his parking space, or battle traffic jams, he elected to catch a cab instead of driving on his own.

Twenty minutes later he was dropped off in the heart of the diamond district, at the 580 building on Fifth between Forty-seventh and Forty-eighth, the exchange floor located between a blue awning OshKosh B'Gosh clothing store and another blue awning retail jewelry store. It was a grand old building – about fifty stories at its high point – holding arched windows with panes segmented by bronze metal in a pattern reminiscent of a child's drawing of a sunrise. American flags hung above plaster molding and gingerbread that included the heads of Roman soldiers complete with helmets. Across the street was Bank Leumi, one of the official banks of Israel.

Years ago, Decker had led a homicide investigation revolving around the murders of a Los Angeles gems dealer and his wife. The case found its conclusion in Israel, specifically on the trading floor of the Diamond Bursa in Ramat Gan, Tel Aviv, so Decker had some familiarity with the industry, giving him context for comparison. Art Deco in style, the 580 building had an anteroom that was smaller than Israel's but larger than the diamond center in downtown L.A. The lobby was more of a hallway, a feast in gray granite, and it was teeming with watchful-eyed people carrying briefcases. Metal sconces lined the dark rock walls, giving the space dots of uplight, but it was still dim inside. Straight ahead were clocks showing various time zones around the world. Security was tight. To the left was the ever-present metal detector, followed by a turnstile, and then a team of four gray-jacketed guards who checked personal belongings as harried people passed into the bowels of the building. To the right was a touch-screen computer directory. According to the listings, the multistoried structure seemed primarily occupied by Jews, but there were names indicating other nationalities as well – Indian, Armenian, South American, and Russian.

The private offices and exchange floor were for the trade only, so Decker knew he'd have to check in with the front desk. After a bit of a grilling, one of the gray guards consented to call up Schnitman. A minute later, Decker held a temporary pass to the eleventh floor *only*, with the name Classic Gems and the suite number handwritten in the spot where the badge had asked for Place of Business. He stepped into the elevators and was taken up to the eleventh floor by an operator with a gun.

Schnitman was waiting for him, a few doors away from the Classic Gems entrance, leaning against one of the walls that made up a narrow hallway. Guards were posted on either side of the foyer, in front of the emergency stairwell exits. In traditional Chasidic garb of a black coat, white shirt, and black hat, he looked older but even smaller. He was stroking his beard, eyes small behind the windows of his glasses. His expression was grave, bordering on hostile. It seemed that Decker made friends wherever he went.

'What are you doing here?' he whispered.

'Thanks for seeing me,' Decker tried out. 'If you don't mind, I'd like to ask you a couple more—'

'I *do* mind!' he spat out. 'I cooperated with the police. I told you all I know. Now you come and bother me at my place of business. Do you *know* what would happen to me if my problems got back to my boss?'

Decker's expression was flat. 'Why would he assume that I was anyone other than a customer? Calm down and let's go find a place to talk.'

Schnitman checked his watch. 'I have a lunch meeting in twenty minutes. I was about to leave.'

'No problem. We can talk while we walk.'

He exhaled loudly. 'Wait here. Let me get my coat.'

It took less than a minute for Schnitman to return. They rode the elevator down in silence, Decker following the young Chasid as he speed-walked out of the building, turning left, hands clasped behind his back, his coat and *payot* flapping in the wind. Schnitman continued to race-walk until he got to Forty-eighth; then he hooked a right.

Decker said, 'If you don't slow down, we can't talk. Then you can't get rid of me.'

Schnitman stopped at the green lettered Fleet building, leaning against the glass, his eyes on his polished black shoes. In front of him was a table overloaded with baubles and clothing festooned with the American flag. The vendor was sitting next to the trinkets, his face hidden by dreadlocks and a copy of yesterday's *Post*. The air rapped out horn honks and engine rumbles.

'Where are you meeting this client?' Decker asked.

'Clients. Fifty-third and Second. They're from Japan, so my brilliant boss figured that I should take them to this Japanese kosher restaurant. It's a good place, but it's kind of like bringing coals to Newcastle. I'm sure they would have preferred a deli.'

'I'm sure you're right,' Decker said.

'What do you want, Lieutenant?'

'You said that Ephraim was edgy right before he was murdered. Any ideas?'

'No.'

'Tell me that again, Schnitman. This time, do it with eye contact.'

The Chasid looked away.

Decker took his arm and held him in place. 'Look, Ari, I can understand your not wanting to say too much in front of the police, that maybe it'll bring attention to your secret organization—'

'It's not a secret organization,' he answered testily. 'We'd just like to assure as much anonymity as possible. Otherwise, people don't come and get the help they need. Believe me, it's hard enough reaching out without cops butting into internal affairs.'

'Which is why you should help me. Right now, it's one-on-one, and maybe I can help you. Turn me away, city police are bound to come back.'

He rubbed his hand over his face and beard. 'Okay. Here's the deal. Ephraim didn't talk to me, but he did talk to someone in the group – his sponsor. I didn't tell you this initially, because I just found out about it last night – at our weekly meeting. Don't ask me for the name, I won't give it to you. You can threaten me with exposure, embarrassment, jail time, the works, but I will not, under any circumstances, break a confidentiality by giving you a name.'

'You're not a lawyer, doctor or pastor—'

'I have *smicha*, so technically I am a rabbi. If I have to use it, I will do that.'

Decker looked around. Scores of people in dark overcoats whistling down the streets, scarves streaming behind them, waving in the breeze like banners. Harsh pewter clouds clotted on the sky's surface like chrome plating peeling from dross metal. The atmosphere was saturated with dirt and the smell of noontime frying oil. Traffic was fierce. A sudden gust of wind whipped up under Decker's coat. He tightened his scarf, suddenly realizing he was hungry. 'What did he or she tell you?'

The Chasid stuck his gloved hands in his pockets. 'That Ephraim was clearly troubled, wrestling with issues.'

'Go on.'

Schnitman said, 'He couched the specifics in *Halachic* terms – what was the Jewish obligation of brother toward brother?'

'Interesting.' Decker nodded. 'Are we talking metaphorical?'

'Exactly, Lieutenant. Usually, Jewish brotherhood isn't blood brotherhood. It's the larger family of *klal Yisra'el* – Jew to Jew. But this time, it was literal. Ephraim was having conflicts with his brother.'

'Business conflicts?'

'Yes, it was business.' Schnitman nodded. 'Ephraim told his sponsor that he had talked several times to his brother about what was bothering him. But the problem didn't stop.'

'And?'

'Ephraim was at a crossroad. Either he had to turn

a blind eye or jump to the next step . . . telling his father about it. His soul was in turmoil.'

'Did Ephraim mention what the troubling practices were?'

'No,' Schnitman admitted. 'But it doesn't take a genius to figure it out. At the stores, Ephraim was in charge of inventory. Ephraim had told us that Chaim had taken some rather sizable loans for expansion—'

'Wait, wait, wait . . . when was this?'

'About two years ago. Ephraim was very excited. He felt that more stores would mean more responsibility, more chances for him to prove his mettle.' Schnitman blinked several times. 'Don't you people do your homework?'

'I just got out here last Friday. I'm not with the NYPD. Talking to you is doing my homework. Now go on.'

'That was rude. I'm sorry.'

Decker looked as his watch. 'You have around six minutes. I don't want to make you late.'

'It's all right. It's an old story, Lieutenant Decker. Old man works up the stores from nothing; then the son gets in with grandiose ideas to make it bigger and better. It appears that Chaim took out loans for expansion; then the recession hit. If that wasn't bad enough, the city was hit with the terrorist attacks. Business fell drastically. So not only was the expansion put on hold, but now Chaim was facing the more pressing question – how to pay back the bank?'

'Chaim stole from the coffers,' Decker said.

The Chasid shook his head. 'Chaim was in charge of the coffers. Stealing from your own store's inventory would be like stealing from your own wallet. You need a third party to rip off.'

'Insurance fraud.'

'Exactly. You put in claims for stolen items that you've never owned. Or you steal your own items out of warehousing, put in claims for them, then resell them on the black market – double-dipping. The problem is that it's all penny-ante stuff – pocket change. Plus, you do too much of it, red flags go up. When you're in real trouble – and I don't know if Chaim was or was not in real trouble – then it's time to hire the professional fire starter.'

Decker regarded the Chasid. 'You seem to know a lot about this kind of thing.'

'Emek Refa'im is a haven for those of us addicted to drugs. Many of us had big problems that led to drug addiction.'

'Things like guilty consciences.'

'Precisely,' Schnitman said. 'Ephraim appears to be no exception. Maybe that's what he was conflicted about, wondering if the store was going to burn down—'

'No,' Decker interrupted. 'I think if Ephraim knew that Chaim was planning to burn the warehouse down, he would have definitely gone to the old man.'

'Yes, you're probably right about that.'

'It had to have been something else,' Decker said. 'You're sure it was business practices that were troubling him?'

'I'm not sure of anything. I'm just repeating what someone told me.' He looked upward. 'I probably shouldn't have even done that.'

'I'd like to talk to the sponsor.'

'The truth is, I don't know where the person lives. I don't even know the last name. Some people are like that, I'm a little more progressive, but even I play it really close to the bone. It's not for my sake – I'm not ashamed of what I'm doing – but if it got out – my problems – my children would suffer greatly, especially in the future. It would be hard for them to find a *shiddach*.'

A *shiddach* – a proper mate set up by a matchmaker. 'Sins of the father,' Decker said.

'Correct.' Schnitman held on to his hat as the wind kicked up. 'But I do want to help. If you come next Tuesday, maybe the person will show up at the meeting. I'll give you an introduction, but that's as far as I'll go.'

'Next Tuesday, I'm back at work in Los Angeles.' He remembered what he told Donatti – sixty hours, now down to less than forty-eight hours. 'But thanks. You helped confirm what I suspected.'

Schnitman regarded Decker. 'You're a good man to come all the way out here to help your fellow Jews. You've probably gotten nothing but grief for your efforts.'

'You're right.'

'Moshe Rabainu got nothing but grief for his efforts as well.' Schnitman smiled. 'You're in very good company, Lieutenant.'

29

It was quarter to one when Decker made it back to the synagogue, but Jonathan was still in conference. Five minutes later, Decker saw his brother walking out of his office with a forty-plus, black-suited woman and a teenage boy. The woman held a balled-up tissue to her eyes, and the kid wore a sullen moue, his eyes focused on the exit door. *Problems, problems, problems.* Jonathan accompanied them outside, returning a minute later, trotting back toward his office.

'Jon,' Decker called out.

The rabbi spun around. 'Akiva. Is everything all right?'

'Yeah, everything's fine.' He did a little jog to catch up with him. 'You were in there for a while. How about some lunch?'

Jonathan said, 'If it's a social thing – and I suspect not – I can't afford the time. If you need me, I'm here for you.'

'Where are you off to?'

'I have to go back to Quinton.'

'Perfect! You can drive and we'll talk in the van.'

Instant hesitancy registered on the rabbi's face. Decker came to his rescue. 'I have no intention of visiting your in-laws. I have other business there – on the north side.'

Now his eyes were curious. 'What kind of business?'

'I'll tell you about it later. How about if I grab a cup of coffee and meet you at the van? It's parked down the street.'

Jonathan said, 'You found a parking space?'

'After a half hour of circling. Go get your things. I'll see you in a few minutes.'

It took more like fifteen minutes. And even when Jonathan did pull out, he couldn't get very far. Traffic was solid steel, distance measured in inches as the van crept over to the Henry Hudson Parkway, horns blaring in protest and frustration.

Jonathan remained stoic. 'There must be some dignitary in town.'

'I read something about a conference – National African Resource Agenda – over at a church.'

'That's right. The Riverside Cathedral is only blocks from the shul. I've been through this before. It's going to take time to get out of here.'

'It's fine with me.' Decker finished his coffee, placed it in a cup holder, then regarded his brother in his heavy wool three-piece suit and tie. Heat was blasting from the vents. 'Why don't you take off your jacket, Jon, while you have the chance?'

'Good idea.' The cars were at a standstill anyway. 'You suggested lunch. Are you hungry?'

'I can wait.'

'I have a couple of sandwiches in my briefcase.'

'In a few minutes, thanks.' Silence. 'Have you talked to Raisie at all?'

'Not since this morning.'

'I won't ask.'

'It's probably best that you don't.'

Decker ran a finger across his mustache. 'I need some confidentiality right now. I have to know that whatever I say won't go beyond these walls.'

'I understand,' Jonathan answered. 'Go on.'

'I talked to some people this morning, Jon. It seems that there was conflict between your brothers-in-law. I don't know the details, but it was over business. In a sentence, I think Ephraim was having some difficulties accepting some of Chaim's marginal business practices.' He recounted the conversation. 'Ephraim was thinking about going to your father-in-law, but then he was murdered. Anything you can add to help me with this?'

'Who'd you talk to?'

'I'd rather not say.'

'Is this person reliable?'

'No reason to lie.'

'I have no problem keeping your words confidential, Akiva. I'm a rabbi; I have privileges. But the confidentiality only goes one way. I'm not as free to talk as you are.'

Decker thought a moment. 'Attorneys have confidentiality. I'm a lawyer. I passed the bar. I even practiced a long time ago.'

'In California. We're in New York.'

Decker grinned. 'It would make an interesting test case, no?'

Jonathan paused, then took out a dollar. 'You're hired.'

Decker turned the bill over in his hands. 'And it looks like I'm reasonable, too.'

'It's no reflection on your legal aptitude.' Jonathan measured his words. 'I don't know much, but I'll tell you what I do know. Chaim was in debt. He actually borrowed some money from me – which I gave him. Five thousand dollars.'

'Not exactly pocket change.'

'No, it wasn't. When he asked for more, I gave him five, six hundred dollars. I told him that was all I could do. And in the future, to please remember that his sister wasn't working and I had three kids in private school.'

'You did your bit.'

'I thought so. He wasn't pleased, but he understood. A few weeks later, he came back to me. He said he knew I couldn't afford any more loans, but what about the shul? Could he borrow from the shul's *gemach* fund?'

'That's the charity fund, right?'

'Yes, *gemach* is the charity fund. However, I didn't consider him a charity case. Also, it was a terrible conflict of interest – bailing my brother-in-law out of debt. I told him it wasn't an option. He got huffy. For a while, he and I weren't speaking. Then about six months ago, we settled our differences. In the main, he apologized. He told me that at the time he was being squeezed by his creditors, that business had been terrible. He'd been desperate. But things had turned around. Business was slowly getting better. It was during Elul, so I figured he was taking stock in what lay ahead for him.'

Elul is the month before Rosh Hashanah. The thirty days served as a wake-up call for those in need to atone for the past year's sins. In Jewish law, everyone fell into the repentant category. Elul usually came around the beginning of September in the English calendar – around six months ago.

'And?' Decker prodded.

'And that's it. We reconciled. Especially after September eleventh, our differences seemed absolutely silly. He had us over for dinner; we had them over for dinner. We took Shayndie for a couple of weekends. Everything seemed all right . . . until this exploded in our faces.'

'What did Chaim do to turn the business around?'

'I was under the impression that he didn't do anything. That things simply improved.'

'So he didn't give you any specifics?'

'No.'

'What about Ephraim? Did he give you any explanation for the turnaround?'

'No, he didn't say anything to me. I always had the feeling that it took all of Ephraim's energies just to be Ephraim. He was dealing with his own set of problems.'

'I'm going to think out loud,' Decker said. 'Don't take offense.'

'I understand.'

'Chaim borrows from the bank to expand the business, then falls into deep debt. Recession hits and business turns terrible. He borrows here, he borrows there – from relatives, maybe from friends, to scratch by, to put the bankers at bay. But it's not enough. He gets panicky enough to ask you to do something illegal—'

'I don't know if he viewed it as *illegal*.'

'It's iffy at best, Jonathan. And even after you explained it to him, which I'm sure you did and in great detail, he balks. He stops speaking to you. Your words, right?'

Jonathan was silent, masking his apprehension by

concentrating on his driving.

'Then all of a sudden, things turn around,' Decker said.

'I don't know if it was all of a sudden,' Jonathan said.

'Business was slowly getting better, you said. Let me parse this out for a moment. Business *slowly* getting better doesn't mean a sudden influx of money – enough so that you're no longer worried about loan officers breathing down your neck. Business *slowly* getting better implies a stretched-out process.'

Jonathan said, 'I'm not following you.'

'That's because I'm working this through as I go along,' Decker told him. 'Okay. We have this slow recovery. But then I'm told that Ephraim was *upset* about Chaim's business practices. So you know what I'm thinking, Jon. I'm thinking that Chaim wasn't relying on his *slowly* recovering business to pull him through. I'm thinking that maybe the guy suddenly came into quick cash – possibly by illegal means. More than likely by illegal means – unless you know of any fortuitous inheritances.'

'You're making major leaps, Akiva.'

'Yeah, that's the fun part of what I do. The messy part is getting evidence to back up my ideas. Now let me play this out for a moment. The easiest way for Chaim to get illegal cash is by insurance fraud. Trouble is, claims take time. The turnabout was rather on the sudden side, correct?'

'I don't know how *sudden* it was.'

'Well, how many months was it from the time he asked to borrow the shul's money to the time you two reconciled?'

Jonathan tapped the wheel. 'About three months.'

'Must have been a hell of a three-month upturn in sales, Jon. Now if it were during Christmastime, maybe. But we're talking from June to September – traditionally slow retail months. Forgive my skepticism.'

Decker's stomach growled.

'Take a sandwich,' Jonathan told him. 'I've got tuna or chicken.'

'Which one do you want?'

'I honestly don't care.'

'Then I'll take the chicken.' Decker rummaged through his half brother's briefcase until he found the plastic bag and the sandwiches inside. 'What do you do when you can't wash?'

'Just make *Hamotzei*. I've also got some fruit, chips, and a couple of Diet Cokes. Raisie has a stake in feeding my gut. Help yourself.'

Decker said a prayer and bit into his lunch. 'Thanks, I'm really starved. Should we continue?'

'You mean should you continue.'

'Yeah, I am doing most of the talking. Anything you'd like to add?'

'Not at the moment.'

'Where was I?'

'Chaim's upsurge in business during the summer-time.'

'You're paying attention.'

'I always was a good student.' Jonathan's voice was bitter.

Decker took another bite. 'So how did Chaim get the money? Like I said before, insurance fraud not only takes time, but also the policyholder sets up a red flag by making too many claims. Now, I was told that when you want big cash from insurance, you destroy the entire stock in one fell swoop courtesy of a professional arsonist. But even if they pay off and you get the cash, it won't get you *quick* cash. For the same reason – claims take time, especially big ones. There would be a major investigation. So I'm asking myself what could Chaim do to generate quick cash.'

'And what have you concluded?'

'Several things.' Decker washed down the chicken-salad sandwich with his Diet Coke. 'This is perfect. Thanks. You're not hungry?'

'Actually, I am.'

Decker unwrapped the tuna sandwich for him. Jonathan said a prayer and took a bite. 'So how would Chaim get quick cash?'

'Money-laundering through his business, possibly. Chaim takes a cut of whatever he cleans. But then I have to ask myself how would Ephraim have found out about a money-laundering scheme since he wasn't in charge of any of the finances, didn't have any bookkeeping records or anything from the bank. So laundering wouldn't be my first choice.'

Jonathan finally made it onto the HH Parkway. It was bumper to bumper. He hoped the traffic would clear once he made it past the city. 'So what would be your first choice?'

'Narcotics. Drugs. Since you're my rabbi – and you're confidentially bound – let me tell you what my brother Randy the Miami Vice cop, told me.' He recapped his conversation with Randy. 'It seems that our brethren have been naughty boys regarding the illegal transport and sales of MDMA better known as ecstasy. As a matter of fact, I recall a big scandal about New York Chasidim bringing in the drug. Am I right about this?'

'It was years ago.'

'About three years ago,' Decker corrected. 'And it did have reverberations in the communities. So what do you think?'

'If I'm correct about this, you're deducing that Chaim got some money by being a courier of ecstasy.'

'Actually, I'm thinking out loud.'

'Then let me think along with you. Wouldn't being a courier imply that Chaim had made frequent trips to Israel or to Europe where the drug was manufactured and then back?'

Decker didn't answer. He knew what was coming.

Jonathan said, 'I don't think Chaim's left New York for the last ten years.'

'Maybe he didn't do it, bit by bit – or trip by trip. Maybe he did it in one big trip with one big score. You wouldn't know if he took a quick trip or not, would you?'

'No.'

'I think the only way to know about his travels would be to check his passport.' Decker smiled. 'Now there's an idea.'

'Forget it, Akiva.'

'What would it hurt?'

'You want me to go over to Chaim while he's sitting shiva for his slain daughter and brother and ask him about his passport?'

'Maybe not.'

'Definitely not!'

'You're right,' Decker said.

They crawled along the parkway in silence, both of them wolfing down the homemade lunch. When the van finally left the city limits – heading upstate via the Sawmill Parkway, traffic eased, and the wheels began turning at a nice clip. Feeling better with food in his stomach, Jonathan resumed the conversation.

'Do you have anything else to say, Akiva?'

Decker spoke carefully. 'Just that *maybe* Ephraim found out about Chaim's drug dealing and considered telling your father-in-law.'

'Ephraim wouldn't . . . *tattle* on Chaim – especially if it were a one-shot done deal. What would be the point? To give an old man heartbreak? Besides, if Chaim did score big – *one time* – it would have been at least six months ago, after Chaim told me that the business was looking up. So how would that fit in with Ephraim's so-called *ongoing* business conflicts with Chaim?'

A good point. 'Maybe he scored more than once.'

'Then he would have made frequent trips abroad. I've already told you that he didn't. We're back to where we started.'

'Well, maybe he was debating another big score, but this time Ephraim found out.'

'And how would Ephraim have found out? Frankly put, the two men didn't like each other. They rarely talked and only to keep peace in the family. Ephraim thought that Chaim was a self-righteous prig, and Chaim thought Ephraim was an irresponsible jerk. They kept their personal as well as private business very separate from one another.'

'But they did intersect in some capacity.'

'In some limited capacity, yes.'

'In business specifically,' Decker said.

'Yes.'

Inventory, Decker thought. *Ephraim was in charge of inventory.* 'Hey, how about this, Jonathan? Maybe Chaim didn't make frequent trips abroad. But maybe his products did. What about the merchandise? Did he import stock from Europe or Israel?'

'The family operates on high volume, low price. They buy cheaper wares that come from Asia, lots of Korean-made—'

'Well, isn't Haifa a major port stop from Asia? Rotterdam too? I mean, how easy would it be to take off the backs of the computers or stereos or VCRs or portable phones or CD players and slip in a dozen bags of ecstasy pills. It wouldn't have to be even that much. Say you bring in ten thousand pills a load, which is not very much to hide in big electronic equipment. At twenty-bucks-a-pop street value, you're talking around a quarter of a million dollars a shipment. And *how* many shipments does Chaim get in a year?'

It was a rhetorical question. Jonathan didn't respond.

Decker said, 'It's much easier to stuff the contraband into merchandise than to bring it across with people. And way more practical. Even if customs were to check for drugs, maybe they'd check one or two pallets. They're not going to go through the entire shipment unless they're suspicious, right?'

Decker was becoming animated.

'Ephraim's doing inventory one day, checking numbers on a list with numbers of the actual wares, and a back falls off a VCR. He suddenly discovers a bag of pills that was accidentally left behind. He knows instantly what's going on because he was a former drug addict. He goes to confront his brother but—'

'Forget it,' Jonathan said quietly.

'What?'

'I said, *forget it*!' Jonathan's face turned hard. 'Screwing Chaim isn't going to bring either Ephraim or Shayndie back to life. The family has already been destroyed, Akiva, do you hear me! *Destroyed*. My wife has been *destroyed*! I will not be a part of this. I will not bring any more misery to my family!'

'Even if there's evidence Chaim set up Ephraim?'

'But you don't have that evidence, do you?'

'Well, no, not yet—'

'I don't believe that for a minute!' Abruptly, the rabbi's face broke, tears rolling down his cheeks, blotted up by his beard. 'If you want to come after someone – if you *need* to come after someone – then damn it, come after *me*!'

'What are you talking about, Jon?' Decker studied his brother. 'What's wrong?'

Without warning, Jonathan jerked the van sideways, swinging it onto the shoulder of the expressway. He almost skidded out as the van bounced on wet dirt and gravel and small patches of ice. He killed the motor, slumped over the steering wheel, and sobbed. When he spoke, Decker could hardly understand him.

'I messed up, Akiva,' Jonathan choked out.

'What? *How?*' Decker touched his shoulder, then slipped his arm around him. 'C'mon, buddy, it can't be that bad. Talk to me.'

'It *is* that bad!'

'Talk to me anyway.'

He lifted his head, his eyes wet and red. 'I messed up . . . with Shaynda. I lied to you. I . . . lied.'

Vehicles were zipping past them, narrowly missing the van's taillights. Heart hammering in his chest, Decker waited.

'She called me – Shayndie called me.'

Decker held his breath. 'When?'

'The morning she was murdered! That's why it was such a shock! I had just *spoken* to her about three hours earlier.'

'Around seven in the morning, then,' Decker said. 'Did she call you at home?'

The rabbi nodded. 'She called me . . .' He strangled on a deep sigh. 'She said she was okay . . . that she was being taken care of. But I couldn't tell anyone – not even her parents, especially not her parents, especially not her *father*. She had sneaked out to call me, but it was against the rules if she wanted to stay where she was. If he found out that she broke the rules, he'd kick her out. So she had to go back really quickly . . . before anyone found out.'

'Who's *he*?' Decker asked.

Jonathan shrugged helplessly. 'We spoke for about . . . one, two minutes. Then she said she had to go. Just please, please don't tell *anyone* that she had called.' He looked at Decker with puffy eyes. 'I begged her to tell me where she was. I begged her to tell me who she was with. Of course she refused. Just that she was being taken care of by someone big and powerful. And that she was okay.'

A long silence.

'I told Chaim,' Jonathan admitted. 'I couldn't help it, Akiva. I just . . . he was my brother-in . . . if it had been *my* daughter . . .'

He turned away, beside himself with despair.

'I told him that he couldn't tell anyone. I told him it was imperative that he kept this between the two of us. But he probably told Minda. Maybe she told the wrong person . . . I don't know. I'm plagued with the thought that I inadvertently set her up.'

'It doesn't sound like it—'

'She begged me not to tell anyone . . . I should have taken it as a warning. Maybe my phone was tapped. Or maybe Chaim's phone was tapped when I called to tell him. I should have pressed her to tell me more, but it was so short . . .'

'If she called you at home, we could trace the call. It's probably a phone booth, but that could give us an approximate location of where she was staying . . . assuming that she walked over to the phone booth.'

'I should have gone to you.' Jonathan wiped his eyes. 'Asked you for advice before I acted. The way I did it . . . not only did I break confidentiality . . . but it may have cost Shayndie her life.'

Decker exhaled, then shrank in his seat. Jonathan misinterpreted his body language. 'You despise me.'

The laughter from Decker's throat was strong and sour. 'Oh my my!' He turned to his brother. 'You think *you* screwed up, guy?' He looked at the van's ceiling. 'I messed up *big time*! I saw her, Jonathan. I saw her and let her go—'

'*What?*'

'I let her go because she was being protected . . . or so I thought.'

'What? *Who?*'

'It's better if you don't know,' Decker said.

Jonathan grabbed Decker's shoulders, fury in his eyes. 'I just bared my soul to you. Your response is not *good* enough!'

Decker's immediate reaction was to punch back figuratively, but he stopped himself. Jon was right. He clasped his hands to prevent them from hitting or shaking. His heart was beating so rapidly, he felt choked off from oxygen.

Steady, steady!

'Okay . . .' He caught his breath. 'Okay, here's the deal. If we're going to sort this out, we've got to lay it all out in the open. But nothing – and I mean nothing – goes beyond the van!'

No one spoke. Cars continued to speed by, front bumpers perilously close to the van's rear end. Decker grumbled, 'We should get off the shoulder before we get hit.'

'In a minute.' Jonathan raked his beard with his fingernails, breathing hard. 'Okay. It stays between the two of us. Who was Shayndie staying with?'

It took a few moments for Decker to get the name out. 'Christopher Donatti.'

Jonathan's expression was stunned. 'Christopher Dona—'

'Ever hear of him?'

'Of course, I've *heard* of him. His father's trial was front-page news for six months! What the hell was she doing with *him*? What the hell were *you* doing with him?'

'I'll answer your second question first. When Ephraim's murder scene was examined, one of the cops mentioned that the hit looked like Donatti's work, but probably wasn't – too low level and too sloppy. But having nothing else to go on, I went to see him.'

'You went to see Christopher Donatti?'

'Yes, I went to see him.'

'Just like that?'

'If you let me explain—'

'You went to see a hit man!' Jonathan was agitated.

'Not just any hit man. You went to call on one of the most notorious *criminals* in mob history whose father ran the New York Family for over fifteen years? And for *what* reason?'

'Could you get the sarcasm out of your voice. It's pissing me off.'

Jonathan looked away. 'I'm just . . . speechless.'

Silence.

'I apologize for my rudeness,' Jonathan whispered.

Decker said, 'S'right. I deserve it.'

'No, you don't. I *assume* you were trying your best . . .' Jonathan blew out air, then wiped his smudged glasses with his handkerchief. '*Why* did you go to see Donatti if you suspected him of killing Ephraim?'

'I didn't suspect Donatti because the cops didn't suspect him.' Decker became morose. 'I went for help, Jonathan. Donatti and I had a past history together. I thought he might be a good source of information . . .' Decker hit the dashboard. 'It was asinine! I'm a stupid schmuck, okay?'

'You're not a schmuck, and you certainly aren't stupid.' Jonathan sighed. 'Who knows what drives our actions? We think we do, but we don't. God is behind everything and He may have had His reasons.'

'That's kind of you to say.'

'I'm certainly in no position to judge, am I?'

No one spoke as cars continued to speed by.

Decker continued. 'I saw Donatti a few times. He told me he had her.'

'What does that mean?'

'Donatti collects runaway kids – strays. Young girls and gay boys with nowhere else to go. He uses them . . . pimps them—'

'Oh my *God*! Did he—'

'No, no. He didn't pimp her. She hadn't been with him long enough. He had picked up Shayndie over the weekend . . . before I got to him. But he didn't tell me right away. We had to play this little cat-and-mouse game first. That's how it's always been between us – head games. Later on, he told me he had her. He said he told me as a favor so I wouldn't worry about her and I could concentrate on Ephraim's murder. At the time, I thought he was being truthful, but you can't tell with psychos. The man is a stone-cold killer and a pathological liar. You work with whatever you can get.'

Jonathan nodded. 'Of course.'

Decker ran his hand over his face. 'I would have sworn it was the truth, Jonathan, because I *saw* her. We arranged a meeting place, and he brought her to me . . . to show me that she was okay. Terrified but unharmed.'

'I imagine she was terrified, being with him.'

'She wasn't afraid of *him*, Jon; she was afraid of *me*! She was in dread that I was going to take her back with me – back to her parents. She was pleading with him not to send her back to her family, begged him to send me away. All she wanted to do was get back to where he had her stashed. She wouldn't let go of him. She was clinging to him like ivy suckers on a brick wall. When he wanted to talk with me privately, he had to *peel* her off him so we could talk alone.'

'It could have been an act.'

'No, it *wasn't* an act. When I asked her questions, she could barely answer me; she was shaking so hard with fright. She *whispered* her answers in his ear and *he* told me what she said.'

'What did you ask her about?'

'The murder, of course. What she saw.'

'And?'

'She said that Chasids took him – Ephraim.'

'Good God, what's this world coming—'

'Or—' Decker broke in. 'Or people dressed up as Chasids. Because they didn't resemble any Chasidic sect that I'm aware of. They wore *shtreimels*. Would you know anything about that? A sect that wore *shtreimels* on weekdays?'

'No.' Jonathan shook his head. 'But there may be one.'

'Or it could be that someone was playing masquerade but didn't have it down perfectly. Like certain Israeli Mafia drug dealers who are wanted in Florida for ecstasy dealing, but rabbited before the Miami Police could make the arrests. Just *maybe* they're hiding in Quinton.'

'What on earth would they want with Ephraim?'

'He might have known something, especially if Chaim was importing.'

'Akiva, Quinton knows every single member of its community. Fugitives couldn't hide there, much less integrate.'

'Unless they have prior connections in the community,' Decker retorted. 'Maybe someone is hiding them. Like I said before, if Chaim was involved in ecstasy importing—'

'Akiva, you have absolutely no reason to connect Chaim to such activities!' Jonathan was shouting. 'Where is any evidence for such outlandish accusations?'

Decker buried his head in his hands. 'No evidence.'

Jonathan covered his mouth, then dropped his

voice to a whisper. 'Even if Chaim was doing something illegal . . . I can't believe he'd set up his own brother! I refuse to believe that!'

'Maybe it wasn't meant to be murder, Jon. Maybe he was trying to scare Ephraim off. Maybe it just got away from him. Maybe I'm totally full of shit! I'm doing the best I can. Obviously, that's not enough. Otherwise, Shayndie would have been alive today.'

Jonathan put his hand on Decker's shoulder. 'Are you certain that Donatti didn't kill her?'

'No, I'm not certain of anything. But it doesn't make sense for him to do it. He knew that if something were to happen to her, I'd be all over his ass. Which was *exactly* what happened. He seemed genuinely shocked when I told him about the murder.'

'Could *that* have been an act?'

'Sure, he could have been snowing me blind, except she did seem so dependent on him. He even said that he'd return her to me intact when things cooled down. I guess I just decided to believe him because it was my only option.'

'What do you mean 'intact'?'

'He screws the kids he pimps. I think he does the boys as well as the girls. He said he wouldn't do it with her.' Decker waved him away. 'I don't know . . . I should have made a grab for her when I had the chance.'

'He would have killed both of you.'

'Probably. You don't want him on your bad side. Although I've certainly pissed him off and he's never done anything to my family or me. I don't know. Psychos like him . . . they're like these half-wolf/half-dogs that people adopt for pets. They're okay for a while. Then they just *turn* on you when the mood hits. Maybe that's what happened. Maybe he just turned. Maybe he considered it biblical revenge against me – eye for an eye, a girl for a girl. He thinks I screwed up his relationship with this girl. This could have been his big revenge.'

'What girl was that?'

'That's irrelevant. It was one of my cases, about eight years ago. When Donatti lived in L.A.'

'He lived in L.A.?'

'For about a year.'

Jonathan sat back in his seat. 'That's not what the Bible means when it states "eye for an eye".'

Once a rabbi . . . Decker said, 'I know. Rina explained it to me. It means monetary compensation. Can you dispense with the nit-picking right now? And let's get off the expressway. It wouldn't be good to make two women widows in one day.'

Jonathan started up the motor and carefully merged into speeding traffic. 'You're angry at me.'

'I'm angry at myself. I screwed up royally. I keep thinking to myself . . . what *should* I have done? Should I have gotten a gun and shot him? Should I have bribed him? Should I have gone to the police? All this Monday-morning quarterbacking. But at the time, I thought I was handling it pretty well.'

'You did the best you could.'

'So did you,' Decker answered back. 'Make you feel any better?'

'No. I feel that God was punishing me for breaking my word. Ridiculous, of course, but tell that to my conscience. Also, I can't help but feel that I set her up somehow. I should have gone to the police. Like you said, at the very least, they could have traced the call to a source. They might have sent out troops to look for her.'

They rode without speaking for several minutes.

Jonathan said, 'You honestly don't think that Donatti killed her?'

'Honestly, no. Because why would he do it?'

'What did he say after you told him that Shayndie had been murdered?'

'First I went into a rage. Then he went into a rage.' Decker pointed to his eye.

'Aha.' Jonathan nodded. 'That makes much more sense than the ridiculous excuse you gave me. Go on. What happened after he punched you?'

'He calmed down. We talked. He claimed that he last saw her around six that morning. She was just like she had been that night – clingy. He was hell-bent on revenge, Jon. I managed to convince him to hold off until I did all that I could do. Last thing I wanted was a professional mob cleaner sweeping around, especially if Chaim's not looking so clean.'

'Akiva, you have no proof!'

'I *know* I have no proof. But if Chaim's involved, it's better that I get to him before Donatti does, agreed?'

Having no comeback, Jonathan maintained silence.

Decker said, 'So this is the deal, Bro. You poke around Quinton and find out if there are any new and secretive people being hosted in the community. I go to the Quinton Police and try to find out if Shayndie was hanging out with the wrong crowd. Remember, Randy told me that there were some local Quinton boys arrested for ecstasy possession down in Miami. If they bought it down South, they most certainly bought it in their hometown. Maybe I can get the name of the distributor. Also, I might go back to Tattlers find out if any of the girls were ever asked to be couriers.'

'And they'd admit it to you? Just like that?'

'Well, no, of course not. That's why it takes a professional lieutenant detective with a genuine gold shield!' He smiled sadly, thinking of a sheltered fifteen-year-old who never stood a chance.

'Stop it, Akiva,' Jonathan chastised. 'You're a good man and I respect you immensely. I hope you feel the same way about me.'

'Of course I do.'

'So let's both stop the flagellation.'

'Deal.'

Jonathan said, 'Am I correct in assuming that you want me to help you?'

'Yes.'

'What you are asking me to do is to go behind my relatives' backs and play spy for you. Even if it means setting up my wife's remaining brother.'

'Yeah, that about sums it up.'

Jonathan was thoughtful. 'I will find out what I can. But I will not serve you Chaim on a silver platter. All right?'

Decker threw up his hands. 'Sure.'

Jonathan glanced at him, then focused on his driving. 'I agreed more readily than you expected.'

'Yes, you did.'

The van fell quiet.

'How far are we?' Decker asked.

'Half hour away.'

'Not so bad,' Decker said. 'Time goes quickly when you're having fun.'

'Indeed,' Jonathan said. 'I hope that I'm a better

partner for you than Donatti.'

'I'm sure you will be for the most part.'

'For the *most* part?'

'Chris has his benefits.'

'Such as?'

'If things get tight, the psycho's familiar with a gun.'

30

Coupling, by its very nature, meant somewhere down the line there would be an uncoupling, and when the inevitable happened, he'd always slip into a deep black funk, knowing that the only person in this entire world who gave a rat's ass about whether he lived and breathed was gone. He knew it was about money – he wasn't stupid – but she faked it well enough so that he could delude himself that some fraction of her heart *cared* even if she didn't love him.

Today was a perfect case in point, because it was good. *Too* good, and that made the loss that much harder, the void that much bigger. His mood was foul, and his dispirited body ached with profound deprivation.

As he lay in bed in a room devoid of any light, courtesy of blackout drapes, he stared at nothing, random thoughts drifting through his brain, a stupor made possible by booze and painkillers.

Yeah, today had been real good.

As measured by her orgasms because that was how he judged the sex.

It hadn't always been like that. She had started out like all the others. For him, sex had always been a one-way street because he didn't give a shit how the girls felt, and 99 percent of them were unable to climax anyway, so why even bother with a pretense. He assumed that Terry was like the rest. He did her like he did all of them, mounting her from behind because it was his favorite position – terrific view, good penetration, and minimum body contact. He abhorred being touched because physical contact in his youth always implied pain. Even the first time Terry had brushed against him, he had stiffened with revulsion. So he did it doggy style, even though almost all the girls he had ever fucked preferred being on top, probably because they felt more in control.

And that was okay for a few minutes. But then they started touching him as they rode him – an instant turnoff – and when it became too much, he'd flip them on their stomachs, pick up their asses, and shove it in from the back. So it was karma when he discovered that on-all-fours was Terry's favorite position, too; marveling at his luck, he believed he had finally found his soul mate in every respect. Then he got to thinking. Maybe she was *too* much of a soul mate, that she probably wanted it from the back for the same reason he had liked it – minimal body contact.

Perversely, that threw him in the opposite direction, where he now *had* to touch her when they made love. He'd lie her on her back, blanketing her skin with his own, smothering her mouth and face with kisses, his hands all over that marvelous body of hers. At first, she squirmed, clearly hating every minute of it, but eventually she calmed down, allowing him to do whatever he wanted – a small price to pay for all the cash he was feeding her.

Then one day, about a year ago, it happened. He was pumping away, looking at her face as he always did because it was so drop-dead gorgeous. Her eyes were closed, and she held a serene expression, yet her body underneath his was keeping time to his rhythm. Then, abruptly, he felt something – a quickening in her movements. In one silken movement, her legs swung about his waist, the heels of her feet digging into his ass as she pushed him deeper inside. Within moments, her breathing had intensified and heightened. Then she came, her face hot and moist as he felt her muscles contract around his cock. The sensation was so electrifying that he exploded instantly, probably not riding out her orgasm as long as he should have. It didn't matter, though, because now he knew what she was capable of.

From that point on, he became obsessed with her climaxing, rating every encounter not by his satisfaction, not even by their mutual satisfaction, but by hers alone. When it was good – like today – the high would last him for months. When it wasn't good, he became angry and sullen, berating her and himself for what had gone wrong, analyzing it ad nauseam. No amount of reassurance would change his brooding state. He had failed, and though she was quick to take the blame, it didn't help. He'd castigate himself, causing nothing but misery for both of them.

Once she tried to fake it just to please him, and that had made him even angrier, the fire so encompassing that he had lashed out at her in a blinding rage, a heartbeat short of hitting her. But he was better than his old man was because he knew how to control it, although she didn't know that. The pure fear on her face had haunted him for weeks. Still, in the end, it was worth it. She had learned her lesson and had never tried to deceive him again.

He knew he was making her nervous, but he couldn't stop himself. He had this self-imposed obligation to satisfy her sexually, to sate her with his cock, and anything less than an orgasm meant he was less of a man.

Today had been a *success*.

Even in excruciating pain, even with the fever and the dehydration, he had managed to bring her to orgasm two out of three times. He would have gone for the perfect record, but she claimed she was sore because it was right before her period or something ludicrous like that. He didn't challenge her because he was wiped out, glad to have an excuse even if it was a lame one. Afterward, he sat while she bathed, watching beads of water fall off her breasts, roll over her flat stomach. He thought about asking her to spend the night, but didn't. Although she'd never refuse him, it wouldn't have been what she wanted.

What she wanted was to get back to the kid.

It was all about the kid.

Which, in general, was okay. He was glad that she was a good mother. But sometimes it did piss him off.

Now she was gone, and he was in agony. He felt as mean as a tethered dog. Once she had loved him totally, had been willing to risk everything to follow him across the country with no promises in return. Then Decker came along and all that changed.

He took a small sip of Scotch from the bottle.

It's not that she wouldn't have found out. Of course, she would have found out. He had just wanted it on his timetable, after he had dug a hole for her that was way too deep for her to climb out of.

Decker.

Goddamnmotherfuckingsonofabitch.

After she had dumped him, he had been consumed with thoughts of revenge against her. He had wanted to pop her but held off because he wanted to do it with style. So he kept his watch, witnessing her steady decline into a deep abyss of debt, looking on as she exhausted all of her possibilities with no one around to bail her out. When she had neared rock bottom, he came to her in the dead of winter, into her shitty jail cell of a tenement – a one-room number with just a toilet and a sink – no shower – and a hot plate for cooking. Around nine in the evening, as he remembered it. The kid had been around three, asleep on the couch, and swaddled in covers. A twin mattress lay on the cement floor.

Fuck, it was cold inside. He had been dressed in a heavy wool suit, a cashmere overcoat, plus a scarf and fur-lined gloves; still, he shivered. He couldn't imagine how she could have slept in such frigid conditions let alone worked. But there she was, sitting at a card table, bundled up and breathing mist, stuffing what seemed like hundreds of letters into hundreds of envelopes, and doing it clumsily because her hands were encased in thick but old knitted mittens. A tape was playing – some college professor droning on about balancing chemical equations. Because she had been clad in layers, her body looked normal. But her face was the giveaway – as gaunt as a ghost.

In that single tick, seeing her steeped in poverty and humiliation, he had meant to pop her. More like put her out of her misery. It was so delicious, his intended revenge.

Except he couldn't do it.

He just couldn't disconnect from those golden eyes filled with degradation, her face awash in shame. Distant memories flooded his brain, and all he could think about was how much he still wanted her.

So he told her to pack her bags. She didn't even own a suitcase, throwing her meager belongings into two plastic grocery sacks. This all went down at a time when he still did occasional favors for his ex-father-in-law, so he still had the trappings – the limo, the bodyguards, a view suite in a posh hotel on Michigan Avenue. He took her to the place, her disgrace keenly visible as they walked through the crowded lobby. He was carrying the sleeping kid in his arms, leaving her like an overloaded donkey to tread through the public areas, burdened under the weight of her clothes, plastic bags, a backpack filled with heavy books, and an oversize purse. When one of his bodyguards moved in to help her, he warned him off with a subtle shake of his head.

Before he took her upstairs, he checked in with the management, saying that she'd be staying with him for a couple of days, that anything she ordered should be placed on his account. The head concierge in charge of customer service – some thin faggot of a guy who looked her up and down with disgust – became fidgety, giving him squirrelly looks, too scared to broach the subject because of *who* he was. The little twit of a man made him laugh aloud. He knew instantly what the stick up his butt was all about.

'Terry, show him some ID.'

With shaking hands and downcast eyes, she pulled out her Illinois driver's license and her Northwestern

Student ID card from a tattered wallet.

The faggot was instantly relieved. His concern had been understandable. She had looked around twelve.

He led her into the elevator to an upper-floor two-bedroom suite holding a panoramic view of the city's skyline. The living area was furnished with several traditional-style couches, a couple of stiff chairs, some side tables and dining-room set – typical run-of-the-mill pieces for a hotel penthouse. But to her, the lodgings must have looked palatial – judging by the size of her eyes. He watched her walk over to a large ceramic vase filled with fresh cut flowers. Still clutching her belongings, she held out a finger and touched a lily. When he told her that it was real, she blushed at her stupidity.

After she had settled the kid into the smaller of the two bedrooms, he asked her if she was hungry, tossing her a room-service menu. Timidly, she requested a dinner salad – the cheapest thing on the list. He ordered a hamburger, and seeing her covetous eyes, gave her half. She ate so slowly, as if each mouthful were her last, it was a torment to watch. When she was done – and it was clear that he was done as well – she took his leftover French fries and wrapped them up in a paper napkin, stowing the bundle along with the mini bottles of ketchup, mustard, and mayonnaise in her purse. He must have been staring because her skin went from pale white to deep crimson when they locked eyes. Instantly, he felt warmth suffuse his face, both of them embarrassed by how basic she had become.

In bed, she was all skin and bones, as shy as a virgin – as tight as one, too – and that only served to stoke his ardor. He was rough on her, all appetite and greed, but she treated him with proper respect and gratitude while still trying to retain some shreds of her massacred dignity. In the end, she couldn't pull it off. After it was over, she broke down and wept openly, her soul broken and futureless. She had whored for half a hamburger and a night out of the cold.

He had quashed her completely, had humbled every cell in her body. It felt okay, but not as good as he had imagined.

In truth, it left him kind of hollow.

Because he still liked her. It bothered him to see her in such distress.

He tried being nice. He smiled. He made small talk. He mussed up her hair and stroked her face. He offered her more room service, but she claimed she wasn't hungry – a bald lie. He sent out for the best champagne in the house. She dutifully sipped her one glass, but in the end, he drank the rest of the bottle by himself. Depleted, he fell asleep only to awaken at four in the morning to an empty bed. Sweat-drenched and in a panic, he bolted up and found her propped up length-wise on the couch, a blanket over her lap and feet, her nose buried in her studies. She had drawn the window curtains open, and it was snowing briskly outside – a sea of white diamonds against a charcoal backdrop.

She greeted him with an innocent face and a radiant smile. She said she was warm for the first time in two months and that her mind was finally able to concentrate on the material. If it was okay with him, she wanted to take advantage of the situation. She was drinking clouded tap water and eating his cold leftover French fries. After much prodding, he convinced her to take a jar of mixed nuts and a bottle of orange juice from the minibar. She ate methodically, a sip and a nut every five minutes so she wouldn't run out. He was leaden with fatigue, but he couldn't take his eyes off her. If she was aware of his scrutiny, she was unperturbed by it, completely absorbed in her textbooks and notes. By his calculations, she hadn't slept more than an hour or two, but she looked as fresh as if she were on vacation. Compared to what she was used to, she probably was. When dawn cracked the start of a new day, it was hard to tell who had actually gotten revenge on whom.

It had all returned to him . . . why he had liked her – no, why he had *loved* her so much. Because now, in the brutal light of morning, as he regarded her calm look and her cool demeanor, he realized that in the space of just a few hours he had lost his grip on her. He had smashed her, raped her soul if not her actual body, and she had sunk to bottom. What could he do to her now short of physical violence against her or the kid, a step he wasn't willing to take? Right now, she had nothing left to lose.

This night wasn't going to happen again. He had caught her off guard, had been given a small window of opportunity to act. Two months ago, she hadn't been as bad off, only a couple of months' arrears in her rent. Two months from now, in order to survive, she'd have to quit school and work full-time. Out in the job market, she'd find men who'd turn hand-springs for her. But as of yet, she didn't know that. Just the type of girl she was, so focused on her own end point of day-to-day living, she had never looked around.

How long would *that* last?

If he wanted her back in his power as well as back in his bed – and he really did *want* that – he was going to have to offer her something, entice her with her own dreams.

He gave her a proposition. She was in her third year of college, struggling to stay afloat. Her goal of becoming a physician was a solid one, but costly, therefore out of reach in her current financial state. Even with scholarships and loans, she wouldn't be able to hack it. Her debts were substantial, and mounting with each passing day. If she expected to continue in her studies as well as raise the kid properly, she would require money and lots of it. So why not take it from the father of her son?

The deal was straightforward – sex for support – as banal as any American marriage out there. While it was true that she could bring a paternity suit against him – that the law was definitely on her side – it wouldn't be to her advantage. He had the money and the lawyers to drag it through the court system for years. And he'd make demands – child-custody rights, weekend visitation, summer months and holidays, too. There'd be lots of animosity . . . irreparable damage. No, it wouldn't be good to get technical about it. It was much better to keep it friendly – more practical, too. His way meant she'd be in charge of the kid's moral and ethical upbringing without his interference. His way meant anything she needed, no questions asked.

Think about it, he had told her. No more debts hanging over her head, no more creditors beating at her door or writing intimidating letters that threatened homelessness if she didn't pay up.

Think about it.

An apartment with heat and air-conditioning, a real stove instead of a hot plate, a shower and a *bathtub*, for God's sake. There'd be money for food, money for clothing, private schooling, and music lessons for the kid, and, best of all, no more menial labor for her. Any job or work that she'd take on would be for her own personal growth, for her own personal *bank* account – money that would be hers and hers alone, funds not needed to fill stomachs or put a roof over heads.

Think about it.

Five and a half years from now, people would be addressing her as doctor. She'd have a time-honored degree and the respect that went along with it. Then there was the *income* that went with the profession, a surefire guarantee of self-reliance.

Think about it.

Holidays. He remembered what a good cook she'd been. There'd be a Thanksgiving table loaded with food – a big fat stuffed turkey, glazed yams with marshmallows on top, plates of fresh cooked vegetables, cranberry sauce, and pumpkin pie for dessert. How about new clothes for Easter mass? And what about a *real* Christmas with a big tree dripping in ornaments, dozens of presents underneath for her *and* the kid? Because this wasn't *only* about her, right? Didn't Gabe deserve to know his *real* father, not just some guy who pretended to like the kid when in reality all he wanted to do was get into her pants? *He* had things to offer Gabe. He knew that their son was gifted musically. From where did she think he had gotten the talent? He had attributes, things he could share with his son. But, of course, he'd *never* get in her way. She'd be the final decision when it came to Gabe's upbringing.

Think about it.

For her, he was erasing the past and all the bad feelings that went with it, replacing it with a secure future instead. And all he wanted from her, all he *needed* from her, was a few days every couple of months. Not too steep a price to pay, considering that there had been a time when she had done it for nothing. It wasn't too much to ask, was it? Some . . . *flexibility* in her attitude toward him? Because, c'mon, be honest, there were still sparks between them. This wasn't *just* about sex; this was about a *relationship*.

She listened intently. She listened without interruption. But she didn't answer him. No matter. He took her silence for acquiescence.

The next day, he went to work while she was in school and the kid was in day care, making his offer a fait accompli so she couldn't change her mind. He found a modest but clean two-bedroom furnished apartment complete with pots, pans, dishes, and utensils, and within walking distance to bus stops and the El. He went shopping for her, stocking the cupboards and refrigerator with food, filling the dresser drawers and small closets with needed clothing: winter apparel for her and for the kid – sweaters, pants, coats, boots, and scarves. He found a Gulbransen spinet piano in a thrift shop. It fit perfectly against one of the living-room walls. When he picked them up in the limo that evening and showed her what was possible, he was 99 percent sure it was over. Then when the kid went over to the piano – wondrous awe in those saucer mint-green eyes of his, tiny fingers tapping out the first couple of bars of Mozart's *Piano Concerto in C Major* – man, he knew he *had* her. He gathered up her mail, took it back with him to New York, and began the arduous process of sorting through her numerous bills.

For five and a half years, she would be his property – his chattel and concubine. And in the process, he figured he'd eventually fuck her out of his system.

A serious miscalculation.

Because it wasn't getting better. If anything, it was getting worse. Every time they parted, it was another knife slicing through his heart, and the knife kept getting bigger and bigger . . . the voices growing louder and louder. He didn't just want her; he didn't just crave her; he *needed* her. When they were together, she silenced his demons: her face, her voice, and her touch more soothing than any drug he had ever taken, more effective than any therapy he had ever gone through. She was his personally designed opiate, and he was addicted to her as surely as if she coursed through his veins.

Two and a half years left.

The thought of her being financially independent, that one day she might leave him yet again, only this time she'd take from him his own flesh and blood, seized him with heart-thumping anxiety. And now she was talking about marriage – *theoretically* – to someone else. His anxiety receded, evolving into uncontrollable rage . . .

What the fuck *was on her mind?*

His breathing quickened, and he knew what was coming. Slowly, the veil of deep depression would lift, converting its energy into unbridled frenzy. Then the urge would overwhelm him. By now, he didn't even try to stop it, knowing full well that there was only one way to quell it.

He reached under his mattress and pulled out one of his many firearms – a Walther semiautomatic. Holding the weapon ameliorated some of the feeling, but that was only temporary. Something more permanent had to be done. With sudden force, he shoved the magazine into the chamber.

Fuck the promises – tacit or otherwise.

He had a *job* to do.

First come, first served.

31

Despite the cold weather and the threatening clouds, there were more than a few joggers in Liberty Park, men and women in sweatpants and jackets, exhaling rapid puffs of mist like fire-breathing dragons. Beyond them lay the steel and glass structure of the Quinton Police Station, all sparkles in the dull sunlight, but as welcoming as a computer chip. Though the van's motor had been turned off for only a minute, the interior temperature was dropping quickly. Decker wrapped his fingers around the chilled metal door handle. He paused before tugging it backward.

'So you have my cell number, and I have yours.'

'Yes.' Jonathan rubbed a stiff neck. 'I don't feel good about this.'

'Don't do anything to your relatives that you can't live with,' Decker told him. 'I'll understand.'

'I'm not worried about myself. I have concerns about you.'

'Me?' Decker furrowed his brow. 'Why?'

'You didn't leave the police chief under ideal circumstances.'

'I'm just going to talk to the man.'

'Akiva, if he's crooked, he's not nice. You're in his

territory. That puts you at risk.'

'I know what I'm doing.'

'Do you?'

Decker mentally summarized the events of the past few days. It was more than a casual question. 'I'll be careful.' Then he opened the door and was out, waving to his brother as the van pulled away. He fast-walked toward the station, hands in his pockets – he had yet to pick up his gloves from Luisa – dodging the runners and the rollerbladers, wondering if he'd ever own the capacity to kick back and let go. It wasn't just this case – although this was personal – it was any case he was on. After turning the big five-oh, he kept waiting for the inevitable diminution of drives. Yet, as much as ever, he was still a slave to his twin obsessions, sex and work, both keeping him vital and sharp witted, but no doubt fueling his overheated engine. It was only a matter of time until he hit maximum burnout.

Precipitation had begun to moisten his nose, dotting the hard ground with distinct wet circles. He put some speed on and made it to the station house before the sky decided to open up. It wasn't warm inside, but the temperature was livable. Better still, it was dry. He went through the usual channels to get to Merrin, but because the town was so small, the red tape didn't take very long. To his surprise, Merrin was in. To his greater surprise, the chief agreed to see him – a promising start considering that Decker had acted like a fool the last time the two had met up.

As he waited, Decker worked on his excuses, playing with the fine points and the details of what he should say and how he should act. When the big man appeared – bulging stomach leading the way – Decker had perfected not only his defense but had also attained, in his mind, the ideal humble look. A glance at the face, then the eyes over the shoulders – an expression that didn't confront, yet held some dignity. He held out his hand as a peace offering. The big man took it, pumped it, then nodded for him to follow. The chief went over to the elevator and pushed the up button. Decker remembered that the office was on the third floor.

Merrin was dressed conservatively – blue suit, white shirt, blue-and-brown-striped tie. His platinum hair was slicked back off his forehead, his ruddy face had that wet look of the recently shaved. Underneath Merrin's belly, Decker could make out the chief's gun harness – a waist holster.

They strolled through the hallways silently, Merrin waving to his officers and detectives as he passed them. His secretary was on the phone, but he nodded to her as he took Decker into his office, closing the door behind. Because of the expanse of picture windows, the room was chilly, actually drafty in spots. Only half of the glass panes had been double hung. But the nip in the air was offset by the perfume of brewing coffee, sending up an aromatic steam that made Decker's mouth water. To distract himself, he looked outward, at the rain pelting the hard brown earth of the pathways, drenching the loose soil of the flower beds. The surface of the lake had become pitted silver. The corner suite afforded Merrin a good view of the park. It was not only pretty, but also allowed the chief to take in most of the area in a single glance.

'Coffee?' Merrin asked.

'If you're taking, so will I.'

'Black, white, sugar?'

'Black.'

He pressed the intercom on his desk and requested two black coffees. A moment later, his secretary came into his office, went over to the gurgling coffeemaker, and poured two cups for the chief – one in his ceramic mug, the second in a paper cup. Why the chief couldn't go over and pour his own coffee was left to speculation.

'Have a seat,' Merrin told him.

'Thank you, sir.' He waited for Merrin to sit, then followed suit. 'I appreciate your seeing me.'

'My imagination, Lieutenant, or do I detect a serious change in attitude?'

'I . . . believe that's an accurate assessment.'

'That's a good start. An even better start would be an apology.'

'I was embarrassed. I was an idiot. Does that suffice as an apology?'

Merrin smiled, his watery blue eyes crinkling at the corners. His mouth held bruised banana-colored teeth. 'I accept.' A sip of coffee. 'Now, what do you need, Decker? You wouldn't come here voluntarily eating shit unless you required something in the way of help.'

Decker raised an eyebrow.

'Yeah, I ain't as dumb as I look.'

'I'm from Gainesville, Chief Merrin. You know we're not all that different. Matter of fact, I use it all the time.'

'Use what?'

'The accent,' Decker said. 'Whenever I'm with a highbrow – someone I perceive as a slicker – the drawl gets thicker and thicker. The things people try to pull once they hear that twang in your voice.'

'Then you shoulda known better. Whaddaya need?'

'A girl's been murdered. Brutally.'

'Brutally, yes, but in New Jersey.'

'I think the reason for her death originated here.'

'Go on.'

'Her death was a side effect of her uncle's murder. And I'm not willing to rule out the family – yet.'

'You want me to investigate the family based on . . . what?'

'Sir, I don't expect *you* to do anything. You've got a town to run. I, on the other hand, have a few more empty days to play with. If possible, I'd like the names of the North Side kids whom Shaynda Lieber used to hang out with. Maybe she confided in someone outside of her community.'

'I doubt that.'

'You're probably right. Nevertheless, I'd like to give it a shot.'

'Unfortunately, I can't give you names. They're minors. While I feel very bad about that girl's death, I believe with all my heart that it had nothing to do with Quinton or its citizens. Sorry, Charlie, can't let you disrupt my town just on a hunch.'

'Well, how about this? Through my wiles and resources, I managed to land a couple of names. Would it get your nose out of joint if I paid them a call?'

Merrin's eyes narrowed, staring at Decker over the rim of his coffee cup. 'What names?'

'Just a few local Quinton kids who were hauled in for possession of ecstasy down in Miami. Correct me if I'm wrong, but several of them might even be eighteen by now.' Decker maintained eye contact as he sipped. 'Of course it's up to you, sir.'

'I suppose I shouldn't ask how you found out about it.'

'We all have our ways, right?'

'You are one sneaky bastard.'

'Coming from you, I'm sure it's a compliment.'

'Which ones do you want to talk to?'

'Ryan Anderson and Philip Caldwell. Both of them have reached their majority.'

'What do you know about them?'

'Nothing.'

'Then I'll tell you something.'

'Please.'

Merrin sat back, eyes on the ceiling, hands resting on his belly. 'Every town, every city has its share of bad boys. For Quinton, it's Anderson and Caldwell – two nasty little pricks who think it's a hoot to throw shit in their hometown and watch with glee while someone else cleans it up.'

'The parents have money.'

'Yes, they do, and we both know that money can buy a lot of janitorial work. But even money can't clean everything.' He put the coffee cup down and leaned over. 'This stays between the two of us, you hear me?'

'I hear you.'

'Those two have done some edgy things in these parts as juveniles. Things I don't need to go into. When they came back from Miami – after I heard what happened down there – I put the fear of God into them and into their families. I do b'lieve we came to a mutual satisfactory agreement.'

Decker waited.

'It goes somethin' like this,' Merrin said. 'I don't

poke my nose in their affairs as long as they keep their mess outside my jurisdiction. That don't mean they can get away with murder. If I seriously thought those two dogs had anything to do with the death of that little girl, I'd have their dicks in a vise so fast, they'd be talking like Alvin and the Chipmunks. But short of the biggies – murder, rape, assaults, robbery – I don't want you messing with their heads. Simply because I don't want those two bothering me or the fine citizens of Quinton. If that seems selfish, I can live with that.'

'Can I talk to them?'

'No, you may not go to their houses and interrogate them. But if you give me a couple of hours . . . well, maybe I can set something up here in the station house. Nice and clean and officially sanctioned.'

'More than fair, Chief. Thank you.'

'I suggest that in the meantime you go find yourself a nice, warm restaurant and nurse a long cup of coffee. Or . . . if your dick needs attention with the wife out of town, go on over to Tattlers and tell them that Virgil Merrin sent you. That way, you can have a good meal and some fine scenery on the house. Tattlers likes to cooperate with the law. It's in their best interest.'

Decker tried to smile wickedly. 'Sounds nice.' He took a calculated risk. 'I wouldn't mind some company. Wanna come with me, Chief?'

Merrin smiled with smoker's teeth, but his eyes never left Decker's face. 'Now that's kind of you to ask, but right now I'm backlogged. Another time, maybe.'

Decker nodded. 'You got it.'

'Maybe I misjudged you, Lieutenant.' Merrin

continued to study the face. 'Or maybe I didn't and you're being cagey.'

'Innocent until proven guilty. That's American jurisprudence.'

'Nah, that ain't American jurisprudence.' Merrin unhooked his holster and pulled out a Beretta. '*This* is American jurisprudence.'

'Are you telling me something, sir?'

'I'm not a man to cross.'

'I figured that out.' Decker got up. 'Thank you. You've been more than accommodating.'

Merrin rose, his belly straining the buttons of his shirt. From a wastebasket, he took out a pocket umbrella. 'You might be needing this.'

'Great.' Decker took it, then extended his hand. 'Thanks again.'

'Not a problem. Always happy to help out.'

They shook hands, extending the routine gesture just a little too long. Grip-to-grip and eye-to-eye, they were engaged in something more than a pissing contest, but hopefully less than mortal combat.

Tattlers wasn't a bad idea. If he could catch a cab, Decker figured he'd be there around three-thirty – after the lunch trade but before the dinner hour. If he were patient and charming, maybe he could slip a few bucks to one of the girls for an interview. Not that they'd admit dealing, but things would come out if he were clever enough. And, if nothing else, it would eat up the time. Merrin had told him to check with him in a couple of hours. If he made it back to Quinton around five, perhaps the chief would have one of the boys waiting for him. Maybe both of the boys.

Or maybe neither.

Because there was something about Merrin that irked him. Actually, there was a whole lot about Merrin that bothered Decker, but specifically that one off-the-cuff comment – an obvious blooper: 'If your dick needs attention with the wife out of town, go on over to Tattlers and tell them that Virgil Merrin sent you.'

If your dick needs attention with the wife out of town . . .

Now *how* had Merrin known that Rina had gone?

It was that kind of throwaway remark that made Decker stand up and pay attention, glancing over his shoulder, checking behind his back. It was that kind of wisecrack that made him wish he had a gun.

Cabs weren't readily available in small towns: They had to be ordered. As Decker walked through the park, umbrella over his head, he found a phone booth under a pavilion and placed the call to the local dispatcher. Twenty minutes later, a taxi came by. Decker shook out the umbrella and slid inside the back. The interior was damp and slightly ripe, but the seats were whole and held workable seat belts. The windshield defogger was going full blast, stale air keeping the front window clear. Decker strapped in and told the driver the address. The cabbie – a thin, young Caucasian with shorn hair, a pierced eyebrow, and a tattooed neck – turned around, his eyes dull and confused.

'Problem?' Decker asked him.

'It's gonna cost about forty bucks.'

'That's all right.'

'Okay, then.'

The driver pulled out onto the road, twisting through the rain-slicked streets of the main shopping district. Water was pouring off the awnings, rushing down the curbsides into the storm drains. Not a soul on the sidewalks, everything gray and deserted. Within minutes, Quinton was a dot in the distance. The cab was creeping down a two-lane highway sided by woodland foliage – heaping piles of naked brush, dripping pines and firs, and copses of leafless trees. Wipers, going full speed, were throwing water off the windshield as fast as the rain was dousing it. Decker felt his eyes closing, only to be yanked open at the sound of the cabbie's voice.

'You going shopping or somethin'?'

'No. Why?'

'The address is a mall. I figured you was goin' shopping.'

'No.'

A few moments passed.

'Tattlers?' the driver suggested.

Decker was annoyed, but an inner voice stopped him from shutting the kid down. He looked at the cab's license. The driver's name was A. Plunkett. 'Why? What's it to you?'

Plunkett scratched his nose. 'Just that . . . for forty bucks you're gonna pay me for transportation . . . I can do better than Tattlers for you. Know what I'm sayin'?'

Decker knew what he was sayin'.

Plunkett sniffed and looked in the rearview mirror. 'You know the girls who work there . . . at Tattlers . . . some of 'em like places where there's a little more privacy.'

Even better, Decker thought. *Get them alone and who knows what they'll admit to*. He counted to twenty. 'And you know a place like that?'

'Sure, I know all the good spots.'

'Local girls, Plunkett?'

The kid stiffened at the sound of his name. 'Is that a problem? Someone local?'

'I wouldn't want things getting around.'

'But you're not from around here.'

'I have friends in Quinton. You can't be too careful.'

'What kind of friends?' Plunkett asked.

'Now, I really don't think that's any of your business.'

No one spoke.

Then the driver said, 'Why don't you tell me what you want?'

Decker thought a moment. 'So it's forty to you and then I fork out for whatever else I want, right?'

'A quick learner.'

'Round trip?'

'Make it fifty and you got a deal.'

Decker took out a fifty-dollar bill and held it so it was visible in the rearview mirror. 'So . . . what would I get over there for . . . let's say a hundred?'

'What do you expect for a hundred?'

The kid was clever, waiting for Decker to speak first. 'I'd like something nice.'

'For a hundred, I could find you something *very* nice.'

He drove a few more minutes, then took a turnoff, the cab bouncing through the hillside as thunder cracked through the air and lightning webbed across the sky. Nothing around except shivering woodland as fierce winds shot through the empty branches. The taxi continued its journey, going deep into the forest. Five minutes later, he started to slow, and Decker saw it – a three-story white clapboard house, complete with tar roof and peeling paint.

'Whoa, whoa, whoa,' Decker said. 'This looks pretty seedy. I gotta wife. I can't afford to risk anything.'

The cabbie was vexed. 'Whatddaya mean? You gettin' cold feet? 'Cause I don't need this shit—'

'I mean, Plunkett, do they take precaution in there? I'm not carrying anything with me.'

'Ah . . .' Plunkett was relieved. 'They got all kinds of protection.' He pulled up alongside the house, missing a tree by inches. He parked. 'You wait here. I gotta clear this, okay?'

The driver opened the door, got out, and slammed it shut, leaving Decker in that awful metaphysical silence. Rain slammed onto the vehicle, suddenly blasting it with machine-gun volley. Decker leaned forward and looked out the windshield. Hailstones were streaming from the clouds. Involuntarily, he felt himself sweating, felt his heart beating too rapidly to be considered healthy. It stank inside. It reeked of bacteria and mold. It smelled rotten.

It smelled like a freakin' *setup*.

Decker took his umbrella, yanked on the door handle, and got out. He made a dash for the house, trembling under the eaves of a wraparound porch. Hail continued to fall, little perfect balls of ice bouncing on the dead ground.

Thinking about his options. Not too much to think about because he didn't have many alternatives. He could stay put . . . or he could run.

Heart going a mile a minute.

Then he remembered his cell phone. Extracting it from his pocket, he pushed the speak button and the satellites sprang up a dial tone – albeit humming with static. Quickly, he dialed Jonathan's number.

Seconds ticked by.

'C'mon, you son of a bitch, connect!'

Another second passed. Then it started ringing.

'Thank you, God!'

One ring.

'Answer, brother, answer!'

Two rings.

'Hello?'

Never had Jonathan's voice sounded so good. 'Hey, it's me and I got a big problem.'

'What?' Across the line, crackle threatened to break communication any moment. 'Can I call you back, Akiva? The connection's bad.'

'Don't hang up!' Decker shouted. 'I'm out in no-man's-land – somewhere up in the hills between Quinton and Bainberry, about ten minutes out of Quinton. As you're going toward Bainberry, you turn left off onto some barely noticeable turnoff; it's a side road—'

'Akiva—'

'Shut up and listen, Jonathan. Follow it up and you'll see a clapboard structure that looks like a broken down bed and breakfast. If I'm *lucky*, I'm at a whorehouse. If not, I'm gonna be shot at really soon.'

'Oh my God!'

'*Listen!* If I don't call you back in five minutes, come out and look for me. And whatever you do, don't call the Quinton Police. Call up the State Police, you understand?'

'Akiva—'

'There's my date. Gotta go.' He clicked off the phone and stored it in his pocket. 'Hey, Plunkett! I'm over here!'

407

The cabbie turned around and came over to him. 'Whacha doing out here?'

'I'm claustrophobic.' Decker's voice shot bullets. 'I'm getting pissed. Yes or no?'

'It's a go,' Plunkett said. 'Calm down, all right?'

Decker exhaled. 'Sorry. Let's go.'

The driver extended his hand. 'Hey, my job's done.'

'Wrong.' Decker grabbed him by the collar. 'You go in with me. I like introductions.'

And then he heard the click. Something in his primal consciousness must have anticipated it because his autopilot instantly grabbed the offending wrist. In a smooth, sharp twist, Decker wrested the gun away, feeling the grip slip from the cabbie's into his own hand. Then he nailed him against the wall, pressing the muzzle of the Smith & Wesson .32 snub-nose against the kid's Adam's apple.

Decker sneered. 'That wasn't at all polite.'

'What the fuck do you want from me?'

'Just what I said . . . an introduction.'

No one spoke, but the breathing was audible, both of them sputtering out big plumes of frosted air, chugging like an old locomotive.

'Why'd you pull a piece on me?' Decker asked at last.

'Why'd you grab me?' Plunkett retorted.

Slowly, Decker lowered the weapon. 'Maybe we just had a gross misunderstanding.'

The driver didn't answer. He licked his lips. 'You're a cop, right?'

Decker didn't answer.

'A friend of Merrin's?'

Within seconds, Decker's heart was battering his

breastbone. 'You might say that.'

Instant relief in Plunkett's eyes. 'Why didn't you tell me that in the first place? You get a discount with that, you know.'

Decker took in the words. Suddenly, Merrin's nomadic job history in Texas made sense. Lots of whorehouses in the small towns. Slowly, he let go of the kid's throat. 'All right, I appreciate the info. Walk me to the door, and you'll get your money.'

They eyed each other; then Plunkett took him to the front entrance.

'Open the door,' Decker told him.

Plunkett complied. Decker took a peek inside. Not much greeting him. A darkly lit paneled lobby with a couch and several empty wing-back chairs. There was a drink cart in back of the sofa holding cups and glasses as well as a coffeepot, an urn of hot water, and a half-dozen crystal cut-glass bottles of amber liquids. Decker thought about asking for the liquor license, but at this point, brevity was the soul of safety as well as wit.

He was face-to-face with a walnut desk and the young blonde who was manning it. Dark blue eyes peered up from a face framed by soft shoulder-length hair. She had decent regular features, but was a step short of pretty; her looks dropped a notch from the remnants of adolescent acne on the cheeks, though the pitting was hidden well with makeup and blush. She wore a short-sleeved hot pink sweater with a plunging neckline, showing off her stunning wares. She looked up at Plunkett, then at Decker, first at his face, then at the gun in his hands. Plunkett smiled.

'I just found out he's a friend of Merrin's.'

'Well, that helps.' The woman smiled with slightly

crooked teeth, the kind that would have benefited with just a touch of orthodontics. 'Come in all the way, sir. Don't be shy.'

Her voice was smoky. Decker placed the gun in his coat pocket and stuffed the fifty in Plunkett's hand. 'You can go now. Don't bother to wait. It may take a while.'

The cabbie looked at him. 'What about my gun?'

'Where's your license, Plunkett?'

No response.

'I thought so,' Decker said. 'I repeat. You can go now.' Eyes still on the woman, he called Jonathan up. 'Call off the posse. Everything's okay.'

Jonathan was screaming. '*Akiva, where are you—*'

But Decker turned off the phone, staring at the woman. If she was in her twenties, it wasn't by much. Her nails were meticulously manicured but with no polish. Decker continued to take in her face.

'What can I do for you, sir? Would you like to see a portfolio of our masseuses?'

Again that breathy voice, raising his heartbeat just a *little* too high. It took him a few seconds to put himself back in job mode. If anyone would have information, it would be the queen bee, not the worker ants. He caught her eyes and bore in. 'I like you.'

She smiled and kept the eye contact. 'Sorry, sir. I'm just window dressing.'

Nice and polite. Someone had taught her manners. 'You know what, darlin'? That's okay with me. Right now, all I want to do is talk.'

Eyes fixed on his face, her expression hardening. 'Against the rules.'

Decker took out a hundred-dollar bill. 'You know, I

bet it's pretty slow right now. We don't even have to tell anyone.' He winked. 'Please?'

Stealing a quick glance over her right shoulder. Decker followed it and made out a small door that blended neatly with the lobby's paneling. Someone was behind there. No doubt someone with a gun. Again she shook her head, her carriage holding the confidence of big-time protection. Merrin had his fingers in a lot of pies. She kept her eyes on Decker's. 'No can do, sir.'

'I'm a very good friend of Chief Merrin's,' Decker persisted.

'I'm glad to hear that, sir, but that's completely irrelevant – other than the ten-percent discount. Which I'm happy to extend to you for any of our massage therapists.'

'So that's what they're calling themselves nowadays.'

Abruptly, her eyes turned gelid, a very familiar expression, though he couldn't quite place it. And then, in a flash, it came to him – that 'Of course, you idiot' sudden brand of insight that made you want to hit your forehead. He smiled slightly, giving her a superior look. 'And what would you do . . . if I told you that C.D. sent me?'

A red wash permeated her cheeks. Again a glimpse behind her back. 'ID, please?'

Decker took out his driver's license. She took it, got up, and locked the front door, hair brushing over her shoulders as she walked. She wore a black leather miniskirt and spiked heels. He watched her rear sway as she disappeared behind the panel-hidden cubby. Five minutes later, she returned. Without a word, she took Decker's hand, leading up the stairs. Her expression had turned blank, not a hint of defiance. There was no eye contact this time. Some mysterious, hidden voice had told her to behave. Failure to do so would have serious repercussions.

32

The suite was at the end of a long, narrow hallway, up two steps and facing the back of the building. Dark and musty, it held yards and yards of draped cloth over the windows and hanging from the ceilings: rich fabric in oxblood velvets and ruby satins. Between the textiles were mirrors – on the walls and on the ceiling. The bed was king size, dressed in gold silk and layered with pillow upon pillow. A crystal chandelier threw disco light over a bedspread vaguely redolent of cigarette smoke and perfume. So prototypical whorehouse, it could have been a movie set. The blonde went over to a mirror and bent down, showing off a nice, tight rear. She pushed in a panel, and a cubby opened up. She took out a portable phone and stood up, extending it to Decker.

'He wants to talk to you.'

Decker paused, then took the receiver. 'Thank you.'

She sat down, perched on the edge of the bed. The mattress undulated. *How neat!* Decker thought. He and Jan had had a water bed during the 1960s when that kind of thing was ultracool. They had to give it away because it had killed his back.

He pushed the talk button. 'Decker.'

'Lay off Merrin. He's a gold mine for me – him and you Jew boys. You kikes are a real horny lot, you know that.'

It took Decker a few minutes to integrate Donatti's words. 'I take it this is a protected phone?'

'I do my best, but nothing's guaranteed. You talk on any line, you take your chances.'

'You don't seem concerned.'

'Why should I be concerned? What's wrong with calling up a massage parlor? I'm not known for my high-class taste.'

'You own the place.'

'Me? I don't own anything like that. Can't get a license being a convicted felon. Terry, on the other hand . . . now there is one rich lady. She owns a string of them.'

'Does she know?'

'She would if she'd bother to read her tax return. You know Terry . . . lives in her head. As it stands, I do the accounting: She's happy just to sign on the dotted line. Anyway, it's not like it's a *bad* thing. Massages are very good tension relievers.'

'You know, Donatti, I see lots of velvet and mirrors here. A big mother water bed. But no massage table.'

'The clients like atmosphere. And if you look in the bathrooms, you'll see we have lots and lots of oil.'

'What do you know about him? Merrin?'

'Not much except that he likes his massages. He brings in other clients who like massages. Because he's such a good referral source, the place gives him deep discounts. All the masseuses are over eighteen, by the way.'

'Comforting,' Decker replied. 'I don't think Merrin likes me.'

'Could be, Decker. I don't like you, either.'

'What else do you know about Merrin?'

'You know, I'm big on delegating. Jen would know more about the locals.'

'The comely blonde in reception.'

'I'm glad you approve.'

'Mind if I ask her a couple of questions?'

'You can ask. I don't know what she'll tell you, even though I've instructed her to be very, very *nice* to you – a big concession because her pussy retired three years ago.'

'I don't want sex, Donatti; I want answers.'

'Sex is always the answer, Lieutenant.'

The line went dead.

Decker handed the phone back to Jen. She took it, stowed it, and sat back down on the mattress, patting it for him to sit down. He sat, setting off a tidal wave. Her hand went to his knee. Her voice was a siren's whisper. 'What can I do for you?'

He took her hand away from his thigh. 'Probably nothing if Donatti shut you up.' He stood and leaned against the wall. She came up from behind and slipped her hands around his waist, pressing her body against his back. It felt nice, but he shook her off. 'I'm married. I don't cheat. Don't touch me, all right?'

He turned around, facing with her puzzled – and slightly wounded – blue eyes. 'What? Did he tell you to seduce me? He's playing games. He knows I don't do that kind of stuff. Sit down.'

She retreated to the bed and sat down with her hands in her lap, as obedient as a schoolgirl.

'Do you live in Quinton?' Decker asked her.

'Rosehill.'

'Where's that?'

'About ten miles east of Bainberry.'

'Separated by woods?'

She nodded.

'What's this area? Like a series of little townships?'

'Exactly.'

'And why did you choose to settle in Rosehill? Did he set you up there?'

'My husband's practice is in Rosehill.'

'Your *husband*.'

'Yes.'

'What does your husband do?'

'He's a physician. Family medicine. He's been in Rosehill for over thirty years.'

'Thirty years.'

'Yes.'

'He's quite a bit older than you?'

'Yes.'

'I don't mean to imply anything negative about that. I'm much older than my wife . . . well, not *that* much older.' Decker began to pace. 'Does your husband know what you do?'

She regarded him defiantly. 'What I do is secretarial work. Nothing more.'

'A few moments ago you were willing to do more.'

Her eyes were steel. 'Doing an old friend a favor, that's all.'

Decker stopped and rubbed his forehead. 'You know a girl from Quinton was murdered about five days ago.'

'Yes. Down in New Jersey. A shame.'

'She was fifteen years old.'

416

'A terrible shame.'

'You get clients from Quinton?'

'Sure.'

'The Jews come in?'

'Yes.'

'Have you ever serviced a man named Chaim Lieber?'

'We keep our clients' names private. People expect that, you know? But since you seem to have a . . . personal relationship with Mr Donatti, I'll answer the question.'

'Thank you.'

'No.'

'A big buildup for a letdown.' Decker laughed. 'He never came in . . . Chaim Lieber.'

'No.'

'What about his brother?'

'Who's his brother?'

'Ephraim Lieber?'

Again she shook her head no.

'Merrin comes in here a lot.'

She grew quiet.

'Nice man?'

'He's always been polite.'

'Good to hear.' Decker began to pace again. This was getting nowhere. 'Let me ask you this, Jen. If I wanted to fly a little, where would I go?'

Her smile was patronizing. 'To the airport.'

'Very funny. Could you answer the question?'

'I wouldn't know. This is a spa, not a rave.'

'A spa?'

'We have a steam bath. Are you interested?'

'No, I've been wet enough for one day, thank you.' Again Decker tried to change tactics. 'So you get some Quinton people in here.'

'Yes.'

'Men who like their privacy.'

'Yes.'

'Probably get some boys in here, too. You know, horny kids looking for some action.'

'All our clients are over eighteen.'

'You card the ones who look underage?'

'Of course. We don't want problems.'

'Merrin get a kickback for looking the other way?'

'I don't know what you're talking about, Lieutenant.'

First time she had used his title. Donatti must have told her.

'You get some bad boys in here, Jen?'

'We get all types of men. But if they want a massage, they mind their *p*'s and *q*'s.'

Nowhere, nowhere, nowhere. C'mon, Decker. You're a professional, for God's sake.

He remembered Donatti's words for snagging the girls: 'tea and sympathy'. How many times had he used that approach with juveniles himself? He sat down on the floor, his legs extended outward, back against the bed. He tapped the carpet, indicating for her to sit next to him. She followed dutifully, tucking her legs under one another, her spine straight up. He kept his eyes on her stoic face, dropping his voice to something soft and soothing. 'How old are you, Jen?'

'Twenty-one.'

'Twenty-one.'

'Yes.'

'My daughter's twenty-five.'

'Really. You don't look that old.'

He smiled. 'I also have another daughter . . . from my second wife. The one who's much younger than I am. That daughter . . . she's nine going on thirty.'

Jen smiled.

'Do you have children?' Decker asked her.

'Yes.'

'How many?'

'Two.'

'How old?'

She swallowed. 'Six and one.'

'Boys? Girls?'

'A girl and a boy.'

'The oldest is a girl?'

She nodded.

'That's great.' Decker smiled. 'Six is a wonderful age, isn't it?'

'Yes.' She stared at her lap. Her black leather miniskirt barely covered her panties. 'Yes, it is.'

'So full of life . . . so full of trust and curiosity.' He sat back, laced his hands behind his neck, and stretched. Then he pitched forward, a concerned expression in his eyes. 'I worry about my little one. It's hard growing up in this day and age, especially because we've seen terrible things. Talking professionally, I've seen many, many bad things up close. Not too encouraging.'

She said nothing.

'All these bad boys, these . . . evil people that I arrest. It jades my perspective. I worry that my . . . my negativity will rub off on her. But you know what?'

'What?' she whispered.

'It doesn't. Kids are remarkably resilient. Don't you find that to be the case?'

Her eyes clouded. 'Sometimes.'

'Well, look at your own little girl. And look at *you*. I

419

mean, it couldn't have been easy having a kid at fifteen. But look how you're doing. You've got a good job. A husband who probably loves you very much . . . right?'

'Right.'

'Two beautiful children. Great fun, huh?'

She nodded.

'Yes, indeed. Just look how well you're doing. You've got a lot to be proud of. I'm sure you're a real role model for your daughter.'

She turned her head away. Her eyes had become wet. 'That was nasty.'

'What?!' Decker threw his arm around her. 'My God, what's wrong? What did I say?'

Burning eyes lit into his. 'Nothing . . .'

'Nothing? You're as pissed as hell. I'm sorry. What did I say?'

'You didn't say *anything*.'

'I'm sorry. Honestly. Tell me what I said?'

She wiped her tears with her fingers. '*Nothing*.' Then she hid her face in her hands. 'Nothing at all.'

'Man, Donatti's going to get mad when he finds out I've upset you.'

'Oh God!' Panic crossed her eyes. 'I'm so sorry—'

'Sorry for what? I offended *you*!'

'No, you didn't! You didn't at all.'

'You're afraid of him – Donatti?'

'No, not at all.'

'Come on, Jen. It's okay. Is he . . . hurting you at all?'

'Of course not!'

Decker watched her as she sniffed and wiped her face, her eyes redder but softer. 'Your daughter?' he asked. 'Is she Donatti's kid?'

She laughed through her tears. '*No*.' A pause. 'I wish to God she *was* his.'

Decker nodded. 'Some jerk took advantage of you, huh?'

She was still furious, but fear made her answer him politely. 'My sister's husband.'

'Oh God . . .' Decker sighed. It was heartfelt. He leaned back and inched away from her. 'I did a lot of Juvenile before I transferred to Homicide. You do Juvie, you deal with lots of sex crimes involving minors. That's what it was, Jen. A sex crime. Because at fourteen, it certainly wasn't anything you did. It was all about what *he* did. And what *he* did . . . was a sex crime.'

The tears going full force.

'They're all the same . . . all of them.' Decker raked his hands through his hair. 'They're all monsters.' Another sigh. 'Raping your wife's fourteen-year-old kid sister. It doesn't get any lower than that.'

No one spoke.

'Yes, it does,' she whispered. 'It does get lower.'

Decker waited.

'No one believed me. My sister . . .' Jen clasped her shaking hands. 'She called me a lying little slut. My father beat me. My mother stood by and didn't do anything. They put my daughter in a foster home. When they tried to force me to sign papers . . . putting her up for adoption . . . I ran away.'

'What a mess! I am so *sorry*.'

'Mr Donatti . . . he took me in. He—' She was choking back sobs. 'He introduced me to my . . . to my husband. He . . . he was one of Mr Donatti's clients.' She wiped her face. 'My husband . . . he proposed to me on my eighteenth birthday. Mr

Donatti told me to go for it . . . to marry him. He told me that he'd take care of me. And he does . . . my husband takes good care . . .' Another sniff. 'He takes *very* good care of me. He loves me very much.'

'I'm sure he does, Jen. Who wouldn't love you?'

She tried to stem her weeping. 'My husband . . . he helped me get her back – helped me get my daughter from her foster parents. He paid for the lawyer; he paid for everything.' Again she broke into tears. 'Oh God, I'm so stupid.'

'Hey, it's okay.'

'No, it's not! When Mr Donatti finds out—'

'He won't find out because neither one of us is going to tell him.'

She looked away and sobbed out, 'He'll find out!'

'So big effing deal!' Decker took her chin and turned her face to his. He looked her in the eye. 'I'll handle Donatti, all right?'

She didn't answer.

Decker let go of her face, riding out her crying. Finally, after it had subsided, he said, 'Jen, that Quinton girl I was telling you about? The one who was murdered?'

'Yes.'

'Did you know her at all?'

'No.' She sighed a sob and shuddered. 'Just what I read in the papers.'

'That's why I'm here. To find out who killed her.'

She didn't comment.

'She was only fifteen, Jen. Just like you when you gave birth. Only she never had a chance to redeem herself – like you did.'

'I haven't really *redeemed* myself. Working day in and day out with ugly men and perverts leering at my boobs and butt, trying to grab a piece of my snatch.'

'You look like you can handle yourself very well.'

'I hate it!'

'Then why don't you quit?'

She couldn't look at him. 'You wouldn't believe it if I told you.'

'He won't let you?'

'No, not at all. I don't think he'd care. He's got others to take my place. And this is actually a *paying* job.'

'Unlike the other assignments he's given you?'

'Mr Donatti has been nothing but wonderful to me.'

Staunchly loyal. Go figure. Decker said, 'Then why don't you quit?'

'You'll think I'm horrible.'

'Nah, I've heard it all.'

She didn't answer.

'Hey, try me!'

She sighed. 'I love my husband, I really do. But he's fifty-six, Lieutenant. And he's not a healthy fifty-six at that. He's had a difficult life. His first wife died after a ten-year battle with breast cancer. He has chronic heart problems ... high blood pressure. We don't do too much ... obviously, we do something. We have a son. But it's not ... you know. And after what I've gone through ... that's really okay with me. But still, there are times ...' A pause. 'Mr Donatti ... he comes here occasionally ... to check up on what's going on. He's ... he's a good-looking guy. I'm still young, you know.'

Her eyes begged to be understood.

Decker smiled. 'Got it.'

Her voice got tiny. 'It's just that I feel comfortable

with him. Protected. I know he used me – that's what those guys do – but he was okay about it.' Silence. 'Not a lot of choices for a fifteen-year-old on the streets. I've heard some real horror stories. I turned out okay considering . . .'

No one spoke.

'We're not that different, you know – me and Mr Donatti. I'm a user, too.'

Meaning her husband. Decker said, 'I understand what it is to feel . . . indebted. I've got a few buds like that myself. One of them . . . helped me out in Vietnam. Saved my life actually. No matter what he does to screw himself up, I always feel obligated to pull him out of the muck.'

'You're a real good listener, you know that?' She pulled her legs straight out, yanked down on her nonexistent skirt, and lay her head on his shoulder. 'Sure I can't do anything for you?'

'You can do a lot for me, and I don't mean sex.'

She sat up. 'So . . . you really want information only?'

'Yes,' Decker said.

'Your wife must be amazing.'

'She is. Tell me about Merrin.'

'Horny old goat. Looks the other way when it comes to this place.'

'Donatti pays him off?'

Her shrug told him he was on the right track.

'Does Merrin look the other way with other things?'

'Like what?'

'Like if I wanted to score ecstasy, would I go to Merrin?'

'I have no idea.' She faced him. 'That's the truth. I

only know Merrin as a client.'

'Well, who would I go to?'

'I don't know. I don't do drugs.'

'What about some of the other girls? I know you have a few here who also work at Tattlers.' Decker took a stab in the dark. 'I've heard you can get a variety of pharmaceuticals over there.'

'Plunkett, right?'

'Right,' Decker lied.

'Figures. He's a real jerk, but he's a good source for referrals.'

'So maybe those girls would know about scoring . . . the ones who work at Tattlers?'

'You'd have to ask them. We don't have anything on the premises, that much I know.'

'Anyone here from Tattlers that I can talk to?'

'Maybe Angela. She'll be free in a half hour or so.'

'Could you set that up *without* calling him first?' A smile. 'Please, Jen?'

She looked at him and shrugged.

Decker didn't push her. 'So you know the people in these townships pretty well?'

Jen laughed softly and bitterly. 'I know the horny ones.'

'What about the boys?'

'Lots of horny boys.'

'Ryan Anderson and Philip Caldwell.'

Her face darkened. 'I know Caldwell. He came in about two months ago. Right when he turned eighteen. Rich threw him out.'

'Who's Rich?'

'The bouncer.'

'The one who's behind the paneling in the lobby.'

Her expression was stunned. 'You don't miss a

425

trick – oh, that's right. I went there to phone Mr Donatti.'

'Yeah, but I figured it out before. You kept looking over your shoulder. So Rich threw Caldwell out. Why?'

'He was roughing up the girl. It was Angela, come to think of it. Rich got to her before the little prick could do real damage. All the rooms have video cameras.'

Decker laughed. 'Oh really?'

She pointed to the crystal chandelier.

'Rich must like his job,' Decker said.

'He's gay and all business.' She looked down. 'Everything's being recorded. Eventually, Mr Donatti's gonna see the video. He's gonna hit the ceiling.'

Decker patted her knee. 'Look, Jen. He wanted you to pump me for information using whatever means, right?'

She was quiet.

'He knows me. Sex wouldn't be an option. That means he knows you'd have to feed me info to keep me talking. My questions will tell him a lot. Was he pissed, by the way . . . Donatti?'

'What do you mean?'

'That this punk Caldwell was roughing up one of his girls?'

'He didn't find out about it until way later . . . when he reviewed the tapes. Mr Donatti doesn't like problems. That's why we're here. So he doesn't have to deal with problems.'

'I see. What about Anderson? Ever come across him?'

She thought a moment. 'If I did, I don't remember. They're all the same, these rich-kid brats. All swagger, all bravado. Each one thinking they're the biggest, baddest dude on the block. They deal in drugs; they show off their guns and knives; they think they're real tough. They think they know what it's like on the streets, but they don't know shit. They don't know how good they have it. They don't know what's important. They have it all, and yet they have nothing.'

The tears had come back in slow, steady droplets, but she didn't appear to notice.

'Sometimes . . . sometimes God is just so unfair.'

33

He had about fifteen minutes to kill before Angela from Tattlers was done with her 'massage' client. Stepping outside into the bracing air, Decker tried to clear his mind. The slashing rain had turned to steady globules of water, the woodland foliage melding into a thick curd of grays and browns as the daylight dimmed. He tightened the scarf around his neck and dug his hands into his pockets, feeling the jolt of iced steel on his fingers. He had forgotten about the snub-nose. He took it out, opened the chamber, and peeked inside. Four bullets. He snapped it shut, then secured the safety latch.

It would have been a perfect time for a smoke and a shot of scotch. He was cold and thirsty and could have used a kick to the system. He was sure that the place had a stash of stag toys, and with Rina absent, he didn't have to worry about his breath or his bad behavior. That was the attraction of whorehouses. Guys could be swine and that was not only acceptable but also expected. Donatti was a down-and-dirty psycho, but the bastard understood married men. It wasn't just a sex issue – though that played a big part – it was a control issue. Men prized freedom. Married men got tired of dealing with their wives because wives were constant reminders of their lost liberty.

In this seedy house of ill repute, he wasn't as alienated as he should have been. In 'Nam, he had frequented brothels, but once he returned to the States, he didn't need to pay for it. It was the 1960s and he was working in a college town. Free love was plentiful, although he frequently lied about his job when he went to bars. Cops were part of the Military-Industrial Complex (whatever that was), pariahs with the flower-power generation. So instead of telling the girls that he was a vet and a cop – hence the short hair – he told them that his hair was short because of lice he had picked up in the Amazon jungle. They bought it hook, line and sinker.

Sometimes, after he screwed them, if he was feeling particularly mean – and back then he often felt *very* mean – he told them what he really was. Far from being turned off, the women were excited by his profession, as if they were cavorting with the enemy. Jan had been one of those types. He had arrested her at an antiwar demonstration. Two nights later, they were humping like rabbits. Three months later, they were married. Six months later, Cindy was born.

Yadda, yadda, yadda.

Then there was that interim period after the divorce. Five years of being single before he had met Rina. The first couple of years were heaven – lots of sex with no emotional entanglements. The years that followed were absolutely dreadful – lots of sex with no emotional entanglements. Somewhere between the job and the sheets, he realized that the good life wasn't endless sexual encounters and a fourteen-hour workday. He knew he was in serious trouble when he preferred his horses to his dates.

Thank God for Rina.

He suddenly missed her terribly, missed her and Hannah Rosie and his routine back in L.A. He wanted to go home. Instead, he was out here, freezing his balls off, trying to help a family that despised his intrusion. But it was too late for him to backtrack. He thought of the Liebers, of the hell they were going through. He wondered if Jonathan could be objective enough to give them pastoral comfort . . .

Jonathan . . .

He'd been out of contact with him for the past hour. Maybe it would be a good idea to touch base. He turned on his phone but couldn't bring up a dial tone. He walked back inside, shaking the cold from his bones.

Jen looked up, then at her watch. 'Shouldn't be too long now, Lieutenant.'

'Could I borrow your phone?'

She pushed it toward him, her chest stretching over the desk, giving him a full view of cleavage. Maybe Donatti had instructed her to give it one more try.

Decker averted his eyes. 'Thanks.' He dialed up Jonathan's cell phone. It connected but was full of static. 'Jon! Can you hear me?'

'Where the *hell* are you?'

Through the electronic noise, Decker could tell his brother was yelling. 'Is something wrong?'

'Is something *wrong*? Everything is *wrong*! I've been trying to get hold of you for the past half hour! I'm driving through the woods here, getting lost—'

'Why? What's going on?'

'Akiva!' he said sharply. 'Where . . . *are* you?'

He turned to Jen. 'Could you give my brother directions to the place?'

'It's off the highway between Quinton and Bain-berry.'

'I know that. What street does he take?'

'I don't think it has a name.'

'Well, can he look for a landmark?'

She shrugged her shoulders helplessly.

Decker was miffed. 'How do you know how to get here?'

'I just know it.'

His irritation turned to frustration. 'Jon, where are *you*?'

'I'm about a mile before the Bainberry Mall.'

'You're too far.'

'Far from *what*!'

'From the access road.'

'*What* access road? I didn't *find* any access road.' The tension cut through the line. 'We have an emergency situation, Akiva. I need to find you *now*!'

Decker felt his pulse rising. 'What emergency?'

'Chaim's missing—' Crackle bit through the line. 'I'm losing you!' Jonathan screamed. 'It's raining, the visibility is poor, and it's getting dark. Give me something to go on!'

'Hold on.' He put his palm over the receiver. 'Jen, can someone drive me down to the highway?'

'Not now. Everyone's busy.'

'How about Angela? You said she'd be done in a few minutes.'

'She doesn't have a car. She gets picked up.'

'What about you?'

'I don't have a car. I usually get picked up also.'

She wasn't being helpful. Decker wondered if that wasn't the idea. 'Jon, I'm going to walk down to the highway. I'm closer to Quinton than to Bainberry, but I don't know how much closer—'

'You can't walk down!' Jen interrupted.

Decker ignored her. 'It'll probably take me a good twenty minutes or so—'

'You can't walk down in the dark!' Jen reiterated. 'One wrong turn and you're lost.'

'It's not completely dark yet.'

'I'll look for you,' Jonathan said.

'Bye.' Decker hung up.

'You can't walk down the road,' Jen insisted. 'I'm telling you, you'll get lost.'

'I don't have any choice.'

'What about Angela? Didn't you want to see her?'

'She'll have to wait.'

'You're going to get lost—'

'You're repeating yourself.' He started toward the door.

'Wait!' She kneaded her hands several times, then opened a drawer and pulled out a storage-size flashlight, a battery-size square with a strong white beam on one end and a blinking red flare on the other. 'Take this. Maybe it'll help.'

'Thanks.'

She bit her lower lip and nodded. She wasn't happy about this turn of events. Maybe she was enjoying his company. He smiled at the ridiculous thought. 'Bye, Jen. Good luck.'

'Same to you, only more of it.'

He laughed but took her words to heart. He walked into the stormy dusk, umbrella in one hand, flashlight in the other, and began to descend the steep pathway that led to the highway. The road was a swirl of rain and mud, which immediately drenched his shoes, the muck rising to the cuffs of his pants. Because of the acute incline, he found that he had to crab-walk across the fluid earth, sidestepping one soaked foot against the other, mud squishing out from under his soles. His toes and fingers tingled with cold.

It was growing darker by the moment, but Decker kept the light off, wanting his eyes to adjust to the dusky conditions. Wasn't much around him to use for landmarks, just endless arms of foreboding copses. A couple of years ago, he had read a Stephen King novel about a little girl alone in the woods. At least, she had the good fortune to get lost in the summertime.

No big deal, he assured himself, just follow the road. Which was quickly turning into a rapid downhill whoosh of silt and slush. He had to walk along the rim, his feet snapping branches and twigs and sliding across the wet detritus that lined the forest floor. As the road became even steeper, he lost his footing and fell unceremoniously on his butt. The good news was he missed landing on the gun.

'Jesus!' He tried to stand up, but the slick soles of his shoes slid out from under his weight. 'Goddammit.'

Dimmer and dimmer.

'Oh Lord!' He took hold of a wet tree trunk and hoisted himself upward, his head missing a low branch by inches.

The road had become washed out, just a stream of thick coffee pouring down the hillside.

Weighing the options, he decided he needed his hands. He folded the umbrella, sticking it into his rear pants pocket, and was immediately assaulted by chilled water oozing down his face. He held the flashlight with his left ring and pinkie fingers and opted to play Tarzan. Grabbing hold of thick branches – whatever would hold his weight – he used them as a purchase to scale down the hill. Arms above his head, hands gripping one limb after another, he oscillated downward as if he were swinging on monkey bars. His movements were slow and deliberate and painful because his fingers were as flexible as frozen carrots. Several times, he conked himself with the flashlight. His language was foul and loud.

Now it wasn't even *getting* darker: Decker had decided it was officially dark. He couldn't see beyond his nose and he could see his nose only because it was good-sized. He turned on the flashlight, arcing its beam through the thicket. In front of him was an endless tangle of denuded brush.

There was no way for him to orient himself except by using the roadway. He'd have to wade through the mud to keep himself from getting lost. Carefully, while still holding on to the tree branch, he stuck his foot into the moving muck – colder and deeper than he thought. It grabbed him by the ankle and threatened to propel him forward while rocks and pebbles pelted his leg. He slid his foot about the ground – as greased as an oil slick. To keep his balance upright, he needed a wide surface area and traction.

It was going to be a breech delivery – legs and butt first. He opened the umbrella and laid it onto the rushing rill. Grimacing, he lowered his butt onto the canopy of vinyl. Using the handle to steer and his feet for brakes, he prayed, then pushed off.

Decker was never big on sledding, probably because he grew up without snow, but he found out really quick that he had a good sense of balance. Once he moved beyond the 'cold and wet factor,' he was able to concentrate on the mechanics of getting down without getting lost or hurt. It was stop and go as he forded the stream, not exactly Washington crossing the Delaware, but it did bring out Decker's more rugged side.

It took around a half hour, and though his backside felt sandpaper sore, he had made it to the highway without so much as a stubbed toe. The umbrella was lunched, about half the spokes broken and the nylon ripped beyond repair, but the flashlight still worked. He waved the flare end with enthusiasm when he saw an approaching set of headlights. The vehicle slowed. A Chevy truck.

The driver, covered by a caveman beard, lowered the passenger window. 'Hop in.'

'It's okay,' Decker said. 'I'm waiting for someone.'

Several moments ticked away.

'Not a lotta cars, buddy.' He looked Decker up and down. 'You *sure?*'

Decker smiled like the village idiot. 'Yeah. I'm fine.' Nodding to convince him. No doubt it made him look even more ludicrous. 'Just fine.'

The driver shook his head, rolled up the window, and left.

It seemed like an eternity, but it was probably only ten minutes before headlights came from the other side of the roadway. It had to be Jonathan because the illumination was creeping over the asphalt. Decker arced the blinking red light across the road-way. The van slowed, then pulled a U-turn, easing over onto what was once the shoulder of the road. Now it was a gurgling flow of mud.

Decker yanked the door open and hoisted himself inside. The two men looked at one another, water pouring down Decker's face. He smiled. 'Can I kiss your lips?'

Jonathan stared at him, his mouth agape.

'You wouldn't happen to have a change of clothes back there? Maybe a towel? I'd take a grease rag at this point.'

'Let's go find you something dry,' Jonathan said.

'First tell me about the emergency. What do you mean by "Chaim's missing"?'

Jonathan inched the van back onto the road. 'Exactly that.'

'He took off?'

'Appears that way.' Jonathan sneaked in a glimpse at his brother. 'Are you all right?'

'I'm drenched and my ass is sore, but otherwise fine. Tell me about Chaim. Details.'

'When I got to Quinton, he was already gone. Apparently, right after *Sha'chris*, he claimed he wasn't feeling well and needed to lie down. But when Minda went to check on him, the room was empty.'

'Any ideas?'

Jonathan had reduced the van's speed to almost nothing. He was still struggling to keep within the lines of the roadway. It was as black as pitch outside with no street lighting. 'About twenty minutes after I arrived at shiva, we received a phone call from Leon Hershfield. I took it.'

'What's going on?'

'Hershfield had just gotten off the phone with JFK airport police and the local FBI.'

'Oh my God!'

'You can see what's coming.'

'He was trying to skip.'

'Those guys you were telling me about . . . the ones Randy mentioned.'

'Weiss, Harabi, and Ibn Dod. They were with him?'

'This was per Hershfield . . . who was sketchy with the facts. Anyway, he told me that they were all set to board an international flight to Israel. Security stopped Harabi and Ibn Dod because apparently something was wrong with their passports or maybe they looked too jumpy or didn't look Chasidic enough—'

'They were dressed as Chasids?'

'Yes, I suppose.' A big sigh. 'You know how tight things are now. Especially El Al. As soon as security was called in, they took off – scattered.'

'Really stupid of them to travel together.'

'Last-minute flights to Israel are always a problem. Airlines have cut their dailies to Israel after the attacks.'

'Did security nab anyone?'

'I don't know, because no one's talking.' Jonathan tapped the wheel. 'Airport police haven't told us a damn thing. FBI hasn't told us a damn thing. The Feds arrived at Minda's house and at the shiva about the same time as the phone call. Hershfield was supposedly on his way to the airport to sort it all out, but . . . but I have the feeling that they *don't* have Chaim in custody.'

'Why not?'

'By Hershfield's questions.'

'What did he ask?'

'The gist? Where would Chaim go if he wanted to hide out? But he was subtler than that. And the Feds basically asked me the same thing.'

'What did you tell them?'

'I decided that after the debacle with Shayndie, I'd talk to you first. So I haven't opened my mouth to anyone. Things are frantic over there. When no one was looking, I took off. My question to you is . . . where do we go from here?'

'Not back to Quinton,' Decker told him.

'No, not unless you want to be detained for hours.'

'Do you know where Chaim would be hiding, Jon?'

'No idea. My first thoughts were maybe one of his stores – in Manhattan or in Brooklyn. I'm sure both places are swarming with Feds right now.'

'So that would be useless.'

'I think so,' Jonathan agreed. 'Maybe we should meet Hershfield down at the airport.'

'Did he ask you to come meet him?'

'No.'

No one spoke.

'Well, what the hey!' Decker slapped his wet thigh. 'Sure, let's try the airport.'

'Think they'll tell us anything?'

'No. But if they have Weiss, Harabi, or Ibn Dod in custody, I'll call up my brother. Those guys are wanted big time in Miami. If I get him on the phone, and he starts in with official extradition processes, it'll give us some credibility.' Decker regarded his sodden lap. 'Before we do anything, I need dry clothing. Since Quinton by now is Fedland, how about the Bainberry mall? Something over there should still be open.'

Jonathan turned the van around.

They rode a few moments in silence. Decker leaned forward and stared out the windshield.

'Your brother will be happy then,' Jonathan said.

'That the police captured these guys . . . if they did capture them.'

Decker didn't answer.

'But Chaim wasn't a part of their Miami ecstasy ring, so far as your brother knew, right?'

Still no response.

'Akiva—'

'Yeah, yeah . . .'

Silence.

'Akiva, did you hear what I—'

'Just a minute . . .'

'What is it?'

'Hold on . . .' Decker's eyes swept from the windshield to the rearview mirror, to the side mirror, then out the windshield again.

'Akiva, what's going on?' Jonathan asked.

'I'm not sure . . .' Decker's mind was reeling. 'There were headlights behind us before you made a U-turn. One headlight, not a pair . . . which I thought was peculiar because it's pouring outside.' Without thinking, he reached into his pocket and pulled out the snub-nose.

'Wha . . . when did you get that?'

'It's a long story, but right now I'm glad I have it. Can I dry the grip off on your jacket?'

'Hold on, I'll take it off.'

'Don't bother, I just need the hem.' He wiped moisture off the gun. 'Since the vehicle was in the distance, I thought maybe it was a car with a busted headlight. Now you just turned around, so it should be facing us. But it's not there.'

Outside, the world was shades of charcoal and black. Even the sky failed to bring forth any illumination, the cloud cover blocking out the stars and the moon.

'Jonathan, cut your lights. Then coast a minute or two and pull over.'

The rabbi killed the beams. They were encased in total darkness. Decker turned on the flashlight and shone it out the windshield. It wasn't much, but it was better than a blackout. 'Coast a few minutes, then pull over.'

A warm flush swept through Jonathan's body. His hands were shaking. 'Here goes nothing . . .'

The van bumped and dipped and finally stopped, askew in the mud, just inches from a tree trunk.

'Switch places with me,' Decker told him.

Jonathan started for the door, then stopped himself. 'You mean I should crawl over you.'

'Yes, of course. Stay down.'

Falling over one another, they switched places. Decker was on the floor of the driver's seat; Jonathan had hunkered down on the passenger's side. Decker could hear his brother breathing hard . . . or maybe he was hearing his own exhalations. A moment ago, he had been exhausted, completely spent. In a few seconds' time, adrenaline had put speed and force into his heartbeat.

'What—'

'Shhh . . .' A pause. 'Hear that?'

'*What?*'

'Listen!'

Finally, Jonathan heard it, the low growl of an engine grumbling through the rain. Decker peered over the dashboard, but nothing came into his field of vision. He lowered the driver's window halfway down, more than enough to liberate the barrel of the snub-nose. Then he looked over the dashboard again.

The motorized whir grew a bit louder, then

abruptly all was silent except for the rain.

'Uh-oh . . . this doesn't look good . . .'

'*Wha—!*'

'Shhh . . .'

Jonathan would have thrown up his hands had there been room. His armpits were soaked through.

'Okay, okay . . . Where's the flashlight?'

Jonathan gave it to him. 'What are you going to do?'

'I gotta see him first.' Decker was talking to himself. He patted the battery pack. 'Let's hope this motherfucker's strong.'

'Who do you think it is?'

'Don't know.' He put the driver's window all the way up, then unlocked the doors. Again he peeked over the dash. He couldn't really *see* anything, but the darkness in front of him seemed to shift, as if the air molecules were rearranging themselves. Could be his imagination playing games. But then something shifted again. 'Get way down, Jonathan. Tuck your head between your legs and your hands over your neck.'

The rabbi did as told. Decker noticed that his brother was moving his lips, but no sounds were coming out – silent prayer. He hoped Jon was saying one for him, too. 'I see something. Hold on, baby . . . C'mon, you mother . . .'

The shape – presumably a human and most probably a male – was nearing the van, walking with a bowlegged gait as if he were about to draw a gun in an old-fashioned Western. Then Decker realized that the legs were straddling a seat. The motorcycle was a small one. Looked to be a Honda . . . something nimble. He was approaching them from the driver's side, most likely because the van's passenger wheels were stuck in a rut of mud right next to the woods.

'C'mon, c'mon . . .' Decker urged.

Inching closer.

'Just a little more, baby . . .'

'Oh God!' Jonathan moaned.

'Hold on.' Decker swallowed hard. 'He's almost here.'

The seconds ticked by.

One . . . two . . . three.

He peeked out again. 'C'mon, motherfucker. Move a little closer to the door . . .'

Four . . . five . . . six.

The Honda was at the front bumper on the driver's side. A figure looking through the window . . . to the dash. Even though Decker couldn't see out that well, he knew there was no way that the biker could see in.

'Keep going . . .'

The figure was walking toward the driver's window.

'A little closer . . .'

Springing into action, Decker hurled the door, clipping the front wheel of the motorcycle, spinning the entire ensemble off balance. Then he aimed the light's beam on the driver's face, features hidden behind a ski mask. 'Freeze!'

Abruptly, something sped past Decker's head.

'Shit!' He dropped the flashlight and ducked behind the safety of the metal door. Vaulting out a second time, he shot from the hip, discharging a bullet at the bike, but a volley of flying metal forced him to retreat another time. The biker's bullets hit the front of the van, sending a deafening clatter throughout its interior, some of the ammo ricocheting off, spitting fire into the wet, raven night. Decker covered his head as hot lead flew past him.

'Fuck!' he screamed. 'Fuck, fuck!'

He leaped out, returning fire: two rapid shots that took off a section of the cycle's back fender. Still, the biker had kicked the motor into gear and sped away, screeching tires that burned rubber even though the asphalt was wet. Decker decided not to waste his last bullet on a fleeing target.

Panting heavily, he would have felt the wetness of sweat throughout his entire body except that he was soaked from the rain. He picked up the flashlight, which had survived the battle without injury, then dragged his body into the driver's seat. 'Are you okay, Jon?'

'I think so . . .' The rabbi whispered. 'Other than uncontrollable shaking, I think I'm fine.'

Decker lowered his head on the wheel, fatigue covering him as oppressively as a sodden blanket. 'I'm shaking, too.'

'Are you all right?'

'I'm whole, and that's all that counts right now.' Decker was trying to steady his heartbeat. He lifted his head up and turned the key in the ignition. The motor coughed lazily then decided to fire up. 'Well, that's a good start.'

Jonathan uncoiled from the fetal position and slithered into the passenger's seat. He belted himself in.

'Here goes nothing.' Decker strapped on the seat belt, then put the van into drive and coaxed it out of the embankment. Once he got it onto the asphalt, he depressed the gas pedal slowly. The car bucked, then limped noisily for about twenty feet before Decker applied the brakes.

'We've got a flat,' Decker said. 'Hopefully, only *a* flat . . . as in one tire. Do you have a spare?'

'I have a spare,' Jonathan said. 'I've never changed a tire, but I'm assuming that you have.'

'You assume correctly.' Again Decker pulled the vehicle by the side of the road. He went out and inspected the damage – a Swiss-cheese hood and one flat tire. Decker didn't bother looking *under* the hood. At this point, it was probably best if he didn't know. Jonathan had gotten out, staring at his newly ventilated car.

'I'll change the tire,' Decker told his brother. 'No sense in both of us getting wet.'

'Nonsense. At the very least, I can hold the flashlight.' Jonathan paused. 'Although I'm still trembling. Think of it as a strobe.'

Decker lay his hand on his brother's shoulder. He was as rigid as a stone post. 'You're holding up great.'

'Thank you.' He turned to Decker. 'Who do you think it was?'

'Don't know.'

'Donatti?'

'Maybe.'

'Merrin?'

'Quite possibly.' He exhaled. 'I also borrowed . . . well, more like swiped the gun from an obnoxious taxicab driver. It could have been him, too.' He brushed rainwater from his eyes. 'I would even say maybe it was Chaim, but I think your brother-in-law has other things on his mind right now.'

Together they pulled out the spare tire and the kit. An hour later, on four inflated tires, they made their way into the Bainberry Mall parking lot. They settled upon the first store that looked promising, a unit that specialized in athletic gear that was GOING OUT OF BUSINESS. They rooted through the deeply discounted items, stocking up on sweats, T-shirts, lightweight waterproof jackets, socks, sneakers, and an umbrella. By seven in the evening, they were back on the highway in dry clothes, wolfing down bagels and sipping hot coffee from paper cups. Warmth on the skin, warmth in the belly: Heaven had many forms and shapes.

Jonathan was driving. 'Where to?'

Decker thought a moment. 'With the car in such poor shape, it makes sense for us to go back to Quinton. Maybe I can squeeze something from the Feds.'

Jonathan blew out air. 'So JFK is out?'

'I doubt if Hershfield's still there,' Decker told him.

'True, true.' Jonathan tapped the wheel of the car. 'If we go back to Quinton, we'll be stuck there for hours.'

'I know.'

'Also, you said this could be Merrin's doing.'

'Possibly.'

'So maybe it's not too safe for us to be there now.'

'Jonathan, if Chaim's house is crawling with Feds, I think we're okay for a while.'

His brother was silent. Decker said, 'What's on your mind, Jon? You have a look on your face.'

'The Liebers have a warehouse. It's in the middle of nowhere – an old converted barn – about twenty miles north of Quinton. So maybe around fifteen miles from where we are. You wouldn't know how to get there unless you've been there before.'

'And you've been there before.'

'Raisie and I get our TVs, VCRs, computers,

cameras, etcetera, etcetera from the overstock – last year's models. Sometimes it's cheaper to get rid of items than to ship them back. We've always gone down after hours.'

'You have a plan.'

'Well, I have a location.' Jonathan finished his bagel. 'I also know where the back door is. I'm sure it's locked and alarmed if no one's there. But if Chaim is there, we can talk to him through the intercom.'

'And what are we supposed to say to him?' Decker asked.

'I don't know,' Jonathan answered. 'Convince him to give himself up.'

Decker laughed. 'A man who set up his brother – and possibly his daughter—'

'Nonsense.'

'Fine. Be delusional. But I will tell you this. Chaim's scared, wanted, and probably irrational. I don't see him just . . . giving up.'

'Well, then, maybe we can convince him that we're a better bet than the police.'

Decker sipped coffee as thoughts tumbled in his brain. 'I suppose we can check it out. Think the car can make it?'

'You're the mechanical one,' Jonathan answered. 'I'm a rabbi.'

'Who said rabbis couldn't be mechanical?'

'Well, I'm not.'

'Fifteen miles one way,' Decker said. 'Then, if we don't find anything, we've got to make it *back* to Quinton. That's forty miles in a van with a shot-out hood and driving on a spare in the rain.'

No one spoke.

Jonathan said, 'I'll willing to try it.'

'Well, we have rain slickers now . . .' Decker ran his fingers through his damp hair. 'All right. Let's give it a whirl.' They drove several miles without speaking. 'And what do we do, Jon, if he resists? What do we do when he starts shooting at us?'

'You don't know that.'

'I know psychos.' Reaching into the glove compartment, Decker took out the snub-nose. 'I have one bullet left. If it's him or me, I go for the kill. Can you accept that?'

'Better he be shot by you than by the police. At least, that way I'll know that the shooting was justified.'

'Maybe better for you, Jon.' Decker felt his jaw tighten. 'Not necessarily better for me.'

34

Everything was stacked against them. The van was straining at thirty, bouncing on a compromised set of tires, each bump and grind sending shock waves up their spines. On top of that, the road was oil slicked, and it was as dark as sin outside. So Jonathan wasn't *sure* if it was the right way. He summed up the situation perfectly.

'This was a terrible idea.' The van landed with a thud as it took a jump over a pothole. The engine stalled for a moment, then continued to chug along. 'I just wanted to reach Chaim before the police. Maybe less chance of his getting hurt.'

'If he doesn't hurt us first.'

'Akiva, I asked you no less than a dozen times if you wanted to turn back—'

'I know you have. I'm conflicted.'

'So am I.' Jonathan gripped the wheel. 'I want to help Chaim. He's my wife's brother. The family has been through hell. I've been through hell. But I don't want to get killed.'

'Succinctly put.' Decker tightened his coat around his body.

'Do you want to go back?' Jonathan asked him. 'Your call.'

'Now there's a switch. The rabbi daring the cop.'

'Not strange at all. Haven't you read the Kemelman series?'

Decker smiled. The rain had abated to sprinkles, leaving the asphalt as shiny as polished onyx. Because one of the biker's bullets had knocked out the heating fan, the windows were kept open to prevent the windshield from fogging up. Arctic cold, but at least Jonathan could see. Since the windows were rolled down, Decker could hear the strong whoosh of water roiling downstream as it cut deep ruts into the roadside mud.

To Decker, New York had always been synonymous with Manhattan. But the state was big and wide and full of open space. Long stretches of glens and valleys sided rolling mountains and dense forest. Because it was dark, the terrain showed only shapes and shadows, but occasionally he could make out a New England clapboard house lit from the inside, or even a small brick structure that sat on the edge of the highway. Once he saw a barn illuminated by several exterior lights, in front of it a hand-painted sign boasting antiques as well as fresh farm products. He could see the mist falling in the light's beam, the sign streaked with water. In the background, he caught glimpses of fields, but nothing appeared to be growing.

Jonathan caught his brother staring out the window. 'It's New York's Corn Belt.'

'I didn't realize it was so rural.'

'Very rural. You should feel right at home.'

Decker laid on the accent. 'Yeah, that there city is too durn big for my blood.'

'I didn't mean it like that.'

'I'm teasing. Mellow out.'

'I'm edgy.' Jonathan clutched the steering wheel with his gloved hands, shivering as he drove. 'I've never been shot at.'

'No one's shooting at us now.'

'*Baruch Hashem*,' Jonathan intoned as he thanked God.

'Good thing, too, with only one bullet.' Decker held the snub-nose. 'That's all right. Guns can give you a false sense of security. Lack of ammo will make us think.'

'Any new theories?'

'No, I'm not holding back. Want me to drive for a little, Jon?'

'No, I'll do it because at least I have some idea of where I'm going.'

Decker tried the cell again. Whereas before he got a momentary dial tone, this time he got nothing.

'The farther upstate, the less likely we are to get a connection,' Jonathan said.

'How far away are we in terms of time?'

'I'd say maybe twenty minutes.'

'How's the gas gauge?'

'Steady. He didn't hit the tank. And I filled up right when I got into Quinton. Gas isn't the problem. We finished those bagels pretty quickly. Are you still hungry?'

Decker was stunned. 'You have *food*?'

'Raisie packed me Danish before I left shiva. She figured that maybe I could use a nosh.'

'She figured right.'

'It's all the way in the back.'

Decker unbuckled his belt. 'Don't get into an accident.'

'As long as no one snipes at us, that won't be a problem.'

Climbing over the backseat, Decker went headfirst into the back of the van and extracted a large paper grocery bag. Sitting in the backseat, he pulled out an aluminum-wrapped bundle. Inside were a dozen assorted Danish. There were also several cans of diet Coke, as if the sugar lacking in the soda compensated for the pounds of sugar in the baked goods. Using contortion and great skill, he wedged himself back into the front passenger's seat. 'I've got cheese, apple, chocolate, cherry . . . what is this?' He smelled it. 'I think it's *mun*—'

'Cheese.'

Decker handed him a pastry. He chose an apple turnover and downed it in three bites. 'Should I pop the top on this soda can for you? This vehicle certainly has enough cup holders.'

'Please.'

He opened two cans of diet Coke. 'Your wife is very smart.'

'All Jewish women are smart when it comes to food.'

'Yeah, I can see Rina doing something like that.'

'Did you talk to her today?'

'Just in the morning. She's probably worried about me. Turns out for good reason.'

They rode in contemplative quiet, Decker trying to figure out Chaim's role in what appeared to be a sophisticated ecstasy ring. Mastermind? Unwitting abettor? Dupe?

'There it is,' Jonathan told him.

'I don't see anything.'

'The turnoff. We're about ten minutes away.'

As they drove, Decker felt a prickling on the back of his neck. Over the years, he had learned not to ignore intuitive pulses.

'Almost there,' Jonathan told him.

Jittery, Decker swept his eyes across the terrain. First he studied what was directly in front of him, then to the right, glancing at the side mirror. He turned around and scanned over his shoulder, along with a check in the rearview mirror, then left for the side mirror.

'We should be right on top of it,' Jonathan announced.

Off the roadway, Decker spotted several glints of chrome, but there were no lights up ahead. 'Jon, pull over and stop.'

'What? Why?' But Jonathan followed instructions, rolling the van over a mud-coated field. 'What's wrong now?'

'Does Chaim's warehouse have a parking lot?'

'Of course.'

'So why are these vehicles parked here, in a muddy field?' Decker pointed to a Jeep Cherokee and a Mitsubishi Montero.

'Maybe the lot was flooded.'

'Why don't I think that's the case?' Decker reached into the middle section of the van and dragged over the bags of clothing resting on the seats. There was a rain slicker for him and one for his brother. Then came the gloves. Lastly, he placed plastic bags around his shoes and tied them over his ankles, instructing Jonathan to do the same. When they were finished, he took the flashlight and opened the door. Not anxious to fall, he took his time getting over to the Cherokee. He tried the door, but it was locked. He shone the light through the side windows, his eyes meticulously observing what was inside.

Jonathan had caught up with him. 'Anything interesting?'

'Young person's car . . . at least, the taste in music is young – my son's age. I can tell by the CD covers on the floor.' Another pass of the beam through the interior. 'Pills on the seat. See how they're stamped – the hearts, that one with a 'toon on it? It's ecstasy. Trash on the floor – beer bottles, cigarette butts . . .' He looked at his brother. 'A couple of Quinton kids got arrested for bad behavior with ecstasy down in Miami – Philip Caldwell and Ryan Anderson. Betcha this baby belongs to one of them.'

He went over to the Montero and peered inside.

'Neat. This belongs to a different animal. A Dwight Yoakam CD cover . . . a pack of Camels . . . nothing much else.' He checked out the rear bumper. 'A D.A.R.E. to Keep Kids off Drugs sticker. Well, well, well. We definitely know who we're working with.'

'Merrin.'

'Someone in law enforcement.'

'Ironic,' Jonathan said. 'I mean . . . if you think he's selling ecstasy. And he has the sticker . . .'

'If I were back home, I could call in the plates. If I were back home, I could also call for backup.' Decker turned to his brother. 'But I'm not back home. We should leave. If Chaim's a willing partner in this, why should I risk my life to save him?'

'And what if he isn't a willing partner?'

'Then he's probably dead.'

'Or being questioned . . . questioned roughly . . .' The rabbi shuddered. 'My wife lost one brother . . .

I'd hate to think that we've come this far only to leave another one behind. But you know better.'

No one spoke.

Decker finally said, 'Show me the warehouse.'

Jonathan took the flashlight and they walked toward the destination. Neither spoke as muck squished under their shoes. Five minutes later, the giant barn became visible because light was coming from a lower window. It was typical in structure – a large parabolic shape that peaked in a roof gable – but someone had modified it for its use as a warehouse. The great door and apron, traditionally used as a passageway to let the animals in and out, had been replaced by a set of double doors that led out to a concrete driveway and loading dock. On either side of the doors were windows stacked three stories high, the lower right window being the illuminated one. Above the great door should have been the sliding doors, but they had been boarded up. The hay doors on the upper level looked to be intact.

The rain was starting to pick up. Neither man appeared to notice.

'What does it look like inside?' Decker asked him.

'Shelves filled with boxes.'

'More than one level?'

Jonathan tried to re-create a mental image. Both he and Akiva were whispering. 'Most of it is on one level with very high shelving. Wide aisles because the guys use a forklift to bring the merchandise up and down. But there is a second level with shelves as well. It's an open loft, I believe.'

'Probably the original hayloft.'

'I suppose. Should we call the State Police for help?'

'I can't get a line out. Even if I could, I'm sure Merrin or one of his cohorts has a multiband radio that picks up cellular calls.' Ideas turned over in Decker's brain. 'Do you know what room corresponds to that lit window?'

'Haven't a clue. But it's not near the entrance I was talking about.' Jonathan stared at the barn. 'That door is on the left side. Right below an outside spiral staircase.'

Each one waited for the other to act. Then Jonathan made a decision, moving toward the structure. 'I want to do everything I can.'

Decker followed. 'If you can say that after what happened in the van, you're dedicated.'

'Or stupid.'

'Sometimes it's one and the same.'

The rain was falling at a steady clip, blocking out the noise made by their shoes trampling over brush. Decker tightened the hood on his waterproof jacket. His hands were encased in nylon gloves. By the time they reached the door, it was pouring. They ducked under an awning as the rain beat tom-toms on the cloth. Decker reached for the door – locked of course. He pointed the flashlight's beam between the metal escutcheon and the door frame.

'It's a latch bolt,' Decker said.

'Which means?'

'I can probably open it with a credit card. The point is . . . do I want to do it?'

'You may only have one bullet,' Jonathan told him. 'But they don't know that. Besides, the lit window is on the opposite side.'

'Someone may be guarding the doors. He'll hear me as soon as I try to spring the latch.' A long hesitation. 'Well, there's a quick way to find out.'

Shoving Jonathan against the wall, Decker covered his brother's body with his, then quietly tapped the door.

Nothing.

Another gentle rap failed to produce any response.

'Take off the plastic from your shoes.' Decker was doing the same thing. 'It makes too much noise.' After the plastic bags had been removed, he handed Jonathan the gun. 'Cover me.'

'You're kidding.'

'Do you see anyone else around?' Decker took out the credit card and gently maneuvered it between the bolt and the catch. A moment later, the doorknob rotated without any hindrance. 'I've got it. Kill the light. Let's hope the alarm doesn't trip.'

Jonathan turned off the flashlight. Decker began to turn the knob . . . millimeters at a time. Finally, he pushed on the handle and the door crept inward.

Slowly . . . slowly . . . slowly.

The door freed itself from the frame.

Nothing sounded.

'The alarm's off,' Decker told his brother.

'Is that good or bad?'

'Don't know, but it's a safe bet that Chaim's inside.'

Slowly, slowly, slowly, Decker pushed the door inward.

Inch after inch.

A quarter of the way open.

Then halfway.

When there was enough room for them to squeeze through, Decker grabbed his brother, pulled him inside, and silently closed the door.

Darkness was the welcome mat. Even after his eyes adjusted, Decker couldn't make out anything distinct. The interior was a vast space of specters and phantoms, of giant shadows and black holes. Rain slithered down the tall windows, dripping like open veins of black blood. A flash of lightning from afar, a clap of distant thunder. Neither man moved or spoke. A few moments passed; then Decker heard blurred background noises – a hint of human speech. It was hard to tell because of the clacking of the rain.

He took several steps in the direction of the sounds. An unwanted smell reached Decker's nose at the same time his sneaker caught on something, pitching his body forward. He barely recovered without making noise. He looked down, then bent down to study the solid object at his feet.

The corpse was fresh. Decker studied the face and decided he had never seen it before. But everything about him said cop: the way he dressed, the type of haircut, the furrows in the face, the roughened hands and fingernails, even his gut. He appeared to be in his forties.

'Someone took care of the guard for us.' Decker stood up. 'Let's get out of here.'

Jonathan nodded quickly.

If timing was everything, theirs was exquisitely off. As soon as Decker turned, he saw him. Jonathan saw him, too, judging by the sound of his gasp. The kid had evil in his eyes, and cold steel in his hand. He had probably heard them come in. He smirked, his face radiating glee at the prospect of killing, of snuffing out human life. Decker reached into his empty pocket, realizing too late that Jonathan hadn't given him back the snub-nose. The seconds became protracted as he watched the teen lift the weapon. Decker felt the horror of his last breath, his own fear mirrored by the terror on Jonathan's face. Too far away to take down, and not enough time anyway. As Satan aimed, Decker looped his arm around his brother's neck, taking them headfirst to the floor and into a puddle of newly spilled blood.

Waiting for the hit.

But nothing happened because the boy's head was suddenly whipped back. Going down in slow motion. The fingers releasing the grip of the weapon, the gun falling from the hand, the knees buckling, and the neat round bullet hole in the forehead. A shadow appeared with outstretched arms, first catching the gun, then the body. Dressed in black, he silently lowered the corpse to the cement floor. He put a finger in front of his lips, then extended them a latex-gloved left hand. In a single swoop, Decker was pulled to his feet. The face was covered with black makeup streaked with perspiration. The entire body reeked of sweat. The right hand was still holding the purloined gun.

After Jonathan was on his feet, the shadow beckoned them with an index finger, then turned his back, expecting them to follow. Wearing a black knapsack, he walked soundlessly and assuredly until he came to a half flight of stairs. He scaled the steps, then nodded for Decker to come up, which he did, helping his shaking brother up onto a platform. It was no bigger than three feet square with an overhead clearance of about four feet. They were compressed, but Decker quickly understood the usefulness of the spot; it had an unfettered view of the warehouse. His thighs bunching as he squatted, Decker scoped out the area.

Several silent ticks passed.

Donatti whispered, 'You can't say I didn't try to warn you.'

Decker wiped blood from his face and blinked tears from his eyes. He had the sudden urge to laugh but refrained. Emotions were reeling inside him. He whispered, 'You shot out the van.'

'Not me, personally,' Donatti replied. 'I thought it would hang you up for a couple of hours, give me enough time to get in and out. You just fucked up everything!'

'We were on our way to the airport.' Decker was still breathing hard. 'To JFK to talk to Hershfield about some drug dealers that airport security had caught. But after the van was shot out – barely on its last leg – Jonathan suggested the warehouse because it was closer. If you had left us alone, we wouldn't have even been here.'

Donatti stared at him, then silently mouthed a series of swear words. 'Might as well make yourself useful.' He handed him the dead boy's gun, then turned his colorless eyes on Jonathan. 'There's more where that came from. Can you shoot?'

'He's a rabbi, not a sniper,' Decker said.

'Then get him out of here.'

'My number one priority.'

'Except you can't go out the way you came in. An alarm will sound.'

'I got in without anything going off.'

Donatti said, 'It's a one-way emergency exit. Trust me.'

'Then how do I get him out?'

Donatti didn't answer. His breathing was labored as water cascaded off his brow.

'You don't look good, Chris,' Decker said. 'What's wrong?'

'Shut up and let me think.'

Five minutes went by, nothing but the sound of the rain.

'You don't look *good*,' Decker whispered, 'but you look *calm*.'

'I am calm. I'm in my element.'

More time passed.

Decker examined the gun in his hands. A Smith & Wesson 9mm automatic, double action. He wasn't sure which model, but it probably had a magazine of about twelve rounds. It didn't smell as if it had been recently fired, the barrel was cool to the touch. Of course, it was frosty inside. Decker could see his breath. He glanced at Jonathan, crouched by his side. He was trembling hard, no doubt from fear, but the physical position they were in was anything but comfortable. Decker placed his hand on his brother's unsteady knee. 'Just another few minutes.'

Jonathan nodded. 'I'm okay.'

'All right, this is the deal,' Donatti whispered. 'There are five doors – front door, one emergency exit on each side, and two doors in the back. The emergency exits are alarmed to go off when you leave and the front door is where the powwow's being held. That leaves the back doors. Go for the closest one.'

Silence.

Donatti continued. 'There was a cop on each alarmed side door, a pair of kids on each back door, and maybe a couple of cops at the front entrance. I've taken care of one cop and a kid – You know, you're damn lucky I recognized you when you came in.'

Decker said, 'It's your artistic eye. Where was that kid stationed?'

'The one I took out? One of the back doors, which means his partner's gonna get antsy if he doesn't come back soon. Let's put some lead in it.' He slipped off his knapsack and pulled out a small set of spyglasses. 'It should be a piece of cake with two of us . . . if your eye is good.'

'Are you asking me if I'm a good shot?'

'Yes.'

'I'm good.'

'Then we're fine, because I'm great.' Donatti handed Decker the infrared binoculars. Through them, the warehouse looked like daylight. 'See that red wooden sign. The letter *N*.'

'Got it.'

'Put it center in the crosshairs.'

'Okay.'

'Clockwise one-fifty degrees.'

'There are two of them. What are they? Like a couple hundred yards away?'

'Yeah.' Donatti looked at Decker's gun. 'You can't use that in the dark.' He took a case out and opened it up, pulling out a pistol. 'Basically, it's a Walther double-action automatic except I've modified it for accuracy at longer range and added an infrared scope and silencer for obvious reasons. Swap you?'

They exchanged firearms. Decker hefted the gun. 'Not too heavy.'

'No need for overkill. Standard nine-millimeter Parabelllum and twenty-two LR. With all the customization, it cost me about fifteen hundred bucks. I'll probably have to lose it after this is all over. Damn shame.' He stowed the kid's gun in his backpack and took out his own customized handgun, complete with scope and silencer. 'We do them; then you can make your move through the back entrance.'

Decker studied the faces in the scope, feeling his heart drop. Two lanky boys, one maybe a couple of inches taller than the other, both of them holding that gaping-mouth confused expression commonly stamped on teenage males. Their cheeks still held a smattering of adolescent pimples. His brain flashed to his own sons. 'They're kids. Eighteen tops.'

'I was that age once,' Donatti pointed out.

A very convincing argument, but Decker wasn't ready to make the jump. 'I'm a police officer. I can't shoot them without warning.'

'Oh, that's clever,' Donatti mocked. 'Why don't you go all the way and paint a bulls-eye on your forehead?'

'I can't shoot them without giving them warning first.'

'You're out of your mind.'

'Donatti, I'll announce myself. If they don't drop immediately, then we can—'

'If we give them warning, they'll shoot, then scatter. Then we'll have a real problem.'

'I'm not going to argue this—'

'You're an idiot.'

'You're repeating yourself.' Decker remained firm. 'Got it?'

'Yeah, I got it.' Donatti picked up a pinecone-shaped piece of concrete and hurled it, the cement whizzing by the bigger of the two boys. As it hit a box and broke into smaller pieces, both of the teens spun around, the taller one raising his gun in Decker's direction. He never stood a chance. Donatti picked them off in two clean shots – *zzzzpt, zzzzpt*. They walked a foot or two, then dropped – *plop, plop*. The shots were so smooth that there wasn't any discernible blood spray. Donatti must have been using hollow points – the kind of bullets that bang around in the skull, turning the entire brain to pulp.

Decker glared at him, his eyes burning with anger.

'I gave them warning.' Donatti was expressionless. 'Self-defense. Now I'll cover you while you get your brother out.'

'That means I walk out with my back to you. I just saw you murder two kids.'

'If you don't leave now, you won't make it.' Donatti adjusted his scope, squatting as still as a stone frog. 'I'll wait a few minutes. If you don't come back by then, I'll just assume that we've parted ways.'

There was no time for contemplation.

'I'm keeping this.' Decker held up the gun. 'Go, Jon. I'll follow you. Be careful!'

'I don't know where I'm going.'

'Just *move*!'

Once they had made it down the stairs and onto the ground, Decker, looking through the scope, scanned the area. Then he grabbed Jonathan's hand. Using the IR lens for visibility, he twisted and turned around aisles and aisles of tall shelving, around boxes and machinery – gingerly and quietly. He dragged Jonathan along as he negotiated the path to the back. Time took on a surreal quality. It was without parameters like hours spent in a casino; in reality, it took only a few minutes to reach the back door.

Pushing it open, stepping over the threshold and then out into a wet and chilly freedom. The rain was coming down in cold, big drops, the ground beneath them slick and filled with mud holes, forcing them to tread with caution. Still, they jogged and didn't stop until they were at the van. Jonathan's hands were shaking as he pulled out the keys.

Decker opened the driver's door. 'Go find a phone booth and call up the State Police. Then call up NYPD and ask for Detective Mick Novack from the two-eight. Don't tell him any details, just to get his butt out here. Don't come back here. The less you're involved, the better.'

'You're not coming with me?'

'I can't leave him alone.'

Jonathan stared at him. 'You can't be serious. Didn't you just tell me this wasn't worth getting killed for?'

'I don't intend on getting killed—'

'You're relying on *Donatti* for protection?'

'If I don't go back, Jonathan, your brother-in-law is *dead*!'

Jonathan looked away. 'My wife's obligation may be toward her brother. My obligation is with my brother. You've got a wife and children. You've got to leave.'

'I can't do that.'

Jonathan regarded him with tears in his eyes. 'And how do I comfort Rina at the shiva?' He hugged him tightly. 'You don't know what's going on. He could be setting you up.'

'Perfectly true. But if I don't return, he'll think I froze. I can't let that maniac have that kind of superiority over me.'

'You're crazy!'

'Then you should be concerned. Insanity is genetic.' He patted the driver's seat. 'In.'

Jonathan paused, then climbed into a damp, cold

seat. Though clammy, it was still better than squatting, taut with terror. He regarded his brother. 'I still have the gun you gave me.'

'I have protection, so you keep it.' Decker shut the van's door. 'With God's help, you won't need it. Go!'

Jonathan placed the key into the ignition. It coughed, it sputtered, it choked, but eventually the pistons kicked in. The motor was breathing albeit asthmatically.

'Drive carefully,' Decker cautioned.

'You be careful,' Jonathan cautioned back.

When the taillights were dots in the distance, Decker started a gentle jog back toward the barn, gun in hand.

Armed and dangerous, he was a force with which to be reckoned.

35

The barren night reminded Decker of funerals, specifically of cops murdered while doing the job. Those left behind – the grieving parents, the felled spouses, and the bewildered children – had a sameness to their wretched faces like the sameness to the color black. In Judaism, Torah is light and light is God. Hell wasn't fire and brimstone and devils and torture. Hell was an abyss without sensation, without end.

Slashes of rain slapped Decker's face. Without the protection of the plastic bags, his shoes and socks had become soaked, but that was of little consequence. There were other things on his mind – Chaim . . . Donatti . . . Merrin . . . Rina and the children. As he neared the back door, he felt adrenaline kick in, his senses heighten.

Opening the door a fraction of an inch. Playing mental games to ward off that terrifying fear of a gun's bore suddenly popping into his face. Only his heartbeat and breathing for company.

A few more inches, then Decker made the commitment. He slipped inside the warehouse and took refuge, hiding behind a stack of three-foot square boxes. Once again, surrounded by phantasmagoric nothingness: by violence lurking behind an eerie stillness. His inhalations were deep. He was sweating profusely, and salt bathed his eyes. He wiped them with the back of his gloves, still wet from rain. He peeked over the edge of the cardboard stack and peered through the Walther's scope, but saw only aisle after aisle of cartons and boxes. Nowhere could he spy Donatti or the platform from where they had been squatting. With no specific landmarks, he was disoriented. He only knew that he was in the rear of the warehouse.

With nothing to go on, he figured he might as well go for the action, to head toward the lit room in front. Hopefully, Donatti – if he did spot him – would look before he shot.

Provided he wasn't after Decker.

Jonathan's words: He could be setting you up.

Donatti had had ample opportunity to pop him, and had yet to exercise the option. But Chris was a pro and picked his scenery like a stage director choosing his set designs. The opportunity had never been better: a headfirst, out-of-town cop trying to rescue his brother-in-law, getting shot in the cross fire.

Again he scoped the place through the infrared lens, scanning the aisles for anything in motion.

Everything appeared inert.

He plotted a path, one that had lots of big cartons and crates to hide behind with plenty of escape routes. Of course, if he could hide behind walls of cardboard, so could a sniper. But maybe they were too busy guarding the door and watching their own asses to worry about an itinerant cop.

He inched out from his current position and gave a

last-minute check to his surroundings. As quickly and quietly as his shoes would allow – he had to tiptoe because his sneakers squeaked – he started toward the other side of the warehouse.

First attempt, he hotfooted it about fifty feet before taking shelter behind a pallet.

Second try, he slithered out another hundred feet, then crouched behind a forklift to reevaluate.

Third time, he found a niche back of a six-foot-high pallet.

His face was hot and wet, and large drops of sweat fell off his nose. His armpits were soaked; his clothes smelled rancid. His breathing was fast and shallow. His rib cage hurt from tension and his oxygen-starved inhalations.

A piece of concrete whizzed by his ear, landing on the ground and breaking into little tippy-tappy noises. Decker whipped around but saw nothing.

Donatti.

But where had it come from?

Decker sucked up oxygen from the frigid air and tried to get a fix on the direction of the projectile. He zigzagged in and out of merchandise, until another stone whizzed by his head.

He veered to the left, then scoped out the new area.

He still didn't see any platform or staircase.

Darting from aisle to aisle, from box to box and carton to carton. He paused a moment, leaning against a pallet marked COMPUTER DESK AND HUTCH. FRAGILE. Sweat was cleaning out his system. The adrenaline rush was subsiding, fatigue taking its place.

Catching his breath . . .

Closing his eyes . . .

Just a moment . . .

His hand dropping to his side . . .

The barrel of the gun pointing to the ground . . .

Just a few more moments.

His eyes snapped open when he heard the voice.

'Freeze, motherfucker!'

Freeze, Decker thought.

Hit men don't give warning.

But cops say 'freeze.'

And good cops usually don't say 'freeze, motherfucker' without provocation. So this was probably a cop and not a nice one.

All this clicked inside Decker's brain within a split second of decision-making. He dropped and rolled, while shooting in the direction of the voice, the semiautomatic spitting out muzzled fire because of the silencer – *pfft, pfft, pfft, pfft*. He scrambled to his feet, but remained stooped behind a crate, his lungs stinging as he panted, his gasping so loud it almost drowned out the moans. Slowly, he rose, but his shakiness forced him to lean against a wooden beam. Unsteady with pinpricks of starlight dancing in his brain, he tried to equalize his balance.

The moaning had stopped.

Decker peeked out.

Of sizable girth, he had fallen with his head back, one thick arm across a padded chest, the other arm extended open and lying over the concrete. The torso had twisted so it was resting on the hip, the stomach spilling onto the floor. The legs were crossed over one another. The face was hard to make out, but the build certainly could have been Merrin's.

Decker inched out from his hiding space.

Donatti was standing over the contorted body, eyes cast downward, arms crossed with a pistol in the left hand. His voice was a whisper. 'See what happens when you give warning. He should have just taken you out.'

'Did you . . .' Decker's heart was beating so fast it threatened to break his sternum. He was still trying to suck up air. 'Did you do it or did I?'

Donatti looked up. 'Take a bow.'

'*Jesus!*' Decker felt his head go light. 'Fuck!'

'Buck up,' Donatti told him. 'Surely, you're not a virgin.'

'Unfortunately no . . .' He swallowed hard, staring at the face. Not Merrin, but definitely a cop. 'Who's left?'

'Just the two pups guarding Chaim's office. I don't know who's actually in the office, because even I can't see through walls.'

'Any more of these?'

'These? You mean cops?'

Decker nodded.

'Not that I know.' Donatti smiled. 'I knew you'd come back.'

'Gotta keep an eye on you, Chris.'

'That's bullshit. Your ego refused to allow *me* to be the one to save your brother-in-law.'

'Can we go?'

With expert precision, Donatti led Decker through the maze of crates, cases, parcels, and boxes. Within minutes, they were within fifty feet of the office, light leaking out from under the door. No one was in view.

Where were the guards?

Donatti stepped back and pulled Decker into the shadows, his eyes in constant motion. They were out of sight, in back of a stack of wooden crates. 'I don't like this.'

'Where are the kids?'

'Don't know.'

'What do you mean—'

'I don't know. They were here a second ago.'

'They're not here now. Where did they go? In the office?'

'Maybe.'

'*Maybe?*'

'I'm not a fucking mind reader. Shut up!'

'Fuck you!' Decker snapped back. His eyes darted from side to side. He looked through the scope of his gun, sweeping the lens across the area.

First there was nothing; then an eye blink of motion flitted out from the corner of his visual field. Reacting before the thought fully registered, he yanked Donatti down and jerked him hard to the left as bullets ripped through a stack of cardboard boxes containing television sets. It set off an explosion of glass and metal, a cloudburst of thousands of slivers and shards that flew through the air and rained down onto their heads.

Deadly silence followed the eruption.

The moments tapped by, punctuated by the rapping of the rain on the roof and the windowsills. Decker lay facedown on the floor, but Donatti was on his haunches, ready to spring. Both of them remained fixed in position, their eyes locked on one another in tacit communication. Decker saw Chris hold up a finger.

The minutes went by . . . two . . . three . . . four . . .

With everyone hidden from view, other senses became heightened. Decker saw Chris close his eyes.

Both of them were professional enough to know not to make the first move.

When in doubt, wait it out.

Five . . . six . . . seven.

It didn't even take that long. That was the way it was with amateurs: overeager because the pups just *had* to inspect their handiwork. They had to *see* the damage, to gloat about it. And with glass crunching beneath their shoes, they might as well have announced their arrival over a PA system. Though Donatti's eyes remained closed, his lips broke into a smile, widening as the noise increased in volume.

The lids snapped open and he patted air, indicating for Decker to stay down. Then he ticked off the seconds with five splayed fingers.

Five, then four . . . three . . . two . . . one.

A quick peek from around the boxes, then two shots fired.

And that was that.

Decker couldn't see them, but he heard them drop, the horrible crack of bone slamming against the cement.

Donatti whispered, 'You can get up.'

Taking great care, Decker managed to balance on his legs, still squatting, still waiting. His hands were crisscrossed with small cuts, his sneakers and rain jacket sparkled like glitter. The darkness abruptly faded; then a wedge of yellowed light cast its shape on the floor. Crunching accompanied the thuds of footsteps along with the sound of something being dragged. Heavy breathing could be heard.

'Caldwell?' A pause. 'Caldwell, are you there?'

Donatti and Decker mouthed the word simultaneously. 'Merrin.'

'Caldwel—'

The smashing underfoot stopped. Donatti shifted his position until the police chief came into view. 'He's looking at the bodies.' He turned to Decker. 'He's got your brother-in-law.'

'What do you mean?'

Donatti took his gun and put it at his temple. 'I'll take him down if you want.' A smile. 'Or do you want to *warn* him?'

Decker's brain was moving too fast to digest his thoughts. 'I'm going to try to *talk* him down.' He got to his feet. 'Stay back, all right?'

Chris shrugged indifference.

'Just be there to back me.'

Another apathetic shrug.

'What does that mean?'

'Time's ticking, Decker. Either do it or let me handle it.'

Decker stepped out and aimed his weapon. 'Hey, Virgil.'

Merrin jumped around, one hand holding a Smith & Wesson .32 caliber pistol with its bore buried in Chaim's temple, the other hand clamped over Lieber's mouth, muting his sobs and wails. Decker's eye went from Chaim's face, over the teenage corpses, then came back at the chief. 'Sorry about your boys.'

'S'right. I got others to take their places.' A piggish grin was plastered across his ugly face. 'It's mighty nice for you to show up. Makes things easier all around.'

'I'm very tired,' Decker said. 'Drop the gun—'

'You can't be serious. Matter of fact, I was going to ask you to do that very thing.'

'Merrin, my nine millimeter is pointed at your chest. Your piece is pointed at Lieber's head. That means I have the advantage.'

'You shoot me; I shoot him.'

'Then shoot him,' Decker retorted.

Merrin's smile sagged, his face registering pure shock.

'So,' Decker told him, 'either drop the gun or I'll shoot you.'

'You're bluffing—'

'Try me, Chief.'

Without warning, Merrin's lips turned upward into a venal grin. 'I suggest *you* drop the gun, Lieutenant, because I do reckon that the odds just shone in my favor.' His eyes went past Decker's head, focusing on something behind him.

No one spoke.

Then Decker said, 'I don't know, Virgil. Donatti's a loose cannon.'

Donatti laughed. 'That's certainly true. Because neither one of you knows whose side I'm on.' A pause. 'Maybe I'll kill both of you.'

No one moved.

'I'm about ten feet behind you, Decker,' Donatti said. 'And, at the moment, *my* nine millimeter is pointed right at the base of your spine. I suggest you listen to the chief.'

Slowly, Decker turned around.

Chris wasn't lying, except now the gun was aimed at Decker's Adam's apple. Donatti shrugged. 'Nothing personal . . . well, maybe a little personal. But primarily it's business.'

Decker looked back at Merrin – at his porcine expression filled with malice and evil, then returned his attention to Donatti. The gun remained on him – a fixed, permanent object.

'If you don't do it now, Decker, I'll shoot you in a five countdown. If you cooperate and *slowly* lower the gun to the floor, you stand a slim chance of talking me out of it.'

Decker weighed his options, two against one – the professional cop and the sharpshooter. Maybe if he ducked, they'd shoot each other. He smiled internally, but found his body had been seized by the shakes. In the end, he bent down and placed the gun on the cement floor. Then he straightened. He'd given the snub-nose and its one bullet to Jonathan. How he wished he had that gun now.

'Keep your hands up and where I can see them,' Donatti said.

Decker raised his hands to his shoulder. 'Is this the part where I try to talk you out of it?'

'No, this is the part where you shut up and listen. Kick the Walther over to me.'

Decker did as told.

Instead of picking it up, Donatti kicked the weapon at least fifty feet behind him, out of anyone's reach. 'One less firearm to go off in my face. Now it's your turn, Virgil. Put the gun in your holster. I don't want any fuckups.'

'You don't want me to do him? The Jew boy?'

'Why would you do him? You've got him precisely where you want him. He'll shit on command for you. Learn to take advantage when fortune shines on you.'

'Now, that's a very good point, Mr Donatti. A very good point.'

'And because I've been so generous with you, you'll send something my way, huh?'

'You better believe it, sir.'

'Can I talk now, Chris?'

'No, not yet. And don't you *dare* act familiar with me.' He shot the floor, an inch away from Decker's foot, pulverizing cement into dust. To Merrin: 'Didn't I tell you to put the gun away?' Donatti became suddenly impatient. 'You're pissing me off. Do it!'

Quickly, Merrin stowed the gun, keeping a firm grip on Chaim's throat.

'Push him on the floor,' Donatti told him. 'Let him feel what it's like to crawl like an insect. Because that's what he is . . . a fucking bug.'

Merrin grabbed Lieber by the collar and pushed him to the ground, stepping on his back to flatten him out. Chaim was sobbing.

Merrin grinned. 'I don't know of any bug that cries, Mr Donatti.'

'Everybody cries, Virgil.'

Three bullets in rapid succession – one in the forehead, one in the throat, and one in the groin. Merrin didn't even have a chance to react. He just stared out of vacant blue eyes, the same hoggish expression on his face, then collapsed onto Chaim, a sprinkler of squirting blood. Lieber let go with ear-piercing screams – uncontrolled and at maximum volume – flailing his arms and legs, pushing the body from his back. Freeing himself from the corpse, Lieber remained on the floor, heaving deep, big gulps as if he were being choked.

Decker could hear himself breathing.

Donatti was speaking to him. 'Back up and keep your hands up.'

'I don't . . .' Decker shut himself up. He was

trembling so hard, it took all his concentration to remain on his feet. He did as instructed.

'Now go pick up your brother-in-law from the ground. He stinks. I think he shit in his pants. Can't anyone take a little pressure anymore?'

Shaking but trying to hide it, Decker went over to Chaim and lifted him to his feet. 'Are you all right?'

Chaim was still sobbing.

'Shut him up.'

'He's terrified—'

'He's giving me a headache. Shut him *up*!'

Chaim clamped his trembling hands over his mouth, his body quivering and unstable on his feet. Tears ran from his eyes. Decker slipped his arm around his shoulders. Chaim melted into his arms.

Donatti went over to Merrin's body, still flowing with rich, oxygenated blood, and plucked the gun from the holster. 'Guess who has all the wea-pons,' he sang out. 'Guess whose ass you'd better start kiss-ing.'

'What do you want?' Decker whispered.

'I'd like your wife, and probably the easiest way to get her is to shoot you.' He stared at Decker, his eyes filled with avarice and hunger. 'What do you think, Lieutenant? Her thick lips around my cock, those gorgeous baby blues looking up at my face . . . Good, huh?'

Decker felt his stomach churn. 'You've got the gun. You're entitled to dream.'

Donatti grinned. 'Nice comeback. You can live another five minutes.' His eyes went to Chaim. 'I just shot a nice piece of my income.' He aimed the gun at Chaim's head. 'To make up for that, you're going to work for me. I need details. You can start now.'

477

Silence.

Donatti shot a bullet at Lieber's feet, making him do a little hop. 'Don't keep me waiting, you stupid kike. Tell me about the operation.'

'I . . .' Chaim cleared his throat. 'I was helping . . . import. I was importing—'

'If you can't stop stumbling over your words, I'm going to kill you. Now try it again. Go on, I'm getting testy.'

'I bring in the stuff . . . in my electronic equipment.'

'From where?'

'Europe . . . Israel . . . Asia . . . all over.'

'And Merrin was your distributor?'

Chaim nodded, breaking away from Decker. He tried to stand straighter, but his legs were still wobbly.

'What's your cut?'

'It works out . . . to about . . .' Heavy breathing. But it was clear that Lieber was calming down. 'I took about thirty percent of street value.'

'Well, now you're down to twenty.'

'Sure . . . yeah. Okay. Whatever you want.'

'Whatever I want, "Mr Donatti".'

'Yes, sure . . . Whatever you want, Mr Donatti.'

'Who did Merrin sell it to?'

'The local kids from the townships . . . *behamas* . . . beasts. Kids with nothing better to do than to go crazy.'

'These vermin over here . . .' Donatti pointed to the corpses. 'They were locals?'

Chaim nodded.

'Merrin sold directly to the boys?'

'He had . . . others in the force to help him out.'

'Good to know. How'd you get into this?'

'Merrin . . . he was using dancers . . . him and the

Israelis and the Arabs . . . but then they got caught in Miami. They . . . needed another way to import the stuff.' He looked at Decker. 'Weiss suggested me because I needed money.'

'You worked with him before?'

'I borrowed some money from him, yes. But I paid it back. I wouldn't have done it.' Again a look at Decker. 'But Merrin found out that I was . . . I was doing things.'

Slowly, Donatti grinned. 'I thought you looked familiar. Course all you kikes look alike when you're naked.'

The videotapes from the whorehouse. Decker raised his eyes. Jen had told him she didn't know Chaim Lieber. And maybe she hadn't known him. Maybe he had come under an alias. Or, just as likely, Donatti instructed her to deny knowing him. And, of course, she'd follow orders. Stupid of him to believe anything she told him. She'd said it herself. She was a user, too.

'Merrin offered you an opportunity, then,' Donatti said.

Chaim nodded. 'He told me it would be just a couple of times. But then . . . the money . . . the money was good.'

A quick glimpse at Decker.

'It's not like you think. I didn't *squander* the money . . . yes, a few massages – but mostly, I used it for business. For *my* business. I used it to feed my large family. I used it to take care of my elderly father. I used it for the local schools and synagogues. Why should I care if I take from the pockets of thugs who crash cars, have sex like animals, and spit when they see you walking down the streets? Why should I care if they blow their brains out on drugs? And why should a self-righteous prick like my brother ruin everything for me? Him . . . the moral do-gooder who has been on and off drugs for ten years. Who borrowed money from me and from my father without ever paying any of it back. Who never raised a finger to help out with my father or help out with the business because he was too stoned to get out of bed. Who had the *nerve* to tell me how to raise my children when he has never accepted responsibility for anything in his life!'

Indignation gave him a certain amount of ill-placed dignity, except that Decker had heard it all before – the self-rationalization and situational ethics to help defend evil actions. 'So you gave Ephraim over to Merrin and his goons because you were resentful?'

'Not to kill!' Chaim spat out. 'Just to talk some *sense* into him.' In a quieter voice. 'And if they scared him a little, so be it.'

'They did more than scare him,' Decker said softly.

'I wouldn't know . . .' Chaim looked away. 'Something went wrong.'

'A bit of an understatement,' Decker said.

'And who gave you the right to be my judge and jury?' Chaim snarled.

Donatti said, 'What happened with your daughter? Did you set her up, too?'

'*I didn't set anyone up!*' Abruptly, Chaim's eyes watered. 'Especially my *daughter*. I loved Shayndalah! She was my own flesh and blood. It wasn't . . . She wasn't supposed to be there. *I don't know what happened!*'

'What happened was they killed her.'

'It was an *accident*!' Chaim cried out. 'They

claimed they knew where she was. They were supposed to bring her back to me. She resisted. A gun went off—'

'She knew them, Chaim,' Decker broke in. 'They killed her because she could identify them. It wasn't any accident.'

Donatti said, 'They don't call you lieutenant for nothing.'

'No, you're *wrong*. It wasn't like that at all!' Chaim protested. 'They said they could rescue her.' He started sobbing. 'They said she struggled, that she was screaming. It wasn't meant to *happen* that way.' He became hysterical. 'I didn't *kill* her. **I DIDN'T KILL HER**—'

Donatti's gun spat three pellets of hot lead, leaving Chaim Lieber with three blood-filled holes in the center of his chest. He was still forming words when he fell to the ground, his lips ring-shaped, mouthing the letter *O*.

The air smothered with its silence. Decker's heart was pounding against his chest. 'What . . . why'd you . . . why'd you do that?'

'*Why?*' Donatti glared at him with stone eyes. 'Because that bitch was *mine*, Decker. It would have been one thing if she left on her own, but she *didn't*. She was taken from me. *Nobody* steals from a Donatti and gets away with it. *Nobody!* Not even her father!'

He was panting like the dog he was.

'Besides, I dislike self-justifying bastards. Asshole's worse than I am. At least, I'm honest about what I do.'

Donatti was holding two guns – Merrin's Smith & Wesson .32 in his left hand, his own semiautomatic in the right. He went over to Lieber's body and tattooed the inert hand with gunpowder by firing off the rest of the magazine from the semiautomatic, in various directions. When he was done, he left the gun at Chaim's side. Several of the stray bullets had missed Decker's feet by inches. When Donatti got back on his feet, he was holding Merrin's revolver in his left hand.

'If anyone would have shot you, it would have been Merrin, don't you think?'

Decker regarded Donatti. He was sweating hard, breathing quickly. Throughout the process, he'd been grimacing in pain. If Decker moved now, if he was quick enough . . .

Donatti read his thoughts and fished out the Beretta from his jacket. He had the Smith & Wesson fixed on his head, the Beretta on his chest. 'C'mon. Don't insult my intelligence.'

The opportunity had come and gone.

Donatti kept the .32 on Decker's head. 'You ever been shot?'

'Several times.'

'Where?'

'Left shoulder . . . arm.'

'Hurts like hell.' The Beretta still in his right hand, Donatti pulled up his black sweater, exposing his bandage.

'Who did that?' Decker asked. 'Merrin? Chaim? One of Merrin's boys?'

Donatti sidestepped the question. 'It wasn't the first time I've been plugged, but I still don't like it.'

'I don't blame you.'

'Hold still.' Donatti pointed the .32 at Decker's chest. 'And I mean *real* still.'

The gun spat fire, grazing Decker's rib cage. He

jumped as pain burst through his body.

'Now we're twins,' Donatti announced.

'Fuck you!' Decker snarled as he grabbed his side. Blood reddened his fingers. Enraged, he bolted forward, but Donatti had taken several steps back, brandishing the weapons toward Decker's head.

'Ah, ah, ah . . .'

Decker stopped and hissed out, 'Go ahead and shoot me, you goddamn son of a bitch! I'm not dancing for your amusement!'

'I'm not making you dance, Lieutenant. I'm turning you into a real live hero.' The next shot grazed his hip. Decker doubled over in pain.

'I think that's enough.' Donatti switched hands, keeping the semiautomatic on Decker's face. Swiftly, he bent down, wrapped Merrin's dead fingers around his pistol, and depleted it of ammunition. When he got up, he wiped his pants with latex-gloved hands, the Beretta pointed somewhere within the vicinity of Decker's groin.

'You should lie down. Losing blood can make you light-headed.'

'Fuck you!' Decker stood up straight for spite. The air reeked of sweat, waste, and blood. His head was on fire. Sparkles danced before his eyes, but he concentrated on his breathing and refused to succumb to the nausea in his stomach and the dizziness in his brain. He'd go out like a man, in full consciousness, face-to-face and eye-to-eye.

Donatti was analyzing the scene. 'Well, it looks to me like Lieber and Merrin shot each other, Lieutenant. Not to mention these two dodos, Merrin's two top runners for ecstasy in the local high schools.'

'Philip Caldwell and Ryan Anderson.'

'You've done your homework. Yes, Caldwell and Anderson. And yes, you're right. They knew Shayndie from hanging at the raves.'

'They took her out of hiding to call my brother,' Decker panted out. 'They figured that . . . that my brother would tell me about it. And that would throw me off for a while. They murdered her . . . but figured I wouldn't even look for the body for a couple of days because of the phone call. It was a good idea except they dumped her in a public place where she was easily found.'

Donatti rolled his eyes. 'Idiots.'

'The boys knew where you had her stashed.' Decker's eyes traveled to Donatti's ice-blue orbs. 'That means *you* had to have known them. Did they work for you?'

'Just the opposite. Caldwell had been one of those pains in the ass who had passed through my portals when I used to take in straight boys. Cocksucker abused my hospitality. Such rudeness has its consequences.' He shook his head. 'He killed Ephraim Lieber in my style, thinking all he had to do to be me was pop the trigger. Well, they say that imitation is the highest form of flattery.'

The room was silent except for heavy breathing.

Decker spoke softly. 'Now what?'

'Well, you can spin it any way you want, but I'd tell it like this: a distraught father/brother avenging the deaths of his daughter and brother from evil drug runners and a corrupt police chief. Let the pissant die a hero. Or you can tell the cops the truth, that Lieber was scum – a sniveling, weak, groveling piece of shit who got blow jobs from hookers and who set up his own brother and his own daughter. Then he tried to cover his tracks, bringing out some hick L.A. cop to pump NYPD for information. When the cop got to be a pain in the ass, he attempted to clean him. But the hick cop happened to be just a little smarter than Lieber thought.'

'I can spin it any way I want . . .' Decker felt sweat pouring off his brow, the left side of his body throbbing in pain. 'You're letting me walk, Chris?'

'Is that a mistake?'

'Probably.'

'I don't think so, Decker. If you come after me, you'll fuck yourself up. Ultimately, it's your word against mine.'

Decker managed to smile, even though the entire left side of his torso pulsated with burning agony. 'I have a little more credibility than you do.'

'Think so? Well, I've got the lawyers, and they're gonna tell a jury this: We were a partnership pure and simple – both of us hand in hand, doing it together, and both of us getting shot in the process.'

He pointed to his own ribs.

'If I go down, old man, you go down. Because all Hershfield has to do is ask you one simple question, Lieutenant. Who came to whom for help?'

The words cut through Decker more powerfully than his wounds.

'And the fact that you're *alive* to tell the story gives *me* credibility,' Donatti continued. 'Because everyone *knows* if I had wanted you dead, you'd be dead.'

No one spoke.

'*And* . . . I'm much cuter than you.' Donatti gave off a charming smile. 'Hershfield's specialty is voir dire. All he has to do is stack the jury with women and a few blue-collar men and you haven't a chance in hell for conviction. The most you'll be able to hope for is a hung jury. Meanwhile, you've not only fucked up your life, you fucked up your brother's family because all the shit will come out. As far as I'm concerned, another trial will only enhance my reputation.'

For a moment, Donatti debated telling Decker that the same motherfuckers who took out Shayndie had also tried to pop his wife. That if he hadn't been there, the lieutenant would be a widower today. But he decided against it. It would give Decker a rationale for letting him go. That's not what he wanted. He wanted to make Decker suffer, humiliated by his own actions and his resulting failure . . . because Decker had humiliated him in Terry's eyes eight years ago.

He started to back away, keeping the gun on Decker's head. 'I'm going to turn around. All the nearby guns have been emptied. You could make a run for the ones behind you, but you'd better be quick and you'd better shoot to kill, because if you miss . . . you're dead. And then I go after your family – one by one by one. If you happen to get lucky with a direct hit, remember your promise to me. You take care of Terry and my son. I really love that little girl.'

Police sirens could be heard in the background.

Jonathan had finally gotten to a phone booth.

'I think that's my exit song,' Donatti told him.

Thinking about the weapons, Decker watched him back away. How his body seared with pain! He was compromised. He couldn't walk without limping, let alone run. Any attempt to seize a gun would give Donatti more than enough time to kill him.

But if he did nothing, then he allowed the murdering scum to walk away. Not just any murderer, a man who had slain his own brother's relative in cold blood and done it as easily as blowing his nose.

Pick off my family – one by one by one.

And even if Decker had the gun in his hand, could he do it? Shoot to kill in cold blood? Just put a bullet through Donatti's brain? The world would be better off. Even Terry and the kid would be better off – *especially* Terry and the kid. Could he make that calculated decision to pop him without direct *threat*?

How did the psycho do it?

Of course, that was the answer: Donatti was a psycho.

At least, the bastard hadn't given him that decision to make. Decker knew he wasn't about to play heroics – not with the stench of his own fresh blood wafting through his nostrils, with this abattoir around him. He owed his family common sense. He owed his family his opting to live.

Decker yelled out, 'You're not playing fair, Chris. You know I can't chance it.'

Donatti grinned. 'The hands are the hands of Esau, but the voice is the voice of Jacob!'

What was he *talking* about? 'I ain't sticking a fork in it, Chris!' Decker continued. 'We're not done yet!'

Donatti gave him a thumbs-up. 'Suck my cock, Lieutenant!'

He turned and broke into a jog.

And then he was gone.

36

It was recorded as Donatti predicted – Rabbi
Chaim Lieber against a half-dozen drug-dealing,
ecstasy-popping animals aided by a corrupted police
chief and two of his lackeys. The slain Lieber had
become a local saint, and Minda, his martyred wife.
It made Decker sick. Days passed, and he was
besieged by endless questions from the police, from
the media, from lawyers, friends, and relatives.
Nights passed during which he was terrorized by
horrid dreams of blood and bodies. For the entire
world to see, he held up well during the ordeal. But
the secrets of his heart told a different story. He was
plagued by his weakness, ashamed by his failure to
confess the truth in all its blindfolded glory.

In the end, after several weeks had gone by, after all
the inquiries and answers were typed up and filed
away, after the newspapers had reduced the front-
page news to a one-column article on page 26,
Decker and his conscience were left alone to brood,
an exclusive club of two that could not be penetrated
by anyone else. Not even by Rina.

Especially not Rina.

Though she begged and pleaded with him to talk,
he kept his incubi private. When things settled down,

he'd see someone. In the meantime, it was all too fresh to deal with, too raw and painful. They would come, the words, but they needed time to form into cohesive deliberations, into articulated introspection.

Who would have guessed that his brother would be the one to give Decker his needed solace? Not Jonathan, who knew only *part* of the truth, but had sworn to take that wedge of it to his grave. Not Jonathan, who tried all the religious medicaments on himself as well as Decker, only to fail miserably. Not Jonathan, who cried, coaxed, and urged, but came up empty-handed. It was clear to Decker that Jonathan couldn't handle him, because his brother could barely address his own demons. Admitting psychological and spiritual defeat – an especially agonizing acknowledgment for a rabbi – Jonathan sought refuge in professional counsel.

No, it wasn't his brother Jonathan who bestowed upon Decker the ability to pick up his head and face another day. It was Randy. Sixteen days after Decker had witnessed slaughter and destruction, he had packed up his bags for Florida: to find peace in his childhood home, to mend his wounds both physical and emotional. The first weekend of his arrival, Randy came down to visit. At six-two, 270 pounds of muscle and fat, his brother had a kick-ass attitude ideal for an undercover cop. His formidable face was slathered by a matted black beard hanging over his chin. His dark piercing eyes demanded to be told the truth.

It started out as small talk: It always worked that way, gradually segueing into Decker's buried guilt. Randy listened without interruption. Then he laid his hand on his brother's shoulder.

'What're you sweating it for, Peter? You know as well as I do, even if you had killed the scumbag, another one would have come along to take his place.'

Decker wiped his forehead. He was soaked with perspiration, even though he was wearing a light-weight, short-sleeved cotton shirt and jeans. It was in the low seventies with blue skies and clear air. 'I don't know, Randy . . .'

'Course you do. No shortage of pissbuckets, Peter. Don't give it a second thought.'

'I should have done something. At the very least, I should have told the cops the truth.'

'And made everyone miserable – the old man Lieber, the widowed wife, the remaining children, your entire half brother's family, you, Rina, your family, even me . . .' He shook his head. 'Truth is a flexible concept, Bro. Didn't you tell me that Jewish-wise, truth means peace.'

'No.'

'Yeah, you did. You told me it was okay to lie to keep peace in the family.'

'Oh, that. *Shalom bayit*. It means fibbing, Randy, not letting murderers go free.'

'Donatti will get his, just like his old man did. In the meantime, you're living to see another day. As they say in the Family, "fuhgeddaboutit." ' Randy leaned back in his wicker chaise lounger. The brothers were resting on the outside porch, drinking lemonade. Damn near idyllic. 'You're a friggin' hero, Peter. You risked your life to save Chaim.'

'It didn't work—'

'So what if it worked or not? It still happened. And you got shot in the process. That makes you a hero.

Furthermore, you made *me* a hero. You know how long we've been after Weiss, Harabi, and Ibn Dod? You *flushed* them out for us. You broke up a major ecstasy-import ring. They're being transported down here for arraignment next week.'

'Like you said, there'll just be more to take their places.'

'Yeah, sure, but it's important for us to *succeed* once in a while. To say to the public, we care about you. We care about your kids and your neighborhoods. And we do care.' He lightly punched Decker's shoulder. '*You* made us look good here in Miami, Bro. You made Novack in New York look good – all the nice things you said in the press about NYPD detectives. Everyone loves you. If you were the political type, you could parlay what you did into chief of police in one of the major cities.'

Decker didn't answer.

Randy brought in the heavy ammunition. 'Peter, you made *me* look especially good. I'm going to get a promotion because of you – D-three. You know how long I've waited for this?'

'I'm happy for you.'

'So stop sulking like a paddled schoolboy. You think Donatti used you? You used Donatti. The psycho was finally good for something other than popping wiseguys and pimping girls.'

But Decker wasn't buying the rationalization. His expression spoke of his skepticism.

'You're still thinking like a Homicide dick,' Randy told him. 'You want Donatti, you gotta think like Vice. You need informants. You need the bad guys to get other bad guys.'

'Donatti's a real bad guy. The bastard shot me.'

Decker's jaw became a ball of tension. 'Worse than that, he humiliated me.'

'Fucking easy for him to make you dance with a gun to your head. Peter, he didn't humiliate you; he played a crooked game. That's being a coward. I'd like to pit the two of you together without the Beretta in his hand.'

The image made Decker smile. 'I should have turned him in.'

'Pete, he ain't worth ruining your life for.' Randy gulped down his lemonade. 'Yeah, it would have been great if you could have taken him under, but the timing wasn't right. The main thing is you're breathing, and that gives you plenty of time to set him up. You want to get Donatti, you need to sting him. You need informants and anonymous tips and wires and videos and surveillance and someone who'll rat him out. That kind of setup takes time . . . maybe years.'

Decker nodded, still consumed with thoughts of revenge. Bastard probably figured the slate was clean for what happened eight years ago. Not so, baby. Now, there was a bigger score to settle. And Randy was right. Maybe it would take years. That was okay. Decker was mature: He was a very patient man.

'Donatti will get his,' Randy repeated. 'In the meantime, look around. It's a beautiful day. Not so bad, huh?'

'No, not so bad.' Decker finished his lemonade.

Randy laughed out loud. 'Just like when we were kids, Peter. I'd screw up and try to convince you why it wasn't all that terrible.'

'You didn't screw up this time.'

'Neither did you.'

Decker didn't answer.

Randy switched gears. 'You're just about healed up and you still got four weeks' disability left. What are you going to do with it?'

'Right now, I'm mellowing out. In a few days, Rina and I thought we'd take Hannah to Epcot—'

'Oh God no!'

'What's wrong with Epcot?'

'Why don't you leave Hannah to me and Sheryl? We'll take her to Epcot and Disney World. She enjoys spending time with her cousins. You go with Rina to the Caribbean.'

'No thanks. Maybe another time.'

'If not now, when? Isn't that a Jewish proverb?'

'It means the study of Torah.'

'Well, you can't study your holy Torah unless your mind is in a spiritual place. In the meantime, the Caribbean is nice.'

'I don't want to go to the Caribbean. I hate beach vacations. I don't tan; I just burn. And I can't think of anything worse than sitting in the hot sun, sweating my ass off.'

Randy exhaled in disgust.

'Rina was also talking about going to Europe for a week to ten days. Mom said she and Dad would look after Hannah. Aunt Millie would also help out. Rates are a joke right now. No one's traveling.'

'I wonder why,' Randy quipped.

'Gotta live your life,' Decker answered.

'Exactly, Peter. Listen to your own advice,' Randy told him. 'Hey. How about if Sheryl and me and the kids come down on the weekend and give Mom and Dad an extra pair of hands?'

'Randy, you've been a peach.'

He smiled. 'I was a pain-in-the-ass little brother,

but you treated me okay. Now I'm rewarding you. Where you two going? Paris?'

'Paris and possibly Munich of all places. She has a close childhood friend who moved with her husband to Germany to start a yeshiva there.'

'Go figure.' Randy slapped him on the back. 'Do it, Decker. Have a good time with your wife, and thank whatever God you believe in that you've got another day with a heartbeat.'

It came in the afternoon, the day before she and Peter were to leave for Paris, a plain white envelope with a stuck-on, pretyped label made out to MRS RINA DECKER C/O LYLE AND IDA DECKER, followed by her in-laws, address, city, and state.

She turned it over. The return address was the same as the front label. Another flip back. The postmark told her it was mailed from New York City. Immediately, she grew suspicious, but who on earth would be sending *her* biological warfare in the mail. Still, she took care when she opened the envelope.

No powder of any kind.

No letter, either.

Only a small single-column newspaper article that had been neatly trimmed – razor cut rather than scissors. There wasn't any mention of the paper's name. Nor was there a date. Rina read the headline.

MAN SLAIN, FOUND ON STEPS OF CHURCH.

On a routine patrol, Officer Willard Greaves discovered a grisly corpse sprawled across the front steps of Medford Methodist Church. The body, sustaining a single shot to the head, was

identified as Steven Gilbert, a computer teacher
at the local community college . . .

The article fell from Rina's hands and fluttered down
to the floor. She could feel her heart pumping blood
clear up to her brain. Her voice escaped her for a
moment; then she called out his name.

'Peter?'

No answer.

She picked up the article and tried to control her
shaking hands. She cleared her throat and tried again,
a little louder. 'Peter?'

Nothing.

She went into the kitchen, the center of her
in-laws' house. Mama Ida had just baked a cinnamon
apple cake, the warm air still saturated with sugar and
spice. 'Peter?'

'Out back.'

She took in a deep breath, exhaled, then went into
the backyard. Peter was grilling their dinner, bass fillets
caught from this morning's fishing expedition. Hannah
had awakened at four along with Daddy, Uncle Randy,
and Papa Lyle. Her daughter was becoming an old-
fashioned country girl – delighted with new adventure
and the open space. It was going to be difficult to
integrate her back into the confined classrooms of her
religious Jewish day school. The only thing that Rina
had going for her was that Hannah sorely missed her
two best friends, Ariella and Esther Ruthie Chaya.

'Hi,' she said.

'Hey.' Decker kept his concentration on the grill.
'What's up, beautiful?'

Peter was wearing an apron. He looked so relaxed
and homespun.

'This came in today's mail.'

Peter looked up. 'What's wrong, Rina?'

'Wrong?'

'You're white.' His face was filled with concern. 'What happened?'

'Nothing, really. Well . . . nothing bad.' She secured the spatula from his hand, and offered him the article. 'Trade?'

Warily, Decker took the clipping. Within seconds, he was aware of his heartbeat. 'Oh my my . . .' Excitement soared through his veins. He couldn't help himself. A smile worked its way onto his lips. 'Son of a gun. Where'd this come from?'

'I told you. It came in today's mail. It was addressed to me care of your parents. The return address was your parents' house.'

'Did you look at the postmark?'

'Yes. It was mailed from New York.'

'New York?'

Rina nodded.

'Not Indiana?'

'No, not Indiana. New York.' She showed him the envelope.

He stared at the envelope, a bit deflated. 'It could be a hoax.'

But Rina knew it was no hoax.

'Well, there's one way to find out.' He looked up from the article. 'You'll watch the fish?'

'I'll watch the fish.'

'Son of a gun. If it is true, we're going to have to tell the boys.' Decker's smile returned. 'Do you want to do it or should I?'

'I think you should do it. I'm . . .' Heat from the grill was baking her face. She suddenly felt faint. 'I'm . . .'

Decker took her in his arms. 'I know, honey, you must be in shock!' He couldn't get the grin off his face. 'Not an unpleasant shock. Here, sit down.' He eased her into a patio chair.

'I'm okay.' She brought her hand to her chest. 'You're going to call Medford Police?'

'Yep.' Decker slapped the article against the palm of his hand. 'I hope this is legit. Because I'm feeling really good right now. Not that I'm one for blood lust . . . but it does have its moments.'

That day in the park . . . hadn't he used almost the exact words? That vengeance had its soothing effect? Rina was quiet, trying to breathe slowly.

'I'll be back.' Decker laughed. 'Incredible. You couldn't make this stuff up. There must be a God in heaven.'

He left her alone and went to make his calls. Still breathing hard, she slowly got up to tend to the fish. No sense ruining dinner over what was done. Examining her feeling, she found that she wasn't sorry about it . . . but she wasn't ecstatic, either. More than anything, she just *was*.

Maybe the news hadn't fully registered.

Her boys . . . they would be relieved. No matter how *over* they thought it had been, now it was *really* over. He was finally gone. Maybe Jacob could finally put the past behind him.

Tears welled up in her eyes.

There must be a God in heaven.

A true statement, but this wasn't God.

God's name was ineffable.

This *wasn't* God.

Because Rina knew his name.

Headline hopes you enjoyed reading Faye Kellerman's STONE KISS and invites you to sample the first chapter of Jonathan Kellerman's THE MURDER BOOK, out now in Headline hardback . . .

one

The day I got the murder book, I was still thinking about Paris. Red wine, bare trees, gray river, city of love. Everything that happened there. Now, this.

Robin and I flew in to Charles de Gaulle airport on a murky Monday in January. The trip had been my idea of a surprise. I'd pulled it together in one manic night, booking tickets on Air France and a room at a small hotel on the outskirts of the Eighth *arrondissement*, packing a suitcase for two, speeding the 125 freeway miles to San Diego. Showing up at Robin's room at the Del Coronado just before midnight with a dozen coral roses and a *voilà!* grin.

She came to the door wearing a white T-shirt and a hip-riding red sarong, auburn curls loose, chocolate eyes tired, no makeup. We embraced, then she pulled away and looked down at the suitcase. When I showed her the tickets, she turned her back and shielded me from her tears. Outside her window the night-black ocean rolled, but this was no holiday on the beach. She'd left L.A. because I'd lied to her and put myself in danger. Listening to her cry now, I wondered if the damage was irreparable.

I asked what was wrong. As if I had nothing to do with it.

She said, 'I'm just . . . surprised.'

We ordered room-service sandwiches, she closed the drapes, we made love.

'Paris,' she said, slipping into a hotel bathrobe. 'I can't believe you did all this.' She sat down, brushed her hair, then stood. Approached the bed, stood over me, touched me. She let the robe slither from her body, straddled me, shut her eyes, lowered a breast to my mouth. When she came the second time, she rolled away, went silent.

I played with her hair and, as she fell asleep, the corners of her mouth lifted. Mona Lisa smile. In a couple of days, we'd be queuing up as robotically as any other tourists, straining for a glimpse of the real thing.

She'd fled to San Diego because a high school chum lived there – a thrice-married oral surgeon named Debra Dyer, whose current love interest was a banker from Mexico City. ('So many white teeth, Alex!') Francisco had suggested a day of shlock-shopping in Tijuana followed by an indeterminate stay at a leased beach house in Cabo San Lucas. Robin, feeling like a fifth wheel, had begged off, and called me, asking if I'd join her.

She'd been nervous about it. Apologizing for abandoning me. I didn't see it that way, at all. Figured her for the injured party.

I'd gotten myself in a bad situation because of poor planning. Blood had spilled and someone had died. Rationalizing the whole thing wasn't that tough: innocent lives had been at stake, the good guys had won, I'd ended up on my feet. But as Robin roared away in her truck, I faced the truth:

My misadventures had little to do with noble intentions, lots to do with a personality flaw.

A long time ago, I'd chosen clinical psychology, the most sedentary of professions, telling myself that healing emotional wounds was how I wanted to spend the rest of my life. But it had been years since I'd conducted any long-term therapy. Not because, as I'd once let myself believe, I'd burned out on human misery. I had no problem with misery. My other life force-fed me *gobs* of misery.

The truth was cold: once upon a time I *had* been drawn to the humanity and the challenge of the talking cure, but sitting in the office, dividing hour after hour by three quarters, ingesting other people's problems, had come to *bore* me.

In a sense, becoming a therapist had been a strange choice. I'd been a wild boy – poor sleeper, restless, overactive, high pain threshold, inclined to risk-taking and injuries. I quieted down a bit when I discovered books but found the classroom a jail and raced through school in order to escape. After graduating high school at sixteen, I bought an old car with summer-job cash, ignored my mother's tears and my father's scowling vote of no-confidence, and left the plains of Missouri. Ostensibly for college, but really for the threat and promise of California.

Molting like a snake. Needing something *new*.

Novelty had always been my drug. I craved insomnia and menace punctuated by long stretches of solitude, puzzles that hurt my head, infusions of bad company and the delicious repellence of meeting up with the slimy things that coiled under psychic rocks.

A racing heart jolted me happy. The kick start of adrenaline punching my chest made me feel alive.

When life slowed down for too long, I grew hollow. But for circumstance, I might've dealt with it by jumping out of airplanes or scaling bare rocks. Or worse.

Years ago, I'd met a homicide detective and that changed everything.

Robin had put up with it for a long time. Now she'd had enough and, sooner rather than later, I'd have to make some kind of decision.

She loved me. I know she did.

Maybe that's why she made it easy for me.

Now you can buy any of these other bestselling books by **Faye Kellerman** from your bookshop or *direct from her publisher*.

FREE P&P AND UK DELIVERY
(Overseas and Ireland £3.50 per book)

The Forgotten	£5.99
Stalker	£6.99
Jupiter's Bones	£6.99
Moon Music	£6.99
Serpent's Tooth	£6.99
The Quality of Mercy	£6.99
Prayers for the Dead	£6.99
Justice	£6.99
Sanctuary	£6.99
Grievous Sin	£6.99
False Prophet	£6.99
Day of Atonement	£6.99
Milk and Honey	£6.99
Sacred and Profane	£6.99
The Ritual Bath	£6.99

TO ORDER SIMPLY CALL THIS NUMBER

01235 400 414

or visit our website: www.madaboutbooks.com

Prices and availability subject to change without notice.